I0762271

COSMIC CHAMPIONS

ALSO BY MARK CALDWELL JONES

The Viper Series (Natalie Nicks)

Book One: NEVER DIE TWICE (2018)

Book Two: VIPER FATALIS (2019)

Book Three: MOONBASE ROGUE (2023)

Book Four: ENDPOINT MATRIX (Coming Soon)

COSMIC CHAMPIONS

COSMIC CHAMPIONS
BOOK ONE

MARK CALDWELL JONES

Title: Cosmic Champions

Subtitle: A LitRPG GameLit Fantasy Adventure

Series: Cosmic Champions Book: Book One

Version: CHAMPIONS_DRAFT17_061723_SAT_1220XM

Published in the United States by Samurai Seven Books.

DRAFT: CHAMPIONS_DRAFT17_061723_SAT_1220XM.scriv

SCRIVENER FILE: CHAMPIONS_DRAFT17_061723_SAT_1220XM.scriv

WORD FILE: CHAMPIONS_DRAFT16_031522_WED_1507XM.docx

VELLUM: DRAFT17_061723_EBOOK_PAPERBACK_FinalEdit

For My Favorite Team Of Champions:

Maverick aka @boogiemansballs
Juliette aka @donnyweb
Hannah aka @garfieldgirl

"There are only two lasting bequests we can hope to give our children.
One of these is roots, the other wings."
– Johann Wolfgang von Goethe

It's precisely when you feel like giving up that you must summon the courage to carry on. It is said: The Creator favors the valiant. Thus, we know the divine powers of the universe grant strength to the bold and help the brave persevere. Never accept defeat and never surrender! Even though it may seem all your dreams are burning down around you, remember that it is by these flames a champion's heart is forged.

— THE COSMOMANCER'S CREED

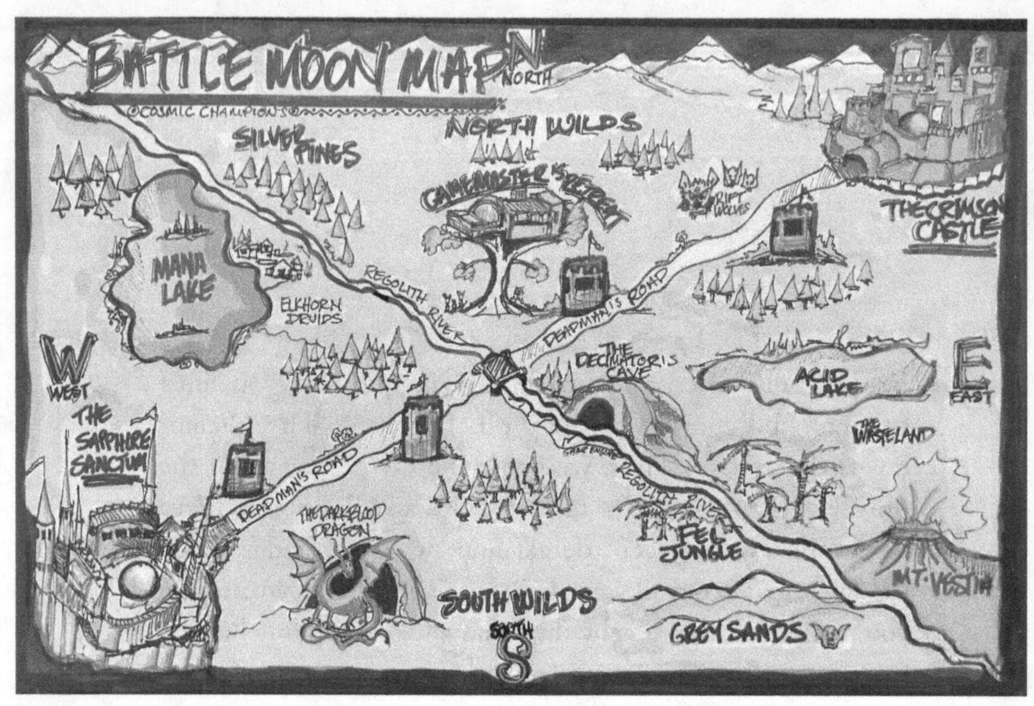

BATTLE MOON MAP
N
NORTH
©COSMIC CHAMPIONS©
NORTH WILDS
SILVER PINES
GAMEMASTER'S RETREAT
RIFT WOLVES
THE CRIMSON CASTLE
MANA LAKE
REGOLITH RIVER
ELKHORN DRUIDS
DEADMAN'S ROAD
THE DECIMATOR'S CAVE
ACID LAKE
W
WEST
E
EAST
THE WASTELAND
THE SAPPHIRE SANCTUM
DEADMAN'S ROAD
THE DARKBLOOD DRAGON
REGOLITH RIVER
FEL JUNGLE
MT. VESTIA
SOUTH WILDS
SOUTH
S
GREY SANDS

COSMIC CHAMPIONS

PART I
LET THE GAME BEGIN

CHAPTER ONE

THE DECIMATOR'S CAVE

Titan knew the one thing that would save his life was inside the cave, and there wasn't a moment to spare. He stepped forward and thrust his glowing sword into the boulder blocking the entrance. The explosion created a burst of light and sound, illuminating and rattling everything within a thousand yards.

He dabbed the sweat off his young tan face, combed the wavy black hair out of his eyes, and examined the results of his attack. He was a powerful warrior, but his first strike had barely made a mark.

He'd have to do better and do it much faster.

Battle Moon folklore told that a corrupt wizard had magically sealed the cave eons ago, ensuring its powerful treasure was protected by the most terrifying of monsters. Could he break through? If he did, would he survive the horrors hidden inside?

Even though he didn't wield magic like his teammates, he had some of the best weapons a champion could own. He twirled his Star-stone Blade and stabbed the boulder again and again.

Boom! Boom! BOOM!

Over and over, the sword disappeared as it cut through the rock. He imagined the fright the cave-dwelling creatures within must have experienced when the shaft of otherworldly magic pierced their dark domain.

Boom! Boom! BOOM!

Finally, the barrier exploded, and Titan stepped through the smoke past the settling debris.

For added protection, he placed his Spartan helmet on his head and peered through its enchanted slits to inspect his surroundings.

There it was, just as the lore described: the ancient Mana Well topped by its fabled stone seal—a large wheel that looked like a macabre Halloween treat. Instead of Rice Krispies and melted marshmallows, this was a disc of human skulls held together by melted gold.

A web of wine-colored strands that seemed to pulse with life covered the shiny disc.

"Altar fungus." Titan smiled and rubbed his gauntlet over the growth. "It only forms on rare magical items. This has to be it."

Using his sword, he hacked away the strange vines to reveal the golden relics. Their radiant color illuminated the walls and stalactites above, allowing him to admire his strange discovery. He noticed the center skull was larger, less human-like, and bore a set of fanged teeth. Something lay in that terrifying mouth, propping the jaws open slightly—a small box perhaps.

"Yes, finally. The Wraith's Skull of Resurrection," he cheered.

He raised his sword over his head as if he'd just won a battle, then recited the artifact's attributes from memory. "Enchanted by the mythic Evercore crystal, this item resurrects the user within sixty seconds of death, regenerating both health and mana to 100 percent. The champion in possession of the skull will manifest the Wraith's Mark in battle. The more mana the warrior spends in combat, the more he heals his nearby allies."

It was the ultimate buff. There was nothing more powerful.

Such artifacts were never easy to secure. Were there more enchantments protecting it? It was time to find out. He was working his fingers around the Wraith's Skull when something moved overhead. The stalactites came alive.

"Cave blights!" he yelled. Every muscle in his lithe, slender frame tensed. "Oh no, not now!"

The giant insects stirred like a nest of agitated cockroaches and skittered down the cave wall to attack, each of them eager to sink their oversized mandibles into his flesh. He raised his shield in defense and stood his ground. Surely, he was the first substantial food source in ages, and they looked ravenous.

He stepped back a few paces, eyeing the entrance.

Since his shield, sword, and armor were a mythical set, he could absorb substantial damage, even from magical attacks. But the blights seemed innumerable. He wouldn't last long against such a large hive.

He may have to run for it. But was that even possible now?

As if sensing his plan, the first wave of blights pounced.

Titan raised his shield, swatting the creatures back across the cave. Curse these bugs! The blights were not giving up, but neither would he. He was determined to have the Wraith's Skull and wouldn't leave without it.

"Started the party without us, did you?" a familiar voice asked.

Titan turned toward the speaker, and a magical force field descended around him just as a second wave of blights attacked.

"Dude, what are you thinking? No one survives this gnarly cave without backup."

Genghis, a young mana-weaving monk, materialized out of the ether only a few feet away. Genghis was both Titan's best friend and the team's healer. He was a head shorter than Titan and wore a wispy goatee and one of his ever-present smiles.

"I've got this," Titan said. "Get back to the base."

"Nah, bro. You're our glorious leader. We can't let these bugs eat you. The entire team's coming to help!"

As usual, Genghis's voice was warm, friendly, and completely free of judgment. He wore ivory-colored leather armor and carried a staff of gnarled wood wrapped in transparent energy.

Its crystal tip glowed with a soft orange light as he produced another one of his protection spells. The sudden formation of the new barrier zapped the blights as they pounced. One by one, they tumbled over, black and stiff like burnt bacon.

"You touched the well before disenchanting it," Aspy, a Quillodian Elf, scolded Titan as she materialized next to the two boys. "It's an obvious trap—if you open that seal, everyone in this cave dies."

"That's why I told you all to hold the line at the Sanctum. If I get this, we'll win the game."

"But that's impossible!" she said.

Aspy had the gleaming look of someone who'd been kissed by the summer sun. Her hair, tied back in braids, was the color of a winter storm. Her eyes glittered like an emerald forest.

She wore elven chain mail and a silver Quillodian dagger sheathed at her hip, but her principal weapon was a recurve bow made of mysterium called the Highguard Claw. It was carved with swirling patterns and runes that flickered like candlelight.

Titan liked her, but he often ignored her ideas, seeing them as too careful. She had named herself The Asp in a failed attempt to assert a dominant persona. It hadn't really worked, and the team clipped the name down to Aspy.

There was no better archer for ranged attacks, but her attempts at leadership muddied the waters. Titan felt she was always getting in the way of what he wanted to do. Like right now.

Aspy muttered a new incantation, causing another magical barrier to drop over the well, blocking Titan from it. As the force field expanded, it pushed the blights back into the corners from where they had emerged.

The bugs scratched and snapped, too furious to give up. Taking another tack, they circled around the champions, sensing somehow that the magic would reach its limit and their dinner would eventually be served.

"Aspy, dang it, we need the Wraith's Skull," Titan argued, pointing at the artifact. "We don't have a chance without it."

Two more teammates materialized behind Aspy, obliterating a cluster of blights as they appeared.

"We're running out of time, people," Ripghoul said.

Though barely visible in the shadows, the young rogue hunter looked formidable, fingering his two shadow-weave daggers. He was athletically built with long legs, a slender torso, and a tan, square-jawed face that others couldn't help but find easy on the eyes.

He was agile, like a cat, and there was a feral intensity in his eyes that burned with a deep-seated desire to prove himself.

"The Cannibals are advancing up Deadman's Road. Our skulks won't hold them off much longer."

"Guys, what are we doing in this nasty cave anyway?" BadMiznus asked.

Miz was a Tykonian Amazon, a foot shorter than Titan and many feet wider. Built for brawling, she was the team's tank. No one enjoyed being on her bad side, including Titan.

She held a torch in one hand and an axe in the other. Her voice was a soft but authoritative one, and raspy from constantly yelling over the sounds of battle. Periodically, she swung her torch to ward off the blights.

"Geez, Titan. They've just destroyed our last tower. I need your help defending the cornerstone."

"He wants to get killed by the Decimator—*again*," Aspy said, as if it were a foregone conclusion.

Titan rolled his eyes. "The Decimator won't be a problem if you noobs would just get out of here."

The Decimator was one of the most feared creatures on the Battle Moon. A notorious monster that hid in caves and snacked on treasure seekers, its nesting place was always changing at random. No one could be sure he'd attack here. And with the skull, it wouldn't matter.

"I know you want to make a name for yourself. That's cool and all," Genghis said, shrugging his shoulders apologetically, "but I don't have enough mana left to save all of us, especially against the big guy. We should clear out while we still can."

"I've got this. Meet me at the cornerstone," Titan ordered, pointing at the cave entrance. "I'm right behind you."

"That's what you said last time," Ripghoul said, snapping his shadow cloak around his body.

"And the time before that," BadMiznus growled.

"Just zip your lips and move out. I can do this," Titan protested. "I don't need anyone's help."

But they wouldn't leave, and another round of bickering broke out. They argued until, without warning, Titan brushed past Genghis, ripped the magical staff from his friend's hands, briefly pointed it at the monk to drain his remaining mana, then twirled the staff around and struck the floor.

The resulting spell created a new force field that expanded outward, gathering Titan's unsuspecting teammates in a net of glowing energy and pushing them toward the cave's entrance.

They yelled and cursed, but Titan ignored all of their protests and pleas.

He wedged the end of the staff into the cave's floor so it stood upright and continued energizing the barrier. Then he turned back to the treasure.

Finally, with his doubting war party restrained and the blights back in their dark holes, he could focus on what was important.

Titan fumbled with the well's seal, trying desperately to get the Wraith's Skull in his hand. It seemed impossible to dislodge. He searched the treasure for runes or magical triggers. All the while, its boney grin seemed to be frozen in a perpetual laugh, mocking his efforts.

Brute force seemed like the only option. He'd have to break the entire seal, hoping the Wraith's Skull would remain intact, and run like hell once he had it in hand.

Sneaking both hands under the edge, he discovered that gold-dipped skulls were very heavy. He strained with all his might and pushed the seal over. It crashed onto the cave floor and broke into several pieces.

A powerful gust of noxious air blasted Titan backward. Following this, a giant purple worm erupted from the opening like a monstrous jack-in-the-box.

The serpent was as big as a dinosaur and as long as a bus. Its entire length was a bloated mass of pulsing flesh, mottled with a purple-and-black-striped pattern. Green ichor and yellow pus oozed from its pores and it smelled like an unholy mix of rotten eggs, spoiled milk, and old cheese.

This was the Decimator!

It slithered over the golden skulls, crunching them underneath its weight. Titan noticed its body ended in a round blob of a head with a gruesome mouth full of razor-like fangs. The mouth appeared to smile when it saw Titan.

"Finally, the dinner bell has rung," the Decimator growled, puffing out its chest and spreading its tiny T-Rex arms like it wanted a hug. "To whom do I owe the pleasure?"

"The name's Titan, foul beast. Return to the UnderRealm or die!"

Titan swung his sword at the creature, but the Decimator easily avoided it then swiped Titan with a claw, throwing him across the cave and into a wall. As Titan collapsed in a heap, the monster laughed in a deep booming guffaw.

"Titan?" it jeered. "What a very pretentious name for a small creature like you. Do you mind? I think I prefer to call you . . . *breakfast*."

The monster roared and showered Titan with a blast of noxious phlegm. The fluid sprayed over his armor and sizzled like acid.

Titan eyed the Wraith's Skull. It was finally free but now lay amongst the debris upon which the monster's hulking frame was slithering and trailing its grotesque slime.

Meanwhile, Titan's teammates, still trapped behind the magical barrier, watched helplessly as the monster closed in.

"Oh, man, he's done for!" Ripghoul shouted.

"Release the force field," Aspy yelled. "We can help you."

"He doesn't want our help," BadMiznus said. "Isn't that obvious?"

"We have to help him. If he dies, we lose the round," Genghis said dejectedly.

Titan scrambled back to his feet and swung his sword wildly at the Decimator, trying to land one blow. But the monster was too fast, dodging and weaving while undulating its snake body.

After several of Titan's expert sword thrusts failed, the Decimator twisted in a graceful spin and cracked its tail like a whip, putting Titan flat on his back. His sword clattered to the cave's floor and spun out of reach.

The Decimator closed in, snapping its venomous jaws, and bit down on Titan's leg. Titan screamed. He could hear the crunch of his armor, the sizzle of the creature's acidic venom, and the breaking of bones as it tightened its jaws. Then it lifted him into the air and shook him like a dog shakes a toy before dropping him again.

Titan fell, banging his head on a large rock as he landed. Dazed but not down, he crawled on his stomach and reached for his sword.

As the monster closed in for another attack, Titan rolled over to find the perfect opportunity. The Decimator's soft underbelly was exposed. He hurled his sword like a spear straight at the evil worm's heart.

The Decimator moved lightning quick and caught the flying sword, then spun and flung it back, with twice the force. The acid-covered blade impaled Titan through the center of his chest.

"No!" Genghis yelled, desperately trying but failing to cast a healing spell.

"Ouch, Breakfast. That's gotta hurt," the Decimator said, exposing its endless rows of fangs in a wide smile.

Titan held up an arm to shield his face just as the Decimator hit him with the final deadly blow.

The mocking laugh of the grotesque creature echoed through the cave until another disembodied voice, like an unseen god, delivered a terrible announcement.

"Your teammate has been slain!"

Slowly, all the color left Titan's face, proving life had drained away, leaving him stiff as the magical armor he wore. Then the Decimator picked him up and ate him like a Hot Pocket.

As Titan's final moments played out, it seemed time and space were torn apart like cloth.

Refusing to watch that stomach-churning scene any longer, reality flew away, past the putrid Mana Well, the unclaimed Wraith's Skull, and out of the cave.

And the retreat continued as if existence were a kite being yanked backward through the air, past Titan's distressed teammates who prepared to fight the still-hungry Decimator.

Faster now, reality rocketed away from the alien jungle, ascending through the Battle Moon's atmosphere into space and beyond.

Until, by some trick of magic, what was real emerged in another realm altogether. Here, a crowd of Earthborn adolescents cheered a scene that played on a giant monitor hanging over an arena filled with thousands of rabid gaming fans.

What had seemed real only seconds ago was to this world just a game called *Cosmic Champions*.

This event was the Eighth Annual Gamecon Western Regional Tournament in Denver, Colorado, United States of America, Earth.

And here a legend was about to be born.

CHAPTER TWO

EIGHTH ANNUAL GAMECON WESTERN REGIONAL TOURNAMENT

Alex Garcia, a handsome fifteen-year-old athletic-looking high school student, sat on the stage tapping his high-end gaming keyboard like he was Eddie Van Halen playing "Eruption." His chestnut eyes were narrowed slits of extreme concentration before bulging into shocked dinner plates. His hands never left the keyboard except to brush his sweaty brunette bangs from his eyes.

The Sparkles Modfia, Alex's five-player e-sports team, wore space-age earphones and matching jackets emblazoned with their team logo—a bedazzled dragon clutching a claw full of sparkling fireworks. They sat next to Alex in large gaming chairs that gave them the appearance of being Formula One racers.

Two teammates sat on one side of Alex and two sat on the other.

None of them smiled.

Instead, they growled and cursed at Alex as they fought to extradite themselves from the deathtrap that Alex had selfishly led them into.

Across the stage near the main monitor was the shoutcaster's table. Cameras streamed their commentary, combining it with the gameplay video and shots of the players in real time. They projected all of this onto giant monitors hanging over the raucous Gamecon audience in the Convention Center arena.

Despite the deafening roars of the crowd, the two shoutcasters continued their play-by-play of Titan's fight with the Decimator.

Shoutcaster Jim Gideon, a bald, bearded fellow who looked like a lumberjack in a banker's suit, leaned into his microphone and gasped.

"Larry, I can't believe this crazy turn of events!"

"A fatal mistake by one of the league's best players," shoutcaster Larry Rizzo replied. The heavyset, curly-headed man hit his forehead with a dramatic dope slap. "I'm shocked, to say the least."

The crowd was shocked too. They let out a collective gasp as they watched the deadly fight within the cave play out.

The video game monster called the Decimator picked up Alex Garcia's avatar, Titan, and ate him. Moments later, it burped, and Titan's ghost apparated out from the monster's big gut and vanished in a swirl of magical energy.

"Titan tried to defeat the most powerful jungle boss—completely alone," Jim said.

"Experienced players know that never works. What was he thinking?" Larry replied.

"Okay, folks. Looks like Titan's death timer is maxed."

"Too bad he won't regenerate in time to save his teammates."

Alex's squad, now no longer looking like a team but a group of tantrum-throwing toddlers, sat on one side of a transparent plexiglass barrier from another five-person team called Creep Cannibals. The Cannibals presented like a team confident they were about to win.

"It's understandable why Titan would want the Wraith's Skull right now," Jim said.

"Yes," Larry nodded. "That artifact resurrects its user to 100 percent."

"Then gives a champion several minutes of invulnerability," Jim added.

"But, as we see here, few players have the skill to acquire it!"

"Alex Garcia, aka Titan, has made a lot of fans by attempting the impossible in his never-ending quest to become a legendary-level player. But that wasn't the move of a champion, was it, Larry?"

Jim eyed his companion knowingly. "I'm afraid you're right, Jim. That strategy doesn't match the spirit of the game."

It was true. The rank of legendary was Alex's undeniable obsession. In the first few weeks of playing *Cosmic Champions*, not knowing anything about the different rewards, he'd lucked out and almost achieved it. While others said his brush with fame was sheer chance, Alex decided it was his destiny and the obsession was born.

Becoming legendary required killing ten champions in ten seconds. The only way it was ever achieved was by acquiring the Decimator buff and immediately taking out an entire team once, then killing them a second time, the moment they respawned.

Legendary status instantly converted your player avatar to a permanent champion. This was like having your number retired in other sports. It forever enshrined you in game lore and the pantheon of competition winners.

The primary reward, a check for $500,000, was the carrot on the stick, along with another stream of income from players who paid for skins and items associated with your champion. This was what Alex wanted most. He didn't care about the fame or the notoriety among other *Cosmic Champions* players. The money was the end goal.

Why? Because the lack of money had torn his family apart. Lack of money was what his two parents argued about incessantly and had led to his father moving several states away. It was the lack of money that had forced Alex and his mom to move into a dumpy apartment on the wrong side of town with little hope of ever affording something better.

In fact, money issues had been so bad that he had to get pet food from the local food bank to feed his dog, Dingo. That moment was the lowest of lows and from that minute forward, he had sworn he'd find a legit way out of their problems. Of all the impossible dreams, becoming a legendary *Cosmic Champions* player seemed the most doable.

But no one watching Alex's current disastrous tournament round knew his backstory. They just saw a kid selfishly and stupidly pursuing his ridiculous obsession.

Larry shook his head in dismay. "There's no virtue in becoming a legend at the expense of your own team."

All eyes turned back to the broadcast to watch the carnage unfold. The Creep Cannibals had ambushed the surviving members of the Modfia as they fled the Decimator's Cave. Now the Modfia were surrounded with minimal health and had nowhere to run.

"Ladies and gentlemen, because Titan drained his healer's mana, the Cannibals are ganking the Modfia with devastating effect."

"It's a slaughter. Titan must feel horrible."

"This will force the Modfia to call good game."

One by one, the avatars for Sparkles Modfia were slain by the avatars from the Creep Cannibals.

When the in-game announcer declared the massacre complete with all members of the team eliminated, Joey "Letch" Yeun, the sixteen-year-old Korean American leader of the Creep Cannibals, stood up whooping and hollering, celebrating the kills.

"I just made the Modfia my bitch!" Letch yelled.

Deadlast, the Creep's second-in-command, pointed an accusatory finger at Alex then laughed and humped the clear divider like a dog in heat.

"Watch your teammates die, Titan! You curly piece of poo!"

Alex slammed his headphones onto the table.

"What's wrong, little baby?" Letch mocked, flashing an exaggerated frown-face. "It's just a game! Right?"

Seconds later, the Sapphire Sanctum's cornerstone exploded, destroying the Modfia's base and ending the round.

Alex's team slumped in despair.

Yeah, sure, it was a game, but the mood said otherwise. This was total devastation. And the game's computer made her last announcement confirming that fact.

"Sparkles Modfia has been defeated!"

Silence hung in the air over the convention center. The entire Gamecon crowd appeared stunned. Even Alex's teammates refused to get up from their chairs or even speak.

This made it worse for Alex as he sat there, shocked, baking in the fiery hell of his terrible defeat. The anguish appeared eternal until the PA system squelched and the shoutcasters resumed their commentary.

"Ladies and gentlemen, the Creep Cannibals win the second round of the final playoff game."

Shoutcaster Larry threw his hands up to emphasize the news, and a wave of applause erupted from the audience. The crowd seemed evenly split. Half the arena cheered for the Cannibals, while the other half booed to support the Modfia.

"Two games down, one to go. Can Sparkles Modfia battle back?"

"We'll take a fifteen-minute break to reset. Stay tuned!"

Inside the Modfia's booth, the pressure of the defeat finally exploded. Jed "Ripghoul" Rivers, a ninja-like assassin in the game, sprang from his chair and lunged at Alex, stabbing him in the chest with a finger like it was one of his magical daggers.

"Idiot! You can't kill the Decimator without the whole team. It's the way they rig the game!"

"I could've done it if you four hadn't panicked like noobs!" Alex shouted angrily.

"You want to be a star at our expense. Slurp my sweaty balls."

Jed was an attractive boy with coffee-brown eyes, long, straight midnight hair, bronze skin, and a square jawline. He was a few inches taller than Alex and thin, with some decent muscles that gave him the appearance of a young basketball player.

He grabbed a handful of Alex's shirt. Alex vaulted from his seat and pushed Jed backward, throwing his headset at him.

"What do *you* know, Jed? You're the worst player on this team."

Jed cocked his fist as if to hit Alex.

Alex's stocky teammate Miz grabbed Jed by the back of the shirt and yanked like she was restraining her pit bull.

"Easy does it, Rivers," Miz said. "Have you lost your dang mind?"

Sixteen-year-old Mizzie "BadMiznus" Howard differed from her game avatar. In real life, she was an African American female who wore bold and bright makeup on her light-brown skin. She had rosy cheeks and hazel eyes. She stood five and a half feet and preferred faded jeans and stylish rock band t-shirts that complemented her curvy figure. A goth punk kinda girl, she rocked pink skull earrings and an aggressive purple faux hawk that matched her general attitude.

As the team's strongest player, she was equipped with an excellent set of muscular arms both inside and outside the game. It wasn't a problem playing team bouncer and stopping the fight before it got worse.

"Let me go, Miz," Jed complained.

"Calm your skinny ass down and I will."

"None of you can handle the pressure at this level," Alex shouted. "I should've known that. Now I'll never become legendary."

"See, he doesn't care about anyone but himself." Jed pointed at Alex accusingly. "That's why he snuck off to the cave."

"We needed that artifact," Alex argued.

"Why? You already have the butt of constant wiping," Jed said.

"And you with the mouth of constant whining," Alex countered.

Jed threw his headset at Alex, striking him hard in the chest.

Alex lunged at Jed.

Then it was a flurry of fists, and fingers, and insults—pushing, shoving, and cussing. When Alex took an actual swing at Jed, the crowd reacted in shock, reminding everyone the cameras were still running. All eyes were on the argument.

The Creep Cannibals, their victorious foes, stood on the other side of the team divider, enraptured by what they saw. The Modfia's meltdown was an obvious blessing in disguise. One of the best things that could happen at this point in the tournament.

And it appeared to be incredibly entertaining to the crowd, who laughed uproariously.

Alex scanned the big screens. He couldn't deny he looked like a complete ass. And it was obvious the others felt the same.

"You know, Alex, Jed is right. I should let him whip your butt. Scratch that, I should help him," Miz said.

Lewis "Genghis" Cho, a slim fifteen-year-old Korean American boy decked out in Rocawear sweats and sucking on his favorite THC licorice, was the team's healer. He looked crestfallen because none of his healing magic was going to fix this mess. But he tried anyway.

"Everyone, calm down. Let this bad energy wash away. What kind of team are we if we turn on each other?" Genghis implored.

"No team at all, but it's not the first time this has happened in the middle of an important competition," Aspy said.

"Yeah, she's right. I vote we make Aspy the team captain," Jed yelled.

Alex shot an angry look at Aspy.

Melanie "Aspy" Wells was a cute, short-haired blonde with green eyes, milky-white skin, and elfin features that matched her game avatar. She was blessed with a treasure trove of intelligence but burdened by a severe lack of confidence.

"Aspy knows that's not a good idea."

"What I know is your behavior is grounds for substitution," Aspy fired back.

"What?" Alex's mouth dropped open.

"Dang straight! Finally, someone is talking sense." Jed clapped.

Miz crossed her arms and nodded. "Don't act surprised, Alex. We've talked about this a hundred times."

"No, guys. Alex is our highest-rated player," Genghis said.

"I know he's your best friend," Aspy replied. "But what's best for the team?"

Genghis and Aspy were the most sensitive players in the Modfia and identified so strongly with their virtual characters they used their nicknames in real life.

"Yeah, Genghis. He did just drain you of all your mana and steal your weapon. Basically, stabbed you in the back," Jed added.

Genghis shook his head. "But I know it's not like that."

Alex puffed out his chest and held up his hands. "Guys, we're in the middle of the championship. If we win this round, we advance to the winner's circle—the big money. You're benching me now?"

The idea was inconceivable.

"We want to win, dickwad," Jed fumed.

"We have an alternate, and he'll do what's best for the team," Aspy said.

Everyone turned to stare at Chuck Chesterton, who was in the corner seemingly oblivious to the war raging around him. The poor kid looked like Napoleon Dynamite and was picking his nose, seriously digging deep for some potential nugget.

"You're replacing me with that nostril goblin?"

"Sorry, Alex, you're out," Aspy said.

"You are such a freaking robot, Aspy. Don't you care how close we are to being real champions?" Alex was furious.

"I don't know what that even means." Aspy was flustered, like she always was whenever there was any conflict. "I just know you broke our trust."

"Really? That's what you're worried about right now—trust? What about winning? I mean, if you're the new team leader, isn't winning your priority?"

Aspy looked around at Alex and the rest of the team with confusion, like she was actually considering that.

"Oh, heck, no," Miz said. "You're not blaming this on her or anyone else."

"Let's not blame this on anybody," Genghis said, raising his hands. "Let's take a deep breath and start over."

Aspy took this literally and pulled out her inhaler.

Meanwhile, Alex was sure they'd reached an impasse. He'd lost the game and now was losing the battle for the hearts and minds of his teammates. He could see it on their faces. They were too angry at him.

This was hard to accept knowing it was his skill that had helped them get into the tournament. He really liked all of them, but they didn't seem to understand his drive.

Beating the Creep Cannibals wasn't the end goal.

The point was becoming the best possible player.

But none of the team saw things that way. They just wanted to have fun, win some money, and go about their lives.

They didn't understand. This was his only chance to make something of his life. This was all he had. If he couldn't secure the legendary rank—and the financial rewards that came with it—all the time and money he'd spent on the game would be wasted.

His whole life wouldn't matter.

Miz stepped in between Alex and Aspy.

"Look, man. This is a team sport. If you can't share the win, you're nothing but a prick! And I hate pricks."

"Burn, baby, burn," Jed teased. "That was a lesbian joke, right? 'Cause you don't like dicks?" Jed reached over to give Miz a high five, but she rolled her eyes and left him hanging.

"Get out of my way, Jed," she said, leaving the team's cubicle.

Dejected, Jed mimicked Miz, shoving Genghis aside and storming out.

"Guys, come on," Genghis called, trailing after them. "Come back. We can work this out."

Aspy stepped toward the door then turned around.

"Maybe you're right, Alex. If I can't get everyone on the same page, I'm no better than you. And if we won't work together, what's the point of having a team anyway?"

She gave Alex one last look of curiosity, as if she was desperately trying to compute the impact of that insight. After a few seconds of awkward glaring, she too turned and left the room.

All the oxygen seemed to leave with her because Alex couldn't breathe. His heart hurt as well. He clutched his chest and prayed it was all a nightmare.

The team was falling apart at the key moment when they needed each other the most.

To make matters worse, they had one more round to play with their rivals, the Creep Cannibals.

The Cannibals were a notoriously vile group of players. Good sportsmanship was not one of their team's values. Alex watched them filing out of their cubicle onto the stage and wondered how to take them down.

Letch was their leader. Then came the rogues' gallery of the most controversial players in the gaming world: Pixel, Starminx, Vertigo, and Deadlast.

Two girls. Three guys. All natural gamers who seemed bred to dominate this kind of competition.

Of all their skills, they were known for one overarching masterful strategy: humiliation. And they seemed intent on using that tactic, no matter how unnecessary it was at this point.

"Man, your team breakdown is evil chaotic," Letch snarled. "Way to implode, loser!"

"Can't get it up on the field or IRL. That trophy and check are ours," Starminx laughed, pointing at the dais and the prize lit under a pink spotlight.

Without warning, Miz was back, stepping in to defend Alex, with her mouth running miles ahead of her normal civility.

"I heard all that trash talk, Creeps. Back your messy rears off my teammate before I thump you," Miz hazed, savoring every syllable of the threat.

"Big talk, black and thick, you're going down," Vertigo replied, slamming a fist in her hand.

"Girl, you did not just say that!" Miz stormed toward Vertigo who was half her size.

"Hey, Creeps," Jed purred.

Everyone turned around to see Jed was hovering over the Cannibal's equipment table. He held a fresh can of soda, beads of sweat hanging on the aluminum can as he cracked it open with a hiss.

"Don't you do that, man," Pixel yelled.

Jed acted as if his hand was possessed, then comically tilted the can, pouring its contents all over their expensive keyboards.

"Oh, dang, I'm so, so, so *not* sorry."

An explosion of curses erupted from the Cannibals as they lurched back to their table in a futile attempt to save their equipment from the soda.

Suddenly Jed's can and the wet keyboards, along with curses and fists were flying around the room. Jed laughed, enjoying every minute of being in the middle of it.

The two teams fought their way onto the main stage, brawling like mad cats, totally forgetting the massive audience was still watching their every move through the jumbotrons. The crowd went crazy, more excited than they had been for normal gameplay—this was real gladiator action, after all.

Even the shoutcasters couldn't resist contributing to the moment. Jim and Larry leaned in, tracking the action while the snowball of players pathetically kicked, flailed, scratched, and screamed as they rolled around the stage.

"Larry, we've got an unscheduled 5v5 melee on stage."

"Dandelions and dipping dots, Jim, the Cannibals just dove on Ripghoul with no damage control whatsoever."

"Genghis has swung a big roundhouse with his headphones, smacking Starminx's backside. That leaves their flank vulnerable."

"Here comes BadMiznus right up the lane. *Bam!* She draws first blood."

"Starminx is down."

"Ripghoul is taking serious damage. Titan moves in with a wet keyboard for the counter-gank."

"Pixel turns tail and bails into the crowd."

"Oh my, folks, look out. Aspy is hurtling insults and water bottles with supreme accuracy, forcing Letch to seek cover."

"Deadlast is white-eyed and has no vision on Ripghoul, who's slipped away."

"BadMiznus is coming down the mid lane with a game chair over her head. She lets it fly. Ouch, direct strike on Vertigo."

"Well, kiss my sweet Halo. That chair attack has ended the battle because here comes tournament security."

The crowd cheered like it was the greatest battle they'd ever seen.

"That's going to be game over," Jim said, slapping a hand on his table.

"I have to say this is one of the most exciting skirmishes we've seen in tournament history," Larry said. "And now some event leaders are joining security on the set."

Alex looked up. Sure enough, various officials were storming the stage. Among them were two people every team feared more than the Decimator—the tournament moderators.

A hush fell over the crowd, and the fighting teams gave in, letting themselves be taken into custody.

Alex wondered how things could go so bad so fast. Only moments ago he'd been on the cusp of his ultimate victory. Now he was being heckled and hauled away for some dreadful punishment like the ultimate loser.

CHAPTER THREE

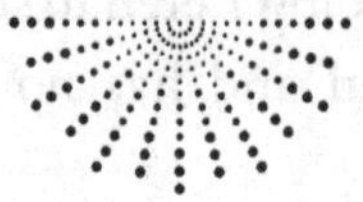

When the team entered the back office, they expected the worst. The room was nondescript, a beige rectangle with five plastic chairs. They sat down anxiously, looking like prisoners awaiting their executions.

The first moderator, who looked and dressed like an adult-sized Charlie Brown, stepped forward and shook his head admonishingly, glancing at each of the Modfia in turn. "Guys, guys, guys," he said. "I think we all agree that things got out of control."

The second moderator had long red hair tied back in a ponytail and radiated a surfer dude vibe. He cleared his throat before introducing himself and his counterpart.

"My gamertag is Slipstream76, and this is BeanFarts69."

He made the introduction straight-faced with no hint of sarcasm.

Moderator BeanFarts69 chugged from a Slurp-Ice cup while still shaking his head. He scrolled through his computer tablet as if searching for something important. When he found it, he nodded to his colleague.

"Well, then," Slipstream76 said. "Let's get started."

Alex and the team didn't know what that meant. They squirmed in their chairs, preparing for the worst.

Moderator BeanFarts69 smiled bleakly and began reading from the tournament rules and regulations manual.

Many minutes later, Alex knew they were in big trouble. The mod droned on with no sign of stopping. His team was being subjected to a verbal waterboarding the likes of which he'd never imagined possible. He had a sudden desire to puncture his eardrums.

"Posting content that is deemed offensive, unlawful, harmful, threatening, abusive, or racially, ethically, or otherwise objectionable—"

Aspy cupped her hands over her ears and moaned. "I know all the rules by heart. Please stop."

"Transmitting content that contains a virus, corrupted data, trojan horse, databot, keystroke logger, worm, time bomb, cancelbot or mine, or scraping personal information . . ." BeanFarts69 droned.

"I can't take another minute of this," Miz groaned.

The entire team was writhing in their seats.

"Stop it! Can't you see you're torturing my friends? You heartless bastards!" Genghis hissed.

"Please don't interrupt us—" Slipstream76 intoned.

"—we'd have to start over," BeanFarts69 finished.

"But if you'd just review the video, I think you'll agree we didn't violate any of the rules you just highlighted," Aspy pleaded desperately with her eyes, as if her argument would make some impact on the two strange men.

Alex tried to help her. "It was self-defense."

Miz pointed an accusatory finger. "They almost killed our rogue."

Jed snickered. "Totally unprovoked, I swear." His swollen lip curled into the half-serious grin of a cool dude enjoying the chaos he'd created.

Alex suppressed a laugh. Jed notoriously cherry-picked the rules he followed. Alex tolerated it because it gave their team an edge.

Aspy continued to try her best to redirect the moderators, which pleased Alex. For once her encyclopedic knowledge of the game might come in handy.

"Please, can you just cut to the relevant infractions?"

Moderator BeanFarts69 cocked an eyebrow. "That is agreeable. We'll proceed to the section—"

"—outlining your violations," Slipstream76 agreed, nodding to his colleague.

"The Champion Code is clear. Severe unsportsmanlike conduct includes intentionally breaking tournament equipment, defacing the tournament stage, or disrupting the venue."

"Check, check, check," Miz said. "Those crazy noodle snorters did all that."

Aspy twisted in her seat. "Miz, you're not helping!"

Miz cursed under her breath. "Yeah, okay. Sorry."

BeanFarts69 nodded and said, "The penalty for any violent behavior is disqualification. In addition, it may be necessary to contact the authorities."

"Or even the Gamemaster, himself," Slipstream76 added.

"What? Guys, c'mon. We're sorry," Genghis pleaded.

"Arrest us, I don't care," Alex said. "Just don't disqualify us. We are too close to winning the whole tournament."

Miz flashed a concerned look at Alex. "Are you serious right now?"

"They're not calling the police," Jed said bluntly.

"Mr. Rivers is correct. For now, we ban your team from any further league play," Slipstream76 said.

"Don't worry, the tournament organizers will file no charges with local law enforcement. But we informed your sponsor," BeanFarts69 added. "He'll be here shortly to take custody of you."

Alex flashed a worried look at the rest of the team. They responded with similar expressions of fear. Their sponsor was worse than the police.

"Well, our job is done," BeanFarts69 said. He stowed his tablet in his backpack, grabbed his giant Slurp-Ice, and turned to leave.

"Don't despair, young ones," Slipstream76 said. "There's a place for budding champions like you in this cosmos. It's just not here—not anymore."

The mods eyed the team one last time, gave everyone a half-smile, and followed each other out of the room.

CHAPTER FOUR

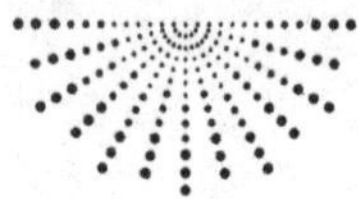

Ray "Sparkles" Malone, wearing dark sunglasses and a Walter White pork pie hat, had a lot on his plate. He was a short, scrawny thirteen-year-old kid navigating the battleground called junior high school.

Clearly, that was enough for the average boy.

Sparkles, however, was anything but average.

His chief priority was his ridiculously lucrative illegal fireworks business, a baked goods side hustle, and a host of other investments that needed managing. He was by all counts a pee-wee-sized godfather who controlled the junior high school black market. If you wanted a case of illegal bottle rockets, he was your man. If you needed contraband candy or cereal, he was your man. Did your parents refuse to buy that latest pair of high-end sneakers? Or the newest video game? Show Sparkles the cash and he'd get you what you wanted.

In the early desperate days of forming the Modfia, Alex had sought him out for financing. It had been a terrible mistake.

"You five losers are a problem I didn't need, not today," Sparkles grumbled.

"Ray, I can explain," Alex replied.

"Not necessary. I understand. You had a fight during your Dungeons & Dragons game? Did I get that right? Someone on the other team hurt your feelings?"

Still in their chairs, the team stared at Sparkles, too scared to say a word. He glared back at them over his black Ray-Bans.

"Who started the fight? Was it mister dog-breath here?" Sparkles asked, pointing at Genghis. "Or do I have the wrong bowl of kimchi?"

Genghis sighed and stared at his sneakers.

Chump, Ray's burly henchmen, dragged Letch, the leader of the Creep Cannibals, into the room.

Jed perked up. "That's him! He started the whole thing!"

"Shut up, Rivers!" Sparkles motioned to Chump, who produced a pan of cupcakes decorated with brilliant blue icing and set them down on the table next to his boss.

"Please don't hurt me," Letch begged.

"Hurt you? Who said anything about hurting you?" Sparkles mused. "These are cupcakes, my man. One of my brand-new business ventures that is really taking off. People love these things. Each one is iced with 99.9% pure cane sugar from the hippie communes of Boulder, Colorado. Nothing hurtful about them."

"Well . . . okay . . . but I actually prefer boba," Letch said meekly.

Sparkles growled and signaled to Chump. "No one turns down my Blue Iced."

Chump grabbed the largest cupcake in the pan then grabbed Letch. Ignoring his pitiful protest, he pried open the lanky gamer's mouth and force fed him the treat. Then he stuffed a second in his mouth, and finally a third. Letch collapsed in a puddle of gooey Twitter-blue drool, moaning like a wounded animal.

"Sweet Geezus," Alex said. "What's wrong with him?"

Sparkles smiled approvingly while opening a small zippered case. "Diabetic coma. Nothing a little insulin won't take care of—if I was *willing* to give him a dose."

He showed the group a syringe filled with medicine.

Letch whimpered a plea for mercy.

Sparkles teased Letch with the insulin, waving the syringe over him as if he might offer it. At the last second, Sparkles coldly dropped it on the ground.

Letch pawed at it, struggling to grab it as if it were an antidote to poison. But before Letch could retrieve it, Sparkles stepped on the syringe, crushing it. Its liquid contents stained the floor. The team gasped in shock.

"That's messed up, man," Miz said, turning away.

"You'd kill this kid over a video game?" Aspy asked.

"He derailed my chance of winning a lot of money!" Sparkles looked at Chump. "How much was it?"

Chump scratched his head and began muttering to himself.

The team snickered as the big bruiser counted on his fingers.

"The grand prize is a quarter million, but there's a 25 percent bonus based on attendance," Chump explained, looking at the corner of the room as he tallied the loss. "If you factor in early estimates, that could be a million dollars."

Everyone stared at Chump, dumbfounded. This Neanderthal was an impressive accountant.

"We can win that money for you, Ray," Alex blurted, thinking there had to be a way out of this. He just needed to think. Maybe talk to the mods again.

"No, Garcia! You can't! And that really, really irritates me because you promised such a big payout. I bought you loads of equipment, five new super-fast computers, bedazzled team jackets with my logo, and paid all the ridiculous entry fees. You're in deep this time and if we don't go along with my plan to make this right, it's Blue Iced for every one of you losers!"

Alex had never seen Sparkles this mad. He was genuinely scared, glancing over at Genghis. Genghis took that as a clue to step in.

"Look, Mr. Sparkles," Genghis said. "We appreciate everything you've done for us. But Alex isn't lying when he says we can still win this. Maybe if we just talked to the moderators again."

"Genghis, you're high as usual, huh? They ejected your butts for good!"

Sparkles was getting angrier by the second. He leaned over Genghis, who winced as spittle hit him in the face.

"Do you have any idea how many junior high bake sales I have to muscle in on to clear a million bucks?"

"One point two million would be more accurate," Chump said.

"Shut it, Chump."

"Just give us some more time. We can win you that money," Alex pleaded.

"No! I'm turning you losers over to new management."

"Without my input?" Aspy was indignant.

"Yeah, Asperger's, definitely without your input."

Sparkles was vicious with his offensive insults and tactics. The middle-school mobster didn't seem to care about hurting their feelings or their lives. He turned and left the room, but it only took a few seconds before he was back with an unexpected solution.

Someone dressed as Bonegrin, one of the most famous characters in *Cosmic Champions*, followed Sparkles back into the room.

Alex felt dwarfed by the champion but also transfixed as he trudged toward them. He was seven feet tall, a solid mass of muscle with bulging veins, and towered over Sparkles like a giant. He breathed through his open mouth, exposing a terrifying set of teeth and two saber-like tusks sticking out either side of his grey-green face.

His crimson leather tunic stood out against the black boots, leather gauntlets, and leggings. He held a macabre trident said to be made from an alien creature's skeleton. It was immediately identifiable as Bonegrin's signature weapon.

Even so, what did this bad cosplayer have to do with Sprinkle's plan?

"Far out, man. That's the best Bonegrin I've ever seen," Genghis said, giving him a thumbs up.

Genghis snacked on a piece of licorice as Bonegrin stepped up uncomfortably close. His thick lips pulled back over his yellow fangs.

He seemed to smile and snarl at the same time as he sniffed the team like they were his next meal.

The glare gave Alex pause. "Man, those eyes."

"A little too real, if you ask me," Miz added, pushing her chair back several feet. "What the heck is going on here? This shiz is getting weirder by the minute."

"I like the costume, but the breath, man, ruins it," Jed said, fanning a hand in front of his face. "Something crawled up inside you and died."

Everyone glared at Jed. The tolerance for humor was gone.

The second person to enter the room was just as frightening as Bonegrin.

Nightbane, who had the elegance of a vampire bat on a wedding cake, was another popular champion. Like Aspy, she was a female elf, but of a much darker, evil race called the Bloodstone Banshee, which was known for their demonic magic.

She stood about five feet six and had a lean, athletic frame. She was dressed in a tight leather catsuit, thigh-high boots, and a leather corset that showed off her moon-white cleavage. Pieces of molded plate mail protected the rest of her body.

Her face was a perfect heart shape with features that seemed chiseled from marble: a perfect nose, lips, and ears. She had alabaster skin and coal-colored hair. Her spooky eyes stared through her thick lashes and glowed yellow like a wolf.

Her only weapons seemed to be a long dagger strapped to one leg and a barbed whip curled and tied to her waist.

"What a pathetic group of losers," she said in her husky growl.

She slinked across the room and sauntered down the line of chairs, trailing the scent of burnt hair. She inspected each of them like a seductive general.

"Talk about a twisted sister," Jed joked as she brushed past.

Nightbane spun on her boots' heels, hissed at him like a feral cat, then rejoined Bonegrin at the front of the room.

"Okay, good deal," Sparkles said. "Seems you bozos recognize your new owners. They said you would."

The team turned to each other agitated, whispering questions. What the heck was this all about? Did he say *owners*?

"Let's wrap this up. I've got more important things to do," Sparkles said, turning to Nightbane. "Did you get the final numbers from Chump?"

"Yes. And we're prepared to increase the offer to ensure absolute discretion," Nightbane said as she surveyed the team. "Your realm's gold is but paper. For your trouble, let's make it two million and throw in a dozen of those cupcakes—they're so delicious."

Sparkles leaned in, licking his lips. "I like how you do business, Ms. Night. You have a deal."

He motioned to Chump to give her the remaining cupcakes.

"Wait a minute. Is this your solution? Dung Breath and Nurse Nightmare?" Alex asked. "I mean, who are they? Two psychotic cosplayers? How are they our new sponsors?"

Sparkles flashed his indignant eyes at Alex.

"Mr. Bone and Ms. Night are scouts for a new team called the Griefers. Most importantly, they agreed to buy out your contract and settle your debt. I would shut up if I were you. You don't want to mess this up."

He pointed at poor Letch, who was still passed out on the floor.

"Come on, Ray. This is insane. The Griefers are old game lore. That's fiction. I've never heard of these guys. If they were legit, one of us would know. These guys are scamming you."

Sparkles ignored Alex and addressed Nightbane. "Just to be clear, they're *damaged* goods. You okay with that?"

Miz was offended. "Hey, what the heck does that mean?"

Nightbane licked her lips. "They will rise to the challenge or be culled."

"Yeah, well, whatever." Sparkles tugged at his imaginary goatee. "Just so it's understood, I don't do refunds."

"We know who and what they are," Bonegrin said matter-of-factly. "The game engine generated profiles about each of them."

"Oh, yeah?" Genghis asked. He looked genuinely curious. "What do the profiles say?"

"That you are the five best *worst* players in the league."

"The five best *worst*?" Miz repeated. "Screw you, crypt keeper."

"Wait." Aspy straightened up like she was asking a question in class. "Have you been spying on us?"

Nightbane walked up to Aspy and leaned in, examining her from various angles as if she were a plant that might need watering.

"No, Ms. Wells, the game engine knows all and sees all. Spying isn't necessary when you spend so much time hiding in the game."

"I don't believe you. How could a game know everything about us?"

Nightbane cupped her hand around Aspy's face. She caressed her cheek for a few seconds then pulled away too quickly. Aspy yelped. Blood trickled down from a red scratch on her cheek.

Nightbane caught the blood with her fingernail and licked it. "I'm happy to show you, little elf."

CHAPTER FIVE

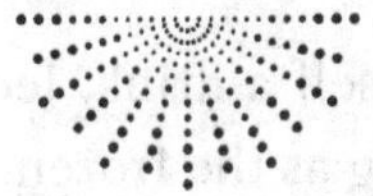

"To begin, we will review your team's wilderness expert," Nightbane said. "Mr. Jed Rivers, also known as Ripghoul. A hunter and a rogue. A thief and an assassin. He's one of your team's most fearless players, one who can't seem to follow a rule to save his life."

Nightbane nodded to Bonegrin. When Bonegrin nodded back, she waved her long fingers over Jed's head, and a tapestry of magical energy appeared displaying Jed's memories.

Genghis leaned back in his chair. "Whoa, man. Far out!"

"Indeed, Mr. Cho. Bloodstone magic can siphon thoughts, dreams, and even nightmares from almost anyone, especially creatures so basic as you, Earthborn."

Alex couldn't believe what he was seeing. He didn't know how Nightbane was pulling this off, but it went way beyond simple cosplay.

Time rewound, and within the mystical blaze of images, a younger Jed Rivers appeared. The team leaned forward as if they'd just sat down to watch a great television show.

The scene cut to a sparsely bearded hipster working the counter of a neighborhood convenience store. It appeared to be late at night. The store was vacant except for one customer—a hoodie-clad kid screwing around with the drink machines.

After several seconds, the magical memory changed its point of view, catching the profile of the customer. It was Jed, and it was obvious he was in the middle of some serious mischief. He perused the Slurp-Ice machines that lined the walls, churning a rainbow of frozen concoctions.

Instead of serving himself a drink, Jed turned on every machine and stepped back, watching as the frozen slush overflowed their spill trays and flooded the floor. When he seemed satisfied with his vandalism, he laughed and headed for the exit.

Just as Jed reached the front door, the store attendant reacted.

"Hey, man! What the heck are you doing?"

The attendant peered over the rows of candy and snacks and saw the mess of frozen sludge and a guilty-looking Jed.

"Hold it right there, kid!"

Jed rushed out, laughing as the attendant slogged his way through the rainbow-colored mess to turn off the machines.

"Ripghoul is an expert at creating diversions," Nightbane observed. "A true rogue with a chaotic neutral alignment."

Bonegrin scoffed.

The scene cut to the backroom of the store as the attendant gathered cleaning supplies and the yellow mop bucket.

From the shadows of the back room, Jed dropped from the ceiling like a ninja and made his way quietly to a box on the attendant's desk. It was full of gift cards. Jed quickly stuffed them into every pocket he had.

"He has potential," Bonegrin growled, as if someone had forced him to give the compliment, "yet squanders his skills on thievery."

Nightbane grinned. "Agreed, but his disregard for the rules gives him an edge."

Before Jed could escape with his loot, two cops entered from the back of the store, surprising him. Without missing a beat, he thrust his hands on his hips and mesmerized them with an impromptu Jedi mind-trick.

"What took you two so long? I called thirty minutes ago!"

The cops couldn't get a word out.

"The vandal is still in the store, destroying my slush machines. He's crazy. Maybe if you move faster, you might catch him!"

Agitated and perhaps embarrassed, the cops rushed past Jed and made a quick arrest of the poor, confused attendant.

Meanwhile, Jed used the confusion to grab more gift cards. Before anyone was the wiser, he slipped out the back door and faded into the night like a phantom.

Now the magical video shifted to images of the *Cosmic Champions* game.

Jed's avatar, Ripghoul, the ninja-like rogue brandishing shadow-weave daggers, hid behind a Warwood tree in the thick wilderness. Nearby, two non-player characters that looked exactly like the convenience store cops had cornered a group of allied skulks.

Ripghoul flung his weapons, killing the NPC's instantly.

A smile curled up over Bonegrin's fangs.

"A cunning and ruthless hunter." Bonegrin grunted his approval.

"Who enjoys the art of deception," Nightbane agreed.

Ripghoul fired a grappling line from a small crossbow and swung away into the forest. Nightbane was satisfied and lowered her hands, ending the magical display.

Nightbane approached Miz next. Her long fingers danced over Miz, and maroon energy swirled around her head, changing the scene.

"Here we have the team tank," Nightbane purred. "Mizzie Summerfield Howard."

The team watched as a magical camera snaked into a crowded dive bar. On stage, a tribute band called Back in Black covered a thunderous AC/DC song.

A drunk headbanger pushed up to the stage and heckled the bassist, which was a terrible mistake because it was Miz.

"The fat dyke can play!" he screamed, throwing up some devil horns.

Without missing a note, Miz leaned over and swung her bass guitar into the skinhead's face, knocking out a few teeth.

When he hurled a racist insult, she leapt like an Olympic diver into the audience. Fists flew. Blood sprayed and bones broke. And when the crowd and chaos finally cleared, Miz stood over the thoroughly beaten punk. She was totally unscathed.

"A worthy opponent," Bonegrin said, nodding approvingly. "She engages the enemy explosively."

"Perhaps she's provoked too easily?" Nightbane wondered. "Such raw power should be used wisely. She leaves herself vulnerable to reprisals."

They watched as the skinhead's angry friends rushed Miz. When she disappeared under a new dogpile, the team gasped and leaned forward, hoping Miz was okay.

But before her fate was revealed, the scene cross-faded to images of the game. BadMiznus, Miz's Amazonian avatar, erupted from underneath a pile of enemy skulks swinging her battle axe like a buzz saw.

It was clear she was in the middle of farming—game-speak for killing skulks, the auto-generated minions that both defended and attacked players. Gold credits spun like she'd hit a jackpot and bodies piled up as she cleared Deadman's Road all the way to the first enemy tower.

"She withstands tremendous damage, making her a tough offensive player," Nightbane observed. "She's the only one of these five who seems to be a natural warrior."

NIGHTBANE THEN TURNED TO ASPY. "Melanie Wells is a smart and beautiful young woman with Asperger's syndrome—a diagnosis that keeps her socially ostracized."

The images of Miz morphed into a flyover of Aspy walking home from school. A montage of several sad scenes played—her alone at lunch, her alone between classes, and her alone in her bedroom at night.

The string of images ended with Aspy in the corner of the school library reading a manual for *Cosmic Champions*. She seemed obsessed with the game.

In the next scene, she attended school cosplaying as her new elf avatar. At lunch, she sat at one crowded cafeteria table. Immediately, she was heckled and humiliated by the other kids and fled the room in tears.

"She's a budding genius but can't process simple social cues."

Bonegrin shrugged. "What good is she if the team rejects her?"

"Her only outlet seems to be the game. Because of that, she's written detailed guides about it. They are very popular among aspiring champions."

To the shock of the team, they see their friend is the writer and blogger behind some of their favorite game content.

"That's you?" Miz said, amazed. "I've got five of your guides. Watch your videos all the time. What the heck, dude? Why didn't you tell any of us?"

Aspy looked at her feet and shrugged.

"Her lack of confidence may be her undoing," Nightbane said. "Despite this, she bleeds strategy."

Bonegrin sniffed her like he smelled something spoiled. "Dangerous, this one. Festering with buried rage."

"Even though she lacks the confidence to lead, her skills are impeccable, her mind unmatched." Nightbane waved a hand. New images flashed before the team.

A female elf swung through the treetops stalking a group of skulks. The skulks advanced through the jungle aggressively until a volley of fiery arrows showered down like a hailstorm.

Flipping out of cover, Aspy landed heroically in the center of an open space to take out the surviving minions. When she drew her bowstring back, three arrows were already nocked.

"Dang, she looks cool!" Jed cheered.

Aspy looked up at him then blushed.

"She captures the imagination of her teammates," Bonegrin said, "but not their hearts."

"Perhaps because she can't accept her true potential," Nightbane agreed.

The images shifted once again. The depiction of Aspy, the badass elf, hiking the jungle trail faded into lonely Melanie Wells navigating her school hallway.

She disappeared into the raucous crowd as the students changed classes.

Bonegrin crossed his arms and scoffed. "Her lack of confidence makes her a weak leader and because of this, the team suffers."

"The team's healer seems to have many of the elf's same flaws," Nightbane said, pointing accusingly at Genghis.

She moved on, conjuring more memories as she did. In contrast to Aspy, Lewis Cho was popular among his fellow students.

"I find it hard to believe this odd, intoxicated knave is the team's main defensive player," Bonegrin said, shaking his head.

"His enthusiasm is disgusting, but he is a highly skilled healer."

Nightbane's images showed Genghis in the center of the school courtyard, sitting in the lotus pose, his hands resting lightly on the buxom chest of a beautiful girl. Many curious onlookers gathered around him, watching.

"I'm passing the healing power of my chi into your third chakra," Genghis said.

"Oh, I can feel it!" the girl said, giggling. "Can you move it any lower?"

"Certainly," he muttered. "Envision yourself under a gentle waterfall. Let the sensation of the warm water envelope your entire body."

"Oh, Gangghey," the girl purred. "You know just what to do."

As the team watched and giggled, the courtyard and high school morphed into a castle, bringing the action back to the game.

In the guise of his online avatar, Genghis levitated off the ground, riding a funnel of mystical energy. As he moved, he spun his staff, weaving new blooms of mana into razor-sharp lotus blossoms that spun out like throwing stars toward a wave of threatening skulks.

In front of him, team Modfia did battle, viciously defending their home base from an onslaught of attackers. As they fought, their health and mana bars diminished. However, Genghis expertly cast one healing spell after another, keeping his teammates in the battle.

"His fellow offensive players rely heavily on his support," Bonegrin observed.

"His deep-seated insecurities stifle him; otherwise, he'd be the heart of the team, making them very powerful indeed," Nightbane mused. "As it is, it's a heart easily cut out."

Bonegrin and Nightbane moved on to Alex, the only team member they hadn't analyzed.

"Alex Garcia, also known as Titan, the team's de facto leader," Bonegrin said. "The elf's got the title, but this one calls the shots."

"Yes, it seems Titan here has more charisma. Isn't that right, Mr. Garcia?" Nightbane asked.

"What did you say? I'm sorry, but Mr. Bone-groin's insanely accurate genitalia distracted me," Alex joked, trying to change the subject. "Shouldn't you wear a better jockstrap or something?"

Everyone on the team laughed, which was good.

What these two creepy cosplayers were saying may be true, but he didn't want to upset the team any more than they already were. Somehow, they needed to stick together long enough to get out of Sparkles's insane deal.

"You know, I've just never thought about champions having boy parts," Genghis snickered.

Bonegrin was surprised, even embarrassed. He glared at them to shut everyone up. When that failed, he raised his trident and zapped the team with a quick jolt of electrical energy. Just enough pain to get their attention.

"Dang, man," Miz yelled, rubbing her arms. "That stung. If you do that again, I'm gonna knock those janky horns off your head."

"Yeah, meathead," Jed yelled. "How are you doing that, anyway? Is there a stun gun jammed up in that crappy prop?"

"This is no toy," Bonegrin roared. "Test me again, and you'll feel the full wrath of the Kraken's Tooth."

Ignoring the argument, Nightbane continued her enchantment, and new images of Alex's life flashed on her magical screen.

The first montage revealed Alex grinding out his job at the mall. A series of dreary days at GameBlaster showed the boy selling expensive games to agitated parents, repairing broken consoles, trading in defective products, and enduring the humiliation of serving entitled, wealthy kids who had no clue what working was really like.

The worst part of it seemed to be Alex's boss. All the GameBlaster employees had secretly named him Bob the Bastard.

It was obvious that Bob the Bastard was a sociopath-in-training, and he loved picking on his underlings—especially Alex Garcia.

"I saw you on Twitch, Garcia. I can't believe you play *Cosmic Champions*."

Bob sneered, not looking up from his task of checking in a stack of returned rentals.

"By the way, you suck . . . big time! I mean, you're one of the crappiest players who ever played that ridiculous game. Your best magic spell must be Butt-of-Constant-Wiping—because all you do is slap diapers on low-level players."

Bob laughed at his own joke. Alex turned red and looked to be on the verge of a meltdown.

All the Modfia were insulted and immediately hated Bob the Bastard.

"Speaking of *Cosmic Champions*, I need a few days off, if that's okay," Alex said, hoping beyond hope Bob might show some mercy.

"What? Why? You're not going to the tournament, are you?" Bob laughed again, but this time it was completely forced—a sign that he was slipping into his one of his sadistic moods. "Don't humiliate yourself, Garcia. Better you stay home, eat tacos, and beat your piñata."

"I'm going to that tournament," Alex muttered. "We have a decent team that's counting on me."

"If you go, you'll embarrass yourself in front of the whole world. I mean, isn't it obvious? Your suckyness is at peak suckage."

"We worked hard and qualified fair and square. Please, it's just a few days."

"No, I don't think so. You're scheduled to close the store that weekend, Cinderella. No ball for you."

"Come on, Bob. I'll close two weeks straight when I get back."

"I'm telling you, Garcia, if you go to that tournament, don't even bother coming back here. You are fired!"

Alex couldn't look. This montage was humiliating. Plus, he'd never told the team he'd given up his job to come to the tournament.

"So pathetic to see a warrior of his potential disrespected in such a foul way," Nightbane said, shivering her shoulders for effect.

"I would rip the spine from this Bob the Bastard and feast on his kidneys," Bonegrin laughed.

"Don't underestimate Mr. Garcia," Nightbane said, leaning in.

"The great Titan has pledged to become the best Cosmic Champion player ever—he wants to be legendary."

Alex said nothing, but the mention of his long-held goal sent a brief panic through him. That dream seemed to slip further away every minute they remained in this room.

"There's only one worthy of that title," Bonegrin said, genuine fear flashing in his eyes. "Pray you never meet our master in actual battle."

"Whatever. No one wants it more than me—you'll see," Alex shouted.

Something in him had boiled over. His teammates looked at him with concern. But Nightbane seemed pleased by Alex's passionate defense.

"That's the spirit, Mr. Garcia! It's that kind of blind faith that creates real champions. Maybe you do have such greatness within you. We shall see soon enough!"

CHAPTER SIX

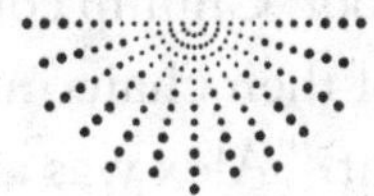

Just as the images of Alex's life faded from view, Sparkles finished a call on his phone. It seemed he'd never once watched the magical display of memories, but he was ready to wrap up the hand-off to Nightbane.

"Just so we're clear," Sparkles said, hooking a thumb in Bonegrin's direction, "Boneface over here has developed a new e-sports league. You guys are going to play for him or you'll end up like this drooling doofus!"

He pointed down at Letch, who was still lying on the floor as if comatose. Blue bubbles dribbled out of the corners of his mouth.

"Barely alive, poor bastard," Genghis observed.

"Understood?!" Sparkles yelled.

Chump crossed his arms and glared for added effect.

Everyone nodded. They understood.

Nightbane appeared ready to close the deal as well.

"Mr. Sparkles, let's finalize the payment. Do you accept Venmo?" Nightbane asked as she pulled out a smartphone.

"Venmo? Heck no!" Sparkles's eyebrows narrowed. "I told you

both no bitcoin, no weird gold. Nothing traceable. I want cash. Cold, hard cash."

"I understand." Nightbane was nonplussed. "But, since I'm not from here, I don't have cash. Bonegrin, can you take care of him, please?"

Bonegrin pointed his trident at Sparkles and Chump and blasted them both with a magical burst of energy. Sparkles slammed into the wall and rag-dolled to the floor. Chump collapsed beside him.

The team jumped out of their chairs, mouths agape.

"What the heck was that?" Alex was amazed but also worried for Sparkles. "Ray! Ray, can you hear me?"

"Mr. Sparkles can't hear you, but don't worry. He isn't dead. He will recover once we're gone," Nightbane said, as if the events of the last few minutes had all been a regular occurrence.

Alex wondered if her had lost his mind. Possibly. Was this all some elaborate magic trick? Then again, everything around him felt very real. He just didn't understand how these two psychotic cosplayers were pulling this off.

"Now that I've scanned each of your minds," Nightbane said, stepping in front of the team, "I know one thing to be true. Each of you desires another shot at winning the game. If we give you that second chance, will you redeem yourselves?"

"Heck yeah, let's do it," Genghis cheered, the eternal optimist.

Everyone glared at him until he wilted.

"Another chance? Redeem ourselves? What does that even mean?" Alex asked. "More importantly, how do we do it?"

That question was quickly answered when Bonegrin produced a familiar object from the game. It was a rare portal key said to open magical doors to other dimensions of existence—the device that allowed everyday kids to enter the game, choose an avatar, and learn the skills necessary to become champions.

The opening of every *Cosmic Champions* game included the animated activation of this key. They'd seen it a million times on their computer screens—but it was quite another thing to see it in real life.

"I'm pretty sure this is an *actual* portal key," Aspy said. She was mesmerized and tried to reach out and touch it.

Bonegrin slapped her hand away.

"I am the designated Herald," he growled. "Only I can wield the portal key!"

Bonegrin raised a hand. The portal key hovered in the air, spinning on its axis before slamming into his flattened palm. Then, through some kind of strange sorcery, it sank into his very flesh. What it left was a glowing sigil. It looked like a golden tattoo of the key. Bonegrin winced as if it was painful but then was very pleased at the result.

"That's not possible," Miz said, stepping back. "This has to be a prank."

"Earthborn are a naïve lot," Bonegrin snarled. "Too young. Too foolish. They'll never make it on the Battle Moon."

He was behind them now, shoving them forward.

"Our job is to find potential combatants for training and get them to the station. Crane and the brothers can sort them out and see if they are truly worthy of battling Malvexus," Nightbane said.

Bonegrin laughed. "Pray you are not, Earthborn. My master will drink your blood like wine."

"Where are you taking us?" Alex asked.

"Surely you can guess by now." Nightbane laughed then nodded to Bonegrin.

Bonegrin thrust his glowing hand forward, and the air exploded with otherworldly color and light. It was nothing less than a mystical portal shimmering in the air before them. It smelled like burning sulfur and gave off a dull heat—something that should have been impossible.

Before they could say another word, Bonegrin turned his trident on its side and used it to shove the entire team through the opening in one clean sweep.

He then stepped through after them, and Nightbane followed. As she disappeared into the magic, the portal collapsed, and they were gone.

PART II
STARWAY STATION

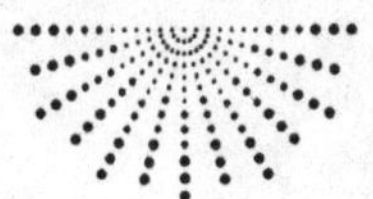

CHAPTER SEVEN

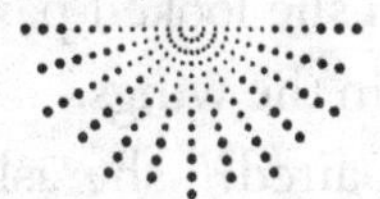

Alex lost all sense of time and space. It was as if he was tumbling, flying, and floating in a bubble of purple slime and slush. There was no pain or fear. He felt completely at ease. One might even say ecstatic. Was that the word for feeling so warm, fuzzy, and thrilled at the same time?

Schlackabakfalloom!

He had arrived.

But where?

Alex walked out of the darkness onto a stage and then into a single spotlight. A few feet away, a beam of intense rainbow colors shone down on a beautiful alien girl.

He recognized her immediately. He had three posters of her tacked on the ceiling above his bed. She was his favorite champion in the game. A fictional warrior whose extraordinary skill was matched only by her exquisite beauty. She was Alex's white-hot nuclear meltdown crush. A fiction, yes, but a true teenage boy motivator.

Her name was Luna Lifestealer.

Alex was in awe.

Luna was staring at him.

He waved awkwardly and immediately regretted it, his entire upper body flushing with shame.

"You . . . you're Luna Lifestealer."

"If you say so," she shrugged.

"If you're not, your cosplay is on point. Wow!"

"Uh-yeah," Luna said. She flipped her coffee-colored hair out of her chestnut eyes, tapped a metallic cuff on her left arm, and perused her heads-up display. Then she looked past him like something more interesting was happening in the wings.

"Are you mentally impaired?" she asked. "Or can you help me out?"

"Uh, I think I'm okay," Alex muttered. "But things are super trippy right now. Am I dreaming?"

"In many ways, yes."

He wasn't sure he knew what that meant, but he didn't really care. Some great music was playing, and he knew the song: "*I Feel Love*" by the disco singer Donna Summer. It was one of his mother's favorites. She played it incessantly when she was cooking dinner.

The music, the lights, and Luna's image kaleidoscoped around him, creating a hypnotic mood. He suddenly felt boiling heat in his nether regions and a powerful impulse to discard his clothes.

Luna hovered nearby, pointing at the horizon with her alien weapon.

He ripped off his t-shirt.

"Getting naked isn't necessary," she said, with no hint of interest.

"Oh, it's no problem. Want to join me?"

"I've already changed my skin. Did they show you how?"

"I think I know," Alex said, pulling off his socks.

He instantly regretted everything he was saying and everything he was doing, but it was as if he'd eaten an entire pack of Genghis's edibles. He just couldn't stop himself.

"You are Earthborn, I see," Luna said, stepping up to examine him in all his glory. "I had expected more, but it'll do."

The sound of Giorgio Moroder's space-age synth swelled. The

voices of Aspy, Jed, Genghis, and Miz came into focus. They were whooping and hollering as if riding a roller coaster. He couldn't see them, but it seemed everyone was as blissed out as he was.

He fell backward into the oblivion of a black hole. He spun into its vortex, and reality warped around the team. Purple twilight stretched out beyond him as he plummeted toward infinity.

Schlackabakfalloom!

Luna and a chorus of alien girls lip-synced to the angelic riffing of Donna Summer. Was this the K-pop video Genghis had insisted he watch before the tournament? Luna spun around him and sang while a million stars rushed by and the Moog synth bumped along like a sonic subway train. No pain, no fear—only wonder.

"What the heck is going on?" Alex asked, slurring his words.

Then the mood shifted as an evil-looking male entertainer appeared, forcing the female chorus offstage. This interloper carried a black sword and pointed it toward Alex. Netherfang, he called it. He wanted to use the weapon to kill Alex's good vibe.

What a villain!

Alex hated him immediately and turned away.

He saw a discernible path now. He raced down it toward the pine trees, which gleamed like Christmas tinsel. While Netherfang's owner shadowed him, he jogged on past the friendly druid children playing near the Mana Lake.

Across the lake now, he swam in the crystalline water, only to see it change and thicken into a horrible oily goo. He stood up, trying his best to wade to shore, waist deep in the muck. Before he stepped free, a hand grabbed him and pulled him back into another black hole.

He swirled around and out of it into a colorful nebula and toward a solar system with an Earth-like world, a familiar moon, and a space station orbiting that moon.

Luna was back now.

"Is that Starway Station?" Alex asked.

"Yes."

"And the Battle Moon?"

"Yes."

"And am I speaking Korean?"

"No, my native tongue, Gladiatorian. But very poorly."

"Who was that creep with the sword?"

"Malvexus. We can't let him win."

"But I'm no champion."

"No, you're much more than that. Much more!"

For some reason, the comment made him emotional. Then Jed was next to him.

"Intergalactic travel is a bitch," Jed moaned.

"Hey, man, we're here," Genghis said. "Wake up, buddy."

"I can't seem to," Alex said groggily.

"I gotcha, bud, hold on."

Genghis stretched across the universe and poked Alex in his third eye, and everything exploded.

CHAPTER EIGHT

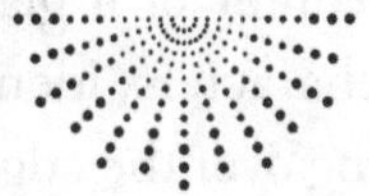

A rift in the fabric of time and space opened, and the Sparkles Modfia team flew through from the other side.

Schlackabakfalloom!

Alex woke up, gasping for air, wildly aware something life changing had just happened.

He and the team had landed hard on some kind of AstroTurf. Their clothes had burned up in transit and crumpled off them like blackened paper, leaving them terribly naked.

But before unmanageable shame took root, they were swarmed by skulk medics who injected them with syringes full of glowing liquid. The magic fluid instantly clothed everyone in basic player attire.

"Modcraft Skindarts!" Aspy marveled.

She tugged at the form-fitting garment. Alex did the same. It reminded him of the wet suits surfers wore in cold water.

"Noob skins, though," Jed complained.

"At least we're not bare-ass naked," Miz said, checking to make sure her lady parts were sufficiently concealed.

Sure enough, they were wearing what every new player of

Cosmic Champions wore when they spawned into the matchmaking lobby.

Alex touched the material. It was a fabric, like spandex, yet sturdier and more durable. Emblazoned on their backs were their gamertags and their team's name—Sparkles Modfia; under that, in a smaller script, it said "Earthborn."

"Look where we are!" Miz said, pointing to their surroundings.

They'd landed in the center of a giant arena, complete with a sparse audience. Real-life characters, identifiable from game lore, sat in the stadium seats and hung over the edges of the walls.

For a minute, the crowd of players closest to them stared, then went back to their business—laughing and telling stories.

One champion was sitting alone talking to himself. Another read a book of spells that levitated in front of them. Another allowed a group of medic skulks to bandage his wounded arm.

"Real, honest-to-God champions, straight out of the game," Jed gaped. "People, we aren't in Kansas anymore."

"No, that's for sure," Genghis said. "But where, man?"

"Starway Station, of course," Bonegrin said, waving a claw at the arena.

Alex had almost forgotten about his new sponsors, if you could call them that. It seemed the team was still in custody.

"More specifically, Spawn Arena," Nightbane added, "where new players are trained to enter the game like real champions ready for battle—and where we leave you to be tested. Be victorious or be culled. Good fortune, Earthborn."

Bonegrin opened a new portal for Nightbane, and the two of them disappeared in a flash.

Alex sighed. "Finally, we're free of those creeps."

"No joke, man," Jed agreed.

Game lore explained that Starway Station orbited the Battle Moon, a planetoid, where the game's primary field of play existed. The Battle Moon orbited an Earth-like planet named Gladiatoria.

The cosmomancers, the game's creators, had discovered Gladiatoria eons ago. It was a planet of war-loving humanoids who were selected to be the game's first competitors and the Battle Moon's guardians.

Starway Station served as the main depot for new teams and the gateway to the moon. Spawn Arena was one of the many parts of Starway Station. New players were trained and tested in the arena.

Also, this was the place single players were paired with others before starting. Once matched, they were teleported down to the Battle Moon in teams of five, where the actual game began.

Still amazed by their surroundings, the Modfia gathered in the center of the field. A buzzer went off and everyone in the stands stared down at them. The team instinctively formed a circle. Standing back to back, they waited for the other shoe to drop.

That didn't take long. On the opposite side of the arena, a monster made of living rock stepped out of a tunnel into the light.

"Who the heck is that?" Alex asked.

"Wow! Dikphite, the elemental rock creature, one of the most feared lore champions in the game," Aspy said as if reading from a manual.

"I know that, Aspy. What I'm asking is who is in the suit?"

"Who's in your suit, Earthborn?" Dikphite laughed.

He picked up a battle mace and threw it. The team dove out of the way as the weapon flew over their heads.

One spectator yelled from the stands, "Way to go, D! Introduce yourselves to the noobs!"

"Now what?" Miz groaned, getting back to her feet.

"Now you prove yourselves, Earthborn!"

Dikphite hurled another battle mace the size of a tree at the team. It missed them by inches and slammed into the turf, creating a deep crater. He trudged forward.

"We have to get out of here!" Alex started backpedaling.

"This should be good. They're not battle ready," a second spectator yelled gleefully. "He'll kill them!"

"Not if I have anything to say about it." A beautiful warrior looking like she just stepped out of an anime film jumped into the arena.

"Luna Lifestealer?" Alex's mouth dropped open.

Luna stepped in front of the team and pulled out her signature chain weapon, called a kusarigama. "Stand down, vicious fiend!"

"Yeah, dick-feet!" Jed said, shaking his fist.

The rock monster looked very annoyed. "Curse you, Lifestealer. Why are you out of your cage?"

"And what of you, Dikphite? Attacking innocents? Does Malvexus hold your leash now?"

"I tire of your interference. If locking you up won't get you out of the way, then killing you will."

"You are no match for me, ogre. I've defeated you before."

"This time, I have help," he said, waving at the tunnel guards. "Bring out the MurkFiend. Let him string Lifestealer's guts out for all to see."

Luna backed up a few steps.

"Despoiler the MurkFiend," she muttered under her breath. "Not good."

The skulks opened a tunnel gate and scattered. Dikphite turned, watching and waiting for the MurkFiend to appear, but nothing happened.

"Hurry, brother, new players to test," Dikphite called.

"Again?" Despoiler shouted back.

"Yes, we're all waiting."

"I hope Malvexus pays his debts," the MurkFiend grumbled.

A second later, a gigantic monster, composed of living vines and plants, stepped out next to Dikphite.

"Oh, no, Despoiler is one of the strongest champions in the game," Aspy said.

Despoiler smiled and puffed out his swamp monster chest. "Isn't that nice, brother? These little monkeys know who I am. Killing them will be a pleasure."

A long spear made of some ancient root grew from the chest of

Despoiler. He broke it off and hurled it at the team, who scattered as the spear zinged past. They regrouped in the center, but Dikphite and Despoiler were advancing now.

Luna turned to the team and motioned for them to back away. Everyone did except Genghis and Alex, who were staring at Luna.

"Garcia, look who it is!" Genghis shouted, excitedly.

Alex didn't need the obvious pointed out. He had been completely gobsmacked by Luna since she had jumped into the arena. All concerns about dying at the hands of Dikphite and Despoiler had been supplanted by some kind of hypnosis. A million dazzling images of Luna Lifestealer stored in a million brain cells seemed to burst forth, flooding the mind's eye, spilling over into the limbic system, and releasing a flood of sweet dopamine. The tiniest bit of drool pooled at the corner of Alex's mouth. He was transfixed and couldn't shake the spell.

Luna glared at Alex, who was awkwardly pawing at her as if to prove she wasn't a holographic projection.

"Oh my gosh, it is you."

He touched her again, unable to break the tractor beam pulling him in.

"Can you please stop touching my hair?" Luna took another step back. "I'm trying to save your life and that's *very* distracting."

"Not to mention super creepy," Dikphite yelled.

The monster had stopped to pick up another weapon and was standing across the field next to Despoiler with one rock-like hand on his stony hip. The arena audience broke out in a raucous laughter, but Alex didn't hear a sound.

Luna scowled at the Modfia. "What's wrong with your leader?"

"He's not the leader," Aspy clarified. "We fired him."

"So you claim the mantle of leadership?" Luna gave Aspy a quick, inquisitive look.

"I guess." Aspy shrugged.

"It seems a poor fit. But so be it."

Luna raised her hand and yelled an exultant war cry.

"Prepare your team for battle!"

"But how do we fight these guys?" Genghis asked.

"With these, of course," Luna said, producing a strange-looking crossbow and firing five new skindarts. Each found their intended targets. Their plungers depressed as if by magic, and the fluid within drained into Alex, Aspy, Miz, Jed, and Genghis. In seconds, they all swooned and collapsed on the ground as if dead.

Luna took the last dart and injected herself. Her eyes rolled back while a strange substance leaked from her pores and poured down her legs and arms, forming a new battle skin. The formfitting armor gleamed in the arena lights. She tapped it with a fingernail, testing the metallic shell.

Meanwhile, modcraft magic spread over the team, clothing them in new outfits, armor, and sheathed weaponry. Slowly they woke wrapped in new skins that matched their favorite avatars. While they kept their recognizable human faces, voices, and most of their original forms, they had somehow morphed into a new amalgamation—becoming the very avatars they played in the game.

Alex was the first to stand up, examining his new skin—a perfect replica of Titan's clothing and basic armor. While that was amazing, he was more impressed with how he felt—stronger and more energized than he'd ever felt in real life.

Genghis echoed that feeling. "Holy shiz! I feel fantastic!"

"So do I! What's in that stuff?" Alex asked. He plucked the dart from his skin and examined the vial.

"We *look* good too," Jed said, marveling at the fit of his dark shadow-weave cloak.

"Game-accurate battle skins," Aspy marveled.

"But how's any of this possible?" Genghis asked.

"It's gotta be Kickstarter," Jed laughed. "Otherwise, I've lost my mind."

"Quickly arm yourselves!" Luna shouted. She pointed at a nearby wall. Every conceivable science fiction and fantasy weapon a geek could dream up hung there, waiting to be used.

Genghis rushed over and everyone else followed.

"Far out!" Genghis grabbed a staff from the wall and found it was a basic match to the one his character carried within the game. He twirled it, doing several skip-catch spins to test its weight. "Hey, man, this is cool!"

Jed found two level-one shadow-weave daggers. His favorite weapons. He stared at them, stunned. "I have a hard-on!"

"Me too!" Miz said.

Aspy looked at her. "Are you serious?"

"You know what I mean, girl," Miz shot back.

"No, I don't, but this place . . . this world," she purred, doing a pirouette with the grace of a ballet dancer taking in everything around them. "It's so much more interesting than some guy's boner."

The entire team doubled over laughing while Aspy ran over to the archery section of the weapon's wall.

"I still don't know what is going on here. Did someone drug us and slap on a pair of virtual reality headsets?" Alex scratched his head. "It has to be a prank."

"Maybe some rich fanboy built a replica of Spawn Arena," Jed said.

"This is the *real* game," Aspy declared. "We've crossed into some kind of alternate dimension or fast-traveled across the universe. That's the only logical explanation."

Alex looked at Aspy, amazed. She had no trouble accepting the impossible. Perhaps because of the unique way her mind worked, she was totally at ease with her conclusion. Somehow, that reassured Alex.

"Yeah, I'm starting to agree with Aspy," Miz said.

"Me too," Genghis agreed. "Even though I know it's completely impossible, somehow we're actually inside the game."

Alex couldn't quite digest it, even though he was thinking the same thing.

Miz pulled a battle axe from its sheath and tapped it against the armored plates on her chest. "Dude, this armor is real, and so are these weapons."

She slammed the axe into the arena ground, and it split the strange AstroTurf open, leaving a massive divot that exposed a metal plate deep underneath the floor's padding.

Aspy stood to one side, seemingly oblivious to Miz and her axe. She was testing the bow in her hand. Retrieving an arrow from the quiver on her back, she nocked it and fired. It flew toward Dikphite, then magically divided into two pieces that flew past him, looped back around, hit him in the butt, and exploded. Dikphite yelped and stumbled to his knees, cursing.

The team whooped in celebration.

Satisfied everyone was ready, Luna beckoned to Despoiler, who was already stomping toward the team.

"You want to fight, MurkFiend?" Luna yelled. "Bring it on!"

Her bravado disappeared when she realized Despoiler was moving too quickly. His giant hand swung with the weight of a wrecking ball, scooped Luna into his swampy mitt, and swatted her across the field toward the arena wall.

Despite being stunned and sailing dangerously toward her doom, she deployed her kusarigama. The sickle flashed in her hand while the attached chain shot back across the arena at Despoiler, lassoing his throwing arm.

When the chain snapped taut, Luna's momentum was reversed. She swung back the other way and crashed into Despoiler with such force that he toppled over, breaking his fall with his own monstrous face.

Luna landed on her feet like a cat, grinning from ear to ear.

The crowd cheered, but Dikphite was on the move. He hurled a new stone mace that whizzed over Alex, barely missing his head.

"Maybe this isn't virtual reality," Alex said. "I felt the heat coming off that mace when it whizzed by. I'm pretty sure we're dead meat if it hits us."

"Exactly right, Earthborn. Defend yourselves or die!" Dikphite barreled past a group of weapons, grabbed a spear, and hurled it at the team.

"Oh, dang it," Jed yelled. "Move people!"

Everyone scattered toward what they hoped was an exit, but they found themselves fenced in by the arena wall.

Alex scanned the crowd. Where was Bonegrin or Nightbane? If he found them, he would insist they stop this insanity.

"Who do you search for, Earthborn? No one is coming to save you."

Dikphite threw another spear at the team.

Genghis grabbed a shield and barely had it on his arm when the spear hit it dead center and splintered apart. "Dank. But totally uncool!" he shouted.

That attack angered Aspy. She picked up a piece of the smashed spear and hurled it at the monster. It hit him square in the head. "Back off, bozo!"

Dikphite scooped Aspy up in his gargantuan hand. "I'm going to eat you for lunch," he snarled.

Suddenly, Luna's magical sickle and chain shot out and whirled around the monster's thick wrist.

"Hands off the strange-looking girl," Luna yelled, jerking the chain. Aspy spilled out onto the arena floor.

"Thanks, I guess," Aspy muttered as she staggered to her feet.

Luna flashed a worried and disapproving look at the Modfia. She didn't seem impressed with their fighting skills.

"Use your numbers as an advantage—half of you, attack Despoiler, and the other half, attack Dikphite," she scolded, turning her attention back to Dikphite and raising her weapon to finish him.

Unfortunately, the monster was one step ahead and hit Luna with a devastating sucker punch. Luna went down just as the team went into action.

Genghis, now dressed like a kick-ass ninja monk, tossed a magical blinding powder into Dikphite's eyes.

Miz hurled her battle axe, hitting the rock creature in the chest, knocking him on his ass.

Without missing a step, Jed pounced, cat-like, whirling his two short daggers, and stabbed Despoiler in his plant-covered hand, pinning one, then leaping to the other and pinning the second in the same way.

Alex, looking like Titan in the flesh, charged with his long sword, yelling and swinging it down like a guillotine onto Despoiler's throat.

"Yield, swamp face, or the head comes off!"

The team circled around the monster, heroically ready to strike again. Aspy helped Luna back to her feet, and she joined them.

But the victory was short-lived when Dikphite, who had recovered, swiped away Alex's sword. His stony arm grated across the pristine blade like nails on a chalkboard.

No longer threatened, Despoiler ripped his hands free, lurched upward to get back on his feet, and hit Luna so hard it seemed to crush her upon impact.

Luna fell onto the turf near the weapons wall and didn't get back up.

Aspy nocked another arrow and fired again. It hit Dikphite center-mass, and he fell to his knees. Alex reclaimed his sword, and the team ran away desperately trying to find cover.

Soon both Despoiler and Dikphite were rushing them in tandem, cornering the team against the wall opposite the weapons.

A perfect trap.

Despoiler reached inside the tangle of his swamp body for a new spear, but Alex lunged forward, swinging his sword wildly, until by some crazy stroke of luck he decapitated the creature.

The monster's head flew away, rolled on the turf for several paces, and stopped to stare back up at his shocked sibling's rocky face.

"No! Brother!" the rock creature cried.

Kablammm!

Dikphite fell over with a hole through his stony chest. Molten blood oozed out, producing a foul stench of sulfur.

Luna stepped toward the team holding the literal smoking gun. She planted one leather boot on Despoiler's body and casually reloaded her weapon while keeping an eagle eye on the creature for any movement. Satisfied both monsters were dead or at least not getting back up, she tossed the weapon away, then raised a fist in victory.

The final buzzer sounded, and the match was over. The crowd erupted in mild applause, but Luna didn't want to celebrate.

"Never ever show mercy to your opponent!" she fumed. "That's combat 101."

Alex stood there, just marveling at her. Even though she was obviously mad, a strange electricity flickered through him. He wanted to eat her like the Cookie Monster eats cookies.

She ignored his stupid expression and leaned in as if she was going to give him her final admonishment. Instead, she whispered a warning.

"Whatever you do, don't trust Crane. Understand?"

"Yeah, sure." Alex was a frozen mass of stupidity.

"How do we get to the Battle Moon?" Aspy asked.

"You don't," Luna said, turning to walk away. "You lot need to be sent back home before you die. None of you are ready to face what's down there."

A new portal opened near the team.

"On that point, we agree," Bonegrin said, stepping through.

Nightbane joined him. After regarding the team with a look of disgust, she clapped her hands, drawing a squad of security skulks onto the field.

When they reached Bonegrin, the leader of the group saluted him and asked for instructions. Bonegrin pointed at Luna.

"Take her to containment," he said. "I've had enough of her insolence."

The security team ran up to Luna, who strangely offered no resistance.

Miz gave Alex a hard stare. She looked mad or about to cry. He wasn't sure. Then she turned her cold stare toward Bonegrin.

"I'm so sick of you two. If you don't get us home right now, I swear I'll beat the living—" Miz stopped, coughed, and then doubled over, holding her stomach.

"Uh, guys, she's gonna toss her cookies," Genghis said.

Miz stumbled a few steps forward, reaching for Jed as her eyes rolled up into the back of her head. Jed caught her as she fell into his arms.

"What the heck is wrong with her?" he pleaded, looking around for an answer.

Then Jed succumbed to the same sickness. He slumped over, unconscious, next to Miz. They lay there in a pile.

"A nap, that's a good idea. I need one too," Genghis said, as he collapsed face-first into the arena turf.

In seconds, the entire team had fallen like dominoes.

The last thing Alex saw before the darkness took him was Nightbane standing over him, smiling.

CHAPTER NINE

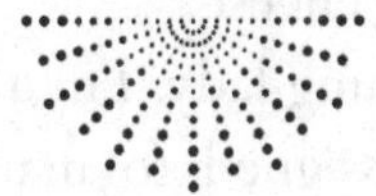

Alex Garcia woke up on a space-age platform that reminded him of a hospital bed. A ring of keys jangled over him like a miniature chandelier.

"Wake up, young man," a voice squeaked.

"Uh . . . where am I?" Alex muttered, rubbing his eyes.

A strange gnome, standing some three feet high and wearing a white lab coat, stood on the side of his bed. He held a magnifying eyeglass, which he was using to examine Alex.

"Take it easy, boy. I'll answer all your questions in due course. Right now, we need to make sure you're not dead."

"Would I be talking if I were dead?"

"Believe me, it happens all the time," Crane replied. "Do you know your name?"

"Alex. Alex Garcia."

"Hmmm. Perhaps that last blow to your head did some damage. Your gamertag says Titan."

Alex sat up. He was back in his basic player uniform. The battle skin and weapons were gone.

"And who are you?"

"Dr. Fester Crane, of course. Who else?"

Crane? Alex knew the name, but barely. Fester Crane was an unpopular lore character in *Cosmic Champions*. The name triggered an unpleasant feeling, but he couldn't reason why.

"You know, the shady Criterion Gnome," Aspy whispered. "The one always trying to steal power from the Gamemaster."

Alex turned to see she was hovering over him, snacking on something that looked like string cheese.

"I beg your pardon, young lady. I'm a respected battle alchemist and the chief engineer assigned to manage all new players and programs at Starway Station."

"A recent promotion, apparently," Aspy whispered.

"My dear, please. Doctor Fester Crane has a mind as strong as a steel trap and a body fit as a Quillodian fiddle." The gnome winked, beating his chest a bit in mock pride. "Pray to the cosmomancers you look this good when *you* are 400 years old."

Skulk technicians buzzed around the room cleaning, sorting, and doing various tasks that made no sense to Alex.

Alex closed his eyes and rubbed his forehead. The last thing he could remember was being on the arena floor and feeling like death warmed over.

Nightbane had been standing over him, examining him with a look of disdain. "I had high hopes for you, Alex of Garcia," she had said.

Her magic-covered fingers tickled the air, and Alex's heads-up display flashed red. The word "defective" appeared in bold letters.

Then his HUD blurred as a squad of chattering skulks surrounded him. Before everything faded to black, he heard Nightbane give her final command.

"Take these hit-sponges away. Perhaps Crane can put them to use."

Alex shook the memory off and opened his eyes again. He was in a large room that was a cross between a posh hotel room and a medical lab. This had to be Spawn Medical where new players healed after battling each other in game tutorials. His teammates were already awake, sitting around a table, eating and whispering.

The old gnome skittered to the foot of his bed, giving orders to his skulk assistants. The little goblin-like creatures wore hooded hospital scrubs. They scurried this way and that, obediently responding to each of Crane's commands.

"Keep that one sedated," Crane ordered, pointing across the room. "She could ruin things for everyone if she wakes up."

Alex pushed himself up on his elbows to get a better look. Luna Lifestealer was on a nearby bed, asleep and snoring rather loudly.

"What's wrong with her?" Alex asked.

"Many things, my lad. Most notably, her brainpan seems fried," Crane said, twirling his finger next to his head. "Several screws loose up in the old noggin." He turned and gave Alex a devilish wink. "Not quite herself these days. No, not at all."

"Will she be okay?"

"Of course, my dear boy. Of course." The gnome patted Alex on the knee as he walked up the bed. He leaned over Alex again. The tip of his finger glowed, and he used it like a penlight to check Alex's pupils.

"Is this Spawn Medical?"

"Of course."

Fester's breath smelled like onions. Alex winced.

"Are you all right, my boy? You look in pain and seem to have forgotten everything about why you are here—or how you arrived."

"I'm fine," he said, sneaking a look at his friends and their table of food. "Just a bit hungry."

"Yes, well, if you feel well enough, please indulge yourself," Crane said, waving his hand toward the table.

Alex got up and joined the team. He took a handful of red grapes. As he talked and snacked, he felt each grape seemed to add to his energy level. He was buzzing with—what was it, adrenaline?

He checked his HUD. The health bar crept across the screen as he ate the grapes. The mana bar that showed his level of magical power was ticking up as well.

Now he knew why Aspy and everyone else looked so happy. They were literally replenishing their health and mana, as if they were characters in the game.

The game.

Wow!

The game really was his world now.

He was a living character in a real-life version of Cosmic Champions.

He didn't understand it, and he still suspected it might be a dream—or some trick of technology—but in this moment and the little moments after it, the game was reality, and reality was the game.

Slowly, he digested this truth along with the fruit. Each grape was strange but sweet, and each bump of mana and health felt wonderful.

"Aspy, what do you think? Is this some kind of virtual reality?" Alex asked, scratching his head.

Genghis looked just as wary. "No, can't be—way too real. So unsettling."

Jed had a different opinion. "Personally, I love it. But we need to get out of *here*. That saggy imp is lying to us. I'm sure of it."

Suddenly, he threw an empty juice can right toward Crane. Alex blocked it and it clanked to the floor.

"Dude," Alex hissed. "Let's get some answers before you start another fight, we can't finish."

Aspy raised her hand like she was asking a question. "I already said that. First, we need to know why we woke up feeling so sick. Also, what about her?" She pointed at Luna. "Why was she trying to help us? And why were those monsters mad at her? And what was in those darts? Did she poison us with something?"

Crane was across the room with his back turned. They had assumed he wasn't listening, but his large gnome ears had heard every word.

"Don't worry, my dear. Modcraft Skindarts aren't dangerous," Crane said.

"Yeah, okay, but what's in them?" Aspy asked again.

"Basic magic spells. Completely harmless."

"Harmless?" Miz repeated. "Is this Grandpa Smurf crazy? I felt like I was dying."

"It takes a bit of time to adjust to the magic, but the cosmomancers have conjured skin transformations for millennia. They are very, very safe," Crane said.

Miz wasn't buying it.

"What happened to us in the arena?" Alex asked.

"You were deemed defective," Crane said. "That's why you were sent here instead of queueing for the next game on the Battle Moon."

Crane wagged one of his little Yoda-like claws.

"But don't worry. Your body and mind will adapt to your new surroundings. And, as they do, your skins and abilities change. You gain access to more offensive capabilities that match your unique personalities and emotions."

"In other words, you level up," Alex added.

"Exactly, dear boy," Crane agreed. "You five have spent a good part of your life playing *Cosmic Champions*, never knowing that the cosmomancers were using the gameplay to train you for something much more advanced."

"A date with a Kardashian?" Jed quipped.

Aspy flashed a look. "Ew. Really?"

Jed shrugged. "I like MILFs, man."

Miz stood up. "Look, Gizmo. We didn't ask to come here. All we need is a way to get home."

"Home? Do you mean Earth?" Crane waved that idea away. He looked at them with widening eyes. "I thought you understood. You're a million light years away from your home planet."

A panel on the nearby wall rose, uncovering a large porthole made of reinforced glass. This revealed a stunning view of outer space. They could see both Gladiatoria and the Battle Moon orbiting nearby. A massive star, some millions of miles away, peaked over the edge of the planet, and a dazzling magenta-colored nebula swirled beyond that.

It was obvious this was not their solar system—and all doubts about being in a space station were put to rest.

"Starway Station is your home now," Crane said, admiring the view.

Alex had seen computer animations of this view many times before. It was the only reason he didn't die from shock.

"You're trying to tell me that's the actual Battle Moon?" Miz asked.

"Yes, of course. What else? The Battle Moon of Gladiatoria," Crane said. "Beautiful, mysterious, and so wonderfully deadly."

The Battle Moon differed from the Earth's moon. While one part remained a grey, barren desert, the other half was a lush, alien wilderness. And from their vantage point, they could see a river and one main road dividing the strange landscape. Two magnificent-looking castles rose at opposite ends of the wilderness.

Alex covered his eyes with both hands and tried to accept the truth, as he now understood it. It seemed the game they had played for years wasn't a fantasy at all, but a meticulous recreation of an alien world. The Battle Moon was a real planetoid many thousands of light years away from Earth, and the computer game *Cosmic Champions* was an incredibly accurate simulation being used by a group of intelligent beings called the cosmomancers as a kind of elaborate training tool. The game prepared would-be champions for the moment they were whisked away across the universe to do real battle with other real players in a real tournament.

Alex took a deep breath and asked, "What about our lives back on Earth? Our families will go nuts when we turn up missing!"

Crane shook his head. "No need to worry, my boy. The Starway warps space but much more. It plucks you out of your reality and places you in a pocket beyond time. A Herald can send you back to the exact place, and the exact moment, you left. You won't miss a minute of your life back on your home planet, and no one will even know you've been gone."

"That's good, I guess. But how do we get home?" Miz asked again, her voice betraying how confused and scared she was.

"The only way anyone ever goes home is as a Champion of the Cosmos. You have to win the game. Fair and square. Defeat your opponents in battle. Then you may journey home and invite your world to join the Cosmic Alliance."

Crane turned from the window, grabbed a new syringe.

"However, I'm afraid your performance in Spawn Arena suggests you are *not* champion material."

"Of course we are!" Alex said, turning on the little gnome.

"I hope for your sake that's true. Your lives and the lives of all Earthborn certainly depend on it."

CHAPTER TEN

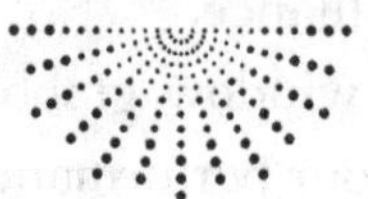

While the team continued discussing the wonders of their new world, Alex got up and walked over to Luna's bed. It seemed she was in a deep sleep, but the snoring had stopped.

He marveled at her once again. Pixels and computer code had come to life like a video-game Cinderella. How completely beautiful she was, more so than any concept art or poster in his room back home.

Was she okay? That was what he really wanted to know. When he turned to look for a nurse, Luna grabbed his wrist.

"Earthborn, heed my warning," she whispered, cracking one eyelid open ever so slightly.

Alex finished her sentence. "About Crane?"

She raised a finger to her lips to quiet Alex, then nodded. "Yes. That's right."

"Are you okay?"

Luna pulled him closer. Alex was so happy.

"The gnome is a liar, and this place is a prison. He's in league with the Griefers and the Crimson Prince. He can't be trusted."

Alex nodded. He wanted to know more, to understand the

passion behind her concern. He opened his mouth to ask another question.

"Take Lifestealer to the isolation cells," Crane croaked. He was back with a squad of armored skulks.

"I'm fine. I don't need any medical attention," Luna said, waving them off.

"Better safe than sorry, my dear," Crane said, pushing Alex away from the bed.

Before anyone could protest, he tossed a fistful of glittering powder over Luna's face. She coughed, sputtered, and finally lost consciousness.

Crane then eye-checked the lead skulk who, along with his squad, somehow magically levitated Luna's bed and pushed it out of the room.

Alex watched Luna go with a heavy amount of trepidation, then returned to the table with the team. Something was wrong. Very wrong. But what to do about it?

CHAPTER ELEVEN

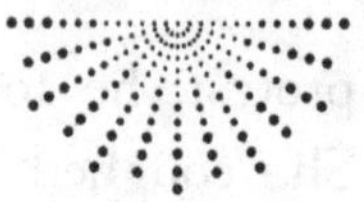

Later that night, the team reclined in their bunks goofing off. Alex strolled in after a shower, a towel wrapped around his waist and one around his head like a turban.

"Time for a team meeting," he said, clapping his hands.

"Get dressed first. You look like a drag queen," Jed joked.

Alex didn't argue. He got dressed and eventually the group gathered around his bunk, eager to talk.

It seemed the team's desire to process what was happening outweighed their bitterness toward him. Even though he was positive their anger was still smoldering below the surface, maybe everyone would move on. Surely, the present problems were more important than the meltdown at the tournament.

"Okay, spill it," Alex said. "What's everyone thinking?"

They collectively glared at him without saying a word.

"You guys always complain that I don't listen. Well, I'm listening," he said. He stared back at them, scanning each face, hoping one of them would crack the awkward silence.

"I can safely say I'm picking up a collective bad vibe," Genghis offered. "As cool as this entire experience has been, my spider-sense is tingling off the charts."

Aspy nodded. "Usually, my radar for these things has zero bandwidth, but Fester Crane gives me the creeps!"

Miz added. "Yeah, this is either the greatest opportunity in our lives, or we're about to die horribly."

"The worst part is no one is going to know," Alex said.

"Wouldn't dying be the worst part?" Aspy asked, cocking her head.

Jed raised an eyebrow at Alex. "Help her with that, will you?"

"The worst part is no one would know," Alex repeated, offering no further explanation. "But yeah, dying sucks too."

"I think we should find a way back to Earth," Miz said.

"I'm pretty sure Bonegrin still has the portal key, but maybe there's another one somewhere," Aspy said.

Alex nodded. "Okay, so one option is to find a portal key and get out of here."

Jed threw his hands up. "What the heck? Running away isn't the answer. If there is anywhere we belong, it's here. We spend all our time playing this dang game. Now we're inside it, living it for real."

Genghis nodded stoically. "Jed is right. I think there is more to see here. Plus, we have actual skills—and if we level up, real magical powers. This is like all of our dreams come true."

"Why do you two assume this is my dream? Huh?" Miz grumbled. "This game isn't my whole life, okay? And I'm nowhere near ready to die playing it."

Jed looked at Alex for help. Alex laced his fingers together, popped his knuckles, and looked up at one corner of the ceiling like he was calculating a math problem.

"I understand wanting to go back home. I agree with Miz and Aspy. Something is not right with our current situation. I've been super freaked out since we landed in that arena. But like Jed and Genghis said, staying might be better than what's waiting for us back home. However, Crane and the others are definitely hiding something. I think we should find out what that is before we leave."

"Yeah, I can get behind that," Jed said mischievously. "Let's do a little secret investigation. See what's what."

Miz folded her arms over her chest. "If it's legit and safe, we can stay longer, but if it's not, we get the heck out, agreed?"

"I'm down," Genghis said. Looking around, everyone else nodded in agreement. "So, what's the plan?"

"First, we need to find Luna Lifestealer," Alex said.

Jed rolled his eyes. "Her again?"

"She saved us from Despoiler and Dikphite," Aspy said. "But I'm not sure we can trust her."

"Yeah, Crane thinks she's sick or crazy," Miz added.

"Maybe, but true Gladiatorian Warriors don't lie. It's part of their honor code. We know that from the lore. They were the first race to play the game for the cosmomancers."

"Alex knows a lot about Luna," Genghis offered. "He curates one of her fan pages on the internet. What's your handle? @LunaLiker99?"

Alex elbowed him in the ribs. "Dude, shut up."

"Did you say Luna *licker*? Oh dang, that's nasty." Miz covered her mouth with one hand, suppressing a string of giggles.

Jed piled on. "Oh, I want to tell her that, like right now."

"Whatever, laugh it up, ha ha ha." Alex laughed sarcastically.

The team erupted in a momentary burst of giggles.

Alex did his best to ignore them, even though he was secretly glad they were all having fun. He didn't want to argue about his plan. He was determined to find Luna. She knew things about this world they didn't. He was sure she was trying to tell him something important before Crane had sedated her.

Alex drew a quick map of the complex, at least what little he had seen and remembered. Jed dumped a few radios on the table next to the maps, which briefly surprised everyone.

"What? I got them from one of the skulks." Jed shrugged. "Genghis, can you figure these out?"

"Yeah, I saw Crane's nurses using them. They seem simple enough."

He fiddled with the radios while Alex explained the plan.

"Okay. Jed and Aspy, you two check out these labs."

He pointed at the east wing.

"Miz and Genghis, you hit the other ones, see what they are really doing in there."

He pointed them to the west wing.

"And I'll check out the detention wing," Alex concluded. "If Crane is keeping Luna a prisoner, we need to know why."

"But we are locked in here," Aspy said. "How do we get out?"

"With these, of course," Jed said. He jangled Crane's chain full of bobbles and keys before dropping them into the center of the table.

Everyone looked at him, amazed.

"What?" he said, smiling proudly. "I'm the best thief in the game. Haven't I been saying that forever?"

Yes, he had, thought Alex.

Jed had gloated about his character's powers for years. Now that they were put to the test, it seemed his confidence was justified. Would that be the case for the rest of the team? Was there a real champion lurking deep within each of them? They were about to find out.

CHAPTER TWELVE

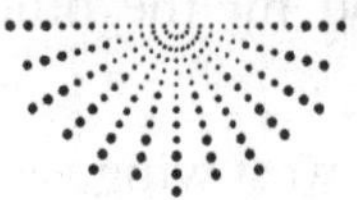

Aspy and Jed had a good view from their hiding place in the restricted lab, and what they saw was very interesting. Fester Crane examined one of the young alien players who had fought and lost in the arena. They had strapped the poor blue-skinned sap to a chair with his head slumped on his chest. The chair was bolted to a mechanical rail system. One end pointed toward an enormous wall full of glowing orbs. This central point was cloaked in the darkest of shadows but appeared to be a tunnel.

Crane was speaking to another champion he called Lackey Lickspittle. Lackey was a frightening Wasteland Goblin with enormous ears that flapped on his head like little sails, a bulbous nose, and nostrils that flared as he spoke. His warty, mottled skin was green like diseased swamp water, and his long pink tongue was barbed at the end. He wore a nose ring made of bone, two enormous gold earrings, and carried a large staff with a crystal orb on the end.

He paced in front of a control panel like he had authority. He fiddled with nobs and levers of various sizes, causing them to buzz with electrical energy. Occasionally, the orbs on the wall would flare to life, illuminating everything in a wine-colored light. The center of shadows extended deeper into the wall, forming a distinct tunnel that had no discernible end. Jed thought it mimicked the strange physics of the Starway.

"I don't understand it. The field warps well enough. It must be your vehicle. There's not enough negative mass," the goblin grumbled. "Malvexus wants a conduit from here to every world he chooses. It must adjust according to his specifications and stay open long enough for safe passage."

"The mass on the vehicle is correct," Crane growled. "You know nothing of these things, Lackey. Out of the way."

"It is wrong." Lackey, who was only a few inches larger than Crane, swatted the gnome aside with his pointed staff. He then waved the staff over the apparatus, and pieces of the machine rearranged themselves, morphing in size and shape.

The alien prisoner groaned as if the rebuilding of the machine was causing him pain.

Meanwhile, Fester Crane was dusting himself off. He cursed in protest and leapt cat-like onto Lackey's back, pulling at the goblin's large ears like a jockey might rein a horse. The two creatures were very similar in stature with different faces. Lackey looked like he was wearing a scary Halloween mask, while Crane had older, impish features that reminded Jed of a dried, shrunken apple.

Their fight might have been comical if they weren't so vicious.

"I didn't give you permission to do that!" Crane screeched.

Lackey snarled, turned on Crane, and grabbed him by the throat. "Who are you to tell me what to do? I'm one of the Griefers."

"You are an idiot, and if you fail to fix this, you will fail to share the reward."

"There will be no reward if we can't open the Starway."

Lackey swatted Crane away again.

"I have fixed your mistake," he growled. "Activate the portal."

"You delude yourself," Crane cursed again. He rushed Lackey and kicked him in the shins. Lackey yelped in pain then kicked the gnome, sending him tumbling across the room.

"You twisted old monkey!" Lackey yelled. "First, I humiliate you by proving you wrong, then I kill you."

He reached for the control panel and threw the largest of the switches.

The orbs flared to a blinding red. It forced Jed and Aspy to shield their eyes.

The central tunnel seemed to come alive and undulated like the body of a giant serpent. An aperture of energy opened, exposing a magnificent view of a star system. The tunnel folded out into space, stretching for the nearest planet.

Then Lackey activated the prisoner's car. It shot out on its rails, jumping onto the fledgling Starway, and promptly pancaked into the wall with such a great speed that it flattened both the chair and the prisoner.

There was a bone-chilling cry of horror, a sickening splat, and the resulting crash. The lights dimmed and the Starway disappeared. There was nothing left of the chair and prisoner but a pile of broken junk and purple-colored jelly dribbling down the wall.

Lackey screamed in frustration. He scurried to the wall, ran a finger through the goo, and tasted it. Then he yelled again.

Crane snickered. "Yes, another spectacular failure," he said, a twinkle in his beady gnome eye. "I'll send my report to Malvexus immediately."

Lackey was already storming out of the room. "Bring another defective player. We try again in one hour."

A team of skulks scurried into the room and began cleaning the wall and the debris.

Fester Crane produced a cigar, lit it, and studied the crash while he took a few puffs, then hurried out of the room.

Aspy turned to Jed with a look of amazement. "I can't believe it. How is any of this possible? It must be a trick."

"But we both just saw it. They just turned that player into jelly."

"Did you hear what he said? The Starway is not working properly," she said. "That could explain the confusion between what we remember about the game and what has been happening to us. They're trying to reverse engineer all of this. Lackey's trying to build a new Starway to bring in more players for this Malvexus guy, whoever the heck that is."

"And we're the guinea pigs."

"This is horrible. If we can't find a real portal key, I'm not sure there's a way home."

Aspy moved closer to Jed, holding his arm in a vise grip. Jed looked at her. He'd never seen her scared before. She rarely showed any emotion, especially not fear.

"You know, you're very pretty when you're worried," he blurted.

She wouldn't look him in the eyes. "If that's true, I should be pretty all the time."

Jed was embarrassed but not enough to hit the brakes. Suddenly, he was fascinated by Aspy's ability to figure out their bizarre situation so fast. He wished he had that kind of mind.

"You're some kind of genius, right?" he asked. "Why spend so much time playing *Cosmic Champions*? You could get rich doing so many other things."

"I'd rather just be normal."

"Who the heck do you know who's normal?"

Now it was Aspy's turn to stare.

Jed had no idea what she was thinking, but she smiled and seemed genuinely fascinated by what he'd just said.

He couldn't believe he'd never noticed how pretty she was. She leaned in. Jed needed no more encouragement. He closed the gap, kissed her, and promptly shoved his tongue into her mouth.

Aspy pulled back and slapped him.

"Gross!"

"Ah, dang. I'm sorry!" he yelled.

The slap had been loud enough to get the nearby skulks' attention. They turned and spotted Jed and Aspy hiding in the corner.

"Save it," she said, noticing they were caught. "We'd better run!"

They bolted out of the door and down the hallway.

CHAPTER THIRTEEN

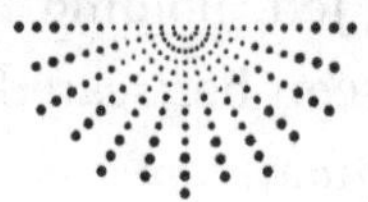

Genghis and Miz hid behind a row of empty crates stuffed into the corner of the large laboratory. The room was abuzz with the sound of whirling fans cooling the monstrous apparatus in the center of the room.

"Look, something's happening," Genghis said.

Miz yanked Genghis to his knees. "Watch it. They may see us."

White light illuminated one wall of the room, and a portal leading to the Spawn Arena opened.

Genghis and Miz observed a team of five goat-headed creatures, who they assumed were aliens from another planet, emerge through the opening. They spilled out onto the stone floor of the lab.

One appeared unconscious. Several were obviously wounded. The last two could stand but looked to be in shock.

"This race has no natural ability in combat. Use them for your machine or let them die. It matters not to me," Bonegrin growled. He was still standing in the Spawn Arena. When the other champion nodded, the portal collapsed, and Bonegrin disappeared.

"You heard him," Kadaver scolded, wagging her bony finger in the air. "The only sensible solution is repurposing their essence."

Fester Crane watched from around the corner. "Are you not concerned about changing eons of tradition, sorceress? Skulks have always been formed magically by the game engine."

The Scourge Elf shrugged. "Unfortunately, skulks are necessary for the operation of the game. Without them, my master will not be pleased."

"Well, we can't fail the great Malvexus now, can we?" Crane said sarcastically.

"All who fail Malvexus will die. This is the fate awaiting every planet that stands against his reign."

"Yes, well, if we succeed, there will be two options for those who oppose your team: die in battle or serve the game as a mindless minion." Crane shook his head.

"Two wonderful options, if you ask me," Kadaver laughed.

Her skulk technicians let out an approving squeal as they clamored around the room, prepping the machine for its next cycle.

First, they sorted the pile of defeated combatants, scooped each from the floor, and one by one deposited them into five large cylindrical chambers that seemed to be the centerpiece of the strange machine.

Next, the skulks connected the chambers by various hoses, tubes, and pipes to another, larger portion of the apparatus—which was actually some kind of animal of gargantuan size.

As the skulks prodded the creature, it revealed its massive squid-like head and roared. The sound was deafening but also heart-sickening. There was no mistake: it was a plea for help.

Genghis and Miz were horrified but watched quietly, feeling incredibly helpless.

Fester Crane and Kadaver continued discussing the procedure while watching the skulks from one corner.

When the cylinders were sealed, the panicked goat creatures slammed their horned heads against their translucent prisons.

Another team of skulks prodded the squid creature with long cattle prods.

The squid bellowed again. This time, it seemed in pain.

Black liquid burst from underneath its massive frame, traveled down the various tubes, and filled the cylindrical prisons.

When the squid's ink spilled into the chambers, the goat creatures bleated as if both enraged and terrified.

In seconds, the chambers were full. The goats, now hidden in their ink bath, struggled to stay alive as more magical energy was applied to the contraption.

A nasty smell akin to burnt hair wafted through the room. The energy surging through the machine swelled to a crescendo and finally dissipated.

The Scourge Elf overseeing this horror show waved her zombified hand. The skulks buzzed around the cylinders like bees, and the ink bath drained away.

When they opened the tubes, nothing recognizable was left except strings of red fiber, black-stained bones, and pools of melted skin.

A collective gasp rose from everyone watching.

"What in the heck is that stuff?" Miz asked.

"One nasty pile of goat-ghetti," Genghis said. "I'm going to hurl."

Even the hideous Kadaver and her technicians were horrified.

"How disgusting," she said.

"And what a complete waste," Crane added, shaking his little gnome head. "This is as bad as Lickspittle's failure in the other lab."

What was left of one goat squirmed in its pile. It looked like something between an arm and a tendril and it stretched out, grasping at the air.

Kadaver stepped out of reach. "By the eye of the scourge," she shouted. "Does it live?"

"Fascinating," Fester Crane said, his ears wiggling with excitement. "Perhaps the concentration of the ink is too strong. You should dilute the next batch."

With a flick of her wrist, Kadaver fired a green blast of energy that turned the melted goat person into a pile of gray ash. In quick succession, she blasted the other four piles, and the horror show was over.

A trio of nervous skulks in biohazard gear appeared, scooped up the remains in a large red bucket, and scurried away, mopping as they went.

"I can't watch any more of this," Genghis said.

"I know. It's horrible." Miz whispered. "But I still don't know what they're doing."

Miz scanned the lab for more clues. One corner of the room was painted gray and seemed to be a blackboard. Kadaver had filled it full of scrawled notes, formulas, and alchemical symbols. At the bottom of all of that, written in bold block letters, were three ominous words:

Independent Skulk Manufacturing.

Miz nudged Genghis and pointed at her discovery.

Genghis read the board then turned to Miz with a look of amazement.

"I can't believe it. They're trying to reverse engineer skulks."

"Those poor goat people," Miz said. "That was a horrible death."

Genghis placed a hand on Miz's shoulder.

"Miz, you were right all along. We need to get out of here as fast as our feet can carry us or we're next."

CHAPTER FOURTEEN

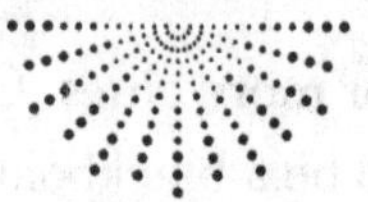

Alex's search led him to an old weapons vault. Mostly it was full of junk, outdated items from earlier versions of the game. He shuffled to the back of the room and rummaged through several ammunition boxes. He pocketed a couple of old vials. One contained a neon-green liquid. The other was clear but frothed when he shook it.

Finally, he grabbed a corroded modcraft gun like Luna had used in the arena and a small quiver of dusty skindarts. When he checked the bigger weapons, nothing he found seemed useful.

Above the shelving was a ventilation system. Based on all the movies he'd seen, he guessed this would give him the fastest route to the prison cells but being extremely claustrophobic, he rejected the idea outright. He'd find another way.

Suddenly, the door opened.

He quickly ducked into the shadows behind the tallest shelf.

It was a skulk guard sweeping his assigned area. It seemed he might turn and leave, but then he spotted one of the open boxes. He stared suspiciously for a beat, looking this way and that.

Alex held his breath and prayed.

The guard gave the room another sweeping glance, peering suspiciously into the darker corners. Then he grabbed one of the older daggers, tucked it under his arm, and left the way he came.

When the coast seemed clear, Alex slipped out of the room and down the hall. He continued around another corner, where he found a large warning sign. It read: "Champion Containment Unit." He had only moved a few paces down the hall when he heard someone whisper his name.

"Titan?"

It was Luna Lifestealer, peeking through the food slot of her prison door. Alex could barely make out the details of her face, but having studied it for so long, he knew it was her.

"What are you doing here?"

"Spying. Seeing what's what," he said. "But also looking for you. Are you okay?"

"Never mind that. If Crane sees you here, he'll kill us both."

The slightest squeak startled them. A pair of skulks were speaking their strange gibberish as they scurried down the hallway.

"Hold that thought," Alex said.

He ducked around the corner, making sure he was out of sight. When the skulks passed, he returned to Luna.

"I assume you'd like to get out of that cell?"

"Yes. But Titan, you need to understand what you are getting into by helping me."

"Save it. Let's get you out of that cage first. Also, you can call me Alex." He flashed a quick smile then turned because he heard more skulks coming down the hallway, a larger group this time. He'd have to make this quick.

Alex motioned, and Luna retreated to the back of her cell. He fumbled with the vials he'd stolen. The one he wanted to use wouldn't open.

"They're coming," she hissed.

The group of skulk guards were loud and seemed to argue as they skittered forward. One was slurping on something that looked like a soda can. The other gestured obscenely with his hand. The entire group laughed when he made a jerking motion. That's when they looked down the hallway.

"You've been spotted," Luna whispered.

The cork on the vial was still stuck, and he was out of time. He jammed the end of the vial into the door's locking mechanism.

"3-2-1, open sesame!"

He kicked the glass vial with the heel of his boot, and it exploded with a loud bang, throwing Alex backward. Smoke and debris filled the space. Luna lunged forward and stiff-armed the door. It swung open, having lost its locking mechanism in the explosion.

She helped Alex to his feet. "You didn't plan this very well, did you?"

"What? That was perfect," he laughed, brushing dust off his chest. "Distilled dragon gas. Works every time."

"And what's the plan for them?" Luna said, hooking a thumb at the guards.

"I guess we improvise."

Luna nodded calmly. She gritted her teeth, ran toward the guards, leapt in the air, and karate kicked two of them in the face.

The rest went down like bowling pins.

"Now what?" Alex asked.

"Now we run!"

CHAPTER FIFTEEN

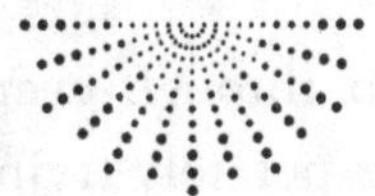

Alex ran alongside Luna, anxiously looking down every hallway and in every open door in search of his friends. They needed to regroup. Things were bad. It was an undeniable intuition he couldn't shake.

"What's really going on in this place?" Alex asked.

"The problems here are just an extension of the problems on the Battle Moon. A rogue champion. He's taken up residence in the Crimson Castle, and his team, the Griefers, are hacking all the game functions and creating cheats to ensure they never lose another game."

"And Fester Crane is helping them?"

"Yes. Crane seems to have turned his back on eons of tradition."

"Where is the Gamemaster?"

"No one is certain. Most likely dead."

"If this is a real-life Spawn Station, there should be some way to reach the Battle Moon from here. Isn't that right?"

"Yes, if you were remotely ready for that, that would be the next step, but death is the only thing waiting for you down there. You'd be a fool to go."

Before Alex could respond, the hallway darkened, red lights whirled and flashed, and one of the loudest alarms he'd ever heard bellowed.

They were in serious trouble.

Where was the rest of the team?

WHILE ALARMS SOUNDED through every corridor, Aspy and Jed raced down the hallway, desperately trying to get back to their team barracks. They turned a corner to discover Miz and Genghis running straight at them from a completely different direction.

Grateful to see each other, they cheered, patted each other on the back, then continued on to the barracks. When they rounded a third corner, Alex and Luna were there, halfway down the hallway, waving them to safety.

"In here, quick!" Alex shouted.

Miz pointed and pushed everyone ahead of her. She turned to guard the rear. Images of the melted goat people flashed through her mind. This was beyond serious now. They had to get home before something like that happened to them.

A glimmer of movement caught her eye. Skulks were rounding the corner.

"Pick up your feet, people!" she yelled. "Get your booties in that room."

Everyone rushed in. Luna quietly shut the door and locked it just as a group of guards scampered down the hallway past the door. For the moment, they were safe.

Miz briefly examined Luna, then turned to Alex.

"Question answered. Your girlfriend was right as rain. Nothing here is good news for us."

"What did you guys find?" Alex asked.

"Horrible things. We need to get the heck out of here," Genghis whispered. "Better we head back home."

"Agreed," Jed said. "Miz is right. We can't stay. Crane is experimenting on players. All his guinea pigs are dead, and we're next."

"Well, that settles it," Alex said.

"But we need the real portal key. That jerry-rigged Starway isn't functioning correctly. It was so horrible," Aspy said, hiding her eyes behind her hands.

Genghis put a comforting arm around her. Alex stared at the floor. What now? Was there another way out of this?

CHAPTER SIXTEEN

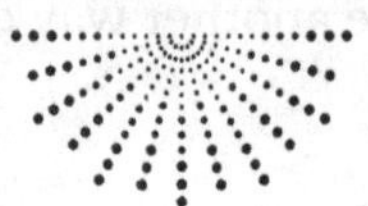

The first wave of skulks to find them banged on the door so hard that the frame rattled. Half the team held the door while the other tried to fashion a worthy barricade.

Suddenly, they weren't alone. Fester Crane had somehow weaseled his way into the room. "That won't last long," Crane said. "Better you surrender now—if you want to live."

"You gross little gremlin!" Jed roared. "You've been lying to us. We saw you and that zombie witch put innocent players in that Easy-Bake Oven of yours. It was heartless!"

"That's an interesting insult coming from you, but I'll forgive it since you have no idea what's going on here."

"Luna does!" Alex shouted.

"Luna Lifestealer is a liar, a low-tier champion, and most importantly, a traitor." Crane sneered. "Siding with her puts you on the losing team."

"You're reaching now, Crane," Alex said. "Luna is going to help us get out of here."

"I don't think that's correct. Ms. Lifestealer knows there is no way out. Isn't that right?"

"This is true," Luna said despairingly.

"In fact, because she can't activate a portal, she had decided to destroy Starway Station, effectively killing everyone here!"

"That wouldn't be necessary if you had refused to go along with the Griefers's plan," Luna said.

"Wait, you want to blow this place up?" Alex was confused and shocked. "Before we even tried getting back home? Are you crazy? We would all die."

"An unfortunate but necessary sacrifice, considering the gravity of the situation."

"I tried to tell you children. Lifestealer can't be trusted," Crane grumbled.

"You're not telling the whole truth!" Luna pointed an accusatory finger at Crane. "There's a tyrant on the Battle Moon—someone who is a lot worse than any of the Earthborn could imagine, someone who wants to enslave everyone they love and every other living being in the cosmos!"

"Such is life, my dear. Danger appears when you least expect it."

Alex narrowed his eyes. "You guys called our team the best worst players in our league. Why would you want us?"

Crane's eyes flashed as if he was delighted, like a spider who'd caught something in his web.

"Because rule-breakers and risk-takers are the ones who always find flaws in any new system," Crane said.

"Rule breaking, we can handle." Jed punched Crane in the nose with a vicious right cross that pounded the old gnome onto the floor.

Crane moaned and reached into his lab coat like he might retaliate with one of his tricks. "I'm trying to help you. I'm trying to help all of us."

"Yeah, right." Miz kicked Crane again, and he spun into the corner of the room, unconscious. "That's for the goats, you nasty little Smurf!"

Jed gave Miz a high five. Aspy and Genghis circled around Alex, leaving Luna on one side of the room alone.

"Alex, I think we've got a new problem," Genghis said. "Luna here wants us to make a righteous sacrifice for a crusade we don't even understand. I'm pretty sure the team doesn't consent."

"If we don't take a stand here, Malvexus and the Griefers will kill everyone you've ever known or loved," Luna pleaded. "Your entire planet will go up in flames or be enslaved. Is that what you want? We can't let that happen. I wish there were another way, but I don't have a portal key."

"And you never will!" A gruesome, clawed hand wrapped in a swath of magical light materialized in the center of the room. The hand formed a hole by turning to the right, motioning like it held a key and was opening a lock. The resulting aperture expanded until it was large enough for Bonegrin to step through. "You betrayed our master, Lifestealer. You'll never be a Herald again!"

Bonegrin's glowing claw flared with light then subsided. The portal vanished, and he pulled out his trident.

"You and the Earthborn will surrender to the skulks now," Bonegrin roared, "or I will slaughter you where you stand."

Surprising everyone in the room, Aspy jumped forward, screaming out a battle cry, and slashed down with a silver Quillodian dagger, slicing off Bonegrin's hand in one swipe.

Bonegrin screamed in anguish, grabbed his wrist to stem the bleeding, and backed away.

Luna jumped forward and kicked Bonegrin in the chin. Bonegrin's head snapped back with a crunch, and he fell to the ground as if dead.

Aspy picked up Bonegrin's nasty green-oozing hand and waved it in the air, examining it like it was a movie prop.

She glanced at Luna, who smiled knowingly and winked.

Alex marveled at Aspy and her new prize.

Aspy twisted and turned Bonegrin's severed hand in the air, creating a rift that bubbled with magical energy.

"His hand is the portal key!" Miz cheered. "Dang, girl, you *are* smart!"

When the magical portal fully dilated, humid air rushed through, carrying the scent of soil, rain, and tropical flowers. Strange animal sounds called from some hidden distance, and the magical energy holding the passage open crackled like lightning.

Miz gasped, "My God, the real Battle Moon is so beautiful."

Alex agreed. Like all these experiences, it was much more than the game could ever convey. Through a window near the doorway, he could see the skulks were about to break through. He looked at his friends and decided on the only logical course of action.

"If this game is truly real, like Luna swears it is"—Alex pointed at the portal and the Battle Moon beyond it—"then that's where we need to be. It's the only place we stand a chance of finding a way homc."

He looked at Aspy. "Do you agree?"

"Yes, let's get the heck out of here." She stepped through the portal and disappeared.

"I don't want to be goat-ghetti!" Miz yelled and jumped through.

"Me either!" Jed shouted and followed Miz.

Luna followed Jed, while Alex waited till the last second. He finally stepped through just as the door busted open and the skulks invaded the room.

The portal collapsed, and they were gone.

PART III
THE BATTLE MOON

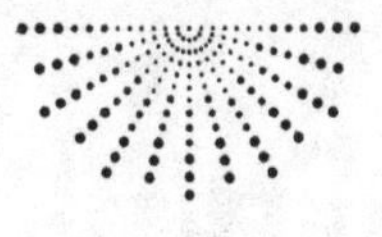

ROUND ONE

CHAPTER SEVENTEEN

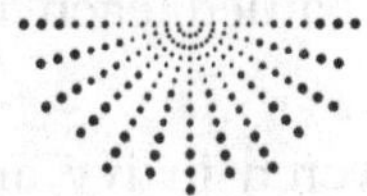

Luna Lifestealer and all five members of the Sparkles Modfia materialized in a swirl of glowing energy, dropping onto a cobblestone courtyard. They were clothed in the basic battle skins they'd worn in the arena. Only Aspy, who carried her Quillodian dagger and some archery supplies, seemed to have any decent weaponry. Miz had one small throwing axe on her hip.

Alex rolled over and jumped to his feet.

"Everyone in one piece?" The team, sprawled beside him, reflexively touched their bodies, making sure they were okay. They turned around to scan their new environment with eyes wide as saucers.

"Wow! This is the real Battle Moon, man," Genghis pointed. "We're in the Crimson Castle!"

What Genghis said was true. They had teleported into a small courtyard in the center of a literal castle—a marvelous, gleaming mound of red stone that fingered toward the sky like a giant's hand. They'd played in the digital version for years. Now, they were inside an accurate 3D rendering that matched that virtual architecture.

The actual castle was the center of a massive estate and had towers, crenelations, parapets, and turrets, all trimmed with soaring flags. The large buildings had glowing scarlet windows that reflected the moonlight and looked like eyes spying on the land beyond it.

The smooth red brick, tiles, and mortar were all variations of the color red—bright red, blood red, cranberry red, melted lava-orange—and had the occasional swirl of gold.

The courtyard was made from cobblestones that reminded Alex of an old European town center. Torches burned on the corner-post, while famous champions battled each other in bas-relief on the portico walls.

Everything seemed covered in ivy and pink bougainvillea and showed little signs of weathering seen in other, similar buildings. Instead, the structures had an artistic flair to them, as if carved from one stone by man or nature itself.

Alex heard a soft creaking sound coming from indoors. Even though there was no noticeable sign of people, he heard the faint echoes of laughter. Each glimpse of the interior seemed to radiate a warm and toasty feeling. The comforting scent of warm cocoa, baked cookies, and hot apple pie wafted on the breeze.

Several units behind them, in the center of the courtyard, sat the estate's cornerstone. Inside its stone vault spun the magical heart of the castle—the Crimson Cosmicron.

Both the blue and red bases had similar structures. Cosmicrons were the power sources that generated all the magical energy the bases needed to function.

The first team to destroy a cornerstone and its cosmicron won the game.

But destroying a cornerstone was a serious undertaking that took strategy, effective attacks, and teamwork.

The cornerstone was the most protected area on the grounds, and the castle defenses immediately killed enemies when they approached. Alex admired the cosmicron and imagined Champions battling through the estate to this very spot.

Without warning, a disembodied voice boomed from overhead.

"Welcome to the game, champions! The Battle Moon awaits! Fare

thee well!"

Luna lifted her arm and tapped a square of iridescent fabric along her wrist. Her heads-up display, a holographic window, projected itself above the square. Several tabs of information popped into existence—most notably, a map of the nearby terrain.

Alex knew the map so well, and yet he didn't *truly* know it. It was one thing to experience something on a two-dimensional screen, and quite another to be in the real, three-dimensional world.

"It smells like sugar cookies!" Genghis laughed.

Luna scanned her HUD again. "Oh, no. This can't be right."

Aspy flashed a look of recognition. It was apparent she was catching on to Luna's concern.

"If this is the real Crimson Castle, then we just spawned into the wrong base, right?"

"Yes, don't play dumb, Elf," Luna snapped, rolling her eyes at Aspy. "I sense you have much more wisdom than you reveal."

"The *enemy* base," Jed shuddered. "You mean we've dropped on the wrong side of the map?"

"Yes!" Luna said. She was spinning around as if expecting an attack at any minute.

"But why would the game start us here?" Genghis asked.

Aspy held up Bonegrin's severed hand. "His hand is the portal key. It was preprogrammed to bring him back here."

Jed checked his HUD's map. "We have to get out of here before—"

The warning was too late. The Crimson Castle was awake now. Magical cannons on the nearby towers rotated and took aim at the team.

"Oh, crap," Alex said. "RUN!"

"I knew I should've gone to the bathroom first!" Miz yelled and dove for cover just as cannon fire blasted the surrounding ground.

The rest of the team followed suit, dodging inhibitor blasts as they ran down a straight cobblestone path leading from the castle's cornerstone to the estate's main wall.

"Head for the West Gate!" Jed yelled, eyeing his map. "Then into the Wilds." He raced ahead, waving them along as he went.

A nearby group of skulks, wearing red armor, turned as they approached. Seeing Luna, they bowed their little heads for several long moments. The team raced by, headed to the West Gate.

A nearby turret turned as if it were a human head inspecting their credentials. Magical energy surged within its cannon. It was about to fire.

The red skulk captain stepped between the cannon and Alex and held up a hand. The cannon blasted him to ash.

Alex stumbled backward into the arms of his teammates.

"I'm pretty sure that was meant for you," Aspy said.

"Let's move it, people!" Jed shouted, pointing to the forest.

The team followed close on his heels. Smells from the nearby wilderness filled Alex's senses while cannon fire blasted overhead. Then genuine fear filled his heart. If they wanted to stay alive, it was time to disappear into the thick woods.

As she ran, Aspy, who was still holding Bonegrin's severed claw, wrapped a spare bowstring around its wrist and threw it over her shoulder. Suddenly, the hand gained a mind of its own. It ripped away from Aspy and hovered high in the air above them, wrapped in a cocoon of magic.

"Oh no, we can't lose that portal key!" Aspy yelled.

Miz and Alex stopped to watch as the hand flew back toward the Crimson Castle like it had suddenly sprouted wings.

"Miz, don't let that claw get away!" Alex yelled.

Miz reacted with the instinct of a practiced warrior. She pivoted and threw her throwing axe at the flying hand. The axe spun out flawlessly, sailing straight for its target—but, despite the good aim, the axe missed and spun on, finally slamming into the cornerstone.

Although it was too far to see, Miz's axe had struck one of the cornerstone's mortared joints perfectly. It cracked ever so slightly, then spider-webbed out into a million additional cracks until the energy of the Crimson Cosmicron leaked through and exploded.

CHAPTER EIGHTEEN

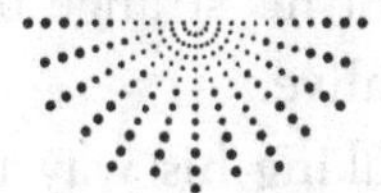

While Alex and his friends marveled at the aftermath of the Crimson Castle's destruction, Bonegrin's hand hovered patiently just outside the base's perimeter. Eventually, the fire and smoke cleared and the magical rebuilding procedure began. While it was a marvelous process to watch, the Modfia decided it was too risky to remain in enemy territory and headed deeper into the forest.

Bonegrin's severed claw flew the opposite way, gliding forward over the Crimson Castle's grounds, through a door decorated with a familiar golden skull motif, and into the opulent inner sanctum.

Several regeneration pods lined one wall of the massive room. As if sensing someone's presence, one pod's translucent dome opened. A cloud of white smoke escaped with a hiss and the hand floated down and gently landed inside.

Once the claw had settled, the pod resealed itself. Hidden mechanisms whirled to life in the deeper bowels of the strange machine.

A set of numbers, familiar to all who played *Cosmic Champions*, flashed on the pod's display. Bonegrin's regeneration timer had begun.

Tentacles of muscle fiber and ligaments grew from the hand and wove together. Soon an arm appeared, then a shoulder.

Finally, the champion's wide muscular torso took shape. This process continued as if a ghost was knitting Bonegrin Banebreaker a whole new body.

The regeneration timer counted down until a chime rang through the castle's halls. Steam hissed as the pod depressurized and opened.

Bonegrin climbed out of his strange bed no worse for wear. He was completely whole and alive.

He wasted no time making his way to the center of the room, where the largest pod was already opened. The pod's former occupant was looking out the largest window.

"Bonegrin," Malvexus said. He took off his opulent golden victor's crown and polished it with the hem of his tunic. "What say you?"

"I've done what you asked, Master," Bonegrin said, lowering his head in an uncharacteristic bow. "We have found a new team."

"Yes, the destruction of our base made that obvious! These cowards have struck a killing blow before the game can even begin. Good, I welcome the deviousness of such a challenge. I refuse to suffer this idleness another second."

Crimson wizard skulks with strange luminescent robes skittered into the room to attend to Malvexus—something that apparently annoyed the champion very much.

"Leave me, you sniveling sycophants." Malvexus spun around, quick as a tiger, slashing and ripping the skulks to shreds, killing them all.

A fresh wave of minions paused at the doorway to the room, took in the sight of their brethren's lifeless bodies, and went into full retreat.

Malvexus licked the skulk blood off his sharp fingernails as he stepped closer to a window. His fangs gleamed in the moon's light.

Bonegrin Banebreaker looked at his leader with pride.

"If the inhabitants of the Battle Moon knew you were watching, the entire planet would shake in terror."

Malvexus laughed.

"As it should."

Suddenly, the game intelligence spoke.

"Stand fast, champions! You have lost the first battle of the game. Round two begins now!"

Malvexus gave Bonegrin a vicious smile, his fangs glistening in the dim light.

"Finally! Let the slaughter begin!"

CHAPTER NINETEEN

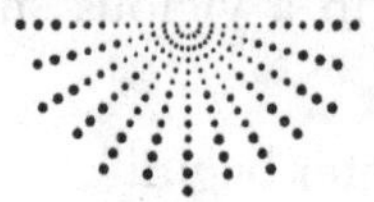

Elsewhere, the Sparkles Modfia raced through the humid wilderness, chased by a myriad of emotions. They were at once scared, exhausted, and confused, but also high on adrenaline, which kept them moving deeper into the heart of the Battle Moon.

The beautiful Crimson Castle had erupted in the biggest explosion Alex had ever seen. Then the game intelligence made a wonderful announcement.

"Sparkles Modfia has won the first round of the game."

"Thank goodness," Alex muttered.

It seemed the rules on the Battle Moon were following the rules of the *Cosmic Champions* video game. Each game was an independent double-elimination tournament with more than one round. The first team to lose two rounds lost the game. In Alex's experience, if the opposite team was good, the game lasted at least three rounds, but it could easily end in two.

Whether it was skill or sheer luck, they were up by one. This relieved some of Alex's anxiety. He knew the next round would be much harder. But this fortunate turn of events gave the Modfia time to level up. They needed to understand everything they could about surviving on the Battle Moon. Whether they liked it or not, it was their new reality.

Alex ran past a row of plants, marveling at the wonders of the alien world they now inhabited. He wasn't sitting in his comfortable ergonomic gaming chair, tapping away at a keyboard, and rolling a mouse around a desk—this was the actual Battle Moon, and he wanted to stop and touch the plants. Smell the flowers, so to speak, and relish for a moment the experience of living in his favorite video game.

Soon he was in a place he recognized. He pushed through the branches of a luminescent fern and stepped out onto a wide, well-traveled road. He twisted his boots in the dark crunchy gravel while examining the familiar path. He'd been here a million times in his avatar form. In game lore, the path was called Deadman's Road. It cut across the Battle Moon map, stretching diagonally from one base to the other.

Arriving here triggered a debate within himself. One part of Alex felt the impulse to turn left and run east toward the Crimson Castle. There, he'd find the battle and engage his new enemies. Attack a tower. Kill a squad of skulk minions. In other words, he could play the aggressive game he'd always played.

The other, more logical side wanted to turn west and lead the team to the Sapphire Sanctum, where he believed they would be safe enough to hide and rest. They'd been traveling for hours, and everyone was exhausted.

He stood on the edge of the road looking this way and that, debating their options, until Luna jerked him back into the cover of Warwood Forest. The team was resting under the thick limbs of a black pine.

"Your team isn't trained well enough to survive the road. Remember, this is the real Battle Moon. You can die here."

"If this is the game I know, we're not really safe anywhere." Alex shrugged. "But I agree, we're not ready."

He checked his HUD. Everyone on the team had a level in single digits and low health and mana. No wonder they were tired.

"We should head to the blue base," Aspy said. "In the game, there's a player portal there. We can use the portal key and get home."

Luna raised a finger. "That is an acceptable strategy, elf. The portal key can be passed to a new Herald, but it must be done at one of the bases."

"Let's do it. And along the way we could train and think, eat, and rest," Miz said. "I'd kill a man for a fruit smoothie right about now."

Alex realized in that moment that no one knew the portal key was gone. Aspy had just assumed Miz's axe had stopped it, and he'd retrieved it. That worried him. He caught Miz examining his concerned facial expression.

"We have the portal key, right?" Miz asked.

"Uh, yeah. I got it. Stuffed it in here." He held up his small leather backpack.

He flushed. Why was he lying? It was like he couldn't help himself.

Jed slapped Alex on the back. "Well, we can't go back to the Crimson Castle, so we hike on to the Sapphire Sanctum."

Genghis was all smiles. "I can't wait to see it, man. Blue is my favorite color."

"It seems the Sanctum is the best place for your team," Luna agreed. "I'm not sure I will be welcome there, but it would be much safer for the five of you."

Alex nodded and raised a finger. "I need to take a quick pee break. Excuse me."

He pushed through the thick cover and walked several units into the forest. He foraged in the brush and came up with a broken tree limb about the length of Bonegrin's missing hand. He then pulled up a bundle of fern fronds and gathered some fallen pine needles under a nearby tree. He wrapped the piece of wood in the needles and tied it with the fern fronds then stuffed it in his pack.

He immediately felt as low as the worms wriggling in the dark earth below him, but he was sure this was necessary. The team wouldn't make the trek to the blue base without the hope of going home.

They needed to believe it was still possible, and maybe it was, he reasoned, knowing somewhere deep down that it was a lie he was telling himself to justify the deception. He tried to think about better things as he made his way back to the group.

After about ten minutes, everyone was ready to resume the journey. When they were back on their feet, Aspy approached Alex.

"I can take the portal key," she said. "My avatar normally carries a heavy quiver, anyway. I need to practice hiking with something on my back."

Alex agreed and handed the bag to her.

She glanced inside and sniffed the contents.

"Pine needles," Alex shrugged. "I thought it would cut the smell."

Aspy nodded, put the pack on, and joined the team as they headed deeper into the wilderness. Alex prayed she wouldn't investigate it further.

"We should follow the lane west," Jed suggested, pointing at the horizon. "Skirt the edge of the road so we don't get lost. That'll also help us steer clear of all the nasty beasties we want to avoid."

No one argued. Jed was the team expert on this part of the map, but they decided Luna would take point since she had the most experience. Jed was next in line, then Aspy, Alex, and Genghis. Miz, who normally led the way, protected their rear.

Despite being low on energy, Alex noticed most of the team seemed relaxed. They were content but wary, since the occasional bloodcurdling howl of some distant monster set them on edge.

That somehow made him feel better about what was in Aspy's pack, and he put it out of his mind. That problem would deal with itself when they made it to the Sapphire Sanctum.

"Hopefully, we'll survive long enough to see this whole wonderful world," Aspy said, talking to no one in particular.

She picked a flower, smelled it, and put it in her hair. She continued walking forward, scanning each and everything in front of her, like a kid on Christmas trying to decide what present to open.

Despite the obvious dangers, Alex had never seen her or any of the team so happy.

CHAPTER TWENTY

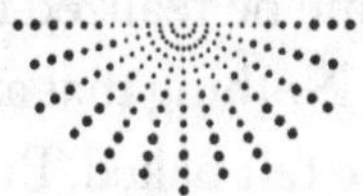

An hour later, the Sparkles Modfia had made it into safer territory. Deadman's Road, which they were still following, had changed. The gravel and dirt gave way to blue-tinged paving stones. It was a sure sign they were nearing the Sapphire Sanctum.

If it was running correctly, then the game intelligence should be able to identify the Modfia as the new blue team assigned to battle the reigning champs on the red team—a group called the Griefers. But all of this was a theory that wouldn't be tested until they approached the perimeter of the Sapphire Sanctum or one of its defensive towers. If they were not attacked, they could take up residence in the blue base and figure out what to do next.

After walking another ten minutes, they crossed the Regolith River and stopped near the bank to rest. While they traded turns with Luna's canteen, a small furry creature peeked out of the dense foliage. It stared at them, panting and wagging its bushy tail.

"OMG, look at this cutie," Genghis cooed. "It's a cat." The team circled around him as he knelt to pick it up.

"Genghis, that's no cat. I swear, dude, you are animal blind," Jed laughed.

It was true Genghis seemed to have an inability to identify animals, especially dangerous ones.

"Still, that has to be the cutest dang puppy I've seen in a while," Miz said. "Hold on, let me get a pic."

She reached around and felt for her smartphone. It wasn't there.

"Never mind," she said, sounding deflated.

Alex reached for his as well. It was also gone.

In fact, it was the first time he realized he had nothing from the real world with him in the game. Nothing that anchored him to home. It was bad not having his phone. He felt naked. But it was worse considering it didn't really matter. What was there for him back home? Boring school classes he was failing. A dead-end job and a sadistic boss who hated him. And a home that was sometimes more unpleasant than his terrible job.

Maybe this was why he was lying about the portal key. Everyone else wanted to go home. They had a reason to. He didn't. Even if this place was dangerous, it was better than what was waiting on him in the old world, which was nothing and no one who really cared about him.

While Alex felt sorry for himself, Genghis was all smiles.

"See, guys, if you just keep your third eye aligned with your universal chakra, life presents you with wonderful gifts. It just proves this place can't be that bad."

Alex couldn't help but smile at his ever-cheerful friend.

He tried to shake off the sudden depression and focus on Genghis and his new pet. The team was having a happy moment. He didn't want to spoil it.

Plus, the little furry guy was a lot like his dog, Dingo. Yeah, this was for sure a dog of some kind. No, not a dog. Too big for that. Something else.

Everyone froze when they heard several low guttural growls from more animals lurking a few meters away.

"Genghis. Drop. The. Dog." Alex whispered.

But it was too late.

Two giant wolves stepped out to guard their pup. They were snarling—viciously.

Genghis saw the creatures and went pale. He swallowed hard and lowered the puppy to the ground like it was a bomb that might explode at any moment.

"Okay, little guy, go back to Mommy and Daddy."

When Genghis stepped back, the puppy seemed upset at being abandoned. He turned on Genghis, whimpering.

"Oh, boy," Jed muttered. "A Rift Wolf just imprinted on Genghis!"

"We need to get out of here," Luna said.

Three more similar snouts poked through the nearby bush—very large snouts, very snarling snouts—which brought the count of dangerous animals to six. Five adult-sized Rift Wolves and one cute puppy sniffing the air like they'd found their next meal.

"Rift Wolves, 200 experience points and 75 gold if slain." Aspy froze and stared blankly at the creatures while she recited the monsters's stats.

Was she in shock? Alex grabbed a handful of her cloak and dragged her backward.

"Attack speed 0.75, movement speed 500," Aspy continued. "One good swipe of a claw could easily hit you for 500 damage."

"None of us have enough mana or health to survive that," Miz said, eyeing Jed for help.

Jed was looking around as if searching for the quickest way out of their predicament, but there weren't many options.

The team backed up carefully, trying to make sure the Rift Wolves didn't completely encircle them.

As they made it through a cluster of ferns, they stepped back into the main road and saw a blue-stoned guard tower, the first legitimate sign they were near the Sapphire Sanctum.

The tower looked like a rook on a chessboard. A blue crystal the size of a basketball hovered magically above it, spinning on an axis, emitting a powerful indigo beam that scanned the landscape like a searchlight.

It wasn't that far away. They could run to it. But would they make it? The tower, as if sensing their presence, scanned them with its strange magic.

"That's one of ours," Aspy yelled. "It's on auto-defense."

"Does that mean it will protect us from the wolves?" Miz asked. She wouldn't take her eyes off the one closest to her.

"Yes!" Alex yelled. He wasn't completely sure, but it seemed worth the risk. "Fall back to the tower. FALL BACK!"

The group burst out of the wilderness onto the open road.

The lead wolf lunged at Jed, who spun on his heels and delivered a roundhouse kick to the wolf's head. The wolf fell back with a slight whimper and yelp.

The other wolves, seeing their leader hurt, bared their teeth and growled, then leapt into action.

Thankfully, the team was already running for their lives straight to the tower. The wolves nipped at their heels.

When they were within firing range, a bolt of blue energy shot from the tower's power stone, out across the lane, over the heads of the team, hitting the lead wolf.

Zzzzzappppppp!

The animal disappeared in a blinding blue flash. A shriek echoed from where it had once been, and a cloud of charred wolf exploded like a dusty firework. The scent of burnt fur wafted down the road.

"Thank goodness," Genghis said, yelling over his shoulder. "It's not firing on us."

"I guess that settles it," Aspy said. "We're officially the blue team now."

The team cheered but kept running while the tower showered the ground behind them in magic blasts.

The wolves skirted the road, weaving in and out of the brush, continuing after the team. New wolves joined the chase, replacing those that had been killed and growing the pack. Suddenly, the tower stopped firing and scanned the environment again as if it had lost its targets.

"Hey, you laggy stack of bricks," Miz yelled. "Peel that tree line apart!"

The sapphire gem seemed to blink as if squinting its magical eye, then opened up. A barrage of brilliant blue cannon fire blasted the tree line, and another Rift Wolf disappeared in a burst of singed fur and ash.

Two wide doors creaked open as the team closed in on the tower. Dim light shone from within.

"Quick, everyone!" Luna yelled, pointing at the entrance. "Get inside!"

The team rushed to the doors, but as they did, one Rift Wolf leapt up and grabbed Jed by the ankle. He screamed. Miz turned on the wolf and kicked it in the head. The wolf yipped and let Jed go.

At the same time, a second wolf attacked Aspy. The wolf's jaws snapped at her arm and missed. Another one lunged and snapped at her neck. Aspy juked left, then right. The wolf clamped down on her pack and tried to jerk it free.

Aspy turned and caught one dangling strap as it slipped away, and suddenly she was several units from the threshold of the tower playing tug of war with a vicious Rift Wolf.

"What are you doing?" Luna yelled. "Let it go!"

The rest of the team had made it just inside the doors, which were automatically swinging shut.

"Come on, Aspy!" Genghis yelled.

Aspy finally gave in. The wolf snatched the pack and scampered out into the middle of the road with its prize, dodging further blue cannon fire. Aspy slipped inside the doors just as they banged shut.

Safe at last, everyone sat down, trying to catch their breath and calm themselves—that is, everyone except Aspy, who was worried sick about what they'd just lost.

"The portal key," she muttered, turning to find the stairs. "We can't lose the portal key."

The team followed her as she bounded up the steps, climbing several levels until she found a large window with a good view of the road.

They arrived just as another blue flash of energy shot out and incinerated a Rift Wolf. Some of the remaining animals were sniffing at the pack. One picked it up as if it might drag it toward the forest.

"Nutsacks. I'd forgotten all about that." Miz hovered behind Alex, staring at him suspiciously.

"Hey, look, weapons." Jed swept his finger across the tower wall. There was an array of ancient equipment covered in dust and cobwebs stored there.

Suddenly, Luna was moving past everyone. "By the Daedroom Sun, I'll get that key." She leapt out of the window and back down into the road.

"Luna, no!" Alex couldn't believe what he was seeing.

The wolves had been content to retreat into the jungle. When the alpha wolf saw Luna, it reversed course and the pack followed. Luna paid no attention to the threat and continued running for the backpack.

The rest of the team decided to help her. Alex was horrified.

"No, guys, get back in the tower. I've got this. I mean, Luna and I can get the pack." He jumped down onto the road.

The team didn't listen and jumped down with him, most of them racing past, determined to help Luna.

Miz had found an old war hammer. Jed had a rusty shield and something that looked like it had once been a spear. Aspy had her dagger at the ready. Genghis stayed behind trying his best to boost their mana levels with the few low-level spells he could conjure.

Meanwhile, the wolves were salivating, thinking they'd just got a second chance at dinner. The alpha wolf stopped and howled as if calling for backup.

Miz turned and confronted the Sapphire Tower again. "Hey, Blue Bricks, protect those badass champions out there." She pointed at her friends.

The tower rotated its cannon and aimed where Miz had pointed, firing like a magical Gatling gun. Blue laser fire strafed the road ahead of Luna.

Luna skidded into the nearest wolf like a baseball runner might try to steal a base. She knocked it over and grabbed the pack with one beautifully fluid movement, then hurled it to Aspy.

Aspy grabbed the bag as it tumbled into her path, then quickly threw it back to Miz, who was now behind her near the tower door.

Unfortunately, now the remaining wolves had surrounded Aspy, Jed, and Luna. One wolf had clamped down on Luna's ankle. She was kicking it in the head with her other foot.

Alex lunged into the fray, brandishing the rusty sword he'd found hanging on the tower wall. He spun around and brought his sword down on the alpha for a devastating blow. The wolf's jaws snapped once before its head left its body and flew off, bouncing and rolling like a soccer ball down the middle of the road.

Seeing the alpha killed so dramatically made the other wolves scatter quickly. Alex grabbed Luna and with the help of the rest of the team carried her back to the tower.

When they were back inside, Miz handed Aspy the pack.

Aspy anxiously pulled out the bundle, hoping to find Bonegrin's hand, and immediately realized it was a fake. She gave herself a dope slap.

"Of course, the hand has been gone since we entered the wilderness. I was so stupid to think otherwise."

"What? That's not right. Alex has been guarding it the whole time," Genghis said.

"No, he was lying," Miz argued. She was an angry tiger about to pounce. "To make us think we still had a way back home."

"Tell her that's not true, Garcia," Jed said. He pointed the rusty spear at Alex's chest.

Alex slapped the spear away, shrugged, and turned to look out the window. "I didn't mean for anyone to get hurt. And I didn't mean to lie. I just kinda forgot about it."

He knew the excuse fell flat. But what else could he say? He didn't really have a reason other than not wanting to disappoint everyone again.

The entire team circled around Alex. They looked like they wanted to throw him out of the tower.

Genghis held up his hands. "Hold on, guys. I'm sure there's a better explanation."

"Genghis, why are you defending him?" Jed shouted. "This jizz-head lies to us about everything."

"Why didn't you tell us the truth?" Aspy asked. "We could've been thinking up another way home."

"I don't know why. I just didn't want you guys to be mad or upset again. I'm sorry, okay?"

Miz was in his face. "I'm so dang disappointed in you, Garcia. How can any of us trust your sorry butt again?" She stormed into one corner and sat down.

"Just remember you're still fired!" Jed added. "We don't want a leader that lies."

Genghis looked sheepishly at Alex. "You just forgot?"

"I knew everyone would freak out and get depressed," Alex muttered. "Since I got us into this mess, I thought I should be the one to find another way home."

"Oh, here we go again. No one's as good as you. You're the best player, the smart one, and we're just your sidekicks. Is that it?" Jed sneered.

"If you guys want to hate me, fine, go ahead," Alex said, waving his hands dramatically. "If Aspy wants to be the permanent leader, she can decide what we do next. But I bet she just freezes up and leaves us hanging."

Aspy stared at the empty pack blankly, then back at Alex, then at the team like she didn't know what to say.

"My mom used to tell me that sometimes the worst weapons in the world are our words," she muttered. "I never really understood that until now."

A few tears formed around the edges of her eyes then slipped down her cheeks. She dropped the bag, turned, and left the room.

Alex looked at Genghis, but he seemed embarrassed and looked away.

Miz was back on her feet and stabbed Alex in the chest with a finger. "You're such a tool, Garcia. I swear to Beyoncé, you're about to get choke-slammed."

Then she followed Jed, who was already chasing after Aspy.

Luna watched everyone for a beat, wincing because of the pain in her new wounds, then closed her eyes as if she might sleep.

A terribly awkward silence fell within the tower.

Alex felt horrible. Despite being surrounded by his team and a new world of unexpected wonders, once again his main experience was the cold, haunting feeling of being completely alone.

CHAPTER TWENTY-ONE

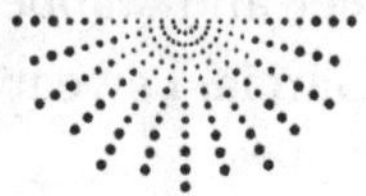

Over the next many hours, the team explored the tower and tried to settle in for the night. According to the game, four defensive towers, two for each team, existed along Deadman's Road.

Each tower was an integral part of the cosmicron network. Being spaced many units away from the main base, the towers served as lookouts and early warning systems. Since most games started with waves of offensive skulks, the towers mainly defended against those early attackers.

Perhaps like all military outposts, the accommodations were meager and only meant to be of practical use. It was dusty and cramped, and all the weapons were rusty, low-level versions of the better ones the team preferred.

Still, Alex was glad to have a sword, and the rest of the team seemed equally pleased to have found some usable loot.

The tower basement was home to only a handful of skulks. The dour little blue gremlins activated upon arrival. They were creepy, like the caretakers Alex had seen in vintage horror movies, shuffling around with dripping candles and mumbling forced pleasantries to their visitors in the middle of the night.

Despite the feeling they were slumming it, it was better than camping in the wilderness—especially with the looming threat of more Rift Wolves.

As the night rolled on and the braziers died down, they sat on their cots and finished the last of their food. A few of them worked to get their scavenged weapons in shape while talking amongst themselves. No one really talked to Alex. The team's cold shoulder was still in effect, but perhaps thawing.

"I wonder if we can find better loot in the next tower?" Miz asked.

"Yeah, or maybe there's some treasure in one of the jungle caves?" Aspy suggested.

Thc jungle part of the wilderness existed south of Deadman's Road. They hadn't yet crossed into that territory.

"Kind of a catch-22 right now. Our weapons are so crappy they wouldn't stand a chance against most jungle creatures, but we won't get better weapons without facing off with those monsters," Jed said.

Genghis entered the room. "Oh, man, gather round, dear children. Look what your favorite gnarly wizard found drying in the rafters." He threw a bundle of old weeds onto his cot.

"What the heck is that? Wheat?" Miz laughed.

Genghis giggled and produced a long Gandalf pipe.

"This, my dear friend, is grade-A Purple Blissleaf. If you were worried about getting a good night's sleep on these janky cots, worry no more."

He broke up the herb and stuffed his pipe.

"Who wants to smoke a bowl with me?"

Everyone laughed, but no one was eager to do it.

"Genghis, you're nuts. You have zero intel on what you are smoking. That stuff may fry your brain," Jed laughed.

"You can't fry what's already crispy, my dude." Genghis waved Jed along. "At least join me on the balcony while I partake. The night air will do us good."

Alex agreed and followed Genghis up and out to the top balcony, which gave a good view of the eastern horizon. Soon the rest of the team had joined them.

Below, on the road, they could see the decomposing bodies of several wolves. Far in the distance, they saw the glimmer of the Crimson Castle shining like a resort on a hill. It was already rebuilt.

The team enjoyed the night air. They discussed plans for tomorrow and made jokes about the smell of the Purple Blissleaf. Just as they were ready to turn in, Miz spotted something strange.

"Is that another puppy?" She pointed down at one of the dead wolves.

Sure enough, a small furry creature, about the same size as the pup they'd seen earlier, was nuzzling the neck of one of the dead wolves.

"Ah, man. Is that thing trying to wake up its dead mommy?" Genghis groaned. "Now I feel one thousand percent worse about killing those things."

Luna stepped out onto the balcony. "Remember, monk. Those wolves would've ripped you limb from limb if allowed."

She peered out at the little creature and hissed.

"Oh, no. That's not a puppy," she said.

"What is it?" Miz asked.

"Only the undead seek blood in the night."

"Undead?" Alex wasn't convinced. "I'm pretty sure that's a chipmunk. Or a squirrel."

The squirrel turned, baring its long fangs, which were coated in dripping blood. The throat of the Rift Wolf was punctured and still pumping from two holes in its neck.

"Oh no, vampire squirrels?" Jed said, looking at Luna for confirmation. "They feed at night. The blood from the Rift Wolves must have drawn them out."

"Not vampires, not now," Miz yelled. "I was ready to hit the bed."

"Practice for your archer," Luna said, pointing at the little vermin. "Kill it before it calls its kind and they overrun us."

Aspy left the team and returned a few seconds later with the bow she'd restrung. She nocked one of the old arrows she'd found and aimed.

Shhhfoosh.

The arrow sailed out and found its mark, hitting the squirrel in the midsection and pinning it to the ground.

"Good shot!" Genghis said, tapping out his pipe.

"For sure," Alex said, giving Aspy a pat on the shoulder.

Aspy looked pleased with herself.

Then the little squirrel started barking—a high-pitched chattering bark that seemed to echo through the tower and out over the wilderness.

"Whoa, that thing is mad," Jed said. "Maybe another arrow in the head?"

"Too late, it's calling its tribe," Luna said. She looked anxious.

Soon the rest of the team understood why. Glowing beady eyes seemed to be everywhere. They were surrounded.

Before Aspy could raise another arrow, the creatures attacked.

"Let's toast these little nut munchers!" Genghis yelled.

Using his pipe like a magic wand, he enchanted one of the few spells at his disposal—a level-one protection ring. A fiery orb flickering like an oversized candle appeared above them. It twirled until it produced a shield of golden energy.

The squirrels tried to advance and were immediately electrocuted by the magic.

The tower tried to aim its cannon, but it was no use. The angle was too severe and the risk of hitting the team was too great.

The few squirrels that avoided Genghis's shield chattered furiously. Soon, the others nearby responded to the call for help.

Genghis twirled his pipe. His shield expanded and dropped over the tower like a magical net.

Swarms of the vampiric creatures broke through the forest and stormed out onto Deadman's Road. Others descended from the night sky. Still others leapt from nearby trees, spreading their little legs and engaging their skin flaps. They flew up high toward the Modfia with fangs out, evil in their enormous eyes, trying their best to find a hole in the team's shield.

"Oh, this is bad," Aspy said. "There are too many of them."

"Agreed," Luna said. "At this rate, they'll destroy the whole tower with us in it. Best if we make a full retreat."

"But where?" Jed asked.

"Yeah, the tower has to be the safest place for miles," Miz said.

"The Silver Pines," Luna said. "They won't follow us there."

"Yeah, the Silver Pines," Alex repeated excitedly. "Quillodian magic enchants that part of the forest. It repels all undead creatures. Deals undead champions 800 hit points in damage every second they stand within the tree groves or on a surface covered in their needles. But we'd have to run at full speed."

"Not sure Genghis can hold the shield that long," Miz said.

"He isn't the only magic user here," Aspy said, stepping in front of the team. "On my mark, we run."

Aspy raised the small bow she'd restrung. The wood was so ancient it was failing, but no matter. She didn't need distance; she just needed the arrows up in the air.

In quick succession, she shot two trick arrows that exploded into a shower of tinier sparkling darts, killing most of the squirrels in melee range.

Some squirrels outside the perimeter were pinned to the ground by their paws and tails. Undeterred, the undead rodents viciously ate through their own appendages and scurried forward.

"Run, everyone!" Aspy shouted. "Run now!"

Aspy shot a third arrow as she jumped from the balcony. The sparks fell like a shower of fire, clearing a path into the forest.

Miz was next out of the tower and for the first time in the game used her Epic Power. One of the rusted battle axes she held came alive, spinning like a magical circular saw. When she hurled it at the squirrels, they disappeared in a cloud of fangs and fluff, giving the impression that a group of stuffed animals had exploded in the middle of the road.

Genghis dropped his shield, and the rest of the team leapt off the balcony and onto the road. They disappeared into the forest, hoping against hope they could make it to the Silver Pines.

CHAPTER TWENTY-TWO

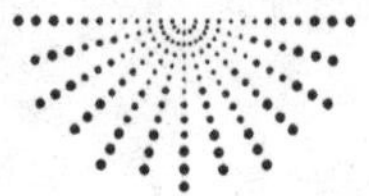

The next morning, the team woke feeling well-rested and grateful. The retreat into the Silver Pines had scared off the vampire squirrels, and once they were deep enough into safe territory, they had made camp and bedded down for the night.

After breakfast, it was decided they would continue toward the Sapphire Sanctum by traveling west through the Northern Wilderness and then to the famous Mana Lake.

When they were ready, they left the Silver Pines through a narrow canyon they found was easy to traverse. Soon they could hear a stretch of the Regolith River echoing in the distance. Chilly gusts of frosty air swept down from the north. Occasionally, pairs of Ash Ravens clucked and clicked as they flew overhead.

While they hiked, they tested their new skins, skills, and weapons. They teased each other about their transformations and dabbled with powers they'd never really mastered in the game.

The reality of manifesting spells and using weapons took more skill than clicking a keyboard or moving a mouse. As time passed, each of them gained more experience points. Sometimes a team member would level up, but their progress seemed glacier slow to

Alex. Despite the agonizing pace, they were all embracing their new life as budding champions.

"Hey, we're making good progress!" Jed shouted. He had raced ahead of the group and was calling down from the limbs of a marsh-bark oak. "This is Elkhorn Druid country. If we continue northwest, we'll find their camp near the Mana Lake."

Elkhorn Druids were a crossbreed—humanoids with elk-like features that included velvet-covered antlers and thick fur that covered their bodies.

"We haven't leveled up enough to take on any of the Elkhorn," Aspy said. "We'd better avoid their camp."

The team stopped to take a break and considered the problem.

"Thc only way we level up is hy challenging higher levels, right?" Miz asked. "Maybe we should take the chance. Pick off any druids that want to fight us."

"Listen to the elf," Luna said. "You lack the skill necessary to make war with the druids. Luckily, I've defeated their leader, Witcheye Mosshorn, in battle many times. Because of this, I am respected in their community."

"What about the rest of the team?" Alex asked. "Can you vouch for us?"

"They often welcome strangers seeking trade. We'll offer them some loot for safe passage."

"But what do we have that's of any use to them?"

Genghis raised a hand. "I know. Any healer worth his salt loves silver pine. The needles ward off dark magic."

"That's not a bad idea." Luna nodded. Genghis looked pleased. They had all stuffed their packs with extra needles in case they ran into more squirrels.

"If they'll let us pass through," Jed said, "we should follow the lake's shoreline south as it bends back toward Deadman's Road."

"Good, I'd prefer traveling on an open road more than continuing this baby-level slugfest through the Wilds," Miz said. She slapped her neck, killing an annoying fly.

Luna shook her head. "Traveling on the open road is not advisable. It will reveal your position to the Griefers."

"That's a glorious name," Genghis said. "Who are these cool *greavers*, anyway?"

It seemed he had missed Luna's earlier warning entirely.

"I'm speaking of Bonegrin and Nightbane and the rest of their team. Your enemies! Why do you think they recruited you? You are nothing more than easy prey. Fresh meat for their deranged leader, who demanded they seek out new players to torture and murder viciously. The Griefers pride themselves on pounding the bones of their enemies to dust," Luna said. "They insist on making all their adversaries suffer excruciating pain. To them, killing is the game."

"Far out, man," Genghis said, lighting up some of the Purple Blissleaf. "But very creepy!"

Luna moved past Alex and hooked a thumb at Genghis.

"If your healer smokes any more Blissleaf, he'll likely float away."

"I sure as heck hope so," Miz joked.

She grabbed the pipe from Genghis and took a puff, which led to a coughing fit. The smoke was too much for her. "Wow. What's in that, anyway?"

"Dreams, druids, and dankness," he joked, giving Miz a bug-eyed stare.

A quick burst of giggles ran through the team, and they got up and started hiking again.

They continued walking for some time and eventually came out of the canyon into a denser grove of marshbark oaks. When Alex noticed the sun falling, he stopped everyone and suggested they set up camp.

"It's getting dark. We need to find a safe spot to spend the night."

"There's a tree line up ahead," Jed said, pointing west. "It would give us protection from the wind and hide a fire if we make one."

Everyone agreed, and when they selected their camping spot, Genghis set up some wards around that area. Miz chopped up some firewood, and Alex built a fire. Luna showed Aspy how to build a temporary shelter, and Jed used his shadow-weave magic to conceal their camp and fire from anyone who might be watching.

"Aspy, you and Miz guard the camp. I'm going to scout farther up this trail."

"No one trusts you right now, Alex. You're not leaving us here while you go off to the druid camp by yourself," Aspy said.

Miz stepped in front of Aspy and folded her arms across her chest. "Yeah, what she said. Someone goes with you, or no one goes."

"Fine," Alex moaned. "Come on, Jed."

Eventually, after much grumbling, they made their way to the perimeter of the druid camp. This was a familiar area to Jed, who often leveled up by hunting monsters around the Mana Lake.

"I've been here a thousand times in the game," Jed said, "but this doesn't look right. Not at all."

"Well, we've never seen it in real life," Alex said, scratching his head.

"That's not it. Something is off," Jed said.

Alex had to agree. He felt a certain unease—and the smell was almost nauseating. He turned to see Luna had joined them.

"The hunter is right," Luna said. "Something about this has changed. And there is no sign of the Elkhorn. We crossed into their land with no resistance or sign of any druid scout. This is not their way."

"We should tell the others," Alex said.

After patiently watching the area for several minutes, they returned to their camp for the night.

CHAPTER TWENTY-THREE

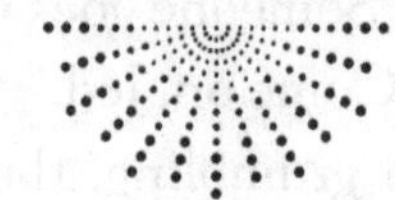

The next morning, the team hiked back to the Elkhorn camp. When they arrived at the edge of a swamp, no one recognized their surroundings. It seemed to everyone that something was very wrong. Not even Jed, who was a wilderness expert, could make sense of the changes.

"It's like the whole map has been rearranged," he said.

"Where are the Elkhorn?" Miz asked, as they skirted the edge of a large pond full of black goo. Bubbles surfaced here and there, making a strange gulping sound.

"Uh, guys," Genghis whispered, "we're looking for the Elkhorn, right?"

"Yeah, doofus," Jed said. "And their camp."

"I think this is it," Genghis replied.

He sounded sad as he pointed at a nearby cave. It was full of the druids' belongings, waiting as if they might return any minute. Still, there wasn't a single Elkhorn anywhere to be seen. The bog bubbled like black pasta sauce, burping stomach-turning swamp gas every few seconds.

The team searched the caves and shoreline as it slowly dawned on them. The field of black rocks near the bog weren't rocks at all. They were the corpses of the Elkhorn Druids. Hardened black goop covered dozens of them.

Jed reached out and held his hand over one body. Magical energy crackled around his fingertips.

"Oh, no," he said gravely. "The whole swamp is full of it."

"Full of what?" Aspy asked.

"Dreadmagic."

"How can you be so sure?" Luna asked.

"I use similar dark magic in the game. But don't ask me how I know it," Jed said, shrugging his shoulders. "For whatever reason, I feel it in my bones and sense it with my mind."

"Wait a minute," Miz said, grabbing the sides of her head. "Is the Battle Moon changing our brains too?"

"Of course, how else do you think we're leveling up so fast?" Aspy said.

"What? No way, man. I was worried about that. This body is a temple, totally GMO free," Genghis said.

"Get off it, man. You'd smoke yourself to higher levels if you could." Jed laughed at Genghis.

"True dat," he shrugged. "But only if it's au naturel."

"This is certainly not natural," Luna said, peering over the bog.

It seemed many of the Elkhorn corpses had died in mid-battle.

"I'm going to check the other side of the lake," Jed said as he jogged off, heading north before circling westward around the lake's edge.

"Dreadmagic is forbidden magic. Whoever did this is evil," Luna said.

Alex raised an eyebrow and stepped closer to Luna.

"If it's forbidden, how is it being manifested in the game?

"I'm not sure," Luna said, looking worried.

Aspy checked her HUD for an explanation. "Maybe we screwed up the game when we teleported here? And we created some kind of glitch?"

This was the first Alex had ever heard of dreadmagic, and it sent a chill through him.

Jed jogged back and he looked worried.

"The entire Mana Lake is infected. This is on a scale I've never seen. It's like a giant dreadmagic trap."

"That should be impossible. It would require an extremely high-level player and all the magical power the game allows to create something like this," Aspy said.

Jed looked disturbed too. "Who the heck is that powerful?"

"And why would they use that power to do this?" Miz asked

"If you were losing, you could draw your opponents here," Alex said.

"Like an ace in the hole," Genghis added, moving closer to the edge of the bog. "Knock your enemy in this goo, and they'd never get out."

"Was this meant for us?" Miz wondered.

"I don't think so," Genghis said. "Look, the trap is already sprung. See, there's something in there."

He pointed into the darkest part of the mire.

Aspy stepped up to see what he'd discovered.

Suddenly, a clawed hand erupted from the black goop and grabbed her boot. Everyone screamed simultaneously.

"Aspy, hold on!" Alex shouted.

He leapt toward her, pulling his sword free of the scabbard, ready to hack into the arm of the attacking creature. But before he could swing his weapon, the clawed hand let go.

Miz pulled Aspy away from the edge, and Genghis checked to see if she needed any healing. Everything was fine. Then another clawed hand emerged from the muck, joining its twin on the bank.

A muck-covered humanoid was trying its best to crawl free of the mire. He pulled himself half-way out, rolled over, and collapsed with his feet still trapped in the bog's goop.

Luna gasped as if she recognized the rack of antlers. "Witcheye Mosshorn!"

"Oh no, it can't be. Who would do this to such a great champion?" Genghis asked. He tried a healing spell, but it was of no use.

Luna reached out to touch the druid, but Jed yelled at her.

"No, Luna! He's infected and it could spread to you."

"I see what this is now," Aspy said. "The druids aren't dead. They are in some kind of stasis spell."

"Aspy is right," Genghis said. Stepping up, he put his hand on Luna's shoulder, comforting her. "My magic can sense it. They are near death but not dead. All of their mana and health are depleted but . . ."

"They aren't able to re-spawn," Miz said, suddenly understanding the situation.

"Yeah, a terrible kind of limbo," Alex added.

"Like bog wraiths," Aspy said. "They're only mentioned once in the oldest lore. In fact, I thought they'd been written out of the game."

"We have to get Mosshorn out of there," Luna said. "He's a fellow champion and doesn't deserve this horrible fate."

"If you touch him, you'll be in the same situation!" Jed said. "I'm not sure what could save him now."

Jed waved his hand and cast a blast of shadow-weave magic that lit up every part of the bog. It glowed a shimmering purple like a psychedelic poster under a black light.

"Look! There must be hundreds of champions in there."

The team let out a collective gasp. It wasn't just the druids—the entire water feature, which had been a pristine body of mana-infused water, was filled with entombed creatures and champions.

"Now I get it," Aspy said. "Usually, this lake is a pure reservoir of mana. It powers much of the regular magic on the Battle Moon. Now, someone has corrupted it—a twisted but genius move if you want to power a dark spell." Aspy's eyes widened, and she stretched her hands out as if measuring the shoreline. "A *lake* full of mana is the *only* magic source large enough to conjure dreadmagic!"

"This is worse than I imagined." Luna's voice cracked.

Alex wasn't sure if she was about to scream or cry. Either way, it was obvious she was very upset.

"This proves he's gone too far. Greed always blinded him. But now he's lost all honor and allowed himself to be corrupted by dark magic. It's so very horrible," Luna said. She put her hands over her face when the tears started. "Malvexus did this!"

CHAPTER TWENTY-FOUR

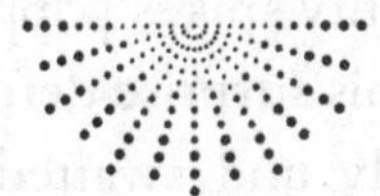

A mood as dark as the water in the bog descended over the team. They milled about on the edge of the new swamp, discussing and debating what they should do, wondering how they could help counter the black magic that had infected the champions and creatures frozen within.

Suddenly, one zombified champion, a robed creature of some kind, rose from the black water and began sloshing toward the team. It moaned as it drew closer.

"Watch out!" Alex yelled. "A bog wraith!"

"Stand back!" Luna shouted. She reached behind her back and retrieved her preferred weapon—a kusarigama. Alex often marveled at the stunning animations showing her mastery of the weapon—a handheld sickle and chain. In the real world, the Japanese had used it to impressive effect, especially with those who needed to be kept at a distance, like the samurai with their deadly swords.

Luna moved her body and swung the chain with the skill of a dancer. The technique seemed more like gymnastics than a tactical move, something Alex didn't understand but respected.

However, this time the bog wraith saw it coming and threw up a defensive spell. The weighted end of Luna's chain, called a *fundo*, was absorbed into the wraith's magical shield where it froze in midair. It then shot back toward Luna with such force it carried her out through the trees with a yelp.

"Holy crap," Jed whispered. "This thing means business."

He was hiding in the shadows near the shore, hoping to flank the wraith. But the wraith was ready for him.

It flexed, and black pointy spikes popped out, giving the creature the look of a porcupine. This surprise defense forced Jed off balance. The wraith turned quickly and swatted Jed into the woods. He landed only yards from a still-stunned Luna.

"You shouldn't have done that, you bony mother trucker!" Miz shouted. "If you aren't already dead, you're gonna be."

She lifted her axe, which buzzed with mystical energy. Her normal weapon was a similar artifact of immense power that required a noble alignment to wield. This axe was a poor substitute, but she forced as much mana into it as possible and attacked.

The bog wraith blocked her first swing. The impact reverberated back through the handle, knocking Miz down. She righted herself, planted her feet, and hurled the battle axe like Thor might throw his hammer.

The wraith screeched and ducked, narrowly missing the axe, and somehow caught the handle. Then it used the weapon's own centrifugal force to spin it right back at Miz, who dove for cover as the axe sailed over her head.

Aspy wasted no time sending a massive volley of arrows into the air. The wraith looked up at them and seemed unimpressed. It flung the cape around itself and in the process blew the arrows back at Aspy, trapping her in her own magical attack.

The wraith slogged through the bog, made it up on the bank, and turned north as if it meant to escape. Instead, it ran right into a sword.

"Going somewhere?" Alex quipped. He had stabbed the wraith in the gut, giving him what should have been a fatal blow.

"I didn't see that coming," the wraith squeaked.

It fell over as if dead, looking like a human-sized hors d'œuvre with Alex's massive sword sticking through him.

As his teammates cautiously circled around, Alex tried to retrieve his sword by putting one boot on the wraith and pulling. It had no effect.

"How inconvenient," the wraith said.

Everyone jumped several feet back, each taking defensive stances or cursing or both. Alex jerked at the sword, this time more out of reflex, not knowing what else to do.

"Easy does it, boy. It hurts when you jiggle it back and forth like that."

With no strategy or plan, the team hit the wraith with a barrage of their best attacks, using every spell and weapon they had.

"Cease fire!" Aspy yelled.

The wraith was silent now and for good reason. Nothing could survive such an onslaught. They waited several beats anyway.

"He's dead," Jed declared. "He has to be."

"Yep, you got me," the wraith said.

The team attacked again in unison, blasting the wraith with another round of devastating magic, mainly out of stunned reflex. How the H-E-double-hockey-sticks was this thing still alive?

"Ouch! Okay, I give up. I'm very, *very* dead. Please put away your weapons."

The wraith rolled over on his side like a dog showing his vulnerable belly. He lay on the muddy bank as still as possible, no longer displaying any threat.

"Who are you, creature?" Luna demanded. "Reveal yourself."

"Most certainly," the wraith said. "But would you first kindly take this old rusty sword out of my liver? Talking would be much easier without this thing sticking through me."

Alex stepped closer, cautiously. He grabbed the hilt of his sword and pulled it out, gently at first then roughly, wiggling it on purpose and stabbing it up and down a few more times for good measure. He hoped inflicting some final damage might permanently incapacitate this creature.

"Yes. Okay. Not very efficient, are you, young man?"

The wraith growled at Alex.

"Thank you very little," he said, when the sword was finally out.

At last, he stood up to face the team, who backed up yet remained shoulder to shoulder in a defensive stance, ready for another attack.

The wraith reached up and pulled back its fearsome cowl. Luna was stunned.

"Gamemaster," she gasped. "By the cratered moon, you are the Gamemaster!"

"Ah, so you've heard of me?" Gamemaster said. "Marvelous."

The old man seemed delighted.

Luna kneeled.

"Get up, my child. That's unnecessary, especially since I did a horrible job of introducing myself."

"Luna, who the heck is this old geezer?" Miz asked.

"Not old, Earthborn," Luna said, remaining on her knees. "More like eons of ancient. One of the first. One of the most high. The Cosmomancer of the Battle Moon."

"The last of them, I fear," Gamemaster said.

He waved his hand like a wand and a magical regeneration cocoon wrapped around Witcheye Mosshorn. The whole package rose from the bog and hovered between the team then flew east, disappearing.

"You warriors six defeated me fair and square. Now I offer my friendship and wisdom in exchange for your help restoring the game."

"And how would we do that?" Genghis asked.

"Wonderful, I hoped you would offer your assistance," Gamemaster said. He grinned, showing a beautiful set of pristine-white movie-star teeth.

"Wait a minute, grandpa, we haven't agreed to anything," Miz said.

She raised her axe. Jed put his arm in front of her.

"Let's hear the offer before we kill him again."

Gamemaster tapped his perfect teeth with a dirty fingernail.

"Offer? Do you mean terms? Game rules? That's quite simple, dear players. If you help me get the game back in order, I will help you get back home."

The team looked at each other. No one offered any argument or protest.

"I'll take that as a yes," he said.

Everyone nodded in agreement.

"Excellent! Now brace yourselves. This is going to hurt!"

He clapped his hands, and the force of the clap reverberated out like an explosion.

Shhhccracckkkk!

The blast instantly killed the entire team. They fell dead at Gamemaster's feet and, after a few seconds, disintegrated in a swirl of magical energy.

PART IV
THE BATTLE MOON

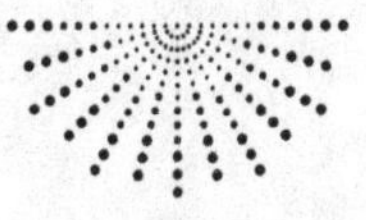

ROUND TWO

CHAPTER TWENTY-FIVE

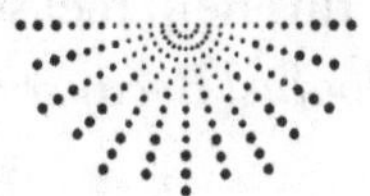

Magical fast-travel was very important for the game. In the computer version, Alex relied on it to dart around and sneak up on foes, but experiencing it in real life made him second guess why he'd ever considered it a good idea.

When he and the team reappeared, it seemed his stomach arrived several minutes before his body, and he gagged as if he might vomit. A spasm of vertigo made him wobble, and he thought for a moment he was going to lose his balance and do an embarrassing face plant in front of everyone. All the green faces confirmed he wasn't the only one feeling terrible.

Where the heck are we? he wondered.

"Sweet Blissleaf," Genghis exclaimed. "This is the Sapphire Sanctum! We're dead, dude."

Dead?

Alex realized he was dreaming.

Or was it something else?

His sense of reality had been so out of whack for so long now, it was hard to know what was happening or what to believe. Best to just roll with it.

Like you're playing a game, he told himself. *Because you are playing a game. A fun game, in fact.*

Was it still fun?

Yes, he said to himself again. *You are having fun. Enjoy playing the fun game.*

Then he remembered.

The bog. The wraith. And the deal. Gamemaster said he would help the team. But why did this help feel so bad?

Because he killed you, doofus! Because you are dead!

No, that can't be right.

Look around!

Look around in a dream. How is that possible?

Turn your crazy head!

Alex turned his head and gagged and choked, then spilled out of the regeneration pod onto the blue-brick castle floor.

"Good morning, honored player," the small gremlin-sized wizard squeaked in broken English. He handed Alex a large towel and waved one strange claw like a game show hostess. "Welcome to the Sapphire Sanctum, your rightful home for the duration of the game."

"Who are you?" Alex asked.

The tiny wizard responded in gibberish that Alex couldn't understand.

"Skularrison Skularney, Master Healer, Sapphire Order," Jed translated, holding one finger in the air. "He's a skulk. He says he's at your service, I think. Still working out that last part."

"Why can't I understand him?"

"He only knows a few phrases in basic language."

"So, how are you translating that nonsense?"

"One of my passive abilities, dude," Jed laughed. "You really should get to know your team better."

Jed was eating a piece of fruit while leaning against the doorjamb of one of several exits from the large round space. He wore a new ninja-styled skin complete with glittering silver chain mail that peeked out from below his black robes. A belt with an array of mysterious pouches and sheathed daggers fit snuggly around his waist. Alex liked the upgrade.

As if sensing it was no longer needed, Alex's pod's dome closed with a puff of white smoke. Some hidden mechanism sloshed clear liquid around the inside of the strange invention. It reminded Alex of a washing machine running through its various cycles. A cloud of steam escaped with a hiss from an exhaust pipe.

"The girl's crypt is on the other side of the hall," Jed said.

Master Healer Skularney squeaked, bowed, and ran behind Alex, then shot him in the left butt cheek with a very large and very painful Modcraft Skindart.

"Hey, man!" Alex screamed. "What's the big idea, shooting a guy down there?"

Jed laughed and offered Alex a piece of his strange blue fruit.

"Hurts, doesn't it? But it beats being naked."

Alex looked down. His new skin was nothing less than awesome. It was a low-level set of armor called Battlegear of the Blueforge. It consisted of a gleaming magical breastplate, spaulders for his shoulders, and well-fitting legplates. The set boosted his attack power by fifty points and improved his chance of striking a critical hit by twenty percent. It seemed leveling up truly had its advantages.

"Can you believe that old fart killed us?" Jed said nonchalantly. He chomped down, taking another bite of the blue fruit.

So it was true. They had died and were now regenerated, something that should have happened when they destroyed the red base.

"Aspy says the game is out of whack," Jed added. "And that geezer was just setting things right."

Alex checked his HUD, where he found the official score. Sparkles Modfia had won the first round. The Griefers showed a big goose egg.

"I'm not sure if he was trying to help us," Alex said, scratching his head. "But at least we're still up my one."

Jed shrugged. "Well, the skulks said this is officially round two. So, I guess we better get ready to face-off with the competition."

Alex felt a buzz of excitement and worry. The game was in full swing now. What would an actual battle with the other team be like?

"Miz, Aspy, and Luna are already awake, skinned up, and exploring the base," Jed said. "Genghis is with them. Come on. Let's go find them and get you some breakfast."

Alex used the posh bathroom, and the two boys set off to find everyone.

The Sapphire Sanctum was more like a cathedral than a castle. Its spires reached higher than the turrets and parapets of a typical fortress, and it had flying buttresses that held the walls like giant fingers. All the stonework was made from various hues of blue, including azure, blackberry, and periwinkle.

There were several bell towers and gargoyles made of blue crystal. Stained-glass windows depicting wilderness creatures were everywhere. They made the entire estate glow with calming light. There was a tranquil mood here that was different from the Crimson Castle. Somehow, it was understood that safety could be found if visitors sought sanctuary peacefully.

The courtyard in the center of the estate featured an opulent fountain in front of the Sanctum's cornerstone, which held the Sapphire Cosmicron. The spinning orb glowed with the color of a morning sky, providing light to the dancing waters and the whole Sanctum.

Solstice roses and hyacinth vines grew everywhere but seemed dense near the fountain. Incense burned by the skulk monks filled the air with a perfume that was both earthen and floral.

Like the other base, all the walls were covered in ivy and indigo bougainvillea, giving the strange cathedral the balance between its more sacred features and the mundane wilderness beyond its massive gates.

Eventually, Alex and Jed found the girls and Genghis. They were getting a tour by a blue-robed skulk named Vicar Skulodius.

"And what is this?" Miz pointed at a large two-pole lever near the main entrance.

Vicar Skulodius responded in skulk gibberish, gesturing his hand in a way that told Miz to flip the switch.

Miz laughed and shrugged. "I have no idea what any of these skulks are saying."

"He said there's only one way to find out," Jed translated. "Pull it."

Miz reached up and threw the switch, and the Sapphire Sanctum seemed to shift into another gear.

"Wow! I think that's the game-on switch," Aspy said. "It's the player's way of activating the base. The skulks switch it off to preserve power when the players are regenerating."

This seemed right. Once the switch was engaged, the cosmicron erupted with fresh magic. Waves of stronger electricity swirled around the sapphire. Now it seemed to pulse like a heartbeat.

Outside the walls, along the perimeter of the main gate, two massive turrets with cannons charged with power. Their gears whirled as the barrels of their guns swiveled back and forth, eagerly searching for a worthy target.

From somewhere below, steam rose in several great gusts of white smoke.

"What is that? Is the base on fire?" Genghis asked.

"That would be the skulk pits firing up," Aspy said. "There's an entire factory hidden below us."

Alex looked down through the street grates to see several vats of sapphire-colored goop bubbling and burping steam. It reminded him of the large pot of spaghetti sauce his mom would make on Monday nights. The contents of that pot filled large copper tubes and flowed through a web of conduits until it was deposited into a series of skulk-shaped molds.

The molds were then pushed into ovens and baked in magic. Eventually, at the end of this process, an entire new wave of sapphire-colored skulks appeared on a slow-moving conveyor. After being skinned in their appropriate attire, each one seemed ready and eager to serve the Sanctum and its new masters.

This batch seemed to be soldiers. As they were produced, they marched up from the pits, out the main gate, and over the drawbridge, where they queued near the entrance to Deadman's Road.

They milled about until a dozen had formed a squad; once aligned in soldierly formation, they marched east down the road.

"Where are they going?"

"Man, this is just like the game. They're headed to the towers," Jed marveled. "They'll defend those structures if attacked, and if killed, the skulk pits will generate new squads to take their place."

Alex stared at the magic and majesty of the blue castle. Every indigo-colored brick, tile, and rivet seemed to hum with a mysterious energy. It seemed alive, like it possessed a mind focused exclusively on defending and protecting their team.

A sense of calm washed over Alex for the first time since they'd crossed over into the new world. No longer worried about his safety, he realized he was hungry.

"Actually, I'm starving," he said to no one in particular.

Immediately, the sanctum responded like an attentive mother. An important looking skulk in a chef's hat appeared and rang a handheld copper bell and pointed Alex and the team to the grand hall.

Once inside, they found a spread that would put any breakfast banquet to shame. The table was loaded with a variety of bacon, sausages, eggs, and a myriad of hot drinks, plus every flavor of juice. And there were desserts—so many, in fact, it looked as if someone had robbed a bakery.

"Hot diggity dang," Miz said, grabbing a donut. "That's what I'm talking about."

"Is it safe?" wondered Aspy.

"Safer than starving," Jed said.

Alex laughed. It seemed to him Jed had never stopped eating since they woke up.

"Baked tofu," Genghis yipped, grabbing a plate. "Heck, yeah!"

The team filled their plates and mugs, found some seats, then began their feast. As they ate, the skulks served them, offering seconds and clearing dishes.

A trio of blue skulks in wizard robes buzzed around, magically manifesting more accoutrements to set the mood. Candles, flowered vines, and music filled the room.

Shhhcracckkkk!

Gamemaster, who no one had seen since the confrontation at the bog, suddenly appeared in their midst. He was wearing a new robe. The black goo from the bog had disappeared. His features were clearer, his silken robe more befitting his stature.

Everyone stood, unsure about his motives. He smiled pleasantly and motioned for them to sit back down. Everyone did, happy to get back to their food.

He watched them eat, sticking his chest out with pride, surveying what had become a quite beautiful room. Then he took up a chair at one end of the grand table opposite Alex and presided over them like a happy father.

"If you like the banquet hall," he smiled, "wait until you see the surprise I have for you."

"Surprise?" Alex said. "The last few days have been one big surprise after another. Everything about this place is a surprise!"

"No truer words could be more appropriate for your first visit here," Gamemaster said. He smiled wide then raised a drink to the team, who responded by raising their own. "My friends, since I have not said it in any polite way, or at all for that matter, welcome to the Battle Moon!"

CHAPTER TWENTY-SIX

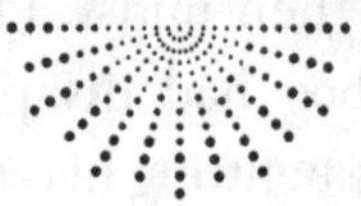

After breakfast, the Modfia team members wandered outside, drinks in hand, and strolled around the main courtyard. They examined aspects of the lush garden and enjoyed the sculptures they found. Each one was of some famous champion that had once called the Sanctum their base.

"My dear Earthborn friends, I realize you are enjoying your respite," Gamemaster said, appearing suddenly behind them. "But I promised you a surprise."

With a wave of his hand, Gamemaster reshuffled the bricks in the nearest wall, producing a room full of magical weapons. A collective gasp rose among the team, and they rushed inside with the excitement of children on Christmas morning.

As they approached the largest display, a magical tapestry unfurled. It read: "GAMEMASTER'S COSMOTASTIC EQUIPMENT EMPORIUM."

The subtitle declared: "Redeem Valor Points Here!"

"Now this is the luscious loot I've been waiting for!" Miz cheered.

Everyone laughed.

Gamemaster regarded them with a wry smile. He disappeared in a swirl of magical smoke and reappeared seconds later behind the counter. He was wearing a Dapper-Dan-type outfit consisting of a wide-brimmed straw hat, a red striped vest, a bowtie, and sleeve spats. His mustache was waxed so that it stuck out a foot on each side of his face. His ever-present wizard staff had transformed into a vintage walking cane that he used to direct his eager customers.

"No pushing. No shoving. And most importantly, no fighting, my dear patrons," he said in his best Willy Wonka impression.

Gamemaster snapped his fingers and a ticket scanner appeared on the counter to his left. Using his cane, he tapped the device affectionately.

"Please place your right hand on the palm scanner. It will read your current player statistics."

Alex beamed with delight.

The weapon's pop-up reminded him of his weekend trips to the arcade. He spent countless hours collecting paper tickets in plastic buckets and then endlessly haunting the winner's circle, where it took even longer to decide how to redeem the tickets. Memories of his father and mother begging him to hurry flashed through his mind. It made him smile. Those had been happier days.

"You, young lady, then you," Gamemaster said, pointing to Aspy then Miz. "If I remember right, it is an Earthborn custom to let females go first."

Aspy looked down at her feet.

"I'm not sure I identify as female. I'm still figuring that out."

"I sure as heck do," Miz said, pushing Aspy out of the way.

"Splendid," Gamemaster said, offering Miz the scanner.

Miz placed her palm down, and hundreds of tickets spooled out. A blue-robed skulk, who seemed to appear out of nowhere, tapped her on the knee and handed her a plastic bucket to catch them as they flooded out.

"The amount you receive is based on the number of valor points you've accumulated thus far," Gamemaster said, pointing his cane at the bucket.

When it seemed the bucket couldn't hold any more tickets, the machine stopped. Miz regarded her treasure with a radiant smile. Excited, she skipped to the bladed-weapon section of the emporium. Her eyes widened at all the magnificent battle axes. It was going to take some time to pick the exact right one.

Aspy was next. She stepped up to the machine with her plastic bucket and another enormous string of tickets spooled out.

Gamemaster gave Aspy a fatherly wink and said, "Each of the weapons is clearly marked with their ticket value. Please calculate carefully. I don't want to be here all night."

Alex was the last in line and seemed to be the most excited of the entire group. He was eyeing one particular sword, which was hanging at the highest point on the wall, out of reach of everyone.

A placard below the sword read: "Starstone Blade of Badassery."

It was a real-life replica of the exact sword he used in the computer version of the game. He'd never seen anything so beautiful.

The value was marked clearly. It cost 500 tickets.

Alex rubbed his hands together greedily. When Jed finished, Alex stepped up to the machine with his bucket at the ready and placed his hand on the valor point reader.

Click!

One ticket popped out of the machine.

"What the heck?" Alex scrunched his nose as if something smelled fishy. "Did your machine run out?"

"Check the panel," Gamemaster responded, eyeing the machine calmly.

Alex scanned it and saw that a single digit flashed on the panel. It was the number two—not one, but two.

"Wait a sec, that can't be right?"

He slapped the side of the machine. The skulk assistant scowled at him and wagged its claw to scold him.

"Really? But even if that's right, it's wrong. The machine only produced one ticket!"

The minion looked at Alex, then looked at the machine. He tapped it once. He seemed to get frustrated, then mimicking Alex, slapped the side of the machine.

A gear within the machine whirled once, and the skulk crossed his arms, flashed a fanged smile of satisfaction, and pointed down at the result.

One more ticket had popped out, dangling there like a tiny pink tongue mocking Alex.

"You've got to be kidding? Two lousy tickets? That's it?!"

"Two valor points. Two tickets. That's how it works," Gamemaster said.

He pushed Alex on the shoulder with his cane, shooing him away from the scanner.

Alex muttered something profane under his breath and ripped the tickets from the slot in one quick jerk—too quick, in fact.

"Or, one and one-half tickets in your case," Gamemaster said, eyeing the torn ticket. "I'm sure you'll have plenty of time to increase your valor score if you choose to make a few changes."

"Oh, really?!" Alex scowled, not wanting a lecture.

"Yes, really. Those deficient in valor need not despair. The spirit has a magnificent ability to expand in strength and fortitude, especially under extreme stress and life-threatening circumstances. Sometimes, losing is truly the best reward."

Gamemaster pointed to the lowest shelf in the glass display case.

"For now, your treasure awaits you here."

He used his cane to point at a collection of toy-like objects piled in small woven baskets.

Alex deflated like a punctured balloon. The baskets held the trash prizes available for players after they had spent all their tickets on the big items.

He looked over at his teammates. They were like sharks in a feeding frenzy, nervously circling the bounty of shiny new weapons.

His head dropped onto his chest while he perused his meager options.

"Well, how about that?" he asked, exhaling miserably. He pointed at the nearest basket. "The pink whoopee cushion?"

"That'll be ten tickets."

"Never mind. How about the X-ray lenses?"

"Twenty-five tickets," Gamemaster growled. "You're headed in the wrong direction, kid."

"Well, tell me already, what the heck can I get for two . . . uh . . . I mean . . . *one and a half* tickets?"

Gamemaster snatched the tickets from his hand, rolled his eyes, and placed a tiny, hinged box down on the counter.

"You can have this. But promise me you won't let your foul mood spoil the fun your teammates are having."

He used his cane to push the box toward Alex like it was radioactive.

Alex nodded reluctantly and took the box.

He fiddled with the latch until it popped open, revealing a simple sticker. It seemed to be some bad artwork—a golden-colored skull of some kind. It looked faded, like it had been misplaced in someone's shorts and washed a few times by accident.

"You're serious?" He gave Gamemaster a side-eyed glance. "A sticker? That's it?"

"Not a sticker. A temporary tattoo." His eyes lit up as he grinned at Alex. "Pretty gnarly one, if you ask me."

"Yeah, great. Who needs a sword? I'll just slap this on my forehead. I'm sure it'll scare the heck out of the Griefers."

The Gamemaster shrugged. "You never know."

Alex took the tattoo and waved it toward his team. "You guys jealous?"

They looked at him like he was an idiot and went back to choosing their new weapons.

"Know this, young man. It will take far more than expensive swords or rare magical artifacts to defeat Malvexus."

"Yeah, is that so? Well, if I'm going to get killed, at least I'll look cool." The sarcasm dripped off Alex's reply as he replaced the tattoo and stuffed the box in his pocket. "Thanks, old man. I don't feel like it's all up to me anymore."

Gamemaster stared at Alex with a mixture of concern and wonder.

"Everyone thinks I'm a loser," Alex muttered as he sulked out of the room. "Maybe they're right."

Gamemaster shrugged, smiling serenely. "That's a problem easily solved."

"Oh, yeah? How do I do that?"

"Prove them wrong, my dear boy," he said. "Prove everyone wrong!"

CHAPTER TWENTY-SEVEN

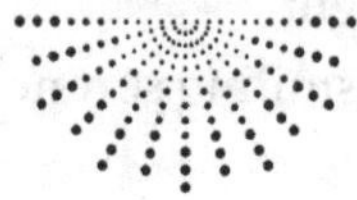

It was decided the rest of the day would be a time to relax, think, and eat.

Luna, who was happy the base considered her friendly, showed the team how to modify the magical creation of food. During lunch, their banquet table was set up with a spread of hamburgers, hot dogs, chicken nuggets, pizza, and french fries.

"I've calibrated the machines to make Earth food as I best understand it," Luna said.

"Heck yeah, chow time!" Genghis yelled, as he almost dove headfirst into the plate of french fries.

After lunch, Luna showed them the portal key gateway that was built into the side of the cornerstone. This reopened old wounds.

"If we had a portal key, this is where you would use it," Luna said. "It seems Gamemaster has promised you one if you continue to help him."

Miz and Jed walked past Alex with withering looks on their faces.

"Interesting," Luna observed. "Your team hates you."

"What else is new?" Alex quipped.

She placed a comforting hand on his shoulder. "I know what it means to bring dishonor to a team."

"Dishonor?" He raised an eyebrow. "That's a little strong, don't you think?"

She looked at Aspy, Jed, and Miz. A dark cloud of sullen animus had descended on the group. Genghis was the only ray of sunshine.

"My people have been the guardians of the Battle Moon for eons. It's our sacred duty to serve and die, if necessary. Many of my kin, whom I once led into battle, look at me now with similar contempt. The path of a true warrior can be quite disheartening and lonely," she said. "But I don't understand why you insist on provoking them."

Alex shrugged. He hated what she was saying, but it seemed true. Something inside him wanted to piss everyone off. He'd always felt that but never put words to it.

"After my parents split up, I spent all my time playing this game. I mean, it was the only thing that made me feel decent. I guess, if I'm honest, it's the only thing I really care about these days," he said, turning away from her to look at the nearby fountain. "When I feel like someone is trying to take it away from me, I get frazzled. Don't think straight. Say things I don't mean. I don't mean to be a dick, but sometimes I just am."

"The Battle Moon is a gathering place, a nexus for worlds to meet and challenge each other through competition. But, above all, it is a test of honor and loyalty—loyalty to your team and the people they represent."

Alex waved her off. "Yeah, yeah. An intergalactic Olympics. If you display honor on the field, you become part of the Cosmic Alliance. Luna, I know the game lore. Are you trying to tell me that applies to the Modfia? I don't remember getting an official invite to be Earth's champion."

"You dismiss me too easily, Earthborn," she retorted. "The cosmomancers believe the character traits you display as a team during the game show the traits you will display as a member of the Cosmic Alliance. Playing without true honor or true valor reflects upon your entire species."

She trailed off. Alex saw tears form around the edges of her eyes, but they defiantly refused to fall.

"Surely this is the tragedy Malvexus inflicts upon my people. He has disgraced eons of heroic play. Now he uses the Battle Moon to orchestrate his own celebrity. He wants to be known as the greatest champion of all time."

"Shouldn't Gamemaster stop him? I mean, if he's breaking the rules, doesn't that invalidate his wins or something?" Alex asked.

"Malvexus has no honor. He doesn't care about the rules. He says the rules are for losers. He'll do anything to prove he's the ultimate champion. And now it seems he'll kill anyone—including the Gamemaster—who gets in his way!"

"Honestly, he sounds like a royal butthole. Excuse my language. Unfortunately, it seems like guys like him always win these competitions."

"It doesn't surprise me you would *admire* him."

"What? What do you mean?"

"You're selfish in a similar way, willing to use people to achieve your own goals."

"Just because I want to win doesn't mean I'm a complete butthole."

"When you try to win at the expense of others, it changes you. That's what happened to Malvexus. Perhaps you're headed down the same path."

Luna walked away and headed toward the girls's wing of the castle. Alex desperately wanted to join her, but it was obvious he wasn't invited.

He watched her go, stewing over all that had been said.

Was it true? Were he and Malvexus playing for the same stakes? Did they approach the game the same way?

As he watched the sun sink lower, he had a hard think about it all.

Could one play and win this game using a more noble strategy? Could he fight a cheater like Malvexus and win? Or even survive? If there was a way, he was blind to the path. And if he couldn't see it, victory was just a stupid kid's dream.

CHAPTER TWENTY-EIGHT

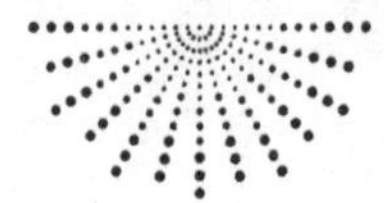

Malvexus stood on the highest parapet of the Crimson Castle and looked out over Deadman's Road and the wilderness that stretched to the west. Even from this distance, the magical glow of the Sapphire Sanctum was visible. The brilliant blue cosmicron spun on its axis, spreading its enchanted light out into the dusky afternoon sky like a miniature star anchored to the earth.

"I want to see that ghastly Sanctum burn before nightfall," he said, licking his fangs greedily. "How absolutely glorious the fires of its defeat would be. I could watch it for days."

The Griefers stepped closer to their leader and looked out toward the enemy base. Their eyes gleamed with purpose, as if they were collectively imagining the destruction their team had seen relentlessly repeated.

Malvexus smiled. He never tired of victory.

"You will smell the smoke of its burning before we return," Bonegrin Banebreaker said.

The great Fel Orc Warrior twisted his reattached claw around his gruesome trident, watching the fingers closely, as if wondering whether the appendage would still obey his commands.

"Yes, the sweet perfume of defeat," Kadaver said, sneering sadistically. The Scourge Elf, who was a sorceress of phenomenal power, twirled her fingers and they flared with purple magic.

"And what of these Earthborn?" Nightbane asked. The female ranger twirled her leather whip and occasionally snapped it at an anxious skulk who entered their room. "They show spirit and ingenuity. It has been ages since our opponents have destroyed our base."

"We'll kill them all," Lackey giggled. The Wasteland Goblin, a creature of mystical science, snapped a pair of goggles over his beady eyes and examined holographic statistics about the Modfia team. "Their first attack was nothing more than dumb luck."

"Or perhaps it was the traitor's plan?" Kadaver asked. The undead elf plucked a maggot from her rotting thigh and slurped it down. "She knows our tactics and our vulnerabilities."

"She will pay for her betrayal," Bonegrin growled.

"Let me kill her, my lord?" Nightbane whispered.

"Yes, Banebreaker had his chance," Lackey sputtered.

"True," Kadaver cackled. "Another of us must rise to the challenge."

Nightbane leaned in, whispering to Malvexus. "Let it be me, my prince. I'll take her head and cast it at your feet as a tribute."

Malvexus grinned at the flirtation then raised a hand to quiet his team.

"I want their destruction to be brutal and just as swift as their first strike on us. Make sure they suffer. But leave Titan and Lifestealer to me."

"As you wish, master," Bonegrin said, signaling to the team it was time to move.

Lackey tapped a button on his HUD and summoned an iron war chariot. It rose off the ground until it parked itself in midair, just beyond the team and the balcony's edge.

One by one, the Griefers leapt into the goblin's vehicle. When they were ready, Kadaver conjured a team of Nightmares with harnesses. Nightbane took control of their reigns and cracked her deadly whip, and the undead horses flew skyward.

Malvexus watched his team ascend into the clouds then tapped his HUD and pulled up Nightbane's conjured surveillance of the Modfia. He scrolled through the various scenes and stopped on the player called BadMiznus. She played a primitive instrument in a band. As he listened to the rock song, energy like he'd never heard before filled his ears. A beat, strong like a gladiator drum, boomed behind the strange Earthborn rhythms of stringed instruments and the resounding clash of cymbals. He loved the music beyond anything he'd ever experienced. He clacked his long, sharp nails on the red stone of the keep's balcony.

This music proved his intuitions correct. As weak as the Earthborn appeared, they had heart, proving there was depth to the simpletons despite their meaningless lives. Eventually, they would rise as warriors and, inspired by things like this music, conquer their solar system then reach beyond into the greater cosmos.

He felt a kinship with their passion.

They were worthy of one last fight on the Battle Moon.

He would kill the Earthborn team, and then, for his own pleasure, enslave their music makers to produce new ballads about his victory. That music would be a soundtrack to accompany his conquest of the Cosmic Alliance.

Malvexus smiled as the next song continued to fuel his devilish dreams.

Below him, the castle's skulks scurried about, obviously frightened by the very champions they served. Soon the fear these dull-minded minions felt would spread to all the Battle Moon and then beyond to every creature, every person, and every planet in the known cosmos.

How majestic would be his reign!

CHAPTER TWENTY-NINE

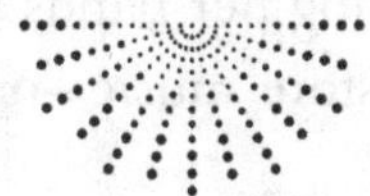

"I'd buy my own *School of Rock* franchise," Miz said. "Give some young people the leg up in the music biz, which I never had. A joint where the kids could jam during the week, and I could rock out on the weekends."

"What would you call it?" Genghis asked.

"Black Is Back."

Everyone laughed.

"Seriously?" Aspy asked.

"No, just kidding," Miz snorted a laugh, a rare thing for the hard-edged tank. "I'm still working on the name."

The more Miz giggled, the more everyone laughed. It was so rare to see her let her guard down, and her joy spread through the entire team.

"What would you do with the championship money, Genghis?" Jed asked.

"I would open a chain of cannabis dispensaries," Genghis said, taking another long drag from his new pipe stuffed with Purple Blissleaf. His beard was longer now, and he'd undone his normally tight samurai bun. Alex thought he was giving off Gandalf vibes. "It would be like a Walmart for good feels. Peace, love, herb, and a five-pound box of *Captain Crunch*."

"Get 'em with the impulse buy," Jed joked. "What's not to love?"

"Right on," Genghis said, giving Jed a fist bump.

"Do your friends get discounts?" Alex asked.

Genghis winked at Alex. "Friends shop for free, my man."

"You know, it would be cool if you sold those Rocawear sweats you love," Miz said, stretching her hands wide like she was stocking the shelves. "And no bad store music—only hip-hop, all day, every day."

"Man, I'm hiring you on day one," Genghis said, giving Miz a high five.

"Speaking of food," Miz said, rubbing her stomach.

"No one was speaking of food," Alex laughed.

"Yeah, well, I'm gonna speak on it. I didn't think I should complain, but the food here has been super disappointing."

"You know, you're right," Aspy said. "I expected so much more."

"Me too. I mean, the game animations always made those spreads look like a banquet," Jed agreed. "But all the entrees I've tasted are Limp Bizkit."

"And it's always cold," Aspy complained. "I was researching microwave spells in my HUD. No luck though."

"You don't think we could get food poisoning, do you? I mean, I didn't see any skulks dropping expiration dates on that milk," Miz asked.

"I think we have enough mana to avoid the old dishonorable discharge, if you know what I mean." Jed raised his leg and let one rip.

That brought on another wave of laughs and groans. Everyone shuffled themselves away from Jed.

"Well, if we're fortunate to last another night, someone needs to teach these little Smurfs how to cook," Miz said.

"Amen, sister," Jed said. "Let's file a complaint with GM the next time he pops up."

"Ab-so-fruiting-lootely," Genghis said.

"Are we high?" Miz asked.

"Maybe. But this is my first time, so I'm not sure," Aspy said, suppressing a giggle.

Her pupils were as wide as two black moons.

Undeniably high, Alex thought.

"Well, I must be baked because I'm definitely tripping," Miz said.

She pointed east where the lengthening shadows were darkening the Wilds. Alex looked and saw movement beyond the gate. He stood up and leaned over the balcony railing. Aspy joined him.

"No, I can see that too," Alex said. "Those are skulks."

"Just not ours," Aspy added.

The concern in her voice ended their late-afternoon slack-a-thon. Suddenly everyone was very alert, shoulder to shoulder with eyes on their new troubles, and there was trouble everywhere they looked.

Luna rushed out onto the balcony. Her battle map had flared to life. The holographic information appeared in front of her, displaying a detailed rendering of most of the immediate area. She seemed most interested in a new signal that had appeared on Deadman's Road. It was pulsing like a heartbeat, and it seemed to get stronger with each second they observed it.

"The first tower on Deadman's Road has been attacked. We must prepare for battle," she said.

Everyone was looking out past the main gate. Something was coming closer.

"What is it?" Alex asked as he tried to squeeze in to get a better look. "More skulks?"

"Much worse," Miz said.

"A whole team of much worse!" Jed confirmed.

CHAPTER THIRTY

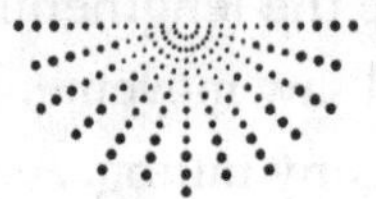

Most concerning was a massive wave of red-armored skulks rambling up Deadman's Road toward the Sapphire Sanctum's palisade perimeter.

Leading the charge was Bonegrin Banebreaker. He was riding a black-furred Rift Wolf decked out in armor. He had the reins in one hand and a Viking war horn in the other.

"Sweet geezus, not this guy again," Alex groaned.

Bonegrin tipped his chin toward the keep's tower and raised the war horn to his mouth.

"Earthborn of the Sapphire Sanctum. Your presence here defiles the sacred ground of the Battle Moon. Prepare to spill your blood in recompense!"

The message boomed from the horn, reverberating through the Sanctum's hall, rattling the windows.

Satisfied they had heard the message, Bonegrin blew into the horn, signaling the start of the battle, then reined his wolf around and returned to the rear of his advancing troops.

"Got his hand back, I see," Jed said grimly. "Wish we'd known that sooner."

He hip-checked Alex and gave him an affectionate wink.

Alex gave Jed a half-smile, but the comment still stung. He had really hoped the portal key incident had been forgotten.

"Yeah, why didn't you tell us you lost the portal key?" Aspy asked nonchalantly. It seemed most of her normal inhibitions were still under the spell of the Blissleaf. "You never really explained your reasoning."

The question seemed sincere, but Alex was annoyed.

Was this really the time to explain himself? Now? Right before a battle? It seemed there was a much more important defense to be made. Bonegrin's wave of red skulks was getting closer by the second.

"Alex is like me, Aspy," Genghis said, putting an arm each around his two friends. "I hate giving people bad news."

"Why would you assume that is bad news?" Aspy shrugged.

The question seemed to stump Genghis.

"Seriously, dude?" Miz interjected, pointing out the window. "What other kinda news is there around here?"

"Nah, bro, news is news," Jed argued. "Don't get me wrong, I'm all for being sneaky, but we five need to be on the same page if we're going to survive this."

"Well, let's debate that later," Miz said. "Look, trouble is knocking at our door."

A Scourge Elf Sorceress appeared on the edge of the Wilds, trailed by a squad of skulk wizards. She raised her hand, casting a frosty blast along the ground of the palisade. Spikes of ice grew like weeds along the structure and then melted. The ground rumbled with life and worms thick as cucumbers wriggled within the soil, loosening the dirt and destroying the foundation. Part of the high fence buckled and failed.

"She's breached the wall!" Alex shouted, pointing at Kadaver. "Our defenses won't hold if her wizards break through."

"Look, behind her," Miz said. "Another line of skulks."

Lackey Lickspittle, the Wasteland Goblin, some three feet high, was driving a small army of skulk soldiers toward the breach. The soldiers swung out of the trees like screeching monkeys.

"He's rigged them with explosives," Jed said, pointing out that each skulk had at least one bomb strapped to its little back.

Lackey raised a silver-tubed rifle and pulled the trigger. Flame shot out in a long stream, singing the skulks, and lighting the short fuses on their bombs.

Perhaps spurred by the flames and the fear of death, they continued through the breach, climbing all over the crumbling structure.

Seconds later, a tremendous explosion rocked the Sanctum, triggering a chain reaction that destroyed most of the palisade and even some of the main gate.

The team was stunned by the amount of damage. It had happened so quickly.

And it wasn't over.

Nightbane revealed her position now. She was directing a battalion of skulk archers who readied their bows. As the Sapphire Sanctum activated its own security, blue skulks of every variety rushed to defend the failing defenses. When they were within range, Nightbane gave the command, and thousands of tiny red skulk arrows rained down like a storm of death, taking out much of the blue skulk army. It would be nearly impossible for the skulk pits to replace such losses fast enough.

When the Modfia saw Bonegrin driving a charge of his own skulk troops toward the gate, they knew it was time to join the battle. The skulks would overrun the base in minutes if they didn't help defend it.

"Time to fight, Earthborn!" Luna shouted.

"Agreed. Ready up, everyone," Aspy said.

With a swirl of magic, she invoked a newly modified battle skin, along with the new quiver and bow she'd chosen at the Gamemaster's pop-up.

"Very cool!" she yelled.

She spun in a circle, trying to catch her reflection in the mirrored tiles along the keep's walls. A stunning warrior elf had replaced the shy girl. She radiated power and magic as she balanced carefully on the edge of the balcony, looking out over the road.

Below them, the Griefers's minions poured into view like an avalanche of evil.

Aspy's eyes lit up as if she were full of new ideas and, more importantly, confidence.

"Focus on the leader. Every skulk squad has one," she said, drawing her magical bow back and nocking an energy arrow that charged with power as she lined up a shot. "Take them out first and the pack will scatter. Then we can pick them off more easily."

"What about Bonegrin?" Genghis asked. "When the skulks are gone, we still have him to deal with."

"This time, I'm taking both his hands," Aspy said. "And his head!"

She scanned the battleground and fired her first grappling arrow. She grabbed the magical rope that dropped in front of her and swung off the balcony with gymnastic grace, flipping in midair so that she landed above them on the very top of the tower's roof.

Every mouth dropped open in amazement.

"That girl is high as a kite," Jed laughed.

"Yeah, literally," Alex laughed. He was completely stunned and impressed. Maybe, just maybe, they had a chance.

CHAPTER THIRTY-ONE

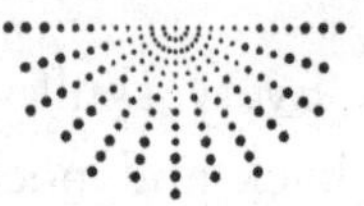

Aspy's transformation seemed to inspire the entire team to make their own spectacular changes. Using their HUDs, they donned new skins and readied new weapons.

Miz invoked a Viking-like battle skin and raised her new axe over her head. She stepped onto the ledge and looked down on the lane.

Jed twirled within a dark cloud of magic, becoming a fully realized version of Ripghoul. His new skin was an impressive ninja outfit that seemed to be made of living shadows. New skills flashed in his profile: First attack advantage, Evasion, and Sneak Attack. Under weapons, he chose: Dual-Wield Short Swords.

Alex had a modified skin because of leveling up, but compared to the rest of the team, he was seriously underdressed and underprepared. The rusty sword he'd found in the siege tower was hardly anything like the sword he used during normal gameplay. But this wasn't the moment to mope around. Everyone had to fight as best they could.

They decided Miz would guard the gate from being overrun. Jed would disappear into the Wilds so he could flank their enemies and gank them before they advanced any farther.

Luna and Alex would take on the skulks and Griefers if they slipped through the main gate. Aspy and Genghis would provide cover and support from a distance.

Bonegrin's skulks were massing near the gate, squealing their strange battle cries.

"I'll plug that hole," Miz said, pointing at Bonegrin.

Alex nodded his approval, and Miz dropped to the ground and rushed to the gate.

Jed checked his short swords, then leapt off the tower, skittering carefully to the edge of the main road.

"Aspy, clear the fog! I'm going in!" Miz ran toward the gate.

Aspy's first shot was a ward arrow. It flew skyward, peaked, then bent back toward the earth like a graceful Olympic diver. Suddenly, the team's vision was magically enhanced, giving them more range and clarity. But what they saw was shocking. The number of red skulks seemed to have tripled from the first wave. Surely they'd be overrun in a few minutes.

"Titan, take point with BadMiznus!" Aspy shouted.

"Roger that!" he said, running out to stand with Miz.

"I'll cover the rear and your flanks." Aspy shot more arrows as she directed the team. "Ripghoul, stay close to the main gate, but out of sight. Kill anyone or anything that breaks through that hole."

Ripghoul adjusted his balaclava, giving himself the fearsome look of a ninja, then flashed Aspy a thumbs up, crept into the foliage, and disappeared.

Luna stepped up next to Genghis. "Give the whole team a mana boost. They'll need it to sustain your defense."

As the primary source of healing magic, Genghis was adept at this move in the game. Could he do it here? Alex wondered and watched.

Genghis sat on the edge of the keep's balcony, legs crossed, head bowed meditatively, and raised his hands skyward. Suddenly, he was levitating. He floated into the air like the mana-weaving monk he claimed to be. Tendrils of Syrinxian magic grew from the center of his chest out toward his teammates. Soon, each of his friends had joined the connection, and a new power flowed into them.

In the game, these kinds of boosts were so commonplace he'd almost taken them for granted. But in this real-life version, they felt truly magical, offering a sense of power, energy, and relaxation all at once—a genuinely wonderful feeling.

"Heck yeah, Genghis. Way to go!" Miz yelled and raised a fist in solidarity. "Feels like I just drank a triple shot latte!"

Soon, Alex realized they would need every boost they could get. The skulks who had come from four different directions had joined together and were now attacking in one unified wave.

Thankfully, Sparkles Modfia seemed similarly unified.

For the first time in the longest time, they fought like a team should, heroically diving into the battle but following Aspy's strategy closely—and they were having fun despite the danger.

After only a few minutes, they had eliminated most of the first skulk wave. Alex looked out into the Wilds and caught Jed's gaze. Jed was actually smiling. Had they won the battle?

"Oh no!" Miz yelled.

She was pointing at a black shape forming down Deadman's Road some distance. Another unstoppable wave of minions was materializing out of nothingness.

"We can't survive another wave, not like that one," Aspy said. "In the actual game, there's always a cool-down period before the minions respawn. We need that to recharge our powers."

"Yes, something is very wrong here," Luna said.

The team was communicating now through Genghis's magical connection. The sound was as clear as a pair of high-end headphones.

"And what would that be?" Miz asked.

"Malvexus has changed the rules," Luna said gloomily. "He's somehow manufacturing additional skulks beyond the game's limits."

Alex thought back to Starway Station and the terrible machines Fester Crane had been creating. It seems they'd found a way to make them work.

Aspy grappled down to where the team had regrouped. The main gate was still on its hinges, but barely. The Griefers held their position outside, amassing fresh waves of skulks.

Despite the Modfia's noble efforts, the brutal onslaught was slowly advancing. When the castle's walls fell, the Griefers would invade, taking no damage, and slaughter the Modfia.

Alex shuddered at the thought.

He watched his teammates watching the Griefers, who were watching their skulks. His friends looked scared.

"What do we do now?" Genghis asked.

"We level up faster," Alex said, raising a mischievous eyebrow.

"Finally, someone's talking sense," Jed said, misunderstanding. "If this Malvexus is cheating, time for us to do the same."

Alex raised his hands to correct Jed. "A *buff* is not a cheat."

"A buff?" Aspy wondered. "Which one?"

"The Darkblood Dragon. It's the closest and the only one powerful enough to make sure we stop the Griefers."

Everyone looked at him like he was crazy—and had he been honest, he would have said they were right to think that. The buff was indeed the only way, but could they kill a monster that powerful at their current levels?

Despite the dire odds, Alex plastered a confident look on his face.

He glanced at Luna, hoping at least she might be in his corner.

"What do you say, guys? Want to help me slay a dragon?"

CHAPTER THIRTY-TWO

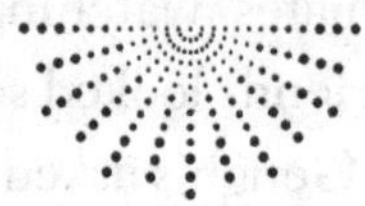

The team quickly debated the plan. Though Aspy doubted the dragon buff would save them, there were no other viable ideas—other than to retreat to the Sapphire Cosmicron where they could make a last stand and maybe get lucky enough to kill the Griefers and reverse course. But that idea was just as much of a long shot.

After much debate, they finally agreed that killing the dragon raised their odds by a sliver, and since time was running short, they decided they'd roll the dice.

Miz, Aspy, and Genghis would stay and defend the Sanctum. They would overcharge the skulk pits in hopes that more minions might delay the fall of the base.

Meanwhile, the buff team, composed of Luna, Alex, and Jed, would sneak away into the wilderness, find the dragon's cave, kill the creature, and secure the buff.

Since the Darkblood Dragon was one of the most powerful monsters in the game, killing it gave the entire team a permanent boost in areas critical to combat—bonus attack damage equal to level ninety, upgrades to player abilities, and increased health of all skulks within close range of the team. At least, that was what Alex remembered. Only one person on the team had memorized the specifics.

"Aspy, what are the exact battle specs on the buff?" Alex asked.

"Slaying the Darkblood Dragon grants the killing team a permanent stacking buff called Shroud of the Darkblood Wing. It doubles all your attacks and allows you to burn enemies for a hundred fifty true damage over five-second intervals, which lasts fifteen minutes. Overall buff accrues to the team and nearby skulks for thirty minutes."

"I say we go for it. I don't want to face those creepy Griefers without the juice to end them," Jed said.

"I have to agree with dick-ghoul." Miz grinned and hooked her thumb at Jed.

"Okay, let's do this," Aspy agreed.

Despite still being novices, the Darkblood Dragon buff would put the team on equal footing with the Griefers. They might win the second round if they used the power wisely—and if they won the second round, they were closer to getting back home.

Once it was decided and they were ready to move out, Aspy fired several arrow volleys to distract the invading skulks, and the dragon team slipped over the southeastern corner of the main wall and into the wilderness.

Alex felt a surge of adrenaline shoot through him. While they knew this territory from the game, it was their first time experiencing it in real life. Everyone considered the South Wilds the most dangerous and inhospitable part of the Battle Moon.

Thankfully, Jed, their guide, didn't appear to be nervous when Luna asked him to take point.

"Lead us, wildsman. We'll follow, deep as you dare."

Jed was up for her challenge. "Your wish is my command."

He produced a pair of magical machetes and hacked through the brush and dangling vines. Alex and Luna followed him into the thick jungle.

Luna turned to Alex. "Perhaps now is the time to prove you can be a good leader."

"Right," Alex repeated. "A good leader!"

He stared blankly at her for a second before she turned and walked on.

It was still hard to accept that he was a bad one, but he'd learned from his mistakes and was ready to do better. He had to.

CHAPTER THIRTY-THREE

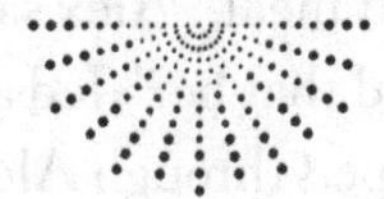

"The Midnight Cave," Jed whispered, pointing at the entrance. "The nest of the Darkblood Dragon."

"Are you sure?" Alex asked.

"Look at that," he said, pointing at a massive pile of bones. The bones lay stacked higher than the actual cave's entrance. "Only a dragon would eat that much!"

"Take cover, Earthborn!" Luna hissed as she slid down behind a nearby boulder. The rock was the size of a compact car, the perfect hiding place for the team.

Alex heard something very large stirring within the cave and decided it was best to follow her lead. He ducked down then peered around the edge of the boulder.

The Darkblood Dragon was indeed there in the center of the cave, curled like a great snake on its treasure horde, proving it was the master of its domain. It was an enormous beast with dark-purple scales, a wine-colored flicking tongue, and fangs that looked like a mouthful of silver daggers. Steam snorted through its wide nostrils.

The team shuffled as quietly as possible into a position that gave them a better view to study the cave.

The Darkblood opened one eye, then the other. It roared, splitting the group's eardrums and rattling the pile of bones littered around the cave's entrance.

"Did we wake it up? Because it sounds pissed," Jed whispered.

Suddenly, the dragon got up. It moved faster than expected, stuck its head out of the cave, and strained its elongated neck. Its golden eyes squinted like it sensed some approaching prey.

"I think it smells its next meal," Alex said.

"Oh, yeah? What would that be?" Jed asked.

"Us!" Adrenaline pumped through Alex, adding a slight quiver to his voice.

Jed peered over the lip of the boulder at the dragon. "On second, third, and fourth thought, I'm not sure we're strong enough to take this thing down."

"The team is counting on us," Alex said.

"I guess it's the only way to survive this round," Jed squeaked. His normal cocky demeanor had vanished.

"A buff doesn't guarantee a win," Luna whispered.

"No, but it's our best chance," Alex whispered, cautiously peering around the rock. The dragon, coiling back into its nest, momentarily disrupted the glimmering hoard and jostled something that caught Alex's eye.

There, in the center of the pile just under the scaly rump of the giant beast, was a very dead warrior. The warrior's skeleton still wore his armor and held his matching weapon—the exceedingly rare Starstone Blade of Badassery.

To Alex, this was the best of all weapons for his class—the best in all the game, really. The one he relied upon while playing the computer version. Now, here was the authentic version—the very thing that might pierce the scales of the Darkblood and kill the creature. He had to get that sword.

The skeleton warrior seemed to wink at Alex. Its ancient yellow teeth glinted as if smiling, and then its old charred armor shimmered with a very familiar glimmer.

"Holy freaking moly, that's the complete Starstone set," Alex blurted. He stood up as if he might rush into the cave.

Jed pulled Alex back behind cover, and Luna clamped a hand over his mouth. Her touch sent an exhilarating shiver through Alex. She smelled like lilacs, vanilla, and girl sweat, all of which he enjoyed for a microsecond, until he realized he'd given away their position.

The dragon roared and stormed out of the cave, heading straight for their hiding place.

"Well, you've done it now, you big dummy!" Jed shouted.

"Quickly!" Luna yelled. "Get on its back."

Alex glared at Luna like she was crazy. But before he could say another word, she kicked him, delivering a spinning kung-fu strike of magic that propelled Alex through the air.

"Oh, no!" Jed screamed. "You overshot."

Alex twisted this way and that, trying to change the trajectory of his fall, but it was no use. Instead of landing on the dragon's back as intended, he'd landed sprawled on the dragon's tail.

He did his best to stab the massive creature with his rusty broadsword, but it seemed to do only minor damage. All it took was a flick and a shrug, and Alex went flying again. Then, as if swatting a fly, the dragon used one giant leathery wing to smack Alex right into the cave wall. Alex ricocheted off the slick stone and landed on the cave floor. Soon he was pinned in place by a very heavy clawed foot.

"We have to save him!" Jed yelled.

He and Luna went into action.

Luna was first in line. Seemingly fearless, she barreled headfirst toward the dragon, who'd been sniffing its new catch. It swung around with a roar.

Luna's sickle was already moving, and the thick Gladiatorian steel slammed into the beast's snout, knocking one fang from its mouth.

Jed jumped out from the shadows with his two short swords and joined her attack.

Luna swung at the monster's mouth again. Another fang was

dislodged, but this time it sailed straight at Jed, who had just turned around. He was immediately impaled and fell to his knees, screaming in pain.

Well-versed in healing potions, Jed gulped a flask of glowing liquid, activating a spell that dissolved the massive tooth into ivory dust. Another wave of magic healed Jed's wound instantly.

The dragon tilted its head back and swirled its snake-like tongue around its remaining teeth. It seemed extremely surprised and annoyed that some of its favorite fangs were missing.

This brief pause allowed Jed to cast a blinding ninja bomb that exploded around the head and eyes of the beast. The temporary blindness allowed Alex to escape the dragon's claw.

He then rushed for the dead warrior, grabbed the sword, threw the armored skeleton over his shoulder, and raced to the cover of a large pile of treasure, where Luna and Jed had retreated to a more defensible position.

The dragon, realizing Alex had escaped, roared again, and threw a monstrous temper tantrum, banging its head, wings, and tail into the walls of the cave. It was done with such force that part of the cave roof gave way. Dust and debris littered down, and moonlight broke through the new opening.

"What do we do now?" Jed asked, frantically looking around. "We're on the wrong side of the way out."

This was true. In their haste to escape the dragon, they'd run deeper into the cave. There appeared to be no way out, other than the main entrance, and the dragon had that sufficiently guarded.

"Help me get this armor on," Alex said.

Jed raised an eyebrow, recognizing his friend's favorite skin.

"A complete set?" Luna asked. "How convenient that is. Very curious."

Alex dressed himself quickly, then unsheathed the Starstone Blade and checked his HUD.

Yes! The addition of the armor increased his magical resistance and added a large bonus to his health. Because he had a complete set of matching armor and the matching weapon, it stacked magical effects into a respectable, passive bonus—and it increased his ability to deal damage to wilderness creatures.

"I think I can take the dragon," Alex said, looking at his hands, which were trembling. He had never felt nerves like this. The realness of the danger loomed beyond the meager protection of his new armor.

"We will do our best to distract it," Luna said, flashing a reassuring smile that wasn't entirely convincing. "Perhaps it will expose a more vulnerable area where you can strike. But strike hard and true. You may only get one shot at this."

Alex nodded. Jed took Luna by the hand and the two of them disappeared in one of Jed's shadow spells. They quietly crept along the cave wall until they had circled back to the entrance.

When he was sure they were in place, Alex took a deep breath and gave the signal.

Jed and Luna reappeared. They screamed and yelled, trying their best to turn the dragon their way. The dragon did so, roaring in frustration when they once again disappeared into the shadows.

Now it was Alex's turn. He rushed from his hiding place, found a suitable spot to make his stand, planted his newly acquired armored boots, drew his new sword, and raised it over his head, ready to try his best to land a killing blow.

"Hey, you big dumb lizard!" he shouted. "Bet you can't get me!"

The dragon roared, charged, and leapt in the air, bounding like a giant dog toward him.

Alex, now looking very much like his avatar Titan, clenched every muscle, bracing himself. He pointed the edge of the weapon squarely at the oncoming creature, aiming as best he could for the dragon's underbelly.

The dragon bounded off the ground, flew forward many units, landed again, and skidded to a halt right in front of Alex. With its front legs down and its dragon butt up in the air, it shook its tail back and forth, panting with strange excitement.

Alex stabbed at the beast, but it danced around in a circle and did its strange little bow again. When it twirled for a second time, its tail hit Alex like a giant whip, knocking him over onto his back.

Instead of pinning Alex with its claw, the dragon sniffed him, then licked him. The slightest bit of purple fire wheezed in and out as it panted, waiting for Alex to make his next move.

The team was dumbfounded. When it licked Alex for a third time, Luna and Jed let out a collective laugh.

"This can't be happening!" Jed shouted. "The dragon wants to play!"

Alex, who knew dogs well, had to agree. The dragon spun around in a quick circle, dropped into another play bow, and wagged its tail fast enough to generate a considerable gust of wind.

Alex thought about the buff and raised his sword to attack the dragon with a killing blow, but he couldn't do it.

"Oh, man, now I feel guilty. This thing wants to be friends."

"But your team needs the buff," Luna argued. "Either the dragon dies, or you do."

Jed turned on Luna. "Come on, Lifestealer. I have an icy heart, but no one is that cold. Look at that thing. It's just a big dog. Heck, I think it wants to play fetch."

Alex grabbed a nearby thigh bone and threw it. Sure enough, the dragon galloped after it, picked it up, and brought it back to Alex, dropping it at his feet.

"I think it's smiling!" Jed yelled.

Alex was gobsmacked. Luna and Jed looked equally amazed. Still, there was a clock ticking. His other friends were expecting help.

The dragon burped, and a brief burst of fire sprayed out, heating Alex's armor and giving him the shock of a new idea.

"He wants to play, right?" Alex asked rhetorically. "Let's let him play!"

CHAPTER THIRTY-FOUR

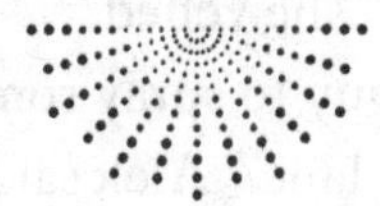

Luna, Alex, and Jed sat in an orderly line along the spine of the Darkblood Dragon as the beast flew west through the cool night air and out over the jungle.

Jed agreed riding the Darkblood was far better than killing it—so much better, in fact, he hoped the ride would never end.

"Genius move, bud," he said, slapping Alex on the back.

Alex smiled. He couldn't believe the plan was working.

In a moment of temporary insanity, he had directed Luna to use her kusarigama and its magical chain to rope the dragon like a cowboy might rope a steer. After wrapping the chain around the beast several times, Jed deployed a Bridle Spell, a low-level hunter trick he rarely used, and the dragon was somehow tamed.

In fact, because it was still in a playful mood, it seemed pleased to fly its new friends wherever they wanted.

"I mean, taming wolves and wild unicorns is one thing," Jed said. "But dragons! Dude! I just never thought it was possible."

Alex was just as amazed.

The combination of Luna's chain and Jed's spell allowed him to steer the dragon up, down, left, right, and with just the right poke, the dragon would burp a blast of magical purple fire.

After a couple of test flights over the Regolith River, they climbed through the clouds and headed back toward the Sapphire Sanctum.

Jed twirled his fingers, continuously casting the Bridle Spell. Alex heaved the magical reins, steering the dragon toward the battle. Luna was the lookout watching for signs of enemy activity.

"There's the front line!" she yelled.

"If we can get this big guy to spray some fire on that new wave of red skulks, we can clear the lane," Alex said.

"Win the lane, win the game!" Jed crowed.

"Let's do it," Luna agreed.

She pointed out Lackey and his new skulk soldiers. Alex reined the dragon. It banked right, and they swooped down toward the main gate.

When Alex reined the dragon lower, Luna raised the sickle end of her weapon and swung it down between two of the dragon's scales.

It barely pierced the gigantic dragon's skin, but the pinch was enough to get the desired result. The Darkblood roared and blew a stream of purple flames. In seconds, Lackey's skulks were completely engulfed.

When they flew back up into the air, they saw a group of bomb-carrying skulks diving out of the nearby trees, sacrificing themselves in the flames. There was a tremendous explosion, taking out the rest of the advancing wave and incinerating Lackey himself. The nasty little goblin disappeared, leaving behind a foul-smelling cloud of smoke and ash.

The team cheered.

"Whoo-hoo! One down, four to go!" yelled Jed.

"Fly down closer to the base," Luna said. "We need to get eyes on the rest of the team."

The Modfia had fallen back to one of the defensive towers. Beams of blue magic shot from a cannon, blasting long swaths of luminous energy straight at the approaching invaders. When the dragon flew by, Alex heard cheers from his teammates and their army of sapphire skulks.

Aspy and Genghis were still fighting from the high ground. Aspy was on top of the highest tower. Genghis hovered nearby on a cloud of magical energy. Defensive spells poured out of him like a storm of lightning.

Miz was on the main gate, doing her best to fight off a horde of skulks who'd built a siege tower. Miz fought valiantly, but she was outnumbered.

"We have to help Miz!" Jed shouted.

Alex nodded in agreement.

"Hit that siege tower first," Luna suggested.

Alex reined the dragon so that it swooped lower. Tightening its wings against its body, it dove toward the structure like a missile. At the last minute, the dragon opened its wings in full expanse and plowed into the tower, slicing it like a sickle. The top of the tower toppled over and exploded.

The team cheered in victory. But then a shockwave from the tower's explosion hit them, and the dragon and the team tumbled in its wake.

Having lost its ability to glide properly, the dragon dropped too low. One claw caught the ground, then they were all crashing into the courtyard of the Sanctum, just inside the main gate.

Alex rolled over with a groan. He'd landed next to Luna, who was staring at the dragon. It was as stunned as the team, but it shook that off. And now it was free of her chain and Jed's Bridal Spell.

Perhaps because it was injured, the dragon seemed to have lost its congenial spirit. Seeing Aspy, Miz, and Genghis for the first time, it roared as if it might attack.

"Retreat to the cornerstone!" Aspy yelled, not knowing if the dragon was still a willing ally. She raised her bow, nocked a new arrow, and pointed it at the creature.

Alex looked up and saw he was too far away to intervene. The dragon would easily take his friends out if they attacked.

Genghis raised a defensive shield as they retreated. The dragon followed.

The last row of cannons activated, rotating into position, ready to attack the dragon—but most of the team was in the line of fire, and the cannons wouldn't shoot until they were clear.

"You guys fall back!" Alex shouted. "I'll try to get the Darkblood under control."

The team didn't argue. They turned to flee and instantly ran into another problem—one much worse than an angry dragon.

CHAPTER THIRTY-FIVE

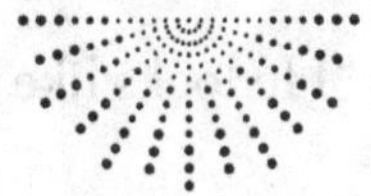

Nearby, the night's darker shadows took the form of a young man. A chilly wind blasted the team as a contemptuous voice, like gravel on ice, echoed from within.

"Pathetic!" Malvexus snarled.

Collectively, the team turned to find the leader of the Griefers.

Malvexus Manslayer was a young male warrior about Alex's age with a slight build that would lead one to believe he couldn't fight for his life.

He was dressed like an evil Elton John in purple sequined leather and silver plate armor. His boots were black latex and had platform heels that added at least six inches to his normally short stature. He carried his sword sheathed on his back in a garish pink scabbard.

He wore a wicked smile on his unnaturally tan face, and his lips were painted the same shade of purple as his leather. His hair was a mop of look-at-me orange combed upward like a rooster's crown. He had a mouth full of vampire fangs and sharp black fingernails that he clicked impatiently on his chest plate.

Malvexus was clearly obsessed with his power, his appearance, and himself. And though he had the authority of a spoiled prince, he carried himself with the haughtiness of an old queen. The hard part was deciding whether his look was a crime against fashion or against nature.

Since the team had never seen him, they were stunned by his overly dramatic appearance.

"Who the eff is that?" Jed asked.

"Yeah, he's overloading my gaydar," Miz cringed. "What's with the horrible costume?"

"I agree," Genghis said. "He looks like a super-villain designed by Dr. Seuss."

"Is that the Helm of Humiliating Bad Hair?" Alex joked.

Aspy doubled over. "My eyes are bleeding!"

Another round of giggles erupted from the Modfia.

Malvexus, their object of ridicule, seemed immune to the banter.

He retrieved his sword and pointed it at the team. A blast of ebony magic shot out and zigzagged through the air until it blasted Alex in the chest. Alex was thrown on his butt several units away from the Darkblood Dragon, his sword clattering to the ground nearby. Alex was sure the attack would have killed him if not for the Starstone Armor.

As he tried to shake off the hit, he wondered how one champion could have so much raw power. Then he remembered the Mana Lake. The fear and sadness in Luna's eyes. And the power she discussed with Jed—the sorcery he didn't understand. Dreadmagic!

The dragon turned and growled at Malvexus, who was already on the move. Malvexus vaulted forward, scooped up Alex's new sword, and plunged it deep into the dragon's skull.

The dragon looked up at the team with puppy dog eyes, as if asking for help, then whimpered in pain before rolling over and dying.

"No!" Jed bellowed. "He stole the kill!"

Malvexus had done one of the worst things any adversary could do during a game. Stealing a kill was unethical, offensive, and poor sportsmanship. Unfortunately, it was also incredibly effective and ultimately fatal for most teams.

"Strange, your mocking tongues are silent now," Malvexus laughed. "Perhaps you finally understand. You've never faced a champion like me. Today, you will learn despair. Today, you'll taste the sting of true death!"

Magic shot down like a laser blast from some otherworldly place —granting Malvexus the Aspect of the Darkblood Wing. Blinding arcane energy enveloped him, bestowing all the great powers the Modfia had hoped to claim. Malvexus then raised his sword and magically blasted the gates into dust and splinters. The explosion threw the team to the ground.

Whilc the team was still stunned, Kadaver appeared and cast a binding spell, imprisoning the Modfia in chains made of icy magic. The frosty manacles burned to the touch. Still, they fought and pulled at the bindings, to no avail.

A flood of skulks and the remaining Griefers stormed through the damaged gates. In that moment, it seemed a terrible darkness had descended and the only thing they could process was a threat from Malvexus that reverberated all around them.

"Prepare to die, Earthborn!"

CHAPTER THIRTY-SIX

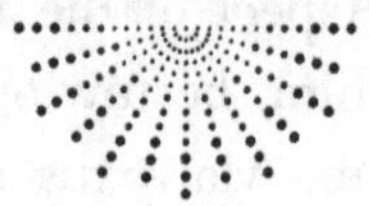

Malvexus turned toward the Sapphire Sanctum's cornerstone and raised his sword. The sleek obsidian blade he called Netherfang churned with its dreadmagic until a stream of ebony energy shot from its tip, cracking the cornerstone's thick stone walls down the middle.

He lowered the sword to recharge it for another blast—one that would surely destroy the structure for good.

When he raised the sword again, a familiar hand lunged out of the shadows and karate-chopped him in the throat.

There was a surge of impotent dark energy as Netherfang clattered to the ground, and Malvexus fell beside it, gasping for breath, his newly won bravado crushed under the violence of Luna Lifestealer's attack.

He stayed on his knees before her, wheezing.

Now it was his turn to be surprised.

"Malvexus," Luna sneered. "I see your corrupt heart only grows darker."

"Oh, Luna, I've been waiting so patiently for our reunion," Malvexus croaked, forcing a weak smile. "Finally, you show your *trai-*

torous face."

"As I told you before, your time ruling the Battle Moon is over," she declared.

The Modfia shot worried and confused glances at each other. Their plan hadn't included outright one-on-one combat with the Griefers and surely not with their notorious leader. But Luna seemed hell-bent on taking the flamboyant madman down. She talked as if she had a history with him. Did she know his weaknesses? If so, did they still have a chance even though he'd stolen the buff?

Malvexus launched himself skyward, pulling his black blade behind him. At the apex, he spun down, attempting to decapitate Luna. But Luna was already on the move. She screamed a guttural battle cry, as if all the rage in the world was being channeled through her, and swung her sickle. The weapons clashed with an explosive metallic clang, magic surged, and the two foes were blown apart.

Luna fell to the ground near the team. Malvexus landed sprawled on the dead Darkblood.

"Way to go, Luna!" Jed yelled. "Stomp that asshat!"

"Yeah, girl!" Miz added. "Take him out!"

The Modfia, still shackled together, anxiously watched the fight along with the Griefers, who had gathered closer.

Malvexus, who was now covered in the dragon's blood, did his best to get on his feet. But Luna got up first, lunged across the courtyard, twirling acrobatically as she went, and scythed into Malvexus's face with her right boot.

He buckled to his knees again, wiped his now bloody nose, and laughed.

Before Luna could line up another kick, Malvexus charged her, spinning in a manner that matched her form, and kicked her in the face. It was almost the same move she had made.

Suddenly, they were fighting like wild animals—*well-trained* wild animals.

Luna proved her reputation as a champion wasn't all fantasy. But

Malvexus matched her move for move, proving he was not only highly skilled but extremely dangerous.

For a time, it seemed Luna would lose the fight. However, even with his stolen buff, Malvexus could never outmatch her.

In fact, giving it one last extraordinary effort, Luna landed a stunning blow to Malvexus's head, and he went down and stayed down, apparently unable to move anything other than his mouth.

"Growing up, you were always the favorite," Malvexus groaned. "They said you would rule the Battle Moon one day."

Alex cocked his head. What nonsense was Malvexus spewing?

"Rule? That's *your* misguided dream, not mine!" Luna shouted. "Perhaps our training warped you at a young age. Or maybe it's this forbidden dreadmagic you now embrace. But something, somehow, has turned you down the wrong path. Before you go completely mad, you must stop this rampage, and restore order to the game."

Malvexus grinned, and a little blood dribbled down his chin. He was still on his knees, gathering his breath.

"I was born to conquer this world, and all the ones beyond it. I'm not stopping until I fulfill my destiny—one way or the other."

"Then, I'll force you to stop," Luna said. She produced a strange gemstone that had hung hidden around her neck. She leaned over and touched the tip to Malvexus's forehead. The enchantment flared with magic and started siphoning his mana. Power flowed out of him into the gem as long as Luna maintained the connection.

"No!" Malvexus bellowed, writhing as if in pain.

"Tell the Griefers to stand down and call good game, or you'll never fight again."

All eyes were on Luna while all ears listened for Malvexus's reply. Finally, it seemed the Modfia might be saved.

CHAPTER THIRTY-SEVEN

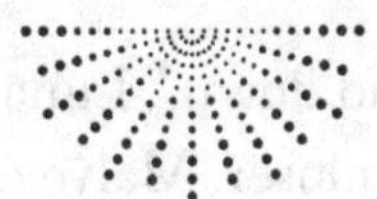

Despite the appearance that Luna was winning, Malvexus wouldn't admit defeat. Alex noticed he was resisting the magic of the Mana Drain. As he fought, he made subtle micro-movements, pulling himself back up into a position from which he might spring another attack. Luna seemed oblivious to the growing threat.

"What are you doing, Luna?" Alex yelled. "Finish him. Combat 101! Remember?! The Mana Drain isn't enough. He's too powerful. Kill him!"

"No, he will submit. He was once an honorable warrior," she said, her voice cracking. "He can be again."

Suddenly, the chains holding the Modfia fell away. Jed winked and put away his lock pick. Not missing a beat, he got to his feet and tried to rush in to help Luna, but Alex grabbed him and held him back.

"What the heck, man? Malvexus said it, plain as day. He won't stop until we're all dead. Dead IRL. Is that computing? If she doesn't end him, he ends us. And she's not getting the job done. We have to take him out."

Alex agreed it didn't look good.

"Kill him, Luna!" Alex yelled, still holding Jed back.

Luna glanced at Alex, but her eyes seemed to stare a million miles away.

The Griefers didn't seem to care that the Modfia had slipped out of Kadaver's binding spell. They were more concerned with Malvexus and Luna and moved in closer. However, they didn't attack. Like the Modfia, they were waiting to see how this duel would play out.

"Accept defeat and stand down," Luna demanded once again.

Luna pressed the jewel closer. Malvexus laughed maniacally.

"You truly are my flesh and blood," he said. "Stubborn to the very end. Yes, just like me, dear sister."

"Sister?" Alex was gobsmacked. "This solid gold douchebag is your brother?"

Everyone on the Sparkles Modfia team was stunned by this revelation.

"I'm sorry, Alex. I wanted to tell you, but I feared your team wouldn't trust me or help the Gamemaster if you knew the truth. No matter, it's okay now. Malvexus will submit. He has no choice."

Luna turned, and for a split second, the gemstone moved off center. It was the mistake Malvexus had been waiting on.

He made his move. Slipping Luna's grasp, he swatted the gemstone away, grabbed her sickle, stabbed her in the back—literally—then picked up Netherfang and sprinted back toward the cornerstone.

It only needed one more good strike from his sword. If he made it there before the Modfia did, it was game over.

Alex raced after Malvexus.

The Griefers disappeared through a portal, allowing them to leapfrog to the cornerstone.

Aspy, Jed, and Miz were on Alex's heels, fighting off the advancing skulks, giving Alex free rein to catch Malvexus.

Alex looked up to see Genghis flying over him.

"I encased Luna in a mending spell!" Genghis shouted.

Alex looked back with concern. "Good man, but we'll all be dead if that dickwad kills the cornerstone."

"We can't let him get near it!" Aspy shouted.

"Your smite spells," Alex responded. "Let's use them together."

Everyone agreed it was a good plan because Malvexus was within striking range now.

Genghis stood shoulder to shoulder with Aspy, and together they conjured the spells. Two large dark clouds formed over Malvexus. One cloud crackled with Genghis's golden-white lightning. The other cloud rumbled with Aspy's emerald thunder. As they waved their arms, the two clouds swirled together, spinning in unison.

"Now!" Aspy commanded.

A massive lightning strike flashed down toward Malvexus.

But at the last second, Malvexus lunged forward, vaulting out of danger, and continued running.

"Again!" Genghis yelled.

Another frightening lightning strike drove through the dark clouds like an arrow. Malvexus, who was now within feet of the cornerstone, paused and dove the opposite way, finding cover from the smite spell. The attack, having narrowly missed its intended target, hit the edge of the cornerstone.

BOOM! The protective stone structure cracked.

Blue energy jetted through. The Sanctum's health bar, which hovered as a holograph over the cornerstone, drained rapidly until only the thinnest red line remained.

At that instant, Bonegrin materialized, stretching out a beckoning claw toward his master. Malvexus dove inside the escape portal. Instead of disappearing, he stopped and turned back with a mischievous grin plastered on his face.

"Don't worry, Titan. The game isn't over yet. You and your team still have plenty of time to die!"

"He's getting away!" Jed yelled.

"Blast him with everything you have!" Aspy yelled.

But before any of the team could attack, Malvexus hit the cornerstone hard in the exact right place. A thousand new cracks spider-webbed out from the original, sending the health bar to zero.

"It's going to blow!" Miz bellowed, shouting the last words any of the team would remember about that moment. "Everyone take cover!"

PART V
THE BATTLE MOON

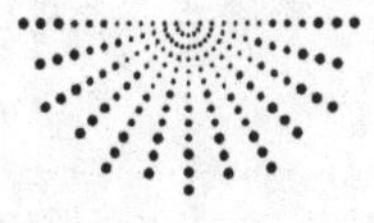

ROUND THREE

CHAPTER THIRTY-EIGHT

The next morning, the team rolled out of their regeneration pods, donned their repaired skins, and shuffled like zombies down to the Sapphire Sanctum's banquet hall.

Everyone was nursing massive hangovers.

"Regeneration sickness blows!" Miz groaned, holding her head.

"Motivates you to win," Jed muttered. "Because losing sucks all kinds of butt cheeks."

In contrast, freshly minted skulks buzzed around the hall, happy as could be. One skittered by with a carafe of mana-berry juice.

Alex couldn't get enough. It seemed every small bone in his body ached, his head pounded, and he might have thrown up if he'd eaten any food. The mana juice was the only thing that satisfied him.

He eyed his HUD, noticing that his levels were still recharging. The more juice he drank, the more they ticked up. After some time, his appetite slowly came back.

"Where's Luna?" Aspy wondered. She was cutting into something that looked like a blueberry pancake.

"No one's seen or heard from her," Genghis replied. "I was

protecting her in a healing spell, but she just disappeared. Man, I'm worried."

"Don't be," Jed said, hooking a thumb at their nearby server. "The skulks say she hightailed it into the wilderness before the base blew. She burned us, bro, burned us bad."

Alex said nothing. He didn't want to think about her or talk about her. Unfortunately, the rest of the team did.

"If Luna hadn't taken so much damage, I would've killed her myself," Miz fumed.

"She wasn't the one who killed the dragon or our base," Alex said. The comment slipped out and he immediately regretted it.

"Yeah, sure, but she didn't stop the guy who did!" Jed yelled.

He was pointing his knife toward Alex aggressively. Alex looked down at the table.

"We shouldn't have trusted her," Aspy said. "I always make the worst mistakes with people like her."

Alex took a mana-berry cake, slabbed it with butter, and poured what he assumed was maple syrup on it.

Part of him wanted to defend Luna. But the other part thought Jed and Aspy were right. In some ways, she'd betrayed them all.

"His *sister*," Genghis said. "I didn't see that coming."

"Me neither," Alex said.

A wave of sadness welled up within him. He felt like he might cry or scream or throw his plate of food across the room. Instead, he waited it out, pushing it back down. If champions could win by suppressing emotions, he would be a legend by now. He shut up, stuffed his face, and thought about all the ways he wanted to kill Malvexus.

After breakfast, the team gathered in the courtyard to discuss the previous day's battle and tried their best to come up with a plan that might counter a new attack. For instance, they might turn the tide by being the aggressors. Could they catch Malvexus and the Griefers off guard?

"We're still too inexperienced to take them on head-to-head," Aspy said. "Honestly, I'm not sure what we can do to win. I think the best plan is getting that portal key and getting the heck out of here."

"What if we concentrated on Bonegrin?" Jed asked. "We could work together and isolate him. Gank him and take the key again. Then, open a portal and jump back home before the others are wise to our plan."

Miz nodded. "I have nothing better. Seems like it's our only shot."

Genghis looked at Alex, who said nothing.

"You guys know best," Genghis said. "I'm with you all the way."

"Running for the exit forfeits the game. That's not quite the cosmic champion way," Alex said.

"We're trying to save our lives," Miz sighed.

"Yeah, I know. I just thought it would end differently."

"Alex still wants a happy ending that fades out with a Rascal Flatts song," Jed joked.

"Who is Rascal Flatts?" Aspy asked.

Miz rolled her eyes at Aspy. "We need to think like our competition. He's broken every rule in the game."

They continued arguing and debating until late afternoon. Nevertheless, the plan to isolate and attack Bonegrin remained the top choice. At dusk, the skulks gathered around the gate, murmuring excitedly.

"What's that all about?" Alex asked.

The team strolled by, watching the skulks. They seemed so happy.

"They say someone's selling skulk treats," Jed said.

"Like a food truck?" Miz laughed. "I didn't know the little guys needed food."

Genghis shrugged. "We should let them celebrate. No telling how much time any of us have left."

Alex nodded. The skulks opened one of the smaller side gates, and a humpbacked old woman rolled a cart inside. The curious vendor parked and raised a tent. A group of skulks queued up, waiting to make a purchase.

The team laughed at the frenzy and walked on, discussing their next steps. It was decided they would enact their plan as soon as the moon rose overhead.

Nightbane smiled. Her deception was almost too easy.

The Earthborn had shown heart in the previous battle. She liked that, even welcomed it. But she also wanted to win. Plus, it was a high honor to be sent on such a mission. One that had such delicious possibilities. The variety of suffering she would conjure gave her goose pimples. How wonderful to kill an enemy slowly and savor their defeat.

She handed out the skulk treats, collected their little gremlin money, and tossed it in the trash. Now it was time for the proper test. Getting the Earthborn to partake in the potions wouldn't be easy.

She handed one senior wizard skulk five flagons of brew and pointed to the Modfia. He bowed respectfully and skittered over to the team.

She watched as they refused.

Then most likely out of something called *guilt*, an emotion she didn't understand or experience, the Earthborn took the tiny cups, made a toast, and drank the potion down.

How incredibly marvelous! A devilish smile curled on her face. Tonight, when sleep came, she would show Malvexus how valuable she was to the Griefers.

Anyone who can control the mind has genuine power, and the Sparkles Modfia would soon know this terrifying truth.

CHAPTER THIRTY-NINE

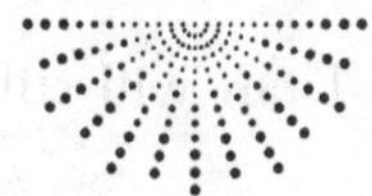

While the mood at the Sapphire Sanctum was literally and metaphorically blue, the vibe on the other side of the Battle Moon was the opposite.

The Griefers were having a party!

The celebration had gone on all night and continued into the next day. They ate and drank their fill at their grandest banquet table.

"We've won so many battles that I was finding victory a bore, but this one is quite sweet," Kadaver said.

"You speak the truth," Malvexus replied. "I felt much the same way. But fighting the Earthborn was different. They proved sufficiently challenging. My blood still boils from the excitement of their humiliation."

"Perhaps Luna trained them?" Bonegrin wondered.

"Not well enough," Lackey cackled, then everyone laughed.

"They have some natural talent and for that deserve a modicum of respect," Nightbane mused. "For instance, their healer is formidable. Thankfully, he doesn't understand this about himself."

"You are right, Nightbane," Malvexus said, leaning forward. "We must get rid of him first. He is the heart of the team and one of the most dangerous. His powers seem to be enhanced by the Evercore energies."

"For some reason, he embraces the Prime Moral Principles that the cosmomancers preach," Kadaver scoffed. "Perhaps because he is young and foolish."

"Could it be Gamemaster guides him?" Nightbane asked.

"Perhaps," Malvexus replied. "All the more reason he must be destroyed."

"But once he is gone, Titan will still be a problem." Lackkey muttered.

"Titan may wish to lead, but the team doesn't respect him," Nightbane said.

"Good, a leaderless team is easy to rip apart," Malvexus said. A slight grin curled around the edges of his mouth.

"And what of Gamemaster?" Lackey asked.

"That old decrepit fool has been taken care of," Bonegrin said. "Snared and infected by the dreadmagic in the Mana Lake. He is weakened and most likely dead."

"No, my Lord," Lackey said, raising a claw. "We have spies in the Wilds. They say that the Earthborn freed him from the trap."

"Yes, I heard this report," Malvexus laughed, raising an eyebrow. "And how was their act of mercy repaid?"

"He killed them! Killed them dead!" Lackey roared. He slapped his little claws to the table, as if it was the funniest joke ever told.

All the Griefers erupted in laughter.

"Ha, yes. I would expect nothing less," Malvexus said, rising to his feet. A nearby skulk refilled his mug of brew, and he continued like a politician practicing his stump speech.

"Here's evidence of the cosmomancers's apathy toward our lives, yet so many dare call me heartless. No, my friends, it is quite the opposite. As I've said from the first day we set foot on this moon, this game is rigged, and we are but its prisoners. These elite, heartless cosmomancers, drunk on power, spin their lies about creating a

Cosmic Alliance, but look around. The citizens of this alliance are nothing more than slaves."

"Hail Malvexus, the first champion to rise and challenge these lies!" Lackey stood on the end of the table and raised a flagon of brew.

Kadaver stood and joined the toast. "If the cosmos wants an overlord so cussing bad, let all voices raise and spread the word—Malvexus is that lord!"

She drank her brew in one gulp and slammed her mug onto the table.

"Down with the cosmomancers!" the Griefers cheered.

"They invaded our world. Imposed their will upon my people. Forced us to channel our warrior blood into this entertainment," Malvexus raged. "Before these aliens came, my forefathers conquered and killed for glory and true honor—not for the pleasure of these puppet masters. I despise their kind. And I will be free of them for all time."

The Griefers cheered again. "Down with the cosmomancers!"

Malvexus unsheathed Netherfang and held it out over their banquet table. Ebony strands of dreadmagic swirled around the blade. His team cowered at the sight of the dark energy.

"Yes, dreadmagic was banned from the game for a reason. I too feared the power, until I understood its purpose," Malvexus gloated. "It is the key to our rebellion. It cuts through the false light. It offers us freedom."

Finally, Malvexus re-sheathed his sword and sat back down.

"Now, we must plan the final round. The Sapphire Sanctum was nearly impossible to invade last time. We need a new strategy."

Nightbane stood up. "My lord, if it pleases you, I have conjured just the thing."

She placed a flask of bubbling purple liquid in the center of the table. Everyone leaned in to get a good look.

"Victory is only a sip away!"

CHAPTER FORTY

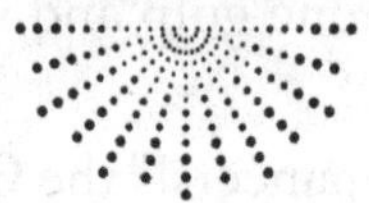

On one level, Aspy knew what she was experiencing was a dream of the night's previous battle. But on another level, her mind believed the nightmare was real. As the battle raged around her, panic gripped her so viciously she was sure she would die. Her teammates were taking damage from all sides.

What could she do? How could she protect them?

The chaos of the fight had trashed every conceivable plan. They were losing, and there didn't seem to be any way to stop it.

The goblin called Lackey conjured a downpour of electric rain, shocking everyone.

Bonegrin hurled his dangerous trident at the team.

Jed tried to block it, but the weapon was too powerful. It punctured his defense and drove through Jed's arm, pinning him to a large Warwood tree.

"Oh no, Jed! I'm coming. Hold on."

Aspy tried to move but couldn't. She felt tears form around the edges of her eyes. Why was her anxiety so terribly paralyzing?

Now the panic was turning to pain and anger. She wanted to cry.

As usual, she was caught in the middle of her feelings but unable to express any of them.

Suddenly, she was enveloped in a dark cloud of Nightbane's telltale magic. The cloud burned her eyes and made her cough until she doubled over. When she tried to stand up, someone rushed by and hip-checked her out of the way.

"Move it, dork!" Rebecca Flanders hissed.

Aspy looked around, surprised to see the battle had disappeared. In its place, a more familiar nightmare had materialized—high school!

Her mysterium battle bow, the Highguard Claw, was gone and replaced by a stack of textbooks, while her tattered Hello Kitty backpack replaced her quiver.

She clutched her books tightly and ping-ponged through a crush of high school students changing classes.

Her classmates pushed, shoved, cursed, shot dirty looks, and yelled awful names. A wave of sensory overload choked Aspy like a thick fog.

She wanted to scream. She always wanted to scream in these situations. But no matter how natural her reactions seemed to her brain, they were never accepted by anyone else. So, once again, Aspy dutifully obeyed her inner mantra—stuff the feelings down or everything will get worse.

She found a dark corner near the soda machine and slumped to the floor to sit. She closed her eyes and prayed the panic would pass—and for a minute, it seemed her prayers were answered. She peeked between her fingers and realized she was alone in the hallway.

Relieved, she stood up with her textbooks and an invisible force raced by, violently ripping the stack from her hands. Then the unseen attacker zoomed the opposite way, spinning her around, tearing her t-shirt, and knocking her cell phone out of her back pocket.

"Neurotypicals are so pathetic," Nightbane cackled, sliding to a stop at the end of the hallway. "How do any of them survive?"

Nightbane was a Bloodstone Banshee Ranger—an evil female elf that could have been Aspy's darker twin.

She sauntered down the hallway. The fluorescent bulbs exploded as she passed. She twirled her Devilmaw leather whip in her hand. Its end, obviously barbed with some jagged metal, scratched at the linoleum as it trailed behind her.

Nightbane exuded confidence and danger like a deranged prom queen. She was everything that Aspy had rejected about herself—feminine, sexy, self-assured. Everything she said she despised but secretly wished she could be.

The Griefer did a cartwheel and cracked her whip hard enough to rip off one of the locker doors off its hinges.

"What are you doing here?" Aspy asked.

"Isn't it obvious? I'm your nightmare—death in stilettos." Nightbane cracked her whip again. This time, it hit Aspy's arm, drawing blood. "Oh, so sorry about that. But you're not really threatened by a little blood running down your arm, are you?"

Nightbane's free hand fingered the dark smoke surrounding her until it magically formed a ghostly image. It was Aspy in her bedroom, holding a pair of sharp scissors to her arm, crying and bleeding.

"Chicken cutter—you never go deep enough. If you'd found a good vein, it would've saved us both a lot of needless effort." Nightbane cracked her whip yet again. It flew back, gathering a fresh surge of energy, and whipped forward once more.

When it hit Aspy in the chest, the impact created a magical explosion, pushing her backward. She crashed into a row of lockers, leaving an Aspy-sized dent in the flimsy metal doors.

"C'mon, you pitiful reject. Bring her out—the *champion,* the real you, not this pathetic mask you wear. Fight me!"

Tears streamed down Aspy's face, but not because she was hurt. No, she was beyond that now. Rage flooded into her like lava as she tightened her fists and transformed into Aspy the Quillodian warrior.

Having replaced the books and backpack with her bow and quiver, she fired a volley of mystical slingers that rained down on her foul-mouthed foe.

Nightbane juked left then right, dodging the first few, but most hit her dead on, turning her into a human-sized pin cushion that sustained serious damage from the strength of Aspy's attack. Her knees buckled as she tried to pull herself into cover behind one of the wrecked lockers.

Aspy, her fear now washed away by rage, kept firing.

Nightbane lashed her whip around an overhead water pipe. With that secure, she bit into the handle and executed the Iron Jaw—an acrobatic aerial spin—one of Nightbane's most powerful counter-attacks.

Undeterred, Aspy continued to fire arrows, but this time her attack was countered effectively. Arrows ricocheted off Nightbane's spinning body and flew back at Aspy with even more force.

Aspy dove out of the way, but several arrows hit her in the back. She doubled over in pain as her health bar dipped from green to red.

Nightbane dropped to the ground and cracked her whip. The tip lashed out, tearing the Highguard Claw from Aspy's hands. A barrage of strikes tore at Aspy's armor, then her skin. Before long, she was slick with blood, pulling herself down the hallway. Only a sliver of health remained as she tried to escape.

Nightbane sauntered like a runway model behind her.

"You're a pariah at school and a beta-suck on your team. Wishy-washy in every way. Just look at how you dress. I mean, what are you, anyway? Male or female? Or just a messed-up, clueless, undecided voter?"

Aspy desperately reached for her magical bow, but Nightbane got to it first and picked it up.

"You're smart, that's for sure. But you'll never be a leader. Why? Because leadership requires trust from the team, and trust requires connection, and no one wants to connect with a freak like you. You were double-dipped in weirdo sauce from birth, and those defects will never change!"

Nightbane pulled back Aspy's bowstring, and a magical arrow appeared, quivering with red energy.

"Don't worry. I'm here to put you out of your misery."

She aimed the arrow at Aspy and let it fly.

CHAPTER FORTY-ONE

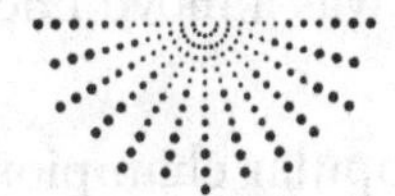

Jed thought he'd gone to bed, but now he was back in the middle of the North Wilds. The Warwood Forest surrounded him, and he could see the Crimson Castle's red glow in the distance. His heart was beating out of his chest. He was sweating and confused. Somehow, he knew he was in danger, but wasn't sure how or why.

A gunshot exploded, and a bullet ripped into a nearby tree. Splinters of wood, chipped bark, and dust blasted him in the face. He dropped behind another tree, hoping to avoid the next bullet.

"I won't miss again," Lackey cackled.

The little goblin skittered through the trees, laughing.

"Oh, yeah? Bring it on, you little wrinkled nutsack!" Jed yelled in response as he pulled out one of his daggers.

Lackey Lickspittle, the evil Wasteland Goblin, was an infamous inventor of deadly gadgets, but none of them had ever impressed Jed. He could see Lackey had climbed into the limbs of a nearby tree and was fiddling with a new weapon Jed had never seen.

"I eat chumps like you for breakfast!" Jed shouted, trying to draw the troll out. If Lackey moved a few paces to the left, Jed was sure he could hit him with one good throw. "Stick that little gross beak out here so I can cut it off."

"You wish, Mr. Nobody," Lackey snorted. "But since you insist, I will show myself. I hope you can handle me in all my glory."

Lackey raised his small staff, and the crystal tip flared to a radiant peak.

Jed shielded his eyes and tried to stare through the brilliance to keep a fix on Lackey. This was a move Lackey seemed to expect and maybe welcome.

"I'm one of the most popular champions in the galaxy. My social media game is off the hook—over a quadrillion fans," the goblin bragged. "Who are you? Some worthless little punk from a backwater planet that's not even in the Cosmic Alliance."

In the next second, he turned the light on himself, and the crystal emitted a series of flashes. It looked like the forest was suddenly full of paparazzi.

Hyper-realistic images of Lackey materialized around Jed. Between the strobe-like effect of the flashing light and the cloned images, Jed was both blinded and confused. He couldn't get a fix on the real Lackey who sashayed through the crowd of his magical clones.

Jed realized the goblin's staff was a glorified selfie stick. What a joke. How was this clown even a champion? He couldn't let this insane creature intimidate him or, worse, beat him.

He reached for a collection of throwing daggers hidden in scabbards on his back and fanned them out like cards, five in each hand.

With practiced precision, he threw them at every Lackey that appeared, but they whizzed harmlessly through the magical projections. None of them found his actual target. That was disappointing.

But the magic of his daggers countered the magic of Lackey's selfies, and they fizzled out like video calls with poor reception, clearing the field of the intended confusion.

"What a buzzkill," Lackey sneered. "No wonder your team hates you."

"Hates me?" Jed laughed. "They love me. They couldn't win without me."

"Seriously? Don't lie to yourself, loser. I've seen your DMs."

"What DMs?"

"Exactly, there are none. Zero. Zilch," he laughed. "No one. Not even your so-called besties give a dang flip about you, do they?"

Jed scowled at the accusation, then spun on his heels and threw a new handful of daggers at the smirking goblin. Lackey's selfie stick strobed bright flashes of magic that pulsed out, deflecting each dagger.

"My team respects me," Jed argued. "You don't know anything." He circled back around, hoping he could attack from the rear.

"I know you are scared and alone. And I know you will never feel the true exhilaration of being loved and admired."

"You're a *literal* troll. Why would I want to be like you? I don't care about bogus social media celebrities."

"What a phony. You lie to yourself. But it doesn't matter because other people on your team are better in the spotlight anyway—your little buddy Titan, for instance. He's everything you wish you could be and more."

Lackey doubled over cackling. The little imp seemed to have the magical ability of self-amusement.

"Laugh it up, Greedo!" Jed yelled. "Alex couldn't make it without me."

"Said the kid living in his shadow." The real Lackey stuck out his selfie stick and projected a holographic movie.

Jed was at home in his bedroom reading about Titan on the internet. He watched game videos about his matches, trying to understand and copy Alex's strategy.

"Look at the receipts, loser. You're a wannabe Titan. How pathetic!"

Jed used his grapple gun to anchor a line to the highest nearby tree and reeled himself up into its limbs. A shower of throwing stars trailed behind him, taking out Lackey's video.

When it winked out of existence, Lackey's mood soured. "Enough with the foreplay. I've sufficiently humiliated you. Now it's time to cut that ugly head off."

Lackey flicked another lever on his selfie stick. The magic orb folded away, and two razor-sharp bayonets telescoped out of both ends. When they clicked into place, Lackey threw the staff like a javelin.

It buried itself in Jed's tree and exploded. The resulting shockwave knocked Jed off-balance. He lost his grip, tumbled from his perch, crashed down through the branches, then slammed into the ground with a devastating thud. Every bone in his body felt broken, and he couldn't catch his breath.

"I'll broadcast your death on your homeworld. At least your bloody corpse might get you some notoriety."

Lackey pulled out a mythic blunderbuss—better described as a hand-cannon. He fired before Jed could move.

The cannonball exploded mid-flight, creating a cloud of red heart-shaped shrapnel that buzzed around Jed in a swarm.

"Take him down, my trolls!" Lackey shouted.

The magical red hearts sprouted arms, legs, and fangs as they morphed into tiny red-skinned gargoyles.

They pounced on Jed, hurled punches and insults too fast to defend against. Jed yelled for help, then screamed again in pain.

Lackey continued to laugh as Jed was swallowed whole by the foaming pile of angry red hearts.

"Yes! Scream, Earthborn, scream all you want! Nobody sees you and nobody cares. Tonight, you die like you've lived—all alone!"

CHAPTER FORTY-TWO

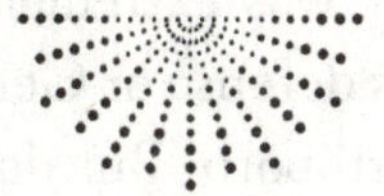

Somehow Miz was in the jungle—more specifically, the unfamiliar territory of the South Wilds. The air was humid from the mist of a nearby waterfall. It smelled of damp soil and rotting plants. Strange parrot-like birds cawed and, God help her, a snake slithered up a nearby tree.

Miz hated the jungle. This was Jed's stomping ground, and she was glad to let him have it. She was a fighter built for battles in open areas where she could see her enemy coming, where power prevailed over the patience one needed to stalk prey, where one could feel a breeze and not worry about dying from a spider bite.

Nonetheless, she was clearly in the jungle. As she tried to figure how or why, she caught sight of a cave many units ahead. Its dark mouth gaped, ready to swallow her into its spooky interior. She studied the entrance, wondering if she might need the shelter while she sorted out her situation.

"Are you curious if your fat butt can fit into that hole?" Kadaver asked. "Maybe it would if I carve you up into pieces."

A burst of icy magic shot past Miz's head and blasted a nearby tree, freezing it instantly. The tree teetered to one side, no longer able to hold its massive weight, then split along the trunk and crashed to the ground.

The Scourge Elf Sorceress stood in the new clearing wrapped in a black cloak. Its cape fluttered in the new chilly wind that seemed to accompany the stranger.

Panic gripped Miz. She hated fighting champions like Kadaver the most. Her skill set was so mismatched against powerful magic users like this sorceress. It was extremely hard for her to land an effective hit without Aspy's defense or Genghis's protection.

"You look worried, Earthborn. But don't be," Kadaver said, as if reading her mind. "I promise not to drag this out. I've got so many more important things to do after I kill you."

Miz didn't waste time either. "Is that right, walking dead?" she quipped, pulling out her axe. "Let's make that flat chest of yours even flatter."

She slashed at the trunk of a nearby tree, then two more, like a lumberjack harvesting timber.

The massive palms fell, hitting the sorceress like a sledgehammer. Kadaver was driven like a tent spike into the soft soil, only to re-emerge behind Miz seconds later, riding a giant white worm.

"Dang, girl, your ugly face creeps me out," Miz said, taking several steps back.

As a heavy metal bassist, she'd seen tons of ghoulish images, but Kadaver was another level of scary. She reminded Miz of Eddie the Head, Iron Maiden's infamous zombie mascot.

"What does a dark creature like you know about beauty?" Kadaver cackled, shooting a blast of icy magic at Miz.

"Black is beautiful, witch!" Miz dodged the attack and threw her axe as hard as possible. It spun out like a massive table saw and cut the worm in half. Kadaver tumbled off her dead mount and disappeared into the jungle.

"The color of your skin is like rotting meat. It disgusts me. I see why the Earthborn hate you for it."

Miz's stomach clenched. Here it was—the other shoe dropping.

The inevitable bigoted smear that always happened at some point, even though she hoped in vain it wouldn't.

Miz loved video games because she could get lost in an alternative universe where she didn't have to deal with real-world prejudices. But even when her racial identity was hidden, it didn't take long before some asshole ruined things by being a racist or trolling her for liking girls.

Now it was happening here, of all places, where the dream of full immersion had become a reality, where she had literally been transformed into her computer avatar. Still, this zombie, who barely had any skin herself, wanted to humiliate her for being black.

Rage poured into Miz like jet fuel. "You think you're the first person to try some racist rant on me? Witch, please. I'm not listening to any of that."

Miz retrieved her axe and threw it again. Kadaver reacted by conjuring a wall of ice. The battle axe chopped into it with a thunk.

Kadaver disappeared in a cloud of magical energy, then reappeared on a hill overlooking Miz's position, wearing an armored skin and holding a wizard's staff. "Loud and proud, is that what you are trying to tell me, muff diver?"

Miz grabbed her axe and leapt forward, swinging her weapon ferociously toward the Scourge Elf's head. Kadaver blocked it with her armored forearm.

They shoved and pushed each other, Miz hoping against hope she could get just enough distance to try another swing. Kadaver, on the other hand, seemed to relish the closeness.

They were nose to nose now, and Miz could see her foe in all her revolting detail. Had the elf robbed a Halloween store? She was wrapped like a mummy in strips of steel armor and wore a black wizard's cloak reminiscent of Santa Muerte.

Around the joints of her armor, where her skin was exposed, Miz could see large loops of what could only be described as surgical thread; her limbs and body parts seemed to be held in place by it, as if she was some victim of terrible plastic surgery. But none of this seemed to matter. Despite looking barely held together, she moved with the skill of a gymnast.

Her body was perfectly in proportion, but at the same time, hideous—a super model cobbled together by some dark magic. Yeah, she'd been pretty once. Maybe. That was up for debate. But now she smelled of rot and ammonia. The only thing she was missing was an autopsy scar and a toe tag. Miz wanted to vomit, but she also felt a wave of jealousy, which must have been obvious to her foe.

"You want to feel me up?" Kadaver purred.

Miz recoiled in shock, and Kadaver hit her with a blast of magic. Miz fell flat on her back, her axe spinning out of reach into the undergrowth.

"Come on, touch me, baby," Kadaver said, running her hands over her body. "I think you like what you see, don't you? My figure has been perfected, unlike whatever you have hiding beneath that costume."

She blasted Miz again. A piece of her armor fell away.

"Let's see. I guess it is a body. But what a disaster!"

She held out her hand as each finger morphed into a glass syringe. Viscous green fluid boiled inside, giving off the odor of formaldehyde, while her nails became long hypodermic needles.

"How about trying my special beauty treatment?"

Miz noticed the magical energy building around Kadaver's hands and rolled for cover just as the terrifying green liquid shot out, spraying the jungle floor. Everything nearby was destroyed by the deadly acid.

Kadaver laughed then coughed. A shower of maggots sprayed the ground. The tiny worms squirmed and wriggled, quickly growing to the size of little guinea pigs. Kadaver picked one up like it was her long-lost pet, tickled its non-existent ears, and ate it.

"Got to keep your energy up. I prefer protein. It's always the best. But you know nothing about dieting, do you, my little chubby foe?"

"I'm going to kill you!" Miz screamed. "And love every minute of it!"

She lunged to retrieve her axe and threw it. Kadaver juked to the left, trying to avoid the weapon, and mostly she did, except for one hand. The axe took it off at the wrist.

"And that'll pay the bills!" Miz cheered.

Kadaver doubled over in pain, holding her arm in a vise grip to stem the blood flow. "That was a lucky move, BadMiznus."

"Yeah? Well, come get some more, beauty queen."

Suddenly, Kadaver was behind Miz. The hand of hypodermic needles flashed like lightning and Miz screamed. Blood sprayed on the jungle floor.

"On the Battle Moon, we play for keeps," Kadaver whispered. "You'll learn soon enough. They call me Kadaver for a reason."

The evil elf slashed Miz again and again. Miz screamed louder this time. She was stumbling, trying desperately to escape into the jungle, but only moved a few units. When she collapsed, warm blood pooled around her.

Kadaver stepped over her and peered down curiously. The sorceress's hair came to life. Thick strands coiled and crawled like snakes down her body, binding her.

Miz gasped for breath, struggling against the terrifying magic. But it was no use. Kadaver had full control, and no matter what Miz tried, the bonds seemed to only tighten.

Kadaver laughed as Miz's eyesight failed. Soon all Miz was conscious of was the echo of her own misery and the smell of blood that marked how real the game had become.

CHAPTER FORTY-THREE

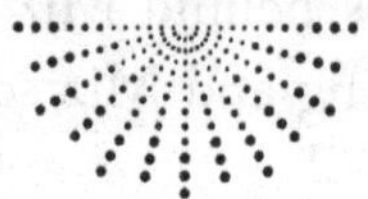

Genghis was so relaxed, like so super comfortable, that he couldn't believe he'd just survived one of the scariest and most difficult battles any kid his age had experienced. He looked around, practicing gratitude for the beautiful grassy meadow and his comfortable spot under the Buddha's Bodhi tree. The limbs above him swayed in the peaceful night breeze, as if lulling him to sleep.

"Oh, man," he purred. "So perpetually groovy."

His lips curled into a satisfied smile, and he closed his eyes, failing to notice the swath of grass in front of him was changing in the most disturbing way. In seconds, the lush green withered into a yellow straw. Soon all the grass was black and dying, turning to ash, and scattering in the wind.

When the smell of the rot was too powerful to ignore, Genghis snapped out of his meditative state. He bolted upright, shocked by what he saw.

The decay was spreading rapidly through the tranquil garden, creeping like black fingers toward him. His paradise was turning into a doomed wasteland.

"What the *what* is happening?" he asked, backing up and trying his best to avoid the approaching disease.

"Just some necessary pruning," Malvexus sneered.

Genghis turned to confront the intruder. But before he could react, Malvexus stabbed the end of Netherfang into the trunk of the Bodhi tree. Instantly, its leaves blackened and showered down on Genghis, cutting his body like broken glass.

Stunned by the viciousness of the ambush, Genghis stumbled back, invoking his own magic to heal his wounds and hold back the infection. But the dreadmagic ate through his spell like acid.

Using banned magic was so far outside the bounds of acceptable behavior it called for disqualification. However, one good thing about the attack was that it revealed Netherfang was the source of the evil.

"Why are you cheating like this?" Genghis shouted angrily.

"Not sure your dope-fueled brain will understand," Malvexus laughed. "But in short, I'm trying to kill you!"

Suddenly Netherfang was flying like a spear. But Genghis was ready for that, flipping forward out of his sandals and away from the danger.

"Fiery coke whites don't fail me now," he said.

Waving his hand at his feet, he conjured a pair of pristine Adonis Sleezy Boost 750 X2 Triple Whites. The magical sneakers rocketed him off the ground, allowing him to strike with a flying sidekick. The attack knocked Malvexus down.

"Take that, Prince Douche!" Genghis rubbed his thumb across his nose like Bruce Lee. "The wicked run to evil, let the good man's feet fly faster."

Malvexus rolled up on one elbow. "Well, you're not a total weakling. But I must ask, is that the worst you can do?"

"Oh, you want moves? I've got moves. For instance, take this sick beat!"

Genghis snapped his fingers, and a magical DJ setup materialized around him. He spun a luminous turntable, and a wall of speakers blasted a thumping, warlike beat.

Malvexus was stunned. It was apparent he'd never seen a DJ in action, and the shock allowed Genghis to carry out the special attack. Enchanted vinyl shot off the turntable like a swarm of buzz saws showering Malvexus in so much damage his health bar dipped into the red.

"If you were an actual warrior, you'd take my weapon and finish me," Malvexus taunted, wiping blood from his nose.

"Nah, brother. You're misguided. I believe in the lore. I play this game because of what it stands for—the Prime Moral Principle. Benevolence toward all. As the Gamemasters of old wrote, adversity tests the champion for those virtues. Playing this game is about more than winning."

Genghis waved his hand, cocooning Malvexus in a bubble of white magic. It tightened down over him, squeezing him like a giant fist.

"No, Earthborn. You mock the old virtues by pretending to be enlightened. In fact, you're a fraud," Malvexus hissed. "You don't transcend your pain. You run from it like a coward. If it wasn't for that Blissleaf you smoke, you couldn't get out of bed."

"No way, you've got it twisted. This dreadmagic has corrupted your mind, man."

"Don't lie. I know the secret you keep. I had a father just like yours."

"Lay off it. I don't have any secrets." Genghis's smile weakened. He didn't like where the conversation was going.

"Your home is the real battlefield, isn't it? Your angry mother is so depressed, she can't stop yelling at you. And your father's even more twisted than my Griefers. You've known his violence since you were young. But no one, not even your best friend, Alex, knows the truth. Do they?"

"Shut up!" Genghis snapped. "You know nothing about me. And if you say another word, I'm going to kill you, you freaking cuss-face-crap-head."

The magical white fist squeezed Malvexus so hard his face was turning purple, but he continued with the taunts.

"Wow, now we're speaking the same language," Malvexus wheezed. "But you're not killing me. Not even close."

Genghis had completely forgotten about the dreadmagic that surrounded him. In fact, the black rot that had spread over the grass field and Bodhi tree had morphed into something more monstrous. It crept up behind Genghis like a giant black scorpion with eight spider-like legs, pincers, and a set of ominous fangs. Malvexus's infected sword, Netherfang, dangled behind it like a stinger.

Before Genghis could defend himself, the dreadmagic scorpion leapt up and grabbed him with its pincers. Genghis screamed, and the fist holding Malvexus vanished in a pop. Then the monster lifted Genghis off the ground and hung him like a prize before Malvexus.

"You're a fraud, Earthborn. If you embraced your true self, you'd be twisted enough for my team. But that's only if you weren't so high all the time! Maybe the best you can hope for is a deep depression. Then you can hang yourself under this ridiculous tree. Either way, you're destined to fail everyone. This I guarantee!"

"Alex will stop you," Genghis wheezed. Tears filled his eyes as the pinchers cut into his arms. Actual blood poured down on the ground.

"Alex? He doesn't care about you!" Malvexus doubled over laughing. "Are you too stoned to see when someone is using you?"

The tears fell now. "No, that's not true! We're best friends!"

"You mean, you are his best bitch," Malvexus sneered. "Your *best friend* will steal all your power and abandon you in a heartbeat if it suits his purpose."

"That's not true!" Genghis sobbed. He couldn't hold back the emotion now.

"You'll see," Malvexus said as the scorpion's stinger came around and Netherfang stabbed Genghis in the center of his chest. "You'll see, soon enough!"

CHAPTER FORTY-FOUR

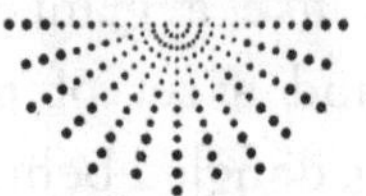

Alex lay in his bed, drifting off to sleep and wondering what the new day might bring. The brew from the skulk vendor had given everyone a buzz, and the mood had briefly turned positive. The game was tied now, inducing a mixed feeling of nervousness and excitement. Could they really win? Or would the Griefers take them down?

If they won, would Gamemaster fulfill his promise to get them back home? Thinking back to the night of valor points and the Gamemaster's Weapons Emporium, he wasn't sure. How would a single temporary tattoo help them beat Malvexus? Gamemaster seemed ready to aid them only if it suited him.

And what plans were the Griefers forming? Malvexus seemed to be merciless in his tactics. The Mana Lake filled with dreadmagic proved that. Would he attack at first light? Or would he use the cover of darkness? When Alex finally fell asleep, the answers to some of these questions were revealed.

In his first dream, Alex walked around the dark mire of the Mana Lake. He looked desperately for any living thing he might rescue or a magical artifact he might recover from the bog. But there was nothing.

He turned to leave and stepped in the water. Soon he was sinking in the inky-black goop, unable to pull himself free. Dead creatures and champions under the water grabbed and clawed at his ankles. Panic set in right as the dream changed.

In the new nightmare, Alex was stuck again. This time he dangled from a great web, along with his cocooned teammates. The mammoth spider that had trapped them spun new silk, wrapping it around Aspy. Bonegrin Banebreaker stood under the giant creature prodding it with his trident.

The silk strands were like steel cables and held him so tightly he couldn't reach his sword, and the enchantments that buffed him did little to loosen the web.

"Are you ready to watch your team die?" Bonegrin taunted.

Alex growled and strained to grasp his sword once again, giving it everything he had, but it was no use.

"I know you thought you were out of our reach. That old decrepit Gamemaster protects you with his magic while he seduces you with his lies," Bonegrin grunted. "The truth is that you will never return home. You will die on this moon!"

Suddenly, most of the Griefers appeared within a cloud of dread-magic. They mocked Alex incessantly.

"Pitiful humans—weak, scared, and totally out of their league," Kadaver laughed. "Lambs to the slaughter."

"I had high hopes for you, Alex of Garcia," Nightbane snorted, pointing at Alex. "Such a disappointment!"

"He's led them to their deaths," Bonegrin said. "What honor is there in that?"

"Loser. Loser. Loser," Lackey Lickspittle chittered in a high-pitch squawk that reminded Alex of a sick crow.

Alex pushed against the web and shouted back the best he could. "Let me go! Give me a chance. I'll take you all down. No problem!"

Bonegrin levitated so that he was hovering in front of Alex. He leaned in as if for a kiss and sniffed the air.

"Is that so? You say you can take me, but I smell your fear!"

His breath was foul, like the sulfur gas from the black bog.

"That smell is you, man." Alex grimaced. "Do you even own a toothbrush?"

"Jokes don't win this game," Bonegrin raged. "And to lose is to lose everything, your life and your homeworld." He slashed down with his trident, and the dream winked out of existence.

CHAPTER FORTY-FIVE

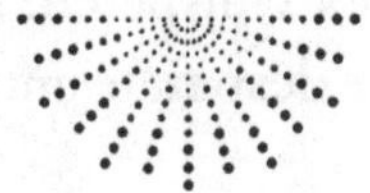

Several minutes later, Bonegrin dropped Alex's limp body against the wall of the Sapphire Cornerstone. Kadaver invoked a restraining spell, and a magical chain called Fetterbane's Web bloomed from the stone and wrapped itself around Alex.

"This one did not sleep as deeply," Bonegrin growled. "Nonetheless, the spell was enough to capture him."

"Only one more to go," Nightbane said, "and we can kill the cosmicron."

Lackey nodded to his teammate. "You've done well, Nightbane. Combining a fear potion with a dream spell was a stroke of genius."

"Yes, it seems Gamemaster fortified this place, but attacking through their dreams broke through all the protections."

Alex shook himself awake and did his best to sit up.

He glimpsed his HUD. There were only slivers of red left on his mana and health bars. It was the same for everyone on the team.

The dream had somehow been real. A true nightmare. He looked around. Miz was chained next to him and still unconscious. Aspy was beside her, and Jed was on the other end of the row. When they'd gone to sleep, Luna had still been missing. He didn't know where she was. But he was most worried about his other teammate. Where was Genghis?

The Griefers had gathered in a circle several yards away. They watched their prisoners carefully while discussing something in hushed tones. Occasionally, they would laugh as if they'd already won.

"Is everyone okay?" Alex whispered. He immediately realized it was a dumb question. The desperate murmurs and groans of pain were an obvious answer.

"I can barely move," Aspy said. Opening one eye, she waved her chained hand. She could only muster a flicker from a illumination spell that cast them in a warm glow.

"I don't feel so good," Jed muttered.

"What a horrible dream," Miz said, finally coming around. She sat up and palmed her face in her chained hands.

"That wasn't a dream," Aspy said. "They attacked us."

She raised her leather armor, showing off deep red gashes that started along her back and continued down the side of her rib cage.

"I'm a mess, too," Jed muttered. He tried to sit up but slumped down, apparently too injured to move much at all. Blood was oozing through wounds on his chest. "I hate to say it, but I just got my ass handed to me. I need Genghis's healing really bad."

"Where is Genghis? Anyone know?" Alex asked. He strained against the chains, looking around desperately to find his friend.

"Here he is," Malvexus said, suddenly materializing in front of them. Genghis was unconscious and slung over the grimknight's shoulder.

"He waged a valiant battle, but alas, it wasn't enough."

He dropped Genghis next to Alex.

Alex was horrified. Genghis looked dead. A dark wound—dried blood, he guessed—spread from the center of his chest.

"I'll bind him," Kadaver cackled. "But it seems this one doesn't really need chains."

The Griefers laughed.

"What did you do?" Alex shouted, straining against his bindings.

"Defeated him, of course," Malvexus said. "That's what champions do."

"Why pick him? Were you too afraid to come after me?"

"Oh, no, Titan. I'm saving you for last," Malvexus said.

The Griefers chuckled again.

Malvexus stiffened and turned on his team in anger. "And why do you four laugh? Has our victory been secured? The Sanctum still stands. I told you I wanted every brick of this place pulled down before we destroy the cornerstone. Total and utter humiliation."

He was in a rage, pointing with his clawed hand toward the main cathedral.

Kadaver looked at him in shock. "But we've already won, sire. Your enemies are at your feet."

"Go now!" Malvexus screamed, pointing again. "I will finish the Earthborn."

"But, my lord, you promised us the kills."

"Do as I command, Bonegrin," he argued. He drew Netherfang from its sheath and pointed it at the orc's chest. "Or the first kill will be you."

The giant warrior raised his hands in surrender while the rest of the Griefers cowered in fear.

"I will not say this again," Malvexus seethed. The veins in his temple flared. "Go! Now! Tear every brick down, then return to me."

The Griefers delayed no longer, turning and running toward the cathedral as they'd been commanded.

Malvexus sheathed his sword. For several moments, he stared at Alex, saying nothing. Alex braced for the worst.

"Are they gone?" he asked in a hushed tone.

"Uh," Alex replied, completely perplexed. "Yeah. They're gone."

"Good."

Suddenly, a cloud of swirling magic stripped away the false form of Malvexus. Gamemaster appeared, staff in hand.

"Then, my boy," Gamemaster said, "we will take our leave of this place before they get wise to my deception."

A mystical light blinded Alex, and they vanished within its flare.

PART VI
THE MODFIA'S REVENGE

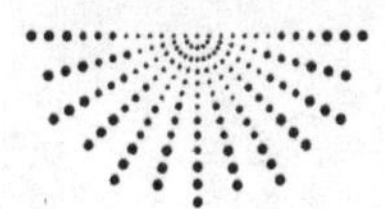

CHAPTER FORTY-SIX

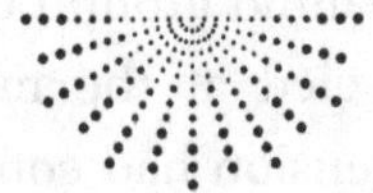

Giant swaths of magenta light fell over the faces of Alex's teammates as the massive object in front of them switched on. Large orbs of mystical energy swirled, glowed, and glimmered, creating a visually stunning representation of something spectacular.

"What is this?" Alex asked.

"This is the Retreat," Gamemaster said. "Your refuge and my home."

"No, I'm talking about this," Alex said, pointing at the moving orbs. "What in the heck is that?"

Gamemaster dismissed it with a wave.

"Oh, that old thing. It's a nuisance, that's what it is. So hard to clean, I tell you. Collects dust like crazy."

"But what is it?"

"That, my dear boy, is a scaled four-dimensional representation of the Cosmomancer's Wormhole Starway."

Now Gamemaster suddenly seemed proud of it. Beams of light shimmered and spun, tracing laser perfect trails across the vast regions of the model's universe.

"Is this, like, for real?" Alex asked.

"Oh, most certainly," Gamemaster said. "My father—or at least, I *think* it was my father—was said to have helped create that."

"You don't remember your father?"

"Well, at my current age, one wonders if one ever had a father or a mother. It was so many millennia ago, it is truly hard to know if it was a story, a dream, or my actual history."

Alex couldn't wrap his mind around any of what the old wizard was saying. Still, he marveled at the model. Somehow, powerful forces beyond his comprehension had connected the entire universe through a network of cosmic expressways.

"So, the portal key opens the Starway?" Aspy asked.

"That's right. That's how you arrived on the Battle Moon," he said. "The key provides both the access and the means of travel—the vehicle, so to speak."

He pointed at one section of the model. When his finger swiped the edge of the holographic orb, it spun to life. A trail of light shot from the Gamemaster's fingertip out and around the edges of two spinning galaxies, to the center of another that looked somewhat familiar—a yellow sun spinning furiously with nine planets orbiting. The blue radiance of Earth came into view as the Starway indicator approached it.

"That's incredible," Miz said, trying to touch the Earth's holograph. "Any chance you can send us back?"

"Like, yesterday?" Jed added.

"Don't worry, you are safe here. The only way Malvexus could break through the Retreat's defenses is if he became godlike. And that's an impossibility while you are hidden here," he said, not really answering Jed's question.

Alex was very familiar with the godlike rules. Four kills in four seconds is what it took. The buff increased speed, power, and health, making a player almost unstoppable.

Becoming legendary—Alex's long-sought-after goal—was similar but exponentially more difficult. It required killing ten champions in ten seconds.

Of course, most people accepted this as an unobtainable carrot that the game company dangled over all players. No one had ever done it, and everyone who played the game declared it an impossibility. Everyone except Alex.

But he'd given up the goal for good now. His understanding of what the actual game was and the real-life consequences of being on the Battle Moon overshadowed all his old goals. Surviving and getting back home seemed much more important. In fact, they were the only things that mattered now.

Jed pointed at another model. "And where does that Starway go?"

Gamemaster smiled and waved a hand. "That, my boy, is something else altogether. Something just as extraordinary."

The key feature of the model looked like a giant glass sphere filled with swirling golden energy. That orb was suspended inside another chamber that looked to be a grey stone wall, but when it rotated it turned translucent, exposing its inner workings. The main golden sphere was labeled the Evercore.

The model showed the Evercore fed two similar spheres—one glowed with a cool blue light, and the other glowed red. They orbited the Evercore like a pair of small planets, representing the game's two cosmicrons.

On the wall above the Evercore model, a collection of large tapestries depicted the transformation of a barren moon into a mythical paradise full of forests, jungles, and lakes. The tapestries also showed two very familiar towers—the Crimson Castle and the Sapphire Sanctum.

"This represents the work of the game engine," Gamemaster said.

"The game's engine? You mean, a computer?" Miz asked.

"Something much more than a mere computer," he said, tapping a finger on the model. "That is the Evercore. A true mystery. I've studied it for eons and still don't understand it. Nevertheless, its magic creates and recreates the world in which we now stand. It blooms the cosmicrons that power the red and blue bases. It charges the regeneration pods, fires the skulk pits, and enchants the intelligence that keeps score and makes all the game announcements. Quite simply, it is the magical heart of the Battle Moon. And I am its official caretaker."

"Does it analyze the rules of the game? Or rewrite them?" Aspy asked anxiously. She had wandered away from the game engine model and was looking at a stack of dusty books.

"Interesting question," he said, raising an eyebrow. "That is a more complicated matter."

"Well, does your library have, let's say, a collection of all the rule books ever written?" Aspy was biting her fingernails again. "I need to understand the evolution of regular gameplay because things have changed dramatically. And, honestly, I don't know what we should do right now. If this were a regular game, it would be over."

"Yeah, it seems we're in some kind of limbo. Normal gameplay doesn't have rules for this, does it?" Miz said. She wiped a tear off one cheek.

Alex ran a nervous hand through his hair. He'd never seen his team so confused.

Gamemaster seemed to notice as well. "I'd say your concerns are quite valid. The normal rules have been thrown out the window," he declared. "Because of that, I will provide you refuge until we rectify this situation."

"Wait a minute," Alex said, throwing up his hands. "Shouldn't you know what to do?"

Gamemaster nodded thoughtfully. "Well, yes. But Malvexus has made radical changes with his dreadmagic. This is the reason it was banned. It is highly destructive, and even well-trained cosmomancers find it hard to counter its effects. Using such an unconventional, rule-busting approach has put Malvexus in a formidable position."

"If that's true, why hasn't he finished the third round by destroying the Sapphire Cosmicron and declaring himself the winner?" Aspy asked.

"Ah, good question." Gamemaster raised one of his bony fingers. "To buy some time, I removed it from the map. Had I not, Malvexus certainly would have won."

"Wait a minute, you cheated?" Jed was amazed.

"Well, if this was a game of Dungeons and Dragons, the Dungeon Master could tweak things on the fly," Genghis offered. "Doesn't a cosmomancer have the same power?"

"Yes, that's somewhat correct," Gamemaster said. He patted Genghis on the shoulder, then looked at him oddly for a second. "Within certain boundaries, cosmomancers are allowed to make modifications."

He walked over to one window and looked out at the real stars beyond the thin atmosphere of the Battle Moon. Alex looked up as well. The view reminded him of how far they were from home.

"In truth, I tried to restart the game," Gamemaster sighed. "But that proved too difficult in my weakened state, so I have removed both the blue and red cosmicrons from the map."

The team was shocked to hear this news and gathered closer to listen. He had their full attention now.

"There is enough energy in the Sanctum itself and in the Crimson Castle to respawn both of your teams one more time. But after that, there will be no resurrection. If you die, you will not regenerate."

"So, normally we destroy the cornerstone to win, but that's no longer the case?" Genghis was confused.

"Correct. I've done something quite surprising, even for myself. I've downgraded the game."

"So, we fight to the last player now?" Aspy added.

Gamemaster smiled at her deduction. "You are very bright, daughter of Earth."

"Last man standing?" Alex asked.

"Or woman," Aspy interjected.

Gamemaster nodded. "Yes. A true battle royale."

"OMG, how's that gonna work?" Miz asked. "This whole situation is messy enough."

"In ancient times, the game was this way. I guess you would say, in your Earthborn parlance, version 1.0 was a battle royale."

"Why did you get rid of it?" Alex asked.

"The cosmomancers believed that form of competition didn't encourage champions to manifest the highest virtues. It tempted players to become too egotistical and too selfish. The gameplay was always about the singular player, not about the team. So, they reimagined the game with a concentration on team play. This seemed to illicit more noble virtues. But as you have experienced yourselves, having a team does not assure one manifests benevolence. In some ways, it complicates the dynamic. Players can hide their greed behind a veil of altruism."

Gamemaster seemed to stare at Alex the whole time he explained these things. Alex flushed with emotion, as if both embarrassed and insulted at the same time.

"So only one person can win?" Alex asked.

"Yes. If the rules are followed. Only one player."

"And what about the former version of the game? Is it gone forever?" Miz asked.

Gamemaster twirled his fingers through his beard. "Well, it is gone, but not forgotten. The game has now been recalibrated to the original version. Surely, this has put the game engine under stress, but I've decided it is best for now. Malvexus is a virus of sorts. If he's not stopped, the whole of the Battle Moon is in jeopardy. He rejects all the rules. Spurns his honor. And this has been going on for some time. The cheating has awakened the dreadmagic's power. The Mana Lake, which was a source of life for all creatures, is now a Bog of Dread, and it grows deeper and thicker with every misdeed. It is now nothing less than a terrible source of infection."

"We found you in the bog," Alex said. "If it's so deadly, why are you still alive?"

"Dreadmagic will kill anyone if the wound is deep enough, or if the exposure is long enough. I foolishly let myself become ensnared while studying the change in the lake. Luckily, my magic was still stronger than the bog when you rescued me. However, we can't count on luck much longer."

Gamemaster's face seemed to darken as he continued to speak.

"It's just a matter of time before Malvexus tries to kill me and take over as Gamemaster. I'm sure he would destroy the Battle Moon, end the game altogether, and try to subjugate the Cosmic Alliance. Rogue champions were always a risk the cosmomancers feared. This is why only the most advanced and noble species were invited to the game."

He waved his hands in the air as if to gather all the stars in his arms.

"You see, the cosmos isn't just held together by the Starways. It's held together by the virtues of the inhabitants, its traditions, and its institutions. These are the things that allow love and justice to be made manifest. Without them, everything devolves into chaos, then entropy takes hold, then the most powerful, dangerous force takes over."

"And what is that?" Genghis asked.

"Death, of course. The scientists call it entropy. The priests call it despair. We call it the *dread*, the terrible power behind dreadmagic."

Gamemaster shook his head. "I never thought until now that this might happen on my watch. But facts are facts. Malvexus will destroy everything if he wins."

"So, what do we do?" Alex asked.

"Well, my boy, you and your team must do what any champions do. You must win!"

Suddenly, energy crackled around the team, and they were transported to another platform. Here they overlooked a room full of books, scrolls, and a plethora of odd artifacts scattered throughout the space. The text on the spines of the books and the open maps seemed to glow and glitter like gemstones.

"This is my library and study. You are welcome to read anything except those books on the top shelf. I wouldn't touch those if I were you."

"Why is that?" Jed asked, a smile curling up on his face.

"Protected by magical charms. Instant death, so I'm told. It's never happened to me, obviously. But you, young man . . ."—he patted Jed on the back—". . . you'd be fried like a reaver rat on a Tambosian spit."

"Whatever the heck that is," Miz laughed.

He stretched his ancient arm out from his robes and waved it with a flourish. They were once again in another part of his strange home.

This magical leap transported everyone to a wooden deck built above an ancient grove of giant evergreens. Here, they could see miles of what appeared to be a primeval forest, lush and slightly humid. The Regolith River cut through the center.

"The great Fantismarune Forest!" Aspy exclaimed, pressing her hands to her cheeks. "The heart of Quillodia."

"Yes, child." Gamemaster seemed genuinely impressed. "Someone has been reading the game lore. How good to know one of you does indeed value the intricacies of world-building. Such attention to detail is surely needed now more than ever."

The ancient man raised his hands with another flourish, and they were all transported once again into a more traditional library.

A massive fireplace crackling with a small fire was the central feature of the room. Plush couches and leather armchairs were neatly arranged around a low table. There were exactly six place settings. Each one had a copper service plate, shiny silver utensils, and a large crystal goblet.

"Once again, Sparkles Modfia, I welcome you to my home. Please enjoy this meal. Rest and relax knowing you'll be safe here tonight."

He waved his hand dramatically, motioning at the table until a banquet of marvelous food appeared.

The spread included roasted meat and vegetables on platters, side plates of various fruits and greens, baskets of bread and pats of butter, and large steins full of frothy liquid that filled the room with their yeasty aroma.

Alex was drooling now, literally drooling.

The team almost fell over each other clambering to claim a seat.

Having tasted the beer, Jed and Alex smiled devilishly at each other and clinked mugs in a happy toast.

Gamemaster took the sixth seat, and the feast began. There was little talking as they devoured their meal.

Alex thought the food tasted a hundred times better than anything he'd eaten in the Sanctum. And once again, he noticed the better food increased his mana and health faster. Everything seemed perfect at that moment, and he secretly wondered if it might be safer to hide here than to re-engage Malvexus and the Griefers. Maybe they could be done with the game and find another way home?

As soon as the eating and drinking slowed to a crawl, and it seemed no one could stuff another morsel in their mouths, Gamemaster asked about dessert.

"Yes, please," Jed said. He seemed to have a bottomless pit for a stomach.

Gamemaster waved a hand, and a marvelous display of cakes and pies appeared, hovering above the table.

"Pick whatever delights you," he said. Then he stood up, magically cleared his place at the table, and replaced it with a clean set.

"Are you leaving us?" Miz asked.

"No, my dear, just making room for your good friend," he said, smiling widely. "And my other guest."

"Our good friend?"

"Oh, yes. Surely, you agree someone that risks their life for yours should be described as such."

He waved his hand behind him, and Luna Lifestealer entered the room. She was bandaged, limping slightly, and looked frailer compared to all the other times they'd encountered her.

"Despite being mortally wounded, this Gladiatorian warrior braved the Wilds, found my home—which is no straightforward task —and explained the dire situation to me. She pleaded for my intervention. Had she not done all these things, I'm afraid I would have failed to rescue you in time."

No one on the team seemed happy to see Luna despite what Gamemaster had said. The tension in the room was as thick as the roasted meat they had just eaten.

Luna held her side and grimaced as she sat down.

Aspy was immediately up on her feet, standing over Luna and pointing an accusatory finger in her face.

"Luna Lifestealer is not our friend. She's a complete butthole!"

Alex's mouth dropped open.

"You're just now noticing?" Jed added.

A collective angry outburst erupted from the team.

Then Aspy turned on the Gamemaster.

"She had a chance to end this and didn't do it—now we're all going to die!" Aspy yelled. "And it's her fault!"

Luna hung her head, saying nothing for a moment. When she spoke, her voice was soft and hollow. "Would you kill your own brother?" she asked, tears welling in her eyes.

"If he was a mass-murdering psychopath, then yeah, sure!" Miz bellowed and stood up next to Aspy. She crossed her arms, as if to further challenge Luna.

Before Luna or anyone else had time to react, Aspy had drawn her bow and a flaming blue arrow; its tip—white-hot with blazing magic—was aimed squarely at Luna's chest.

"Stop it, Aspy!" Alex yelled. "If anyone gets to kill Luna, it's me!"

Alex grabbed Aspy by the shoulder and squeezed it affectionately. She turned briefly to look at him with tears in her eyes, perhaps expecting more jokes, but Alex was just as upset. Aspy lowered her bow.

"I idolized you," he said to Luna. His voice was on the edge of cracking. "I swallowed all that warrior crap you were preaching to us, but it seems it was all bull. You betrayed the team."

"I thought he'd listen to me," Luna said. "I'm his sister."

"Yeah, which you conveniently forgot to tell us from day one," Alex said. "Anyway, it seems the only family that matters on the Battle Moon is your team—the ones who don't lie and will defend you from the insane killers on the other side."

Alex drew his sword halfway from his scabbard.

"You need to leave—and leave now. We can't trust you anymore."

Luna could barely get out of her chair, but she did it and hobbled across the rug.

"Wait a minute, Luna." Genghis held up a hand. "Alex, didn't you hear what Gamemaster said? She tried to make up for what she did. If she hadn't asked for his help, we'd probably be . . ."

Genghis stumbled toward Luna, who had stopped on the threshold leading to the next room. Suddenly, he fell to one knee and mumbled something about needing to go to bed.

"Genghis, what the heck, bud?" Miz shouted. "You drunk or something?"

"Or something," he said, slurring his words.

He had one hand under his shirt, touching his chest, then he slumped to the floor.

Miz rushed over just as Genghis's eyes rolled back into his head. Jed knelt beside her and placed two fingers on his friend's neck.

"His pulse is weak," Jed said.

"How do you know that?" Miz asked.

"My uncle was an Army medic." He pulled back Genghis's collar. "Dang, look at that. That's not good."

Everyone leaned in. Black lines stretched along Genghis's skin. The source of the problem was a wound on Genghis's chest. From there, the infection stretched out like a black hand, reaching up his neck, toward his brain.

"Geezus, what happened?" Alex asked. He dropped to his knees opposite Jed and squeezed Genghis's arm.

"Help me get his shirt off," Jed said and looked at Alex, who hesitated. It seemed weird to undress his friend. "Come on, man. He's hurt. We gotta see how bad it is."

When they lifted Genghis's shirt, everyone gasped. The wound had grown three times the original size. It seemed every vein on his torso was filled with black ink.

"Malvexus attacked him," Aspy said anxiously.

"Yeah, this is the same stuff from the bog," Jed said, holding his hand over the wound. "I can sense it. Dreadmagic."

"Unfortunately, you are very right." Gamemaster leaned over Genghis, investigating the illness. His fingertips emitted green light, casting a glow that seemed to make Genghis look even worse.

After a few minutes, Genghis slowly opened his eyes. He attempted a smile and tried to sit up when he recognized his friends, but it was too great an effort.

"Ugh. Did I smoke too much Blissleaf again?"

"I wish that were the problem," Miz said, squeezing his hand.

"I'm sorry, son. This doesn't look good," Gamemaster said, his brow creased with concern.

"Can he use his own healing spells to take care of it?" Aspy asked. She stepped closer, reaching out timidly to stroke her friend's shoulder.

"Intelligent solution, dear girl. He could try such a thing, but it would only suppress this necrosis for a short while. Perhaps it might come back stronger if he failed to keep it at bay."

Gamemaster raised a hand and waved it over Genghis. "Sleep!"

Genghis went limp. He snored loudly, wheezing with each new breath.

"Malvexus has done this on purpose," the cosmomancer said, checking Genghis's HUD. "His blade, Netherfang, must be corrupted with dreadmagic."

He swirled one arm, and a mystical construct approximating a dragon's claw appeared. It closed over Genghis, forming a cocoon of healing, then lifted him into the air. Gamemaster then swirled his other arm a few times, producing a magical portal the size of a door.

"Quickly, we must get him to one of the bedrooms." He pushed Genghis through to the other side and stepped one foot in. "Gather to me, little champions."

The team, including Luna, followed, and they all disappeared.

CHAPTER FORTY-SEVEN

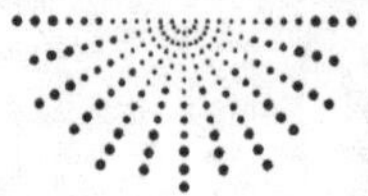

Over the next many hours, each individual member of the Modfia wandered in and out of Genghis's bedroom, hovering over him and checking on his healing progress. They gave quick worried glances to each other then restlessly floated away to haunt other rooms like heartsick ghosts.

"Genghis is seriously hurt," Miz said. She looked at Alex with tears welling in her eyes.

"You mean dying, don't you?" Alex said. Buried emotion crawled up from somewhere deep within him and grabbed him by the throat.

"Yes," she cried. "He may not make it through the night."

"Don't lose hope, young ones. He is strong and wants to live," Gamemaster said. "The healing spell has been set. Now we wait for his body to respond and fight the infection."

Luna suddenly left the room, saying nothing.

"Where's she going?" Aspy asked.

"Who knows and who cares? Let her go. This is her fault," Jed said. "If she'd stopped Malvexus, Genghis would be okay."

"What can we do while we wait for him to heal up?" Miz asked, directing the comment to no one in particular.

"Beat the crap out of the bastard who did this," Alex said. He stared out one window, refusing to look at anyone.

"I wish we could. Malvexus is a monster," Aspy agreed. "He purposely attacked Genghis to sideline our healer. He wants us to suffer so we have to beg for mercy."

"Mercy?" Jed snorted. "That's something he won't give any of us. Our fights with his creepy crew proved that."

"We're going to take Malvexus down," Alex said, clenching his fists. "We'll do everything we can to make sure of it."

Aspy raised her hands in exasperation. "The thing is, we won't survive another direct attack. We can't resurrect, we can barely heal, and our mana is at the bare minimum."

Miz wasn't so sure. "I don't know. I'm so angry right now I feel like I could take Malvexus down all by myself."

"I hear you, but we can't go off alone," Jed said. "On the other hand, I have to admit, I'm all out of ideas. What do you think, Alex?"

"We have to lie low. Try to hold out. Keep Genghis alive and replenish our mana and health. While we camp out, we figure out a good way to win this. Most of all, we need to pray Malvexus gets frustrated and screws up."

Eventually, the team ended up in the kitchen, perched on stools and gathered around a large island, trying their best to keep their hopes high. They snacked on bowls of elf apples, jungle plums, baskets of warm bread, and jars of jam.

But their favorite thing, by far, was Gamemaster's beer. A floating pitcher of the brew materialized magically and hovered in the spaces between them. It filled their mugs as if they were being served by a ghost. A honey-colored foam bubbled off the top of each mug when it was poured.

Jed nudged Miz. "Give this a try, dude. It's so good."

Soon everyone had a mug of the stuff. Beer bubbles randomly floated into the air and magically took on the shape of a symbol, which Alex recognized as their character sigils. The happier the mood at the table, the clearer, more colorful, and more solid the sigils grew until each cast a dull, barely visible aura of mystical light down upon its chosen host.

Even though it was hard to be cheerful knowing that Genghis was so sick, time slowed, and they found themselves lost in a small pocket of happiness.

Alex felt a tingle of something pleasant. It was the buzz of excitement mixed with the energizing glow of anticipation—a longing to ride into the next chapter of their adventure and lasso their destiny, no matter what danger may be waiting.

It was as if they were finding their purpose in being a family. And this purpose was flowering into a new ambition, one he'd never really had back home or in their strange new world. He was no longer obsessed with just winning the game for winning's sake. He was in touch with something more, but he couldn't quite define it. It wasn't simply the need to survive. It wasn't a desire to get back home. No, there was something new—like an anchor of meaning—that reassured him he was on the right path, that they all were. And this assurance filled him with something stranger than magic: the power of new purpose. Alex felt it become stronger than he'd felt anything before, and he was sure the others felt it as well. They wanted to win the game not just for themselves but for each other.

After a while, Gamemaster joined them. "How about a song?" he suggested.

"But we're having such a good time," Miz laughed. "Let's not spoil it."

"I'd like to hear a song . . ." a familiar voice wheezed.

Everyone turned and stood up excitedly. It was Genghis. He looked terrible and had dark circles under his eyes. He could hardly stand and propped himself up on one of Gamemaster's walking sticks. But they didn't care. They were so happy he was alive.

"Genghis, my God," Aspy gasped and threw her arms around him, almost knocking him over. Miz and Jed joined in.

Alex gently slapped his friend on the back and gave him the standard half-hug boys his age used to show affection. Perhaps for the first time, Alex could see and feel how important his attention was to Genghis. Something about the way Genghis looked at him so admiringly made Alex feel both ashamed and sad.

Even during Genghis's worst moments, when he was truly suffering, he gave away what little energy he had to Alex. Alex had never once considered how lucky that made him, and how unfair it was that such things were not reciprocated.

"This healer may be the strongest of you lot," Gamemaster said. "He's on the mend. Your team's magic is holding his infection at bay."

"Our team's magic?" Alex asked.

Gamemaster just smiled. Alex immediately connected the comment to the strange feeling and insight that had hit him earlier. Yes, something magical was happening, even if he didn't fully understand it.

Alex looked back and caught Gamemaster watching him.

"Like I said," he added, grinning, "there's power within this team. You just have to tap into it."

Everyone looked at each other, not understanding the comment.

"How crazy did you say this old geezer is?" Jed chuckled.

"Nobody asked that question," Gamemaster said, cocking an eyebrow.

"I just did," Jed laughed, pulling Genghis to the table and serving him some of the beer.

Genghis drank the first mug down in one long continuous gulp, slammed the mug down, and let out a belch of Olympic proportions. Everyone laughed.

As they celebrated the reunion by talking, eating, and drinking with each other, music crept along the walls from the corner of the room. Despite their lack of enthusiasm, Gamemaster sang his song and, as he did, the sigils grew in clarity and size, hovering higher over their heads now.

At first, they were oblivious to this, but at some point Alex noticed the melody. It sounded like the seventies soft rock his mother played when she was working around the house. The lyrics told a story about the Battle Moon's creation. Gamemaster had a surprisingly pleasant singing voice.

Genghis pointed at the sigils that danced over their heads. He swiped at them as if they were actual objects and they spun on their axes, shimmering, and buzzing with radiant energy. Soon they tightened their orbits, and as if gravity were dragging them closer, they joined in a flash of brilliant light. For a moment, everyone turned away or shielded their eyes. When they turned back, a new symbol was there.

"A team sigil," Genghis said. "I've always wanted one of those."

"Yes, you have," Gamemaster said. "Hopefully, the rest of your friends will see the wisdom in such a thing."

Genghis pulled up a chair and filled a plate with food. "That reminds me, guys. While I was in snoozeville, I had a vision," he said, chomping on something that looked like a chicken leg. "I want to share it with you."

CHAPTER FORTY-EIGHT

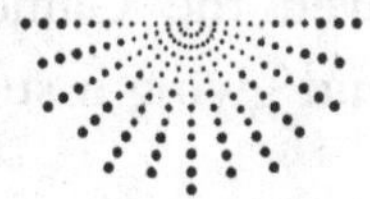

"Guys, you know I hate bringing the energy down," Genghis said hesitantly, "but I have something important to tell you, and tonight might be my last chance to do it."

"I don't think trying some new weed is the best idea right now," Jed joked.

Genghis grinned and motioned for them to tighten their circle.

"Are you going to make us hold hands?" Miz asked, shivering at the thought.

"Or meditate?" Aspy wondered, looking up anxiously.

Genghis shuffled over to Gamemaster and pointed at the old wizard's staff. "You mind if I borrow that for a few?"

The ancient man winked at Genghis then whispered over the staff, ever so briefly, and handed it over. "You may have this as a gift. I have many like it."

"Wow, thank you, sir."

The cosmomancer smiled and nodded.

Genghis fingered the grooves of the staff carefully, holding it out in front of himself like an orchestra conductor might wave a baton. Slowly, the tip warmed until it was glowing. The light brightened and projected magical animations out into the space above the team's gathering.

The five Modfia members stood on the edge of a grassy knoll posing in battle-ready stances. Suddenly, magical versions of their foes materialized and attacked. Five battles began, each one a replay of the last dream-like confrontations with the Griefers.

Just when it seemed they would have to endure the humiliating defeat again, Genghis waved the Gamemaster's staff. "Freeze it there," he said, his free hand giving a subtle flourish as if he were pressing a pause button.

He walked around the scene, then leaned in, studying each individual battle.

"Do you guys notice anything interesting about our enemies, besides them being class-A bungholes?" He pointed. "Look at their faces."

Intrigued, everyone stepped closer and inspected the scene.

"Oh, man, that's freaking creepy," Jed said.

"What is?" Miz asked.

"They all look like us!" Jed said, sneering with disgust.

Alex gave himself a dope slap. "Wow, what does that even mean?"

"Nightbane's magic did a number on us. She crawled around in our heads, found our most negative emotions and our biggest fears, then attacked us with the one Griefer who could exploit those weaknesses the best. They were buffed by our shadow-selves."

"I don't get it," Miz said.

"I do," Aspy said. "It's like the Griefers used our worst fears as a weapon against us."

"So we got paired with the one Griefer who would be the hardest to stop?" Alex asked.

Genghis nodded. "Yeah, that's right."

"Reminds me of rock, paper, scissors," Jed said. "Rock smashes scissors, paper covers rock, scissors cuts paper."

"If I'm the rock," Miz said, "Kadaver was definitely paper."

"Exactly," Genghis said. "That's how they beat us last time. Rock smashes scissors. But what if our scissors fought like a rock?"

"I think I get what you're saying now," Miz said. "We fight dirty like they did."

"No, not exactly," Genghis said, raising a finger. "We need to change the dance completely."

"Now I'm confused again," Alex said, glumly.

"First, we change dance partners." Genghis waved his wizard's staff and spun their foes into new positions. Each Modfia member got a new Griefer to fight. "Then we change how we dance."

"I don't get that part," Jed said.

"I do," Aspy said. "Try this: Think about the one person on our team, in this group here, that you clash with most."

"That's easy enough," Jed said. "You and me, Genghis, we're like oil and water."

"Yeah, that's a good example," Aspy said. "But what would happen if Genghis started fighting more like you?"

"He'd be a badass," Jed laughed.

Aspy nudged him in the ribs. "What it would mean is that Genghis would embrace his darker side."

"He'd stop being the nice guy all the time," Miz said. "He'd fight dirty when it suited him."

"Yeah, you're getting it. I'd have to embrace that part of me I reject because it scares me. Because it's a lot like my father, who is . . . well . . . he's not a good man." Genghis stopped and looked down at his feet. "But that's exactly what I'm saying. The Griefers will attack our weaknesses again if we let them. To win, we must change how we think about ourselves."

"Are we doing therapy now?" Alex groaned.

"No, dickweed," Jed said, stepping up next to Genghis and putting an arm around him. "We are learning how to stack the deck."

"Yeah, flipping the script," Aspy said.

"Malvexus hacked the game to win," Miz concluded. "We can't do that. But we can hack ourselves."

"You got it!" Genghis cheered.

There was a pause in the conversation as they considered the new strategy. Genghis hung his head, like he was suddenly very depressed.

"What's wrong, buddy?" Alex asked. "You okay?"

"Sorry, thinking about killing Malvexus makes me emotional."

He paused for a beat. When he raised his head, he wore a devious smile.

"And that emotion is pure joy!"

CHAPTER FORTY-NINE

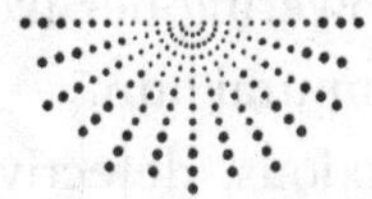

Lackey Lickspittle sat in front of the largest vault he'd ever found on the Battle Moon. The amount of gold inside would be more than he would ever need if he could just get it open. His magical lock-picking device spun the dial of the ancient combination lock until a distinctive click reverberated through the dense steel casing.

He stopped, laced his fingers, cracked his Wasteland Goblin knuckles, adjusted his goggles, then steadied his nasty little claw.

"Ah, okay, now for the final tumbler," he said aloud, as if coaching himself. "Must be calm. The slightest ripple in my concentration will set off the traps."

Just as his fingertips touched the dial, the loudest fart he'd ever heard rattled everything in sight.

The disturbance immediately triggered the vault's defenses. A rapidly spinning blade sprang from some hidden place and cut off all of Lackey's fingers on one of his hands. They dropped to the ground before he even knew he'd lost them. When they wriggled on the dirty floor like dark-green worms, Lackey screamed a bloodcurdling scream.

"Oops, sorry about that," the farting intruder said.

Lackey grasped at his wounded hand, looking around the room.

Aspy sat above the large vault, waving a hand in front of her face. "That last mug of beer really didn't agree with me."

"I knew I smelled an Earthborn," Lackey grumbled. "Who dares challenge me? Is it you, assassin? Or has the stupid monk come to fight?"

"Just me," Aspy said, lowering her ivory hood and revealing her long hair pulled back in a samurai bun.

"What?! You? The anxious, defective one?" Lackey gaped. "I never expected such vileness from a she-elf."

"Yes, that was the point," she said.

"No matter," the goblin sneered. "Killing you is easily done."

Lackey, who was still losing blood, health, and mana from his wounded hand, waved the other one, and magically produced a pair of poisoned-tipped daggers. He threw them with deadly accuracy.

When the daggers closed in, Aspy executed a perfect crescent kick, and sent them flying back toward their owner.

Surprised, Lackey desperately tried to twist out of the way, but slipped and fell. The poisoned knives hit him perfectly, puncturing his legs like a pair of fangs.

"How did you do that?" Lackey screamed. His health bar was down to a mere sliver now. "Nightbane defeated you so easily. Surely, I can too."

A flourish of mystical music rang out as Aspy laced her fingers into a meditative pose. "There is no failure in defeat unless one gives up," she said, her voice calm. "And this she-elf never gives up!"

In another lightning-quick move, she bounded up into the air, and like a graceful bird in flight, floated for a moment before delivering one of the most devastating kicks she'd ever executed.

Lackey's health and mana were depleted completely.

"But how?" he wheezed, drawing his last breath. "You're the weakest of them all!"

"How?" Aspy smiled. "The stupid monk. That's how. He's my

good friend, and he taught me something. There's power in our weaknesses if we just embrace them."

She bowed to her dead foe.

"Couldn't have done it better myself," Genghis said. He was behind Aspy on a nearby ridge, watching from a higher vantage point.

"Now it's my turn!"

Genghis raised his new staff and disappeared in a blinding flash.

CHAPTER FIFTY

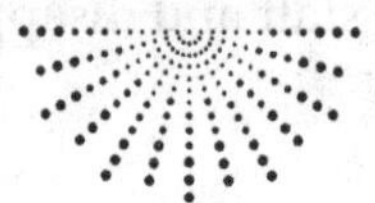

Elsewhere on the Battle Moon, in a small collection of crystalline buildings called Mirrorstone Manor, Kadaver, the most grotesque of the Griefers, had just started her spa day.

"This facial better work," the murderous Scourge Elf mused. "The last one only clogged my pores. The blood was too old."

"Yes, your gorgeousness, we have made sure this blood is fresh."

"Prove it," she demanded. "I'm paying good gold for this."

The female skulk snapped her fingers and a squad of anxious assistants skittered across the room. One pulled back the silk room divider, revealing three helpless Lava Trolls. They were tied upside down. Tubes of all shapes and sizes stuck into their bluish veins while their strange green blood flowed out into one giant collection tank that hung over the facial table where Kadaver now sat.

Jed wasn't sure using a strategy out of Miz's playbook would work, but he was down to try.

Normally, he'd stick to the shadows, phasing in and out of the darkness, taking his foe down one subtle cut at a time, but today, he'd confront this Kadaver chick in a new way—and have some fun doing it.

As the skeletal Kadaver relaxed under a new application of her blood mask, Jed plugged in. Seconds later, an ominous bass sound thumped from the shadows of the spa. Slowly but surely, the slow funky groove enveloped the entire room.

"Turn it off, curse you!" Kadaver bellowed, waving hysterically at the nearby skulks. "Don't wreck my beauty treatment, or it'll be your blood in that collection tank."

The nervous attendants scrambled around the room, trying to silence the music. But it was no use. They didn't know where it was coming from.

Jed turned it up another notch.

"What is that horrible noise?" Kadaver screamed, ripping her mask away and sitting up.

"That's one badass bassline," Jed chuckled.

He materialized from his shadow-weave spell perched on top of a column of magical speakers. When he saw Kadaver's face, he grimaced.

"Girl, hope you didn't pay money for that beauty treatment because it most seriously did not work."

Kadaver shrieked when she caught her reflection in a nearby mirror.

"Facial fail on aisle one," Jed laughed. "This witch is gonna need a refund!"

Instead of his normal ninja skins, he'd donned a white t-shirt, snake-green pants, and a hot-pink leather jacket. He wore oversized sunglasses and a red feather boa wrapped around his neck.

A replica of Miz's battle axe had replaced his knives, except this one was a sleeker purple model that he had the strength to use.

Like the instrument, he looked wholly different. His hair was dyed purple to match the axe. His face glowed with expertly applied makeup. He had fresh fingernail polish.

This was unlike anything he would have ever dared before, but it filled him with joy. He was the center of attention, no longer hiding in the shadows, and he felt free.

"What's wrong, Kadaver?" Jed taunted. "Worried my hot look is going to melt your face? Nah, that ugly mug is already bad enough."

"How dare you confront me, Earthborn. Soon I will bathe in your blood."

"I don't think so. I've got some pretty cool new tricks!"

Jed spun the dial on his magical amp, then stomped a foot pedal and started playing one of the funkiest riffs he'd ever heard. The sound waves erupted from the enchanted speaker and shot out across the room in a wave of fiery energy.

When the attack slammed into Kadaver, it instantly stripped away her remaining skin. The bassline was melting her face, literally!

Jed had always looked down on Miz's moves, but now he understood the power of her playbook. If he could be brave enough to put himself out there, a brutal frontal assault had its merits.

He blasted Kadaver with wave after wave of magical power—and in-between the attacks, he dropped a few juicy putdowns.

Kadaver screamed, trying her best to fight back, but her health bar was burning down rapidly. The wall of magical sound was too much, and Jed easily dodged the few counterstrikes she managed.

Jed stood his ground even when she threatened to advance. He just turned the volume up, making the attack even deadlier.

Eventually, it was too much for the Scourge Elf. She dropped to her knees, helpless in front of Jed. The effects of her beauty treatment had been obliterated and her health and mana were mere slivers.

"Stop, please, I beg you!" she screamed.

"But the song's not over." Jed peered over his sunglasses. "You should have never listened to Malvexus, zombie girl. You picked the wrong side of this fight, and now you pay the dues."

Jed stomped the last pedal and played another funky flourish until Kadaver disintegrated and finally disappeared.

CHAPTER FIFTY-ONE

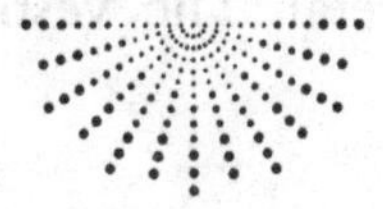

Nightbane sat alone at the banquet table, surrounded by at least ten silver chalices of wine. The gray-haired troll, the owner of the Wasteland Tavern, huddled in one corner, pretending not to watch the taste test. None of the selection seemed to suit the Bloodstone Banshee. He pushed the young orc barmaid toward the table with another unopened bottle.

"That's the finest in the cellar," he hissed, slapping her on the rump. "Don't spill a drop."

Now that the sun was down, the tavern was lit by candles and the fire in the hearth. The flames flickered, making the long shadows dance along the walls. Three old Vestian Dwarves, famous for making their home in the Volcanic Mountains, sat in one corner playing music.

"Are you sure this is the best?" Nightbane complained, pushing the newest goblet away. "Because so far, these are a complete disappointment."

The owner grimaced. He didn't know what to do to make the entitled champion happy. Surely, he'd be killed—and his establishment burned down—if he dared challenge one of the Griefers. They were now the de facto rulers of the Battle Moon. He couldn't cross any of them.

Suddenly, the door of the tavern burst open. A gust of wind blew inside, extinguishing some candles, and a cloaked figure glimmering with moonlight entered and sauntered to the fire.

The stranger stood in front of the hearth, watching the flames dance. Slowly, her cloak absorbed the light of the fire and radiated a golden hue like molten metal. The Vestian Dwarves were amazed and stopped their singing.

WHEN MIZ TURNED to face Nightbane, the champion looked confused, then extremely worried. This pleased Miz and she flashed a very uncharacteristic smile that seemed to brighten the dim tavern.

"BadMiznus of the Earthborn. The tank who talks trash," Nightbane growled. "Kadaver told me your size is both an embarrassment and disadvantage in combat. No wonder you hide yourself in that cloak."

"And you're Nightbane, the deranged coward who attacked my friends while they slept!"

"Yes, that was me," she laughed, her lips curling around her tiny fangs like two purple worms. "You were so easily beaten."

"You shouldn't have messed with us like that," Miz said. "Now I'm going to do something I normally would never do."

"And what's that?"

"Hurt you real bad," she grinned. "Real, *real* bad!"

Miz cast aside the cloak, revealing her new bedazzled catsuit. It was the tightest thing she'd ever worn. It sizzled hotter than the fire behind her. A new, intimidating confidence radiated as she spun in a slow circle, showing off every detail of her curvaceous body.

Nightbane made a sudden movement to grab her whip, Devilmaw, but found herself frozen in place. It seemed the catsuit was enchanted and the magical light projected from the glimmering beads was hypnotic, trapping Nightbane in an unexpected trance.

Miz's hand went up, leveling a pistol crossbow at the demonic elf. Two magical bolts glistening like ivory flew across the room and tattooed her forehead.

Ka-shunk, ka-shunk.

Nightbane tumbled over, crashing in a heap. Spilled wine poured down like a shower of blood.

The Vestian Dwarves rushed for the door while everyone else, including the old tavern keeper, tried their best to hide. The barmaid screamed, but the loudest screams came from Nightbane herself.

"Don't worry," Miz laughed. "I'm just getting started!"

CHAPTER FIFTY-TWO

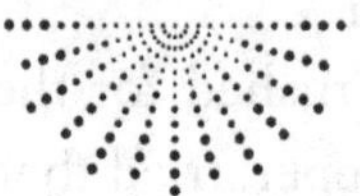

Bonegrin Banebreaker was furious. He raced out of the Crimson Castle past the first protection tower and opened a rift portal to Lackey's last-known position. The distress ping had been sent from somewhere in the Southlands. Specifically, near the Acid Lake on the border of the Grey Sands. An abandoned Wasteland Troll goldmine, most likely.

The door on the other side of the portal opened, casting a crackling, deep-blue glow over one of the grey dunes. Several yards in front of him, he saw Lackey face down in the sand. He lay still, as if dead.

"Lackey," he growled. "Who did this to you?" He clawed at Lackey's shoulder, attempting to lift him out of the sand.

Kaboom!

The hidden bomb exploded. Magical shrapnel tore through Bonegrin's dense armor, ripping into his flesh, and throwing him up in the air. He fell back down, crashing into a rocky outcropping with a sickening thud.

Genghis stepped up next to the wounded Fel Orc. According to his HUD, the bomb blast had depleted nearly all his health and mana.

"I want you to know," Genghis said, "you brought this on yourself."

He raised his staff high as a magical bayonet appeared at one end. Then he thrust it down, impaling Bonegrin through his hard heart.

"I'll kill you, monk!" Bonegrin groaned and clawed at the staff as Genghis twisted it deeper. "All of your pathetic friends will suffer!"

"Attacking us again would be a mistake," Genghis said, absorbing all of Bonegrin's remaining mana.

This was a move he'd never considered before, finding the idea too aggressive, but he was following his own plan—changing his dance partner and how he danced. Something about it felt right, perhaps even justified.

Bonegrin looked back at him, completely helpless. Drool dripped over the side of his grey cheek.

"I swear I'll . . ."

"Oh, shut up!" Genghis shouted. He spun the bladed staff around and lopped off Bonegrin's head with a sickening wet snap.

A minute later, Bonegrin's body levitated, returning to its assigned regeneration pod within the Crimson Castle. Genghis watched for a moment, wondering how much power those pods might still have.

Gamemaster had guessed only one more resurrection would be possible for both teams. He prayed the Crimson Castle was out of mana.

When he clicked his heels together, his magical sneakers activated, and he flew away, hoping he'd seen the last of Bonegrin Banebreaker.

CHAPTER FIFTY-THREE

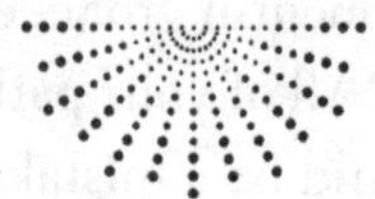

On a ridge overlooking the valley that cradled the Crimson Castle, a grove of ancient oaks swayed in the breeze. Alex and Luna sat beside each other on the highest branch.

"Yes!" Alex cheered, nudging Luna. "They did it. I can see four of the regeneration pods are active."

"Let me look," Luna said, reaching for the enchanted spy glass. "By the cratered moon, you're right!" She raised both eyebrows. "Your team has gained much honor today!"

Luna looked at Alex. Alex looked back. It was hard to ignore the buzz of good vibes between them. No doubt his feelings about her had been on a roller coaster ride. He'd started with a volcanic hot crush, but that had been frozen by a glacier of anger after her screwup with Malvexus. Now, he'd settled in a happy tropical climate full of warm emotion.

Of course Luna had found it hard to kill her own brother. Most normal people would. But the Modifa team was made up entirely of only children. None of them had siblings. This made them less sympathetic to Luna's dilemma.

Also, Luna had braved the Wilds by herself to warn Gamemaster, and she petitioned him to intervene, which pretty much wiped out the previous debt.

However, it was her care for Genghis that stoked Alex's fire the most. He saw her concern about his best friend.

Best friend? He rarely admitted that to himself. But it was true. That was how he felt about his buddy.

Finally, Luna was proving extremely loyal to the Modfia. She'd stopped short of offering to fight Malvexus again, but she had willingly helped them plan the current ambush by offering up all the intel. Having once been a Griefer herself, she knew their secret haunts, their strange proclivities, and their weaknesses. All of that information had proved invaluable. Now, thanks to her, they had a chance at winning.

"We need to report back," Alex said.

"The rendezvous point is just over this hill. Come on, let's go."

They watched the castle for a few more seconds then climbed down.

"I hope everyone is okay," Alex said, creasing his forehead.

Luna stopped and looked at Alex like he'd just said the strangest thing.

"You continue to surprise me. When we first met, it seemed you only cared about winning. About becoming legendary. Something has surely changed."

"Maybe." He shrugged.

"Well, the game isn't over yet," she said. "Who knows what lessons we will learn before we defeat our adversary?"

"Our adversary?" Alex wondered. "You sound like one of those crazy Earthborn kids. Are you Team Modfia now?"

Luna said nothing more but was smiling. It was a smile as wide as the Battle Moon.

They climbed onto two enchanted sky horses and took to the air. As Alex watched her fly away, her hair swaying in the cool air, her subtle laugh echoing back, he had an important realization.

This moment.

This very moment was his favorite moment in the game so far, and even though he wasn't sure how much longer he might live, he was sure he'd never forget that smile.

Never.

CHAPTER FIFTY-FOUR

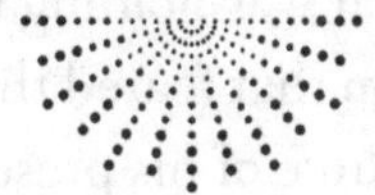

Malvexus brooded as he stood in the center of the throne room's grandest window. He looked out at the darkening clouds, noticing something had changed. Without the Crimson Cosmicron, the Crimson Castle no longer glowed with power. It seemed lifeless and weak, as if his adopted home were sick.

Never one to care that much about the living, he marveled at his own empathy. Was he getting soft? Was this some kind of enchantment? An infection from his fight with the Modfia healer? What sinister plot was unfolding now?

Surely, it was the cursed enslaver. The cosmomancer was breaking eons of tradition to help the Earthborn. Perhaps his uprising was having its desired effect? Finally, power was slipping from the ancient invader. Was the Gamemaster scared?

The deaths of his worthless cohort were much easier to understand. They'd been beaten quite badly because of false bravado and pure laziness.

The Earthborn had a reason to fight. They wanted to live, and they had attacked out of desperation. His team had lost such noble motivations many battles past.

The humiliation burned within him. He would not let this ragtag group claim his victor's crown. They were inexperienced children from a worthless race of beings no smarter than a planet of monkeys.

Of course, he was young—not that much older than the Earthborn's leader, Titan. Many, including his father, had looked down on him because of this, but the glory of being a champion made age of no real consequence.

What *was* consequential was holding the victory and steeling his mind against any part of him that feared the next battle.

Perhaps this was the source of his present darkness?

He was dwelling on the hardships of war and forgetting the joys of victory—the smell of spilled blood and the exquisite sight of his enemies' defeat along with the sound of their pleas for mercy, and the thrill of offering them none.

This was the call of a true warrior.

This was the glorious burden of a king.

But with the map changed and the cosmicrons hidden by the Gamemaster, the Crimson Castle was without magic. The next battle with the Modfia would decide everything. He could not lose or every grand aspiration would be forfeit.

Too bad his pathetic team had forgotten how to fight.

"My lord, our lookouts say they have spotted the Earthborn spying on us here at the Crimson Castle," Bonegrin pleaded. "It is of the utmost urgency that we hear your new plan."

Malvexus gazed with contempt upon his once great teammate.

"Dear Bonegrin, is that doubt in your voice?"

"Absolutely not, my lord. I simply ask that you lead us into battle. With you by our side, we will defeat these upstarts and be done with them once and for all."

Malvexus tilted his chin as he considered the request. Occasionally, he glanced at the other Griefers who had joined Bonegrin in the lineup—Nightbane, Kadaver, Lackey. All of them had regenerated for the last time unless he could take control of the game engine himself.

"Bonegrin Banebreaker, you have been my ever-faithful servant, always willing to make any sacrifice."

"Of course, my lord, only ask and it shall be done."

"Tell me, what are the game's rules for becoming godlike?"

Nearby, several red skulks squealed with delight. They huddled in the dark corner, eyes fixed on Bonegrin and Malvexus. They seemed to sense that Malvexus's question signaled something quite dramatic was about to happen.

The Griefers on either side of Bonegrin shuddered, giving quick nervous glances, seemingly worried they were in the line of fire.

"Sire, you must eliminate at least four champions within four seconds."

"That's it," Malvexus said. He nodded approvingly as a devious smile curled up on his lips.

"Difficult for all, but not you, sire," Bonegrin said. His head hung low, staring at Malvexus's enchanted boots as if afraid to meet his master's gaze.

"Ah, you flatter me," Malvexus said, drawing Netherfang from its scabbard. He played with it, occasionally sticking an imaginary opponent with mock jabs. The tip of the sword trailed dark dreadmagic through the air like smoke. "Though I am the best of all the champions who've played this game and my skills are unmatched, becoming godlike is nearly impossible, even for me. That old goat, Gamemaster, rigged it that way. It adds an element of random drama to the game. In other words, becoming godlike doesn't take skill. It requires blind luck."

"Surely, you have both on your side, sire." Lackey Lickspittle groveled.

"No, you are wrong," Malvexus said, his anger rising. "Luck has abandoned us. Your pathetic defeat proves that."

He turned away, looking back out the window. He took a deep breath to calm himself and softened his voice.

"But here's my stroke of genius. I just realized there is a simple way to harness the godlike power." His voice rose, dripping with devious delight. "That is, if I'm *ruthless* enough."

Suddenly, before any of the Griefers could comprehend what was happening, Malvexus had run his sword straight through Bonegrin's chest. The thrust was so quick that instead of pain Bonegrin reacted with a look of pleasant surprise, as if his master were playing a joke.

Then Malvexus drove his hand through the open wound and pulled out Bonegrin's orcish heart. He presented it to his loyal ganker to inspect. The heart continued to beat.

Bonegrin groaned, then fell over dead.

"Killing my team is the quickest route to becoming godlike. And since you've each failed me and proven just how worthless you are, at least you can give me this."

Malvexus turned on Lackey, severing his little goblin head in one violent slash of his sword.

Kadaver screamed in horror and cast a powerful blast of ice magic, which Malvexus easily blocked. The storm of icy daggers ricocheted off his force field and rained back down, impaling Kadaver, draining her of all remaining health. She slumped to the ground with a look of shock on her face. Netherfang struck, lopping her head from her body.

Nightbane fell to her knees, begging for mercy. Malvexus threw his sword like a spear and her pleas turned to a bloodcurdling death-rattle. In seconds, the Griefers lay slaughtered on the ground.

As the bodies of his former teammates dematerialized for the final time, the screams, the blood, and the mercy not given filled Malvexus with inspiration.

Nothing would stop him now. Nothing. For he was a god now in every way that truly mattered here on the Battle Moon. He would kill the Earthborn. Kill the Gamemaster. Take control of the game engine and its power source, the Evercore. Then the infinite bounty of the Cosmic Alliance would be his.

PART VII
THE BATTLE ROYALE

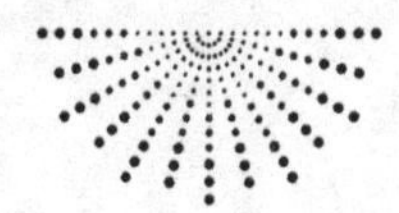

CHAPTER FIFTY-FIVE

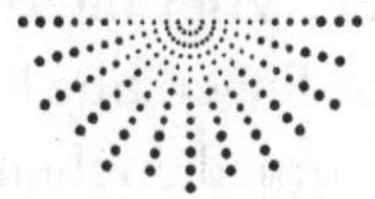

On the other side of the Battle Moon, back in the safety of the Gamemaster's Retreat, the Modfia's self-congratulatory celebration was going strong. For once in their long history, they were actually enjoying a victory. Of course, this was inextricably linked to Alex *allowing* himself to celebrate the moment. That good mood had infected everyone.

"More beer, bro!" Alex laughed, nudging Jed. "We need more beer!"

"I think you've had enough," Aspy laughed. "But, okay, here's a bit more." She held her thumb over the top of one bottle and shook it until it sprayed everyone.

"Aspy!" Miz giggled. "Can't believe your crazy ass just did that."

The two girls gave each other a bear hug.

"Maybe, just maybe, we are a good team after all," Jed laughed. "Good at drinking, at least!"

Chime!

Suddenly, the game intelligence made an unexpected and ominous announcement: *"An enemy has become godlike!"*

Everyone froze in stunned silence. They stared at each other, hoping their collective confusion would give birth to an explanation for this sudden, incomprehensible plot twist.

Miz was the first to break their silence. "How's that even possible?"

"There are only two ways that's possible," Aspy said. She gulped the rest of her drink and set her mug down. "One of the Griefers killed all of us."

"Well, that didn't happen," Alex interrupted.

Aspy was holding up one finger. She hadn't finished her thought.

"Or one of the Griefers turned on their own team."

"That mothertrucker Malvexus killed his own team," Jed said, throwing up his hands in disbelief. "That's ice cold, man. Ice cold!"

"If Malvexus is godlike," Genghis said, "he'll be coming for us next before the buff wears off."

"We need a new plan, fast," Alex said. "None of us can take him on individually. We'll have to strike together."

"Actually, that's what he's counting on," Aspy said. "If we attack as a group, we'll make ourselves more vulnerable. With godlike power, he just needs to hit the team hard enough to stun us, and then he can pick us off one by one. It'll be as easy as knocking over a house of cards. But I think there is a way we can take him down."

"How?" Miz wondered, nervously grabbing for her weapon.

"Remember the old breadcrumb maneuver?" Aspy asked.

"Yeah," Jed said. "Spread out. Wear the attacker down. Fight on the run, right?"

"Yes, exactly," Aspy said. "Make him use up the buff before he gets all of us. Then whoever's left can attack on a level playing field."

"Geez, man," Jed said, looking up. He had a glum expression on his face as he gazed out at the stars beyond the Battle Moon's thin atmosphere. "I was just about to be happy for a change."

"We still can be," Miz said, her voice warming the conversation with an uncharacteristically compassionate tone. She brushed up behind Jed and nudged him in the shoulder. "Let's get rid of this asshat for killing our good vibe. Then we settle in to the longest extended party this floating rock's ever known."

Jed turned and gave her a half-hug. For a moment, it seemed he might break down. That triggered some buried emotion in Alex. He did his best to stuff it back down and took the last swig of beer left in his frosty mug.

Everyone circled around Aspy as she laid out the specifics of the new plan. When she suggested Alex's part, everyone gasped. But Alex quickly agreed. It was logical and if it worked, it would double their chances of taking Malvexus down.

"If we go now, we might have a chance," Aspy said, turning around. Her fingers danced above her head, activating the battle map. When it materialized, she pointed to the infected Mana Lake. "Our chain of breadcrumbs will lead Malvexus to this spot. Hopefully, when he arrives, he will be at his weakest."

"We need a fast travel spell," Alex said.

"My thoughts exactly," Genghis said. He twirled his wizard's staff and manifested a pair of dope-looking sneakers for each member of the team.

"Grail kicks for everyone. Slap them on, my friends. There's no reason we can't look good while spanking ass," Genghis said.

"Fiery coke whites, no way!" Jed yelled.

Miz was amazed. "Dang, son, I wanna keep these."

"Wait until you break 'em in!" Genghis gave her a thumbs up.

Genghis enjoyed their excitement as the team levitated off the ground—running as if they were on an invisible high-speed walkway. They tested the shoes, practicing what was possible. They cut along the ground, up the tree trunks, down branches, and literally ran through the air. Surely, this was a major enhancement that would allow them to rival Malvexus's intensified speed.

"Far out!" Jed yelled. He sped past the team so fast he was nothing but a blur.

After making sure the shoes would work, they reviewed the complete plan, then chose their places on the map. One by one, they would confront Malvexus. Alex and Luna would be the final breadcrumbs leading to the Mana Lake, hoping they might use the dreadmagic bog to their advantage.

"Are you sure this will work?" Miz asked Aspy.

"No, but it's the best idea I've come up with."

"Okay, I'll give Mal-*ass*-head a good reason to come here first," Miz said. "Aspy, you and Genghis wait for my signal flare. I'll hold the line here as long as I can."

Aspy looked at Miz with concern, but instead of saying something she leaned over and gave her friend a hug and a kiss on the cheek.

This shocked everyone.

"Be careful," Aspy said.

Miz waved and raced off.

Genghis took a drag on his pipe, shoved it back into his pocket, and headed out.

Jed donned his newest shadow-weave armor. Then, like a bolt of lightning, he shot from their presence toward his agreed upon spot.

Aspy waved to Alex and Luna and followed Jed.

"Now for my part of the plan," Alex said.

"The Decimator is nearly impossible to kill," Luna said, shaking her head.

"Believe me, I know," he said grimly. He thought about how being eaten by that hideous worm had started their whole adventure. "Unfortunately, *nearly impossible* is the only thing we've got."

CHAPTER FIFTY-SIX

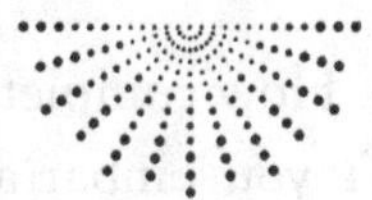

Miz climbed onto the Retreat's roof. She found the highest peak with the best view of the surrounding wilderness and took a defensive stance, gripping her magical bass. Her fingers danced along the strings, producing a steady, booming thump. It echoed out across the jungle toward the Crimson Castle.

In seconds, a dark figure appeared on the horizon. It was Malvexus flying on his winged mount—a Nightmare—a pegasus tortured with dreadmagic. The fearsome beast reared against its reins and galloped straight for Miz.

"Come and get some, you pathetic little skulk pimp!" Miz yelled.

She plucked the strings harder, producing the grungiest, nastiest bassline she'd ever played. A wall of sound erupted from her enchanted speakers and radiated out, creating a dangerous wave that seemed to grow in size and power with each note.

The mystical attack would shred anyone who approached it. Malvexus wouldn't know what hit him.

Alex couldn't believe it. This fight with the Decimator was more disastrous than the last one. Even with his higher level, real-world experience, and the enhanced power of the Starstone Armor and weapon set, he couldn't kill the monster.

"I know what you're thinking, little boy," the Decimator growled. "You're wondering why you came alone."

The bloated creature clacked his fangs and sprayed smelly green pus as it laughed.

"How arrogant you are. How completely stupid. No one can kill me by themselves. Haven't you embarrassed yourself in this cave already? Don't you know the rules of this game?"

"Fortunately, I don't," Alex muttered, "you big, ugly worm."

He rolled over, got back to his feet, took a new defensive stance, and raised his sword.

"Why don't you come teach me!"

Miz raised her bass just as Malvexus swung Netherfang. The block was perfect, but he was so powerful that the resulting explosion propelled her through the air. She slammed into a nearby tree and crumpled to the ground.

Despite her valiant effort, she was hopelessly outmatched because of his enhanced godlike power.

Using her last bit of strength, she raised the end of her bass. A magical flare burst from it and sailed high into the sky, exploding like a firework.

Hopefully, Aspy would see it and understand.

Aspy saw Miz's signal, and panic wriggled down her spine. The flare shot high above the tree line, burst bright, and slowly twinkled out.

Miz had been the first tripwire, and this sign confirmed she was down for the count or, worse, had been killed.

Now, it was time to step up and take on one of the most fearsome players the game had ever known. She was smart enough to know she was no match for Malvexus. He would plow through her with ease, but she hoped Miz had taken him down a peg and prayed she could do the same.

The godlike buff was a finite power, so any reduction in his mana and health bars would be important during the last battle.

She had to make her contribution count.

Suppressing her normal instinct to snipe from a safe distance, she grabbed the Highguard Claw and the rare arrow she'd never dared fire—the Celestial Spark—and stepped out into the clearing, making herself an easy target.

The power of the special arrow would surely make a dent in Malvexus's health bar. Could an accurate head shot take him down? She would try her best.

She thought about all that had happened here on the Battle Moon. It was beyond anything her imagination would've ever conceived. And now it seemed she was making her last stand.

The only thing that comforted her was the thought of her team. For the first time in their entire history, they were truly cooperating and following an actual plan.

Her plan.

That thought made her smile.

Now she would see if all her haranguing and arguing for cooperation made a difference. Could they take down this bloodthirsty maniac?

Malvexus was coming now, fast and strong. Death on a dark horse. She readied the Celestial Spark and aimed for his head.

Back in the Decimator's Cave, the situation was worse. Alex was on the verge of giving up. The Decimator was punishing him physically and emotionally.

"Such a pitiful pattern, Earthborn," the Decimator laughed. "You rush in to fight me, you suffer, you die, and then your team dies. How completely pathetic."

The evil worm swept its massive tail across the cave, hitting Alex solidly and sending him flying into the opposite side. He crashed into the slick cave and slid down into a heap.

"Yes, it's my fault," Alex said, spitting out some blood. "The team hates me, and I hate me. I've been completely selfish. I've put us all in this situation. If I had good sense, I'd give up."

He pushed himself up on one arm and crawled behind the nearest rock formation, praying it would give him some cover from the creature's fearsome claws. He wouldn't withstand another direct blow.

"Then go ahead, Titan, you ridiculous waste of armor. Give up!"

"I said, 'if I had good sense.' I don't! My bad decisions are making bad decisions!" Alex wrapped one hand around his aching ribs and found his chest was wet with blood. "Come on, worm, I still have enough health to make things a lot worse!"

Genghis laced his fingers, flexed his wrists, and twirled his hands in a circle. A magical viewing portal appeared at eye level, revealing images of Aspy fighting Malvexus, playing out the battle in real time.

"Come on, girl!" Genghis cheered. "Kick that maniac's butt."

Aspy stood her ground dodging blasts of dreadmagic.

Then the Celestial Spark was loose, and it rocketed skyward, expanding as it flew. When it reached the size of a missile, it hit Malvexus and detonated like a nuclear weapon.

It forced Genghis to shield his eyes.

The Nightmare mount disintegrated in the blast and Malvexus plummeted down, impacting the ground in an explosion of dust and dirt. But when he finally clawed his way out of the deep crater, he was laughing.

"Well met, Earthborn," Malvexus chuckled. "That tickled."

He stood up, dusted himself off, twirled Netherfang in his hand, and with sudden inhuman speed rushed across the field straight for Aspy.

Aspy fired a final barrage of arrows straight above her own head, a move that both horrified and amazed Genghis—a courageous act meant to sacrifice herself to weaken their foe.

The arrows rained down, creating a blinding explosion.

Genghis's viewing portal collapsed.

He turned, looking over the wilderness in the battle's direction. Surprised by his tears, he wiped them away, just as a single magical flare burst above the jungle canopy and twinkled away to nothing.

Luna Lifestealer fingered the control stick on her glider and banked left. The cannon fire burst like a fiery comet over the starboard wing, blackening the hull. She pushed the throttle and opened the flap to dive toward the Crimson Castle. Another blast of cannon fire shot past, heating the cockpit to an almost unbearable temperature.

Sweat erupted all over her body, dripping down her arm, making the controls harder to handle.

If her brother was to be stopped, eliminating the Crimson Castle was the only option. She wasn't even sure if that was possible.

Would some hidden mechanism created by the Gamemaster rebuild it immediately? Or could the entire system be destroyed if she hit it with a critical blow?

That was the hope anyway.

The glider swooped closer. She was now within yards of the castle's perimeter.

So far there was no resistance from the Griefers, which was amazing.

She had expected Bonegrin or Lackey to oppose her.

Even the red skulks seemed to be elsewhere.

That was when she saw another flare. The first, she had assumed, was from BadMiznus. Was this Aspy's signal? Was all now lost? Were any of her friends still alive?

Friends?

Could she even call them that?

She banked right, then left, avoiding another shot of cannon fire. She pulled the stick toward her. The glider packed with explosives had to hit the right tower. If it did, it would likely bring the castle down for good.

Unfortunately, there was only one way to make sure her aim was true. She'd have to hold the controls for as long as possible.

Inverting the glider, the craft took on a new trajectory, zooming straight for the room holding the regeneration pods.

Whatever she called the Earthborn, they deserved her help. She owed them that. And she always paid her debts—even if it cost her everything.

The sword swished through the air so dangerously close to Genghis's face he could smell the pungent oily magic that clung to the blade.

He rolled away, springing to his feet, his shoes now blazing with the speed of every arcane buff he'd been able to muster. He fled deep into the Quillodian Forest.

Near a grove of ancient trees, he cast a protection spell, drawing on the magic of the old timbers and the dryad spirits that inhabited the forest. A pleasant fairy melody erupted from the roots and vibrated along the limbs, swelling the leaves with green energy. Seconds later, a canopy of magic protection covered Genghis. He readied himself, knowing Malvexus was close.

"I can smell you, Earthborn," Malvexus growled. He was above the trees now, hovering as he inspected the force field.

Had it been any other situation, Genghis would've taken pride in the impressive magical spell, one of the oldest in the game. It both hid the conjurer and gave a substantial shield that would withstand almost any attack. But this wasn't a normal situation. Netherfang plunged down, splitting the largest of the ancient trees.

The dryads inside screamed with rage.

The spell partially collapsed, and Malvexus descended to the forest floor while Genghis readied his most powerful offensive spell.

"You've taken the name of a great warrior," Malvexus said, his tone dripping with condescension. "Strange choice, since you're the weakest of your pathetic pack. But I will admit your spellcasting is quite admirable."

"I'm not done yet!" Genghis yelled, throwing a white-hot plasma spear. It rocketed toward Malvexus like a missile.

But Malvexus spun and knocked it away with such ease it was as if he were swatting a fly. The spear tumbled backward out of control and exploded. Genghis was blasted so far into the woods he disappeared from view.

"Don't worry, healer. Soon your skills won't be needed," he said. "I'm about to make sure there's no one left to heal!"

Jed watched as the last flare from Genghis twinkled and faded away. He paced, circling the large rock he'd been resting on.

"You can fight, Prince Douche, just like you fight everyone, or you can try something different for a change."

He turned his head as if arguing with the imaginary version of himself who had posed that decision.

"But why should you suffer? Nobody on this team really cares about you."

He turned his head the opposite way.

"No, that's not true. They do. But if you use that spell, you won't have anything left to protect yourself."

His head ping-ponged back and forth as the internal argument heated up.

"Yeah, and that's going to hurt like hell!" the doubting side said.

"It's the right move," the nobler side said.

"Yeah, it really is."

Jed stopped pacing and pulled his two favorite daggers from their scabbards and crossed them in a ritual gesture. He did this again and then a third time. When the two blades touched for the final time, a black spark of shadow-weave magic erupted from the center of the intersection.

The spark elongated into a dark thread and swirled like a funnel cloud until it took shape. Jed moved around the nebulous cloud, pushing and pulling the magic with his gloved fingers.

Slowly but surely, the shadow energy took the shape of a horse—a horse that grew one horn from its head.

Suddenly, the dark unicorn neighed and stamped a hoof on the soil. Jed stroked the animal and whispered in its ear. The shadow-horn neighed again as if agreeing to the suggestion.

Then, with no warning, Jed smacked the magical animal on the rump. The horse reared on its hind legs then charged off into the jungle.

Jed smiled, watching it gallop away.

He took a step forward and collapsed.

"You just gave away all your mana, big dummy," Jed's doubting side said.

"Yep, it's in that unicorn," Jed said, smiling blissfully. "And here comes Mal-penis-head. Let's hope I've finally done something that matters!"

Both aspects laughed, ending the internal debate. And Jed's laughing continued, despite death descending like a dark angel.

ALEX SWUNG his sword with all his might. Simultaneously, the Decimator swung the tip of his long barbed tail. The two weapons met and the force of the impact blasted Alex backward into the cave wall once again. His sword clattered to the rocky floor and spun out of reach.

"Now, my dear boy, you will die again," the Decimator said. "Do you prefer I roast you before eating you or shall I just swallow you whole?"

"How about neither?" Alex said. "I'd rather cut you open, you fat bloat-hole."

Alex dove across the cave, reaching out for the hilt of his sword.

Another well-timed swipe of the Decimator's tail swatted at him. This time, Alex rolled out of the way and continued to scurry toward his weapon. For a very brief instance, he saw something else move near the cave's entrance.

"As I've said, if you wanted to defeat me, you shouldn't have come alone," the Decimator roared. The massive beast jumped high and slammed his full weight down, pinning Alex in place.

"I never said I was alone!" Alex sputtered, keeping his eye on the cave's entrance.

The Decimator, catching on, turned to face the unexpected threat.

Jed's unicorn charged out of the cave's shadows at a full gallop. Before the Decimator could move, the unicorn rammed his long sharp horn into the great snake's soft underbelly. The Decimator roared as he was impaled, and clawed at his attacker while the horn sank deeper into his guts.

"Ah, no," the Decimator moaned. "This is going to hurt really, *really* bad!"

Alex slipped out from under the Decimator and dove for cover behind a large row of stalagmites. Jed's unicorn flared with magical energy and exploded like a grenade.

When Alex looked again, the green and blue goo of the Decimator's guts covered everything in sight. He stood up, retrieved his sword, sheathed it, and walked over to the center of the cave to examine the remains of his dead enemy.

Suddenly, a portal opened above him. A cloud formed, and a bolt of magic struck him like lightning, doubling all his powers, and pushing his health and mana into overdrive.

"Congratulations, Champion," the game intelligence said. *"You have received the Aura of Decimation, one of the most powerful buffs in the game!"*

Alex felt another form of magic spread through his body.

Gratitude.

He thought about each of his teammates, especially their last moments laughing together at Gamemaster's home. Then he thought about Jed, hoping he was okay.

He spun in a circle, looking for any sign of the shadow-horn. The only thing left was its strange antler, which rolled across the cave floor toward Alex as if the spell was still in play.

Alex picked it up and examined it, then heard a familiar voice reverberating from inside like the ocean waves might echo from a seashell.

"Get ready, man," Jed said. "Malvexus is coming your way. Make sure you give him hell. And win this one for the Modfia!"

CHAPTER FIFTY-SEVEN

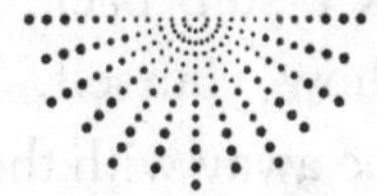

The former Mana Lake that had once been the joy of so many creatures—and a principal source of magic for the northern wilderness—was now a horrible place that offended all the senses. Starlight revealed the once pristine reservoir was an ink-colored marshy bog. Pungent swamp gas bubbled up from the goo along with the murmurs and moans of the undead imprisoned below the corrupted waters.

Still, the champion maintained her position, hiding behind a stand of overgrown reeds. From here, she could see both the more verdant hills in the distance and the well-worn path leading down to the bog. It was the highest ground the swamp offered and the best place to make her final stand.

Without warning, the game intelligence spoke.

"A champion has acquired the Decimator buff."

Before she could celebrate this news, a new sound boomed overhead, and a crimson-colored comet burned across the sky. A sonic boom exploded when it passed. The comet then corrected course, zigging and zagging over the bog as if searching for something.

Finally, it plummeted to the shore with such tremendous force that all the black sand was melted into volcanic glass.

"Where are you, Titan?" Malvexus called, stepping out of the comet's smoking crater. "I can sense a champion's energy here. Don't be a coward. Come out and face me."

"You'll find no cowards here, brother," Luna Lifestealer said, stepping out to face him. "Only your just reward—death and doom!"

Malvexus startled, took a step back, then shook his head as if disgusted. "Finally, you show yourself. But way too late. Surely you've guessed that I've done away with the old team."

"No desire to share the glory?" Luna sneered. "Is that it?"

"Far from it, dear sister," Malvexus said, clutching his hand to his chest as if her insult had wounded him. "You are my blood. My family. When I kill you, I promise to immortalize you as one of the best ever conquered!"

Malvexus leapt skyward. Luna did the same, and they crashed into each other.

His first punch felt as if it might knock Luna's head loose. The second one felt as if some strange god had dropped a mountain on her. She rocketed down to the ground and crashed into the sandy shore.

Malvexus flew down and hovered over her. "You could have shared in this honor. Helped me kill the cosmomancer. Freed our people for all time. Now you're nothing but a stepping stone. My greatest victory made possible by my greatest regret."

"But, brother . . . I'm not here to fight you . . ." Luna spurted, the rest of her words fading to a whisper.

Malvexus turned his head, listening intently. He floated closer, lowering himself within inches of her. Luna couldn't move.

"What was that, sister?" Malvexus laughed. "Not here to fight? Then why are you here?"

Luna opened her eyes and sat up. "I'm the bait!"

Titan exploded from the bog with a force field of green mystical energy shimmering around him. Shocked, Malvexus turned to face his new foe.

But Luna was ready for that, kicking him as hard as possible. The impact threw Malvexus to the ground, where he lay sprawled on the edge of the bog. His face was only inches from the blackest mud.

Titan flew forward, creating a large enough ripple in the bog that a decent sized wave of dread-goop splashed up and over Malvexus. The dangerous magic seemed to be alive, wrapping hundreds of its strange black tentacles around him.

He cried out as if he were being burned. He tried to stand and shake it off, but it was a futile attempt. Soon, Malvexus was completely cocooned in it. Alex could hear it sizzling as it burned into his skin.

"Ouch," Alex winced in sympathy. "That has to hurt."

As if to confirm Alex's theory, Malvexus screamed again.

Meanwhile, the mass of goo worked on pulling Malvexus into the bog. Long black tendrils shot out, methodically dragging Malvexus toward its depths.

"Using my sister as bait," Malvexus sneered. Suppressing his pain made him work for each word. "You have the same drive to win that I do, Titan. You'll do anything to strike the killing blow, won't you?"

Concentrating all his remaining power, Malvexus punched through the goop, freeing one hand and then a leg, giving him enough leverage to lunge for Alex. But Alex was watching carefully and side-stepped the attack.

Malvexus tumbled past, and as he did, Luna threw her sickle and chain. With one tremendous yank, the sickle's blade sank into Malvexus's stomach. With another hard jerk, the sickle completely impaled him. The curved blade jutted out of his back, giving him the appearance of a fish caught on a hook.

As Malvexus struggled to free himself, Alex attacked, attempting to take an arm. The clang of Malvexus's sword blocked the blow. But Alex swung again, and this time it found its mark. The hand holding

Netherfang was severed, and both the hand and the sword tumbled into the bog, falling below the dark water.

Meanwhile, Luna had wrapped one end of her chain around a massive boulder. When she was sure it was secure, she karate-kicked the giant rock, sending it tumbling down the hill, straight into the heart of the bog. The boulder dropped like an anchor, pulling everything but Malvexus's head down under the infected water.

"Honestly, you look so much better in black," Alex sneered.

"I'm going to kill you!" Malvexus shouted.

"Not if *they* kill you first," Alex replied.

All of Malvexus's undead victims schooled around him like sharks smelling blood. The most vicious ones grabbed and clawed at their old foe while the others moaned in pain or screeched in delight.

"*Finally . . . we . . . have . . . our . . . revenge!*"

Luna stepped to the edge of the bog. "I tried to warn you, brother," she said, shaking her head in pity. "Your viciousness would have consequences. Who will show you mercy after what you've done?"

Malvexus attempted to say something but choked on the black goo. He coughed and spit, trying to free himself from the muck, but it was impossible now because a seemingly endless number of hands had found him. Slowly but surely, they pulled him under, drowning him in the dreadmagic.

"I can't watch this," she said, too heartsick to look.

Alex stepped up beside her.

"Don't worry, I'll watch for all of us."

The bog boiled as if a school of starving piranha were feeding for the first time, and a dull crimson glow illuminated the frenzy as it sank to the bottom of the bog, finally out of sight.

Alex, satisfied that Malvexus was gone, turned away. Luna put her arm around him to steady herself, and the two wounded heroes pointed themselves east and limped away into the dark wilderness.

PART VIII
THE DREADHORDE

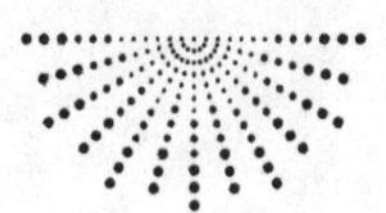

CHAPTER FIFTY-EIGHT

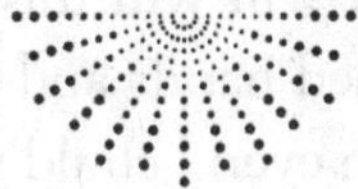

Unbeknownst to Luna and Alex, the bog was undergoing a most unexpected transformation as Malvexus's former victims encircled him, feeding off his residual godlike power. In only a matter of minutes, the brackish pond looked as if it had suffered a withering drought. Almost all the water had receded, leaving nothing but the tar-stained sand and rocks that had once hidden below the surface.

But this unfamiliar landscape was inconsequential compared to the host of undead creatures that remained. Angry champions and vicious monsters animated by the godlike magic they'd absorbed from Malvexus stumbled around in the muck, growling, groaning, and howling for revenge.

Having been drained of all mana, and with only the tiniest sliver of health, Malvexus pulled his body across the muddy bog, clawing his way back to the shore. All his beauty and glory had been stripped from him. What remained was blackened skin stretched tight over a bony frame—a pitiful creature that looked like a living skeleton.

Alex and Luna, who heard the horrible shrieks, came racing back and saw the army of undead champions and monsters, drunk off their newfound power, milling about. The creatures roared and screamed as if still in pain. A murderous look filled their eyes.

Alex felt someone had punched him in the gut. He couldn't breathe, couldn't think. That this could happen was a complete shock. He didn't understand how, but it seemed Malvexus had exploited another bug in the game. Their victory had been premature. And worse, it may have created another disastrous situation.

"One way or another, I will win this!" Malvexus clawed at the oily mud with his mummified hands and laughed maniacally. "Now you'll die more horribly than even I could've imagined."

Alex stared at Luna, who had tears in her eyes. Before he could say a word, she grabbed Alex's sword, leapt into the air, and attacked Malvexus again, driving the sword through his back and through his heart. His health bar went to zero.

But now they had a bigger problem.

This strange collection of monsters seemed to be of one mind and determined to find another source of magic to feed upon. All undead eyes looked at Alex and Luna. But, finding no inspiration there, they turned and stared at each other.

CHAPTER FIFTY-NINE

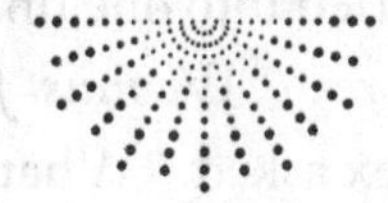

Alex and Luna watched as the mass of undead creatures squirmed around each other like a swarm of confused ants, unsure what to do with their newfound hunger.

Empowered by the dreadmagic, the strange mob crowded closer and closer together until they congealed into a mass of flesh. This new monstrosity assimilated everything into one chimeric creature. Its freakish shape seemed to shift as it moved, arms becoming tentacles, bones morphing into hundreds of fang-filled mouths, and heads turning into large bloodshot eyes.

Its terrifying form changed, mimicking the face of Malvexus. Eyes scanned the surroundings with murderous purpose, as if searching for someone or something to feed upon. Another part of the undead swarm formed a giant hand and pointed to the east. A horde mouth opened and screamed, having found its target.

"I've never seen this kind of magic," Luna said, holding her hands to her face. "What kind of corruption is this?"

"I don't know," Alex said, his hand gripping his sword.

"Malvexus's evil. It's infected them. The godlike buff transferred to the horde."

"Or he's exploited some bug in the game. Controlling all of them at once."

"Or they're controlling him?"

"I don't know what to make of this, but it seems to be searching for something. Look!"

Alex pointed as the swarm's central throng propelled itself forward using its new tentacles, blabbering in every alien tongue until the cacophony of words settled into one unified voice.

"*Feed . . . Feed on the core . . . We must feed on the Evercore!*"

"Feed on the core?" Alex asked. "What does that even mean?"

"Bloody blades, only my brother's twisted mind would think of that," she gasped, raising a hand to her mouth.

"Think of what?" Alex asked, grabbing her shoulder.

"The Evercore is the power source for the game engine and the Battle Moon. If this horde consumes it, everyone and everything will be destroyed!"

CHAPTER SIXTY

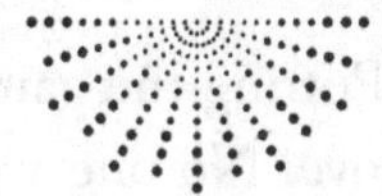

Luckily, their magical sneakers, albeit a bit scuffed, were still working. Luna flew alongside Alex, staying out of attack range of the monster but following closely behind.

Neither Luna nor Alex had ever seen anything like this before—not even the lore said anything about such a creature. The horrific monster was a gigantic malformed starfish mowing down the wilderness like a living buzz saw, jonesing for the one power source that was surely off limits.

Luna was certain her brother's demented mind had mixed with his dark magic and infected the *Dreadhorde*, as she called it.

Alex agreed both the name and her theories about its origins were reasonable. The monster seemed intent on killing or assimilating every living creature in its reach and destroying everything that got in its way.

"It's moving like it smells the Evercore," Alex said.

"Yes, but where on the moon is that?"

He debated whether the horde might be headed for one of the two castles, but its movement toward the center of the map said otherwise.

"The Decimator's Cave," Luna suggested, answering her own question. "It's long been rumored the cosmomancers built the game engine under that cave."

Of course, that made sense.

The Decimator was the most powerful monster on the Battle Moon. It was the perfect guardian. And the Mana Well penetrated down deep below its cave into what the game lore called the UnderRealm.

Yes, that had to be it. Putting the game engine underneath that cave would be a genius move. No one would dare disturb it. That cave was one of the most dangerous places in all the Battle Moon. Not only did the Decimator live there, but it was full of other deadly creatures, like that nasty colony of cave blights. Alex had died there countless times before even cracking open the Mana Well. He couldn't imagine making his way into the UnderRealm. Surely no living champion ever had, thus anything built in that place would remain hidden.

The Decimator's Cave was in the approximate center of the map. They needed to follow Deadman's Road to where the Regolith River curved north, avoiding a perilous chasm that cut down south into the jungle portion of the wilderness. The cave hid in the thick overgrowth on the east bank of the river.

Alex looked at the map and noticed that one could draw a straight line from the Decimator's Cave to the Gamemaster's Retreat in the North Wilds. Was this placement on purpose? Did one of the Gamemaster's secret passages connect his home to the game engine? Another reasonable guess.

The more time passed, the more accurate their guess seemed. Soon they were in sight of the Regolith River. The Dreadhorde cut across Deadman's Road, down into the jungle chasm, and stopped on the east bank opposite the notorious cave.

Alex and Luna landed on a hill overlooking the action.

As a Gladiatorian warrior, Luna was always equipped with rally markers. "Loci Convium!" she shouted, staking the ground with one.

A brilliant sapphire beacon exploded skyward like a geyser of light. The bright beam pulsed in a steady rhythm, signaling all nearby allies to rally to their location.

If the other Modfia team members were alive, they were no doubt suffering from regeneration sickness, having just respawned for the very last time.

At least, that was the hope. It had never been a surety there was enough magic left in the Sapphire Sanctum.

With a desperate heart, Alex scanned the sky, looking for any sign of his friends. After several long minutes, he saw movement on the horizon. Miz was the first to appear, followed by Aspy and Genghis. Finally, Jed arrived, riding the Darkblood Dragon. Alex screamed with joy like he'd never screamed before.

When the Sparkles Modfia reunited at the rally point, a joyous celebration full of hugs and high fives began.

"I can't believe we did it," Aspy said, reaching out to hug Jed.

"I'm just happy we're alive," Jed laughed. He ruffled Genghis's hair.

"Bring your messy asses in here. I need to get codependent for a few seconds." Miz squeezed Jed and Alex into a group hug with Aspy and Genghis squished in the center.

Even Luna got her share of high fives and handshakes.

They were alive and victorious. Malvexus and the dreadful Griefers were gone. And they deserved a helluva party. But the celebration would have to wait. The Dreadhorde was crossing the river to attack the Decimator's Cave.

Since the team had the high ground and sufficient cover, they could watch as the horde rose on strangely formed wings and swirled like a funnel cloud above the cave.

When the creature's twirling had reached peak momentum, it formed a singular, monstrous claw that stabbed down like a spear.

The resulting explosion destroyed most of the cave and part of the cliff. The shockwave flung the Modfia to the ground.

As the debris cloud cleared, Alex could see the Mana Well had been obliterated and pieces of the golden skull seal were strewn across a swath of the jungle. The strike had done its job.

"Look, I know it's hard to see but I think that's the game engine," Aspy said, pointing down into the exposed UnderRealm.

Using his enchanted spyglass, Alex took a closer look. He immediately agreed with Aspy's assessment. What he saw reminded him of the model he'd admired in the Gamemaster's Retreat.

The engine had a million magical gears, levers, and rings that ticked and chimed like an antique grandfather clock. Giant silver dials with numerous rings embossed with strange alien symbols, runes, and numbers spun both clockwise and counterclockwise.

In the center of the engine was a boulder-sized golden crystal, glowing like a tiny star. It was obvious from the way the magic energy pulsed that this crystal was the power source—the Evercore.

The cosmomancers had constructed a massively thick retainer wall to protect all of this—the shape of which suggested a nuclear power plant.

Unfortunately, this protective shield was now cracked open so that Alex could easily see the game engine and the Evercore inside. He wasn't the only one who saw it.

"*Feed . . . feed on the core . . . We must feed on the Evercore!*"

The Dreadhorde had found its main target.

CHAPTER SIXTY-ONE

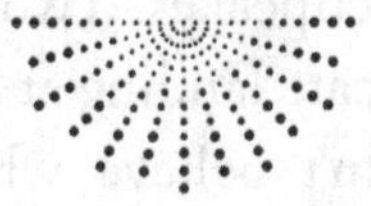

As the team discussed how to stop the Dreadhorde, something else was happening overhead. Lightning flashed and thunder boomed, and the sky fractured, opening a new Starway portal.

Alex braced himself, wondering what new monsters this wormhole might reveal, until a very familiar group flew through the opening.

Luna tensed, ready for more fighting, but Alex laughed. He recognized every crazy-looking person. Some rode winged creatures, others were using magical artifacts or spells to fly.

It was the Creep Cannibals in all their obscene glory.

Letch, Starminx, Deadlast, Pixel, and Vertigo.

Though he had hated their Korean rivals with a passion only days prior, he now welcomed them like divine angels coming to the rescue.

They circled around the portal, which flashed like lightning each time a new player teleported through.

"The Creep Cannibals!" Jed laughed, delighted beyond belief. "No freaking way!"

"Cannibals?" Luna asked, raising an eyebrow. "Are they dangerous?"

"Uh, under normal circumstances, yes," Alex chuckled, a wild smile covering his face.

The most surprising arrival was Sparkles Malone.

"Hello, little bitches!" he shouted.

He zoomed past on a magical flying motorcycle. Chump sat on the back, throwing some of their most dangerous fireworks at the horde. When the pair rocketed over Alex and Luna, Sparkles laughed and tossed down a pair of cupcakes. Two little parachutes deployed, bringing the treats to a delicate landing at Alex's feet.

Luna and Alex couldn't believe what they were seeing. She raised one to smell it. The gooey blue icing squeezed through her fingers, shocking her with a jolt of energy.

"They're enchanted," she marveled, licking at the blue frosting. "Who is this wizard?"

"That's Sparkles and these are the best Earthborn treats ever made," Alex said, stuffing one cupcake in his mouth.

Alex had never been so happy to see someone he hated. He raised his hand and gave the kid a thumbs up.

"Eat up!" Sparkles said, tossing a dozen more for good measure. "You and that hot bimbo need all the mana you can get. Your health bar is about as small as your . . . oh, never mind, just stuff your face, dude. Looks like you need it."

"I think I will kill that one," Luna said, pointing at Sparkles.

"Yeah, maybe later," Alex laughed.

Letch zoomed down, cut the engine on his high-tech jet pack, and landed. "Garcia, you've been holding out on us, man. A real Battle Moon. Wow! Mind if we join the fun?"

"We need all the backup we can get," Alex said, tossing the cupcake wrapper. "But this isn't a game, man. It's deadly serious. We must stop that thing!"

Alex pointed at the undead horde.

"Evil chaotic, dude!" Letch said.

Starminx, Deadlast, Pixel, and Vertigo landed beside him.

"You have no idea," Alex said, offering a fist bump to all the Creeps. "So you guys came to help?"

"Yeah, man. Don't ask me how we got here. It was a blur. But once we landed in the training arena, some creepy gnome named Crane helped with weapons and training. He said to tell you he'd had a change of heart."

Alex couldn't believe it. "You sure you guys are up for this?"

"Heck, yeah." Letch slapped Alex on the back. "Do we look like noobs or what?"

Aspy stepped between the two boys.

"We're glad you guys are here, and we appreciate the enthusiasm, but we can't screw this up. So, drop the ego and listen."

She explained everything that had happened over the last few days, hitting the most important points and ending with their theories about the Dreadhorde. When she finished, the harsh realities of their situation had appropriately tempered the mood of their reinforcements.

Everyone agreed on the basic plan and the talk turned to the next steps.

"Look at that wall around the engine. We have to hold the line down there," Miz said, stepping up on a nearby boulder. "One of the magic users needs to set up a force field around the engine. I'll take all the tanks with me down to the river's edge."

She pointed to the Regolith that snaked through this portion of the jungle.

"Who has alchemical abilities?" Aspy shouted. "Pixel, transmute that water to something more deadly. This thing won't have vision on its flank, so we'll have the advantage to start."

Miz got into position and produced a protection totem, then stuck it in the ground behind her. The magic would enhance their force's efforts while she defended the line.

Jed said, "Focus like we're defending our cornerstone. We need to break their line. Better we hammer one spot and maintain pressure."

"Oh, shizzle, what are those things?" Vertigo asked, pointing to the west.

It seemed a million skulks had turned up. Blue ones from the Sapphire Sanctum had covered the east side of the mountain, while red ones covered the west side. Despite normally being at war, they greeted each other with waves and gleeful chattering.

Each clan sent a representative to talk with Alex, who they guessed was the leader of the war effort. One larger blue wizard spoke in Skulk. Alex didn't know what he was saying. He shrugged and turned to Jed for help.

"He says Luna's rally marker drew them. They are here to help save the Battle Moon."

Alex climbed on the tallest rock and the remaining champions gathered around. A hush fell over the crowd. Red skulks and blue skulks mingled side by side. So familiar they were with taking orders that they looked up expectantly at Alex as if he might be their new master.

"I know none of you have ever been given the credit you deserve. But all of that changes today. Today, the skulks matter more than anyone!"

A massive cheer erupted from the crowd.

"Our foe intends to destroy not only the game engine . . ." Alex said, pointing down at the Dreadhorde, ". . .but the entire Battle Moon!"

The skulks booed.

"If that monster consumes the Evercore, we all die. No respawn. No regeneration. It's game over. Forever."

The skulks all gasped, looking back and forth at each other. Their murmuring rose to a dull roar.

"The cosmomancers built the game engine below the Decimator's Cave. So this is where we make our last stand," Alex said. "I know I ask a lot of you. This next battle may be the hardest one you've ever fought—but it's also the most important. Help us and we will be indebted to you, as your champions."

The skulks cheered and, knowing their duty all too well, turned from the gathering and marched off to do battle.

Now it was time for the champions to do the same.

PART IX
THE LAST STAND

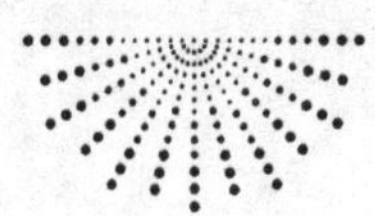

CHAPTER SIXTY-TWO

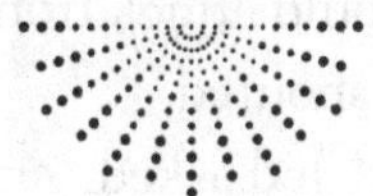

As they had for ages before, the skulks led the players into battle. First, they formed a defensive line along the retainer wall, then created a protective pocket for those champions with ranged weapons, like Aspy, Deadlast, and Pixel.

Most of the skulks formed battalions to attack the outer edge of the advancing horde. With both red and blue standing side by side, it was reminiscent of an American flag going into battle.

The skulks fought with their normal fearlessness and resiliency, but the horde viciously mowed them down. Even with the added support of the champions attacking from the air, the horde somehow advanced.

After a long time of fighting—and when two-thirds of the skulks were dead and gone—Alex, Luna, Sparkles, and the rest of the Modfia and the Creep Cannibals regrouped on the edge of the ridge overlooking the retainer wall.

"We're taking too much damage," Letch said. "I'm not sure we can stop that thing."

"We don't have a choice. We have to or we're all dead!" Alex argued.

"But look at that health bar!" Jed yelled. "We've barely made a dent."

"Its defenses are too tough," Miz said, shaking her head. "Even at my strongest, I couldn't break through into the center of that."

"The center," Aspy said, raising her finger in the air. "That's it. This thing is like a storm, like a magical hurricane full of undead champions and monsters. But every storm has a center. If we could get in the middle of it, we could attack from the inside out."

"That's brilliant," Alex shouted.

"So, how do we do this?" Jed asked.

Genghis smiled. "A hammer throw special?"

"Yes, that's it," Alex agreed. "A hammer throw special!"

"What the heck is a hammer throw?" Sparkles asked.

"Just the most iconic champion tag-team move ever conceived," Genghis said.

"One champion, always the strongest of the team, throws the smallest but deadliest member into the center of a battle," Alex explained.

Aspy raised a finger. "Statistically, if it's a bullseye shot, the impact does massive damage, but it also stuns the enemy for several seconds, drops all shields to zero, and allows for even more up-close injury that rapidly degrades the opponents even if they are buffed or being assisted by a healer."

"Exactly what she said." Genghis winked at Aspy.

Aspy smiled and added. "But the throw has to be dead-on accurate, otherwise it is instant death for the one attempting the throw."

"But even if we threw a champion into the center of the horde, they wouldn't last a minute," Luna said.

"They would if they had support," Aspy replied.

"No one can support a fighter who's inside that thing," Luna argued.

"That's why the healer and the fighter—Genghis and Alex—must go in together. We hammer throw both as a team. Once inside, Alex can lay waste while Genghis protects and heals," Aspy said, crossing her arms as if resting her case.

There was no argument. The plan would be genius if it worked. But *would* it work?

LUNA STEPPED up into position while Alex and Genghis each tied on a fresh pair of enchanted sneakers.

"Grab the end of my chain," she said.

Alex took hold of a long length of it, then wrapped it around his armored forearm, cinching it as tightly as possible. Genghis jumped onto his friend's back for a piggyback ride.

Letch zoomed by on a winged dactylbeast. "We'll set 'em up. You take them out."

"You got it!" Alex shouted, throwing up a fist in solidarity.

"Eye of the Storm maneuver!" Pixel yelled, pointing to the middle of the Dreadhorde.

The Cannibals zoomed up into the sky, dropping dozens of magical Molotov cocktails, burning back the creatures, and clearing a space in the center of the monster mass.

The Creep Cannibals made a rapid descent, landed back near the engine's retainer wall, then formed a defensive line so that they might fight shoulder to shoulder.

Jed was next. He wrapped his shadow-weave cloak around the two boys, then invoked a binding spell that enveloped Alex and Genghis in the enchanted garment.

"Ready?" Luna asked.

Both Alex and Genghis nodded.

"One hammer throw special coming up!" Luna shouted. "May you crush our enemies to bone and ash!"

Genghis looked at Alex and laughed.

"Man, your girlfriend is so intense. I love it!"

Alex smiled. *Girlfriend, was that for real?* His heart thrilled at the thought.

Miz stepped up. "Give 'em hell, guys," she said, and swung her battle axe like a golf club, hitting them with the flat side, and the two boys shot out into the air.

Luna's chain whipped forward with a crack. At the peak of its arc, the chain tightened, and Luna spun them around. With each revolution, their speed and momentum increased until it was so fast Luna couldn't control it any longer and she released the chain.

Alex and Genghis flew forward, shooting out over the monster, arcing high into the air. When gravity caught hold, they plummeted, rocketing down into the center of the Dreadhorde like an artillery shell.

The ground exploded, and when their magical cocoon fell away, they found themselves on their backs in a crater about three feet deep. The hammer throw special had hit the target perfectly—literally dead center in the middle of all the action. A true bullseye.

They stood up in the hurricane's eye, with the undead swirling around them, still unaware of their presence. Now they could attack from within.

"Come on, brother," Genghis laughed. "Let's drink some tears!"

Alex laughed too as he twirled his sword and raised his shield. Maybe, just maybe, they might stop the horde after all.

Alex gave Genghis a fist bump, and said, "Let's do this."

Genghis nodded, then cast an impressive spell over the two of them.

As it enveloped them, the magic brushed Alex's skin with the lightest of touches, giving him a sort of buzz and the confidence that he was completely safe from any damage.

Alex spun into the nearest undead monster, lopping its head clean from its body. Genghis hovered nearby, completely focused on shielding both of them; at times, he assisted with his own kills while still maintaining a bubble of magical protection around them both.

It was a shame the two boys weren't competing in a tournament because they were playing the game like never before. No matter what champion or monster struck, Alex met them with skill. Weaving, dodging, and spinning, he shredded every attacker with exquisite precision.

Occasionally, they would hear or see one of the Creeps or Modfia fly above them. The combined effort meant they were now attacking on both the inside and outside of the horde, and the damage was making a serious dent in the health bar.

The situation that had been so dire only minutes ago now seemed manageable.

If they could keep this pace, it might force the horde to retreat, and they might save the game engine and the Evercore.

CHAPTER SIXTY-THREE

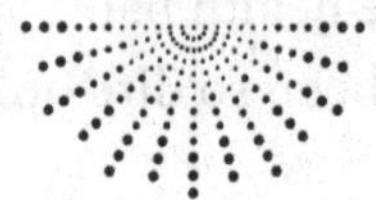

When its health and mana finally dropped into the red zone, the worried Dreadhorde turned its attention to stopping Alex and Genghis.

Despoiler the Murkfiend, whom they'd last seen in the arena, stepped out of the horde, holding his long corruption sword. It was a complete surprise to see him as part of the undead.

"Titan, we hate you most of all," Despoiler hissed, swinging his giant sword.

Alex raised his shield and attempted to rush the swamp monster.

At the same time, two long tentacles from an undead slimesquid wrapped around his ankles and pulled his legs out from under him. Alex tripped forward, losing his balance, and fell right into the path of Despoiler's blade.

The corruption sword sliced through his armor into his back. Alex screamed from the pain. His health bar dropped dangerously low. It was a devastating blow.

Meanwhile, the slimesquid had turned on Genghis, wrapping its poisonous tentacles around his arms, legs, and waist. All of Genghis's energy turned to his own defense. The shields around Alex dropped away, leaving him more exposed.

"You may have defeated me," Despoiler laughed, echoing Malvexus's voice and mannerisms. "But I will have the last word. The Evercore will be mine, and nothing will stop me!" Despoiler raised his sword high.

Suddenly, a new tentacle wrapped around Alex and pulled him back just as the corruption blade plunged down.

Alex looked behind him to see Genghis holding the other end. He'd killed the slimesquid and used one tentacle to save him, but Genghis was nearly out of mana, and so was Alex.

As the horde moved in, Genghis conjured one of his best special attacks, called The Holy Hand Grenade, and threw it at the weakest part of the horde. It detonated, blowing a hole through to the outside. The boys rushed through and tumbled onto a nearby grassy knoll. They were down for the count and nearly dead.

Team Modfia and the Creep Cannibals were huddled together in eyeshot of the knoll. They had cut the horde down to a quarter of its original size, but every player was wounded and near death.

It seemed Malvexus would win no matter what they tried. The Dreadhorde continued moving toward the Evercore.

CHAPTER SIXTY-FOUR

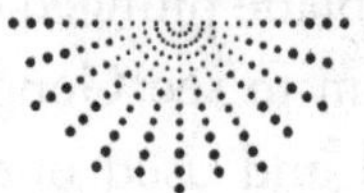

Alex and Genghis were down on their backs.

Both were dying—this time for real.

Alex felt the specter of panic hovering over him. In a few more seconds, it might possess him fully, and he would freak out and become of little help to himself or anyone else. He had to do something.

He looked at the horde. The health on the monster was solidly red—near the danger zone, but still strong enough to resist another attack. Genghis only had enough mana for one good spell. Alex had enough health for maybe one more attack, but the horde was sitting pretty with enough power to withstand both.

He glanced over his shoulder and could see the rest of his friends.

The Modfia and the Creep Cannibals were helping each other retreat, tending to each other's wounds, and arguing amongst themselves about what to do next.

They were all in the same position—only slivers of health left. Any additional damage could kill them, and it would be over.

There was only one option that made sense, but it was gut-wrenching. Could he do it? Would he do it?

Alex crawled as close to Genghis as he could get.

"Got any fight left in you, buddy?" he asked.

"Barely," Genghis groaned. He was holding his ribs and winced every time he moved. "How about you?"

"My mana's down to zero," Alex said. "Hardly enough health to stand up."

Genghis couldn't even raise his head. "I'm sorry, Alex. This is the end. We're not gonna win this one." Genghis looked at him sheepishly as if he was ashamed of his efforts during the battle, like he'd failed Alex. "I know winning is so important to you. I hate that it ends like this for you."

Alex immediately felt the crushing weight of shame. It was as if years of guilt might smother him. Tears welled in his eyes.

"For me?" Alex's eyes widened in disbelief. "Dude, you have it so wrong. That's not why I'm upset. No way, not now."

"It's okay, brother. You don't have to explain anything to me." Genghis looked away as if he might cry.

Alex grabbed Genghis by the arm. "Now listen to me, man. The only person who's failed during this whole adventure is me."

Genghis turned back to face his friend, the emotion obvious on his face.

"I've been the biggest jerk ever," Alex continued. "I get it now. I'm the one who screwed up. This game has been the only thing I've cared about. And I guess it's because winning is the only thing I've ever done that's mattered. I have zero other skills. Nobody cares about me when I'm not playing this game. This is all I've got."

Alex raised his hands then winced. He pulled something from his pocket, opened it, and put it in his mouth.

"At any rate, that's what I thought until I saw you so sick. I couldn't believe I was going to lose you. You're my best friend," he paused and looked away, wiping a few tears from his eyes. "At least, I hope you still are. And, well, you're the reason I still play. No one else celebrates me winning like you do." He patted Genghis on the shoulder. "By the way, thank you for being that kind of friend!"

"You don't have to thank me," Genghis wheezed, raising an unsteady hand to first wipe some of his own tears, then to give Alex a weak fist bump. "Bros forever, my man, bros forever."

"You're wrong though. I do need to thank you. I should've been a better friend to you. You deserved so much better."

Genghis held up one hand and Alex took it. They squeezed and Alex used the leverage to roll up on one elbow and pull himself closer to Genghis.

"I appreciate what you're saying, dude, but stop talking like that." Genghis looked at him with concern. "You're scaring me."

Alex decided he would start being a better friend right now by easing some of Genghis's anxiety. He plastered a goofy smile on his face as he dragged himself closer.

"Now, we don't have much time. So promise me you won't tell anyone I did this."

"Did what?"

"This."

Alex stretched his hand out over Genghis and invoked a mana draining spell. There wasn't much to drain but, thankfully, it was enough.

Both the Modfia and the Cannibals, now taking cover behind the retaining wall, clambered over each other, trying to see what the heck was going on with Alex and Genghis.

"What's happening? What are they doing?" Luna asked.

"Alex is—*oh no*. I think he's doing it again!" Miz shouted.

"What?" Jed asked.

Aspy shook her head. "He's stealing the rest of Genghis's mana!"

"He's lost his dang mind!" Miz shouted.

Everyone shielded their eyes. An explosion of light and power erupted between the two boys.

When they looked again, Alex was up, but Genghis was still down on his back.

Miz couldn't believe it and burst into tears. "I really thought he'd learned his lesson, that he might be different now."

"No, you see," Jed raged. "He only cares about himself."

"Oh my God," Aspy said, "we have to get over there. He's killing Genghis!"

From their vantage point, it seemed that Alex had absorbed all his friend's remaining magic and was now doing something even worse.

This was too much for everyone. They were defeated, and now they were being betrayed by one of their own. All hope drained from the group.

Alex could barely look Genghis in the eye as he drained his remaining mana. Genghis was speechless, dumbfounded by the sudden attack.

"I'm sorry about this, buddy," Alex said, hovering over the boy as Genghis's health bar ticked down to nothing. "But that spell isn't the worst of it. So really forgive me for what comes next. And please, please never tell anyone I did this, okay?"

Genghis, now panicked and extremely weak, tried to push Alex back.

"Did what?"

"This."

Alex bent over and licked Genghis's forehead.

Genghis was so surprised he laughed.

"You've gone completely bonkers, Garcia. Who's the high one now?"

Alex smiled, hooked one finger in his mouth, and pulled out a small translucent piece of wet paper.

"Sorry for the non-consensual tongue action, but I've lost all my spit. I've been sucking on this thing the whole time we've been talking."

He activated the temporary tattoo he'd gotten from the Gamemaster with the stolen mana, then he pressed it to Genghis's forehead, using one of his dirty thumbs. Next, he rubbed and massaged it until it was transferred and in place. Once the slick paper backing was off, he brushed it aside and blew air over the resulting tattoo.

It was a familiar image—the Wraith's Skull of Resurrection!

"What the heck, man?" Genghis said, gently touching his forehead. Alex cast a quick reflection spell to give him a look. "I appreciate the adornment. It's a gracious gift. But I don't really think this is the time to worry about decorating our skins."

Suddenly, golden light burst from the skull tattoo. Genghis stiffened as a bolt of magical energy surged through his body.

He grabbed Alex.

Alex grabbed him.

Genghis started convulsing as if something had electrocuted him. His health and mana dropped to zero.

"Now he's killed them both!" Jed slapped his forehead in exasperation.

"No, look. Something else is happening!" Aspy yelled.

Genghis rose from the ground. He hovered like a glowing angel above the battlefield, then he suddenly blasted Alex with a new healing spell.

"He's alive!" Miz yelled. "That beautiful blunt-smoking bastard. He's alive and higher than he's ever been!"

It was true. Genghis was literally glowing like the Evercore itself. He pivoted and flew straight to the rest of the team. He zoomed up and hovered over them while newly sprouted wings on his heavenly-white shoes flapped furiously.

"What's up, my sweet homies?"

Everyone cheered to see him alive.

Genghis had manifested the Wraith's Mark, which proved he had received the Wraith's Skull of Resurrection, a regeneration artifact made from an Evercore crystal. The item resurrected the user within five seconds of death, regenerating both health and mana to one hundred percent. It was one of the best artifacts a healer could get. The more mana the possessor spent in combat, the more his nearby allies were healed. It was the ultimate buff.

Genghis's character bars verified this. They were shining like brilliant emeralds, proving the Wraith's Skull had maxed out both his health and mana.

"We thought Alex had killed you, man!" Jed shouted.

"Alex?" Genghis shrugged. "No way, dude. That guy is our friend!"

Alex was indeed trying to be the best friend possible. He threw himself into the battle, attacking a fresh wave of the Dreadhorde, whooping and hollering as he went.

"He's fighting to save us!" Luna shouted, marveling.

Despite the obvious dangers, everyone cheered. Relief flooded over them, along with more tears and squeals and yells of happiness.

While they celebrated, Genghis folded his fingers, stirring the air as if seasoning a bowl of soup, slowly forming a molten ball of chakra energy. It was one of the most powerful regeneration spells he'd ever managed.

"You ready for some juice?!" Genghis asked.

Everyone cheered again.

"We don't have much time, so brace yourselves. This will tickle!"

A wave of refreshing magic shot from his hands and washed over the two teams. Instantly, their health and mana were maxed out.

Genghis, still hovering above them, turned toward the horde where Alex was plowing through the undead like a human weed whacker.

"Come on, guys. Let's melt some butts!"

The teams let out a collective battle cry and charged.

CHAPTER SIXTY-FIVE

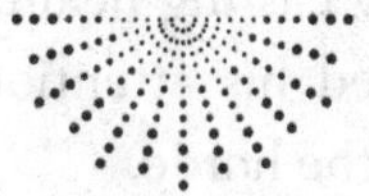

As the team fought, Genghis rose high above the battle, where he could easily track the movements of everyone he intended to support. His green eyes were wide with rapturous delight. All the negative effects of the dreadmagic had disappeared.

He was completely healed, but more than that he had somehow tapped into the Evercore itself. Through some strange magic, it seemed as if the core had possessed Genghis, embodying itself in one champion to help fight back against its dark enemy.

Genghis embraced the union.

The mind of the Evercore was wholly benevolent and, dare he say, worried for the champions; it was even compassionately empathetic toward the creatures trapped in the Dreadhorde's morass.

The Evercore wanted to save everyone.

Within his mind, Genghis heard a voice saying, "This is the real game of life, young man. One must figure out how to live fully while helping all other sentient beings do the same."

Genghis touched the tattoo that Alex had pasted to his forehead.

Surely, Alex could have used this power himself, but he had given it away. Why?

"Your friend made the right choice—a very creative and noble choice. Celebrate the sacrifice," the Evercore said, giving Genghis a new insight. "Share this power with your friends. For this is the greatest of the virtues: that a friend would lay his life down for the other."

Genghis smiled serenely.

Yes, this was everything he knew in his heart to be true and right.

He began methodically casting healing and buff spells upon his teammates. Then he turned his attention to Alex. His friend had fought back into the eye of the horde.

Taking careful aim, Genghis threw one of his best spells. The mystical energy missed Alex, glanced off the scaly back of some lizard-like creature, and dissipated into the ether.

Genghis tried again several more times.

But no matter how expertly he cast the spell, he couldn't reach Alex.

Thankfully, for the moment, Alex was fighting so well he didn't need the help, but a shudder of anxiety flowed through Genghis. It seemed both he and the Evercore felt concern for Alex. How long could he last?

Genghis forced his attention back on the other team members. They had to stay fully charged if the horde would be put down.

The cosmos depended on their victory. He prayed Alex could stay in the fight.

Meanwhile, Alex was lost in the dance of war. He'd never felt so clear-eyed, so focused. All his anxiety was gone. It seemed as if something had kicked his abilities into overdrive. He was making a sizable dent in the Dreadhorde by once again cutting from the inside out.

His teammates were making their own progress. The consciousness that had corrupted the horde was distracted by its outward defense and its unwavering desire to consume the Evercore. Alex was, in many ways, being ignored, but that didn't lessen the danger.

"This is for Miz!" he yelled "This is for Aspy!"

He spun around and faced an undead monster brandishing two battle axes. "This is for Jed! This is for Genghis! And this is for Luna!"

He fought on with a single-minded purpose—*save my friends*!

CHAPTER SIXTY-SIX

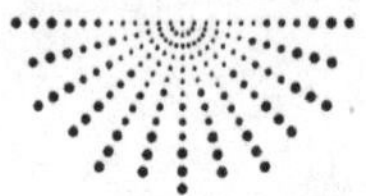

Unbeknownst to Alex, the two teams were also fighting the best they ever had. Having faced each other several times in competition play, they knew each other's tactics, and slowly but surely each team adapted to those eccentricities, becoming one larger team that seemed to maximize their skill in all the right ways.

"I can't stop this one!" Miz yelled. She'd lost the bladed head on her battle axe and her magical bass was mere splinters and completely useless.

Letch and Starminx zoomed in to help.

This freed Miz up to tank through the next layer of the horde.

And so it went.

Genghis flew overhead, channeling all his core-energy into the team.

Alex kept chopping from the inside out.

The Sparkles Modfia and the Creep Cannibals continued to trim the size of the monster until the creature seemed to sense its impending defeat.

Ever the cheat, the spirit of Malvexus seduced the horde to make one last massive push. The monster rose into the sky on a column of undead creatures, angled down, and threw itself like a spear toward the retaining wall. A tremendous explosion mushroomed up and the blast knocked most of the team to the ground. However, when the smoke disappeared, the result was clear. The horde had failed!

Miz, Aspy, Jed, and Genghis stood together, arms locked at the elbows. A glowing, glittering ball of energy shimmered around them, acting as an impenetrable shield.

The horde's spearhead had sunk several units into the team's magical cocoon and now, by some reverse magic, the Modfia was draining all the remaining power from the monster.

Within several seconds, the morass of undead creatures collapsed like a house of cards, littering the field with the shriveled remains of the now truly dead.

The residual dreadmagic filtered out of those remains like a doomed spirit, screaming in painful protest. Then it flew away like an angry ghost, disappearing in the dark sky.

When it was clear they'd won, Genghis lowered the shield, and the team cheered. Already standing together, they drew each other even closer in one massive team bear hug. Somehow and someway, they'd done it.

The game's fragile voice sputtered.

"Your enemy has been defeated!"

Another collective cheer that seemed to come from the Evercore itself roared across the Battle Moon.

CHAPTER SIXTY-SEVEN

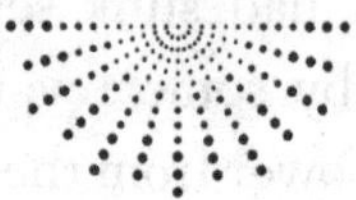

"Where is Alex?" Genghis asked, triggering a collective panic. Their teammate wasn't with them celebrating. He wasn't even on the battlefield—at least, nowhere nearby.

"Look, there!" Deadlast pointed. "Is that him?!"

In the far distance, at the tail end of the debris field, a pile of corpses lay in a gruesome stack. Alex's glowing Starstone Blade that had been thrust into the top of the pile rose majestically skyward, like a cross. Still glittering with magic, the sword's energy cast a light upon the face of their missing friend.

Alex lay on his back, sprawled on top of the pile—lifeless and unmoving.

"Oh no!" Luna yelled as she ran forward.

Genghis gathered the two teams in a bubble of energy and lifted them into the air, flying them to Alex's resting place.

When they landed at the foot of the pile, Miz and Aspy and Jed climbed to the top. The Creep Cannibals spaced themselves out to form a human chain so they could slowly and carefully move Alex down the pile and onto a clear patch of the grassy knoll.

"Alex, can you hear us?" Jed asked, resting his head on Alex's chest, desperately listening for a heartbeat.

"Oh no," Miz said, holding her hand to her mouth. "Look at his stats."

Both the mana and health bars were completely drained, devoid of even the slightest bit of energy.

"No, not like this!" Aspy cried. "It can't end like this!"

PART X
CHAMPIONS OF THE COSMOS

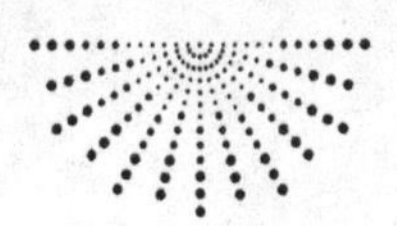

CHAPTER SIXTY-EIGHT

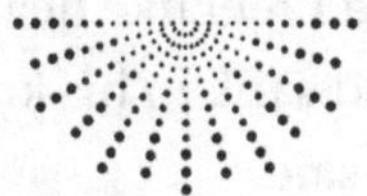

The feeble voice of the game engine made another announcement.

"Your teammate has become legendary!"

Alex's lifeless body shuddered, then levitated above the ground. It paused for a moment, hovering over the debris of the battlefield, then slowly floated past his teammates, into the nearby wilderness, and disappeared.

Luna Lifestealer stepped up next to Aspy.

"By the heart of the cosmos, no one in the game's long history has ever become legendary!"

"You mean, not until now," Aspy said, wiping tears off her cheek.

Luna nodded her head in agreement.

"Wow, Alex, you did it," Genghis muttered under his breath.

Jed put an arm around his shoulder. "Yeah, that crazy bastard really did it!"

The teams watched over the horizon, hoping against hope they might see some sign of Alex respawning in the dim sapphire halls of the Sanctum.

As the team continued to grieve, Alex rematerialized behind them. He tried to take a step forward, then stumbled and cursed. Everyone turned around, amazed.

"No freaking way!" Genghis cheered. "Alex, you're alive!"

"Uh, are you sure about that?" Alex asked, squinting at the surrounding faces. "Because I feel like death warmed over."

Alex stumbled again and sank to his knees.

"You look it too," Letch said.

Jed promptly hit Letch in the ribs to shut him up.

Then Genghis, Miz, Aspy, and Jed dogpiled on top of their friend like a pack of wild Rift Wolves, smothering him in a cacophony of hugs, laughs, screams, tears, and cheers.

"But how?" Alex asked, searching their faces for an answer.

His eyes landed on Luna's smile—her marvelous, incredible smile that shined like the cosmos itself.

"How am I alive?" he asked again. "I know I should be dead."

The Gamemaster appeared in a swirl of magic next to the team, then knelt down next to Alex. He reached out and stroked Alex's head affectionately.

"Quite simple, my brave champion," he said, offering a fatherly smile. "Legends never die!"

CHAPTER SIXTY-NINE

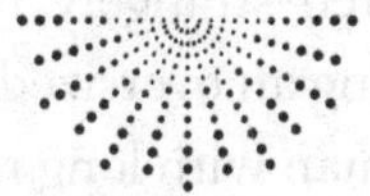

The only sign of life left in the horde was the champion who had started the whole debacle. Having dug himself from beneath the horde's remains, Malvexus, nothing more than a living skeleton now, struggled, clawing his way into a stand of ferns growing several yards from the edge of the battlefield.

As he reached out, grasping at the nearby tree roots, Luna stepped in front of him.

"Hello, brother."

Malvexus looked up, straining to respond, but found he didn't have the energy or power to do anything but stare helplessly at his sister.

"Thought you should know," Luna said, conjuring a last spell that produced a gleaming silver artifact with mystical runes carved along its outer rim, "you've finally won a prize no one else possesses."

The large ring opened along a hinge. Luna placed it around Malvexus's neck and clamped it shut. The runes flared with magic, and the collar tightened in place. A length of chain telescoped out of the manacle. Luna picked it up as if she were about to take her pet for a walk.

"The Silver Runestone Collar of Eternal Imprisonment," Luna said. "I knew it would fit you perfectly!"

Luna snapped her fingers and hundreds of tiny flags appeared holographically all over Malvexus, giving him the appearance of a porcupine. Luna snapped again, and the flags illuminated red with a resounding ding.

Suddenly, two young cosmomancers materialized on either side of Malvexus. They appeared strangely familiar. One was a rather short and plump man holding an oversized cup of pink Slurp-Ice, and the other was a tall skinny man with long red hair tied back in a ponytail who took his glasses off and cleaned them with his faded *Cosmic Champions* t-shirt.

"Slipstream76, at your service, Ms. Lifestealer. This is my co-mod, BeanFarts69," the tall moderator said in his surfer bro accent.

He waved a hand at his partner, then gave Luna a quick, bored glance.

"Did you call for a moderator?"

BeanFarts69 stared at Luna gulping his slushy loudly.

"Uh . . . yeah," Luna said, pointing down at Malvexus.

Suddenly recognizing who had been collared, they both showed immense interest.

"No way!" Slipstream76 pushed his glasses back on his nose.

BeanFarts69 dropped his giant cup and pointed excitedly at Malvexus. "Well, tickle my sweaty undercarriage. We've been trying to catch this troll for ages. He keeps changing his gamertag."

Slipstream76 crouched next to Malvexus, taking a closer look.

"Ouch, you don't look so hot, dude."

"This is the champion responsible for nearly destroying the entire Battle Moon, the game engine, and the Evercore itself," Luna said. "Please make sure you lock him up and throw away the key. Justice demands it!"

"Don't worry, with this many flags and that collar, he's never playing this game again," BeanFarts69 said. He produced a magical tablet and gave it a few taps, then he handed it to Slipstream76 for approval.

"Thanks for bringing this to our attention," Slipstream76 said, raising one finger high. "By the way, we're obligated to tell you we may need further information to close this case. If we do, we'll contact you in two business days."

"But don't worry," BeansFarts69 said, winking at Luna, "this banishment is a slam dunk."

BeansFarts69 handed Luna a roll of emporium tickets and patted her on the shoulder. Luna looked at him like he was crazy. He gave her a weak smile and stepped up next to Malvexus and Slipstream76.

"Come on, Skeletor," Slipstream76 said, taking the collar from Luna. "I'm afraid you've been banned for life."

"In other words," BeanFarts69 said, "game over, loser!"

A mystical portal opened behind the two moderators. They stepped through, pulling Malvexus along with them, and all three disappeared with a snap.

CHAPTER SEVENTY

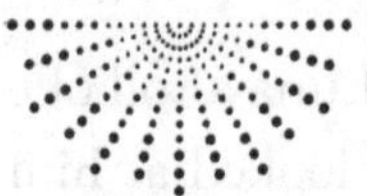

Two days later, the Battle Moon showed zero signs of the calamitous fight with Malvexus and the Dreadhorde. The Sapphire Sanctum gleamed in the early evening starlight, and at the opposite end of the long Deadman's Road, the Crimson Castle sparkled and flickered like a magical candle.

There was one notable change to the map: Gamemaster had constructed a gleaming stadium in the heart of the wilderness. It was filled to the brim with representatives of the Cosmic Alliance—humanoids and alien creatures of every shape and size. Banners of their favorite champions billowed in the evening breeze. The occasional crack of fireworks mixed with music and cheers as each of the alliance's most famous champions was presented before the crowd on a floating dais that hovered over the center of the field.

The Modfia and the Creep Cannibals were invited to the backstage of the dais, where they gathered in their teams and peered through the curtains at the stadium.

"This has to be the best party ever," Genghis declared, awe in his voice.

Everyone agreed.

"What's wrong with the beanpole?" Chump grunted and hooked his thumb at Letch.

Sparkles shrugged, not bothering to turn around. Those who looked had noticed something was off—Letch's hand was flickering in and out of existence.

"Whoa, dude. You're glitching!" Starminx shouted.

Her head phased in and out of reality.

"You too!" Letch pointed. "Oh man, that's totally weird!"

Suddenly, the phasing had spread like a virus to the entire Cannibal team, including Sparkles and Chump.

"It's not happening to the Modfia," Aspy pointed out. She shot a glance at Pixel, whose lower half was missing. "We seem to be immune."

"Garcia, is this your doing?" Sparkles demanded, half his face gone in a glitch. "As soon as my foot reappears, it's going straight up your . . ."

"No need to be alarmed, my young friends!"

Gamemaster appeared in a whoosh of magic. He raised both hands to calm the group. "This condition will be resolved momentarily and all will be put right."

"What's happening to them?" Miz asked.

"Is it some side effect of the dreadmagic?" Aspy wondered.

"No, I'm afraid this is my fault," Gamemaster said, placing a comforting hand on Vertigo's glitchy shoulder. "Allow me to explain."

"By all means," Sparkles snarked as his lower half vanished again.

"It's no surprise that during the last battle, my abilities were pushed to their limits. With the enormous number of enemies attacking the Evercore, I had only enough energy left for one powerful spell and used it on a very ancient one."

Aspy's eyes widened. "What's this spell called?"

"Summon Deus Ex Machina."

"Summon dude's macaroni?" Jed wondered.

"Close, child, something like that."

"Should I be impressed or not?" Jed laughed.

Gamemaster gave him a weak smile and continued. "Cosmomancers are only allowed to cast the spell once a universal cycle, which means roughly every millennium. The last time I did it, I nearly respawned myself."

"What exactly does it do?" Genghis asked.

"The spell conjures an unexpected solution to an unsolvable problem, but the cost is high, and the effect is completely unknown."

"So, that's how the Creep Cannibals and Sparkles got here," Alex concluded.

"Yes, it seems so," Gamemaster said.

"But why us?" Vertigo asked.

"For some reason, the Evercore felt you were the right team for that moment, perhaps because of your great friendship with Alex and the Modfia. The magic would not have chosen you otherwise."

"Er . . . well . . ." Deadlast stammered. "That's strange because the last time we were together, we were trying to kill each other."

Gamemaster laughed. "Ha! That proves it. No doubt you are a genuine family of friends. Only those who care deeply bicker so passionately."

"If you say so." Letch smiled, then shrugged his invisible shoulders. "I mean, I guess it's true. The respect has always been there, even though I would never tell Alex or the others. They're the best I've ever played. That's why I wanted my team to beat them so badly."

Gamemaster smiled. "Yes, you see, like magic, friendship takes many forms."

"So, what's up with this glitching?" Alex asked. "I'm sure they'd like their faces and bodies back in one piece."

Everyone with a visible head nodded in agreement.

"This effect is totally normal as the countdown on my spell approaches its final revolutions," Gamemaster said, waving off any concern. "In a few seconds, the spell's magic will fade and this glitching will be resolved."

"What the heck does that mean for us?" Pixel asked.

"You will return safely to the time and place from which you came. Unfortunately, you may not retain any memory of your visit to the Battle Moon."

"Dang, man. That sucks," Letch said. "I love it here!"

"Yes, I'm afraid it's not ideal," Gamemaster said, patting the boy on the shoulder. "But to sweeten that bitter pill, I offer you a magical reward, hoping your possession of such will eventually reawaken your memories of the great deeds you performed here, and most of all, our deep appreciation of your bravery."

Gamemaster waved his staff over the Cannibals as well as Chump and Sparkles. After stirring the air above them for several seconds, magic radiated out, caressing them gently like fingers. When the strange light faded, a golden tattoo adorned each of their wrists. Everyone stared curiously at the pulsing symbols.

"What is it?" Deadlast asked, rubbing the arcane mark.

"Your reward," Gamemaster said. "A special faction seal called Knights of the Cosmic Alliance."

"Oh, man, my mom is gonna freak," Pixel said. "She hates tattoos."

"This will not be visible to your mother, dear. But when needed, a faction seal will magically identify you as a special friend of the Cosmic Alliance. If and when a Starway is opened on Earth, the seal will trigger a summoning spell, putting you first in line to the Battle Moon."

Before anyone could say anything further, a countdown timer appeared holographically above the Cannibals, counting down from ten to zero seconds.

"Farewell, my friends, the alliance thanks you for your service!"

The Modfia waved to their friends, who were swept up in a mystical twirl of magic. They glitched magically one last time before disappearing.

"Wow, I hope they're okay," Miz said.

"They very much will be," Gamemaster said. "I guarantee it." He stepped forward and peeked between the curtains. "Now, my friends, please excuse me," he added, stepping through and onto the main stage. "Today's most important duties await!"

MOMENTS LATER, Gamemaster stood in the center of the floating dais. He addressed the stadium's audience, his face mirrored on a host of gigantic screens.

"Dear citizens of the Cosmic Alliance, the game engine is restored. The Evercore is out of danger, and the Battle Moon regenerated. The glorious tradition of our game has been saved!"

A raucous cheer burst from the crowd for several minutes.

"It is with immense gratitude that I present to you the players who made this possible—a team who, through their valiant efforts, showed our grand collective of unified worlds that the virtues our traditions revere, and our game reveals, still exist even in the darkest corners of the universe. Their bravery and camaraderie prove goodness continues to hold our cosmos together and can be found in the most unlikely of places."

A spotlight beamed down on the Sparkles Modfia, and they stepped out from behind the curtain, waving to the audience. The crowd roared with tremendous applause until the old cosmomancer raised his hands.

"In ages of old, when the Battle Moon was new, the cosmomancers had a cadre of elite protectors. As the eons passed, the need for such guardians diminished and the tradition faded into the shadows of memory. However, recent events have shown such warriors are needed once again. So today, I announce this tradition's restoration."

Gamemaster pointed his magical staff at Luna and the Modfia as new golden insignias appeared on their uniforms.

"Thus, I declare the foundation of the Cosmic Honor Guard. I have recruited these six champions you see before you for this commendation. Fate forged them in the most epic of battles, and henceforth, they will stand ready to protect the cosmos if such danger ever comes again."

This time, the eruption from the crowd was so thunderous, Alex wondered if the stadium might collapse in on itself.

While Alex and the team waved to the crowd, a parade of skulks holding brightly colored sparklers marched onto the stage and began a musical number that included a marvelous display of acrobatic choreography, musical instruments, and melodious lyrics that no one except Jed seemed to understand.

As the skulks entertained, the Modfia and Gamemaster huddled together near the back of the stage. Gamemaster leaned in to share more news.

"Because of your team's tremendous bravery in the face of certain death, we will invite the people of Earth into the Cosmic Alliance," he said.

Gamemaster then turned to Jed with a mysterious twinkle in his eyes.

"I hereby appoint you Jed Rivers as Earth's official Herald. It will be your job to recruit new Earthborn players for future contests. Will you accept a portal key in recognition of that honor?"

"Me?" Jed was flabbergasted. "Are you sure about that?"

Gamemaster waved a hand to produce the portal key and it hovered in front of Jed.

"I know of no one better than you young man, to find players who will honor the *rules* of the Battle Moon," Gamemaster said, winking at Jed. "Your loyalty to your friends was an unlikely inspiration to the rest of the team. Without your steadfastness, surely the team would have been lost."

Jed nodded his approval and held out his hand. The key spun as it magically descended into his palm and created a glowing tattoo.

"Wow, that's cool. Thank you!"

Gamemaster patted Jed on the shoulder and stepped down the line.

With a flourish of magic, he produced another portal key and gave it to Miz.

"What? Are you serious?" she asked. "Why me?"

Gamemaster pointed at Jed.

"I'm sure your friend will need some assistance as the new Herald. I can think of no one better to back him up. Plus, of all your team members, you seem to have the strongest connection to your birth-world. With the portal key, you'll be able to return home whenever you so desire."

Miz was on the verge of tears as she accepted it.

"One more thing for you, young lady," Gamemaster said.

With another flourish, the cosmomancer conjured a new magical bass guitar and handed it to Miz.

"I'm afraid part of the Cosmic Honor Guard's duties include ceremonial music. I hope you are up to the task. This fine instrument shall replace the one you lost in the battle. It is enchanted to ensure that it's indestructible and never goes out of tune."

Miz took the bass. "Heck yeah, I can handle that," she beamed.

Gamemaster patted her on the shoulder and moved on to Aspy, to whom he handed a small plastic card.

"What is this?" she asked

"Your brilliance saved the day, young lady. A growing mind, such as yours, needs all the nourishment it can get. To that end, I gift you with a card for my library. I've never given one out before. It entitles the holder to check out any item from my entire collection."

He winked at Aspy. She nodded her head in appreciation, marveling at the glimmering card.

"You know, cosmomancers sometimes take on apprentices, if you should ever be interested."

Aspy's mouth dropped open.

"Think about it," he said, moving on down the line. "We can discuss the details after the ceremony."

"Dear Luna," Gamemaster said. He swept back a fold of his cloak and retrieved a sword with an ornate scabbard. "I want to gift this fine blade to you. It is made from impeccable Gladiatorian steel and enchanted with tremendous magic. It seems the blade may cut through almost anything in the cosmos. I call it Dreadbane."

Luna looked up at the Cosmomancer. Her eyes glistened as she nodded and took the sword.

"It's extraordinary," she said, marveling at the exquisite gift. "Thank you so much, sir."

"It's my hope that you will lead the Cosmic Honor Guard with that sword. That company needs a captain and I want you to take the position because I can think of no other warrior worthy of it."

Luna bowed her head again. "Yes, sir. It will be my honor."

"No, dear one, the honor is all mine."

He patted her on the shoulder, then turned and stared toward stage right. He motioned to a group of skulks waiting in the wings. When they saw his signal, they scurried out.

"Finally, let's not forget what's owed each of you."

Alex recognized two of the lead skulks from the Sapphire Sanctum: Vicar Skulodius and Skularrison Skularney. Vicar scurried up to Jed and dropped a rather large leather bag on Jed's boot.

"Whoa, little dude," Jed winced. "That could break a man's foot!"

Jed leaned over to examine the bag. Skularrison looked up at Jed, smiling and chattering in the skulk language while pointing his little claw at the bag.

Jed translated for the team. "He says it's a special bonus loot drop." Jed opened the bag. "Oh, my sweet noob nuts! It's full of gold coins!"

The two skulks proceeded down the line, dropping similar enormous bags of gold in front of each team member.

"There's enough gold in here to last a lifetime!" Alex exclaimed.

"Yes, I believe so," Gamemaster said. "Certainly enough to provide generously for yourselves and your families. No one need worry about lack of treasure, ever again."

Alex was overwhelmed and suddenly had a burning urge to rush home and show his mother. Finally, their biggest struggles would be behind them. Finally, he had a reason to go home.

But that journey would have to wait for a few more minutes because the skulks' brief show was over and the stadium crowd of thousands erupted into deafening cheers. They were chanting the team's name.

Gamemaster raised his arms and the crowd immediately fell silent.

"Thank you to our performers." He turned toward the skulk entertainers and said, "Your music and aerial feats were outstanding."

The skulks bowed and exited the stage as the crowd cheered again.

Gamemaster waved his staff. "Now, my dear citizens of the Cosmic Alliance, once again, please join me in celebrating our newest champions—the pride of all Earthborn—the Sparkles Modfia!"

Each team member stepped forward and one by one took their assigned places at the edge of the platform while the crowd continued cheering.

"In addition to the honors already bestowed, I declare one of these exceptional champions as the Most Valuable Player. That honor goes to Lewis Cho, better known to all of you as Genghis the BadVibeKiller."

Using his magical sneakers, Genghis levitated above the dais, spinning like a breakdancer in the air. The crowd roared with delight.

"And for the first time in our monumental history, one of these celebrated champions has secured *legendary* status. His personal sacrifice restored my faith in the game and all that our alliance stands for. Everyone here knows his name now: Alex Garcia, or as we shall call him, Titan Hordeslayer!"

The eruption of adulation was so incredible that Alex wanted to cry, but the embrace from his own team overwhelmed that momentary emotion, leaving him with one heartwarming thought—team hugs might be the best prize of all.

Gamemaster's voice boomed over the Battle Moon, calling their names one last time. "Titan. Genghis. Aspy. Ripghoul. BadMiznus. Luna Lifestealer."

Gamemaster swept his hands in the air producing a new burst of colorful fireworks above the stadium.

"My dear alliance, I give you the greatest Champions of the Cosmos!"

PLEASE LEAVE A REVIEW!

That concludes COSMIC CHAMPIONS, I hope you enjoyed it.

If you liked the book, you'd make this writer very happy if you'd please leave an honest review on Amazon.com (or the other store where you bought it). Reviews are critical. They feed the algorithms and allow more eyes to see my books. Despite being a bit of a hassle, they are essential to my success.

So, please take a moment to leave a review. If you do, I promise not to send The Decimator to the location of this reading device. Thank you very much!

— Mark

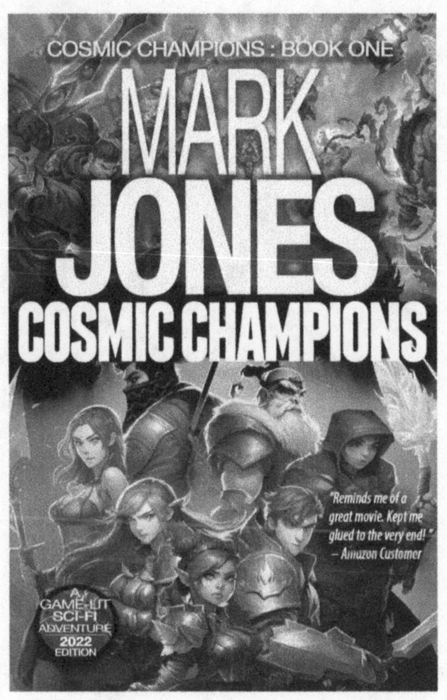

The SPARKLES MODFIA wants you!

If you join the SPARKLES MODFIA TEAM you'll be the first to know when the next book is out. I'll send you information about my Advanced Reader Group and the chance to read all my new books free of charge!

Click Here To Join:
http://jonesmarkc.com/teammodfia

ACKNOWLEDGMENTS

Thanks to the team of people that helped me finish this book and supported me along the way: Steve Bonczyk, Ron Thomason, Jim Stiles, JR Palma, Jason Letts, Malorie Seeley-Sherwood, Diane and Larry Jones, Laura Kate and Jonathan Brandstein, Hannah Jones, Juliette Jones, and Maverick Jones. Thank you!

ABOUT THE AUTHOR

Mark Caldwell Jones is a novelist and screenwriter living in Los Angeles. *Cosmic Champions* is his most recent book. Learn more about Mark and get free content like news about, *Moonbase Rogue*, the next book in his spy thriller series, by visiting him online.

For more information:
www.jonesmarkc.com/bookclub
mark@jonesmarkc.com

www.ingramcontent.com/pod-product-compliance
Lightning Source LLC
Chambersburg PA
CBHW010356050826
48979CB00052B/2821/J
9780991037698